KW-220-262

Miss
Winter
in the
Library
with a
Knife

ALSO BY MARTIN EDWARDS

THE LAKE DISTRICT
MYSTERIES
The Coffin Trail
The Cipher Garden
The Arsenic Labyrinth
The Serpent Pool
The Hanging Wood
The Frozen Shroud
The Dungeon House
The Crooked Shore

THE HARRY DEVLIN SERIES
All the Lonely People
Suspicious Minds
I Remember You
Yesterday's Papers
Eve of Destruction
The Devil in Disguise
First Cut is the Deepest
Waterloo Sunset

THE RACHEL
SAVERNAKE SERIES
Gallows Court
Mortmain Hall
Blackstone Fell
Sepulchre Street
Hemlock Bay

FICTION
Take My Breath Away
Dancing for the Hangman

NON-FICTION
Catching Killers
The Golden Age of Murder
*The Story of Classic Crime in
100 Books*
The Life of Crime

Miss
Winter
in the
Library
with a
Knife

MARTIN EDWARDS

An Aries Book

First published in the UK in 2025 by Head of Zeus,
part of Bloomsbury Publishing Plc

Copyright © Martin Edwards, 2025

The moral right of Martin Edwards to be identified
as the author of this work has been asserted in accordance with
the Copyright, Designs and Patents Act of 1988.

All rights reserved. No part of this publication may be: i) reproduced or transmitted
in any form, electronic or mechanical, including photocopying, recording or by means
of any information storage or retrieval system without prior permission in writing from the
publishers; or ii) used or reproduced in any way for the training, development or operation
of artificial intelligence (AI) technologies, including generative AI technologies. The rights
holders expressly reserve this publication from the text and data mining exception
as per Article 4(3) of the Digital Single Market Directive (EU) 2019/790.

This is a work of fiction. All characters, organizations, and events
portrayed in this novel are either products of the author's
imagination or are used fictitiously.

9 7 5 3 1 2 4 6 8

A catalogue record for this book is available from the British Library.

ISBN (HB): 9781035910588; ISBN (TPB): 9781035918959
ISBN (E): 9781035910595

Cover design: Gemma Gorton | Head of Zeus

Typeset by Siliconchips Services Ltd UK

Printed and bound in Great Britain by
Clays Ltd, Popson Street, Bungay, NR35 1ED

MIX
Paper | Supporting
responsible forestry
FSC
www.fsc.org   FSC® C018072

Bloomsbury Publishing Plc
50 Bedford Square, London, WC1B 3DP, UK
Bloomsbury Publishing Ireland Limited,
29 Earlsfort Terrace, Dublin 2, D02 AY28, Ireland

HEAD OF ZEUS LTD
5–8 Hardwick Street
London, EC1R 4RG

To find out more about our authors and books
visit www.headofzeus.com

For product safety related questions contact productsafety@bloomsbury.com

Dedicated to my editor Bethan Jones,
whose enthusiasm for this book has been so motivating.

The Players in the Game

Visitors to Midwinter
Harry Crystal
Carys Neville
Baz Frederick
Poppy de Lisle
Zack Jardine
Grace Kinsella

Midwinter Trust
Jeremy Vandervell
Bernadette Corrigan
Chandra Masood
Daisy Wu
Ethan Swift
Frankie Rowland

And YOU?

Rules of the Game

Nature of the Game – Miss Winter in the Library with a Knife is a game within a murder mystery. Take nothing for granted. Are people simply making polite conversation – or giving you vital clues?

Aim of the Game – The aim is to solve the mysteries of Midwinter, a village unique in the United Kingdom.

Game Set-up – Six players are already on their way to Midwinter to play a mystery game. The winner will qualify for membership of the Midwinter Trust. You are invited to take part in the game remotely.

Game Play – Remote players may, either from the outset or at any time subsequently, retire from active gameplay and follow the story as external observers ('readers') or analysts ('reviewers'). Someone at Midwinter is playing a deadlier game than the one that the six guests have been invited to play. Remote players are invited to use their detective skills to deduce what is going on. Clues may be found throughout the text, including the supplementary materials (such as the official Midwinter website and the unofficial history of Midwinter), and these are set out in a Cluefinder at the end.

Looking at the Cluefinder before you reach the end will disqualify you from winning.

The six guests will be given 'warm-up' puzzles to develop and test their problem-solving skills, and solutions are supplied as the game progresses. However, these puzzles do not contribute to the solution of the mystery game or of the other mysteries of Midwinter.

In addition to the main text, there are supplementary materials, some of which are relevant to the mystery game and some of which cast light on the mysteries of Midwinter itself. Remote players may wish to consider these materials – for instance, comparing information on the Midwinter Trust's website with the unofficial history of Midwinter – as well as studying the main text for clues to the over-arching mystery that may be found in the Cluefinder. Puzzles and other elements of the game that are *not* related to the over-arching mystery and the clues to be found in the Cluefinder are on the pages marked with a border.

Winning – For the six guests, winning entails solving the mystery game. For remote players, the target is to spot as many of the clues in the Cluefinder as possible.

Less than 10 clues spotted: maybe concentrate on enjoying your reading?

10 to 30 clues spotted: well done – you are a good detective in the making.

30–39 clues spotted: move over, Poirot.

40 or more clues spotted: perhaps you should expect an invitation to Midwinter…

Strategy Tips – Trust no one.

Disclaimer – The creators of *Miss Winter in the Library with a Knife* accept no legal liability in relation to people who play the game including personal injury or death.

Invitation

*The Midwinter Trust requests the pleasure of
your company as our guest at a unique all-expenses-paid
Christmas break.*

Arrival: 23 December – Midwinter Halt, North Pennines

Departure: 27 December – Midwinter Village

Transport will be provided to and from the station

Dress code: smart casual.
There will be a Christmas-themed fancy dress dinner party
on Christmas Day and your participation is cordially requested

*You are invited to play a mystery game created especially for the
occasion. A special prize is on offer to the winner*

λ η ρ ρ υ η μ σ γ π η μ

σ ζ γ κ η ω π ψ π χ

υ η σ ζ ψ ι μ η δ γ

*if it's all greek to you,
then just clear your head
go two letters forward
and forget about z*

RSVP: Chandra Masood, Head of People,
The Midwinter Trust, North Pennines

Email: chandra.masood@midwinter.org.uk

Introduction to Baz Frederick's draft script for the Black Death podcast, episode #13, 'Evil under the Snow'

The snow lay deep and crisp and deadly.

Scrambling over the crest of the fell, the two searchers came to a halt and scanned the countryside below. Where did moorland end and sky begin? They saw only an infinite white shroud.

Their quarry had vanished.

Both searchers carried backpacks and were equipped for arctic conditions. Visibility was hopeless and the cold gnawed at their bones like a terminal disease. Yet this wasn't some Siberian waste, but perhaps the highest stretch of English landscape. And certainly the loneliest.

The woman lifted her goggles, hoping for a clearer view. Flying slivers of ice stung her cheeks and made her eyes wet with tears.

'Could be anywhere.' The snow deadened sound, so she raised her voice. 'Anywhere!'

'Can't have gone far,' her companion said. 'Not in this weather. Not without landmarks to guide the way. Not in a dizzy and disorientated state. Bad enough to be a bag of shredded nerves in Midwinter. Out here in the wilds, you'd be scared to death.'

'We must call for help.'

He faced her, turning with care so as not to lose his

footing. The compacted snow was treacherous, the ice beneath their boots as slippery as polished glass.

'No!'

His ski mask formed a perfect disguise. She couldn't guess what was in his mind. The prospect of imminent disaster had stretched her own nerves to breaking point.

'We'll never do it.'

'Giving up isn't an option. We must keep looking.'

'But—'

'I don't have a choice.' A pause. 'This is *personal*.'

Without another word, he picked his way down the slope as if edging through a minefield. She knew he was following the safest route, but without crampons he'd never have kept his balance.

She stood motionless, hypnotised by the whiteout. In hollows of the landscape, the blizzard had carved the drifts into strange and ominous shapes, like surreal works of art dreamed up by a demented sculptor. She imagined them coming to life, snow monsters ready to devour everyone in their path.

Her temples pounded as the earthy smell of the snow seeped into her lungs. She longed to head back to safety, but he was right. They'd come too far. She dared not surrender to fear.

What was that? Could it be...?

She shifted her hat, made of thick wool with a waterproof lining, so it no longer protected her ears.

Yes, she hadn't imagined the sound. That eerie noise in the distance was the thrum of a helicopter, somewhere in the opaque sky. Marine commandos airlifting food and medicine to stricken communities cut off from the rest of the world.

Should she wave her arms in a wild attempt to attract attention? Or was she as invisible to them as the chopper was to her? Her companion would never forgive her. She dared not betray his trust.

As she strained her ears, the thudding of the rotor blades grew fainter until at last she heard nothing more. The helicopter was heading for the upland villages on the far side of the fell. Her head ached, bludgeoned by the silence. Had she squandered a lifeline or dodged disaster by the skin of her teeth?

Nothing for it now but to keep going.

She adjusted her goggles and hat before following in her companion's footsteps. The slope was pitted with ridges and cracks, and in places, the snow was unstable. She moved with exaggerated caution, desperate not to provoke an avalanche.

He glanced back, as if he'd calculated to the second how long she'd take to overcome her doubts and stick to the plan. He knew her too well.

When she caught up, he said, 'Hear the copter? Time is short. We need to keep moving before someone else beats us to it.'

'So where do we look?'

'Nobody could get far in these conditions. Think about what you'd do. Search for a stone shelter. Huddle up with the sheep and try to keep warm.'

'I don't see any shelters.'

'They'll be under twenty feet of snow,' he said patiently. 'We need to figure out where they are. Then we start digging. That's why I brought the snow shovels.'

In the past, she'd have smiled and said: *You think of*

everything. Now she scanned their surroundings, searching in vain for that lost horizon.

The wind gathered strength again, regaining its voice, ready to threaten livestock or people foolish enough to get in its way. The roar was as fierce as the snow whipping into their faces, blinding them to what lay ahead.

She had no idea how long they kept on walking. Five minutes? Fifteen? Thirty? Time became a blur, like the snow-smothered landscape.

Suddenly her companion halted and raised a gloved hand.

'Seen something?' she bellowed, trying to make herself heard above the blast of the gale.

He pointed.

Striding forward, she got a better view. They were standing above a gash in the terrain, a crevasse beneath a narrow overhang. Snow filled the bottom of the gully, with a small mound piled in the middle, its shape unnatural and yet sickeningly recognisable.

She gasped the words – she couldn't help herself – 'A snowman!'

But not a happy, smiling snowman with a battered hat, a carrot nose, and eyes formed from black buttons.

This snowman was stretched out on the ground. Arms and legs outstretched, beseeching and forlorn.

Even before they began to dig, she knew the truth.

They'd found the person they were looking for.

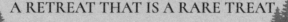
Midwinter is a very special place. This tiny village – barely more than a hamlet – nestles high in the rugged landscape amid panoramic views of outstanding natural beauty. The settlement dates back to its creation by Marcus Midwinter, a man of great enterprise and imagination, more than one hundred years ago. His aim was to provide jobs, homes, prosperity, and recreation for this sparsely populated local community.

Originally conceived as a model village for people who worked in the local mine, Midwinter was gradually transformed after the Second World War by Marcus's son, another high achiever blessed with vision, flair and idealism. Sir Maurice Midwinter founded and endowed a Trust which reinvented the village as a secluded, nurturing, and immersive retreat.

Today, the Midwinter Trust continues to perform an invaluable role as custodian of a village like no other, preserving its heritage and maintaining the values laid down by Sir Maurice while promoting diversity and inclusivity.

The private and tranquil surroundings offer a serene and wonderfully relaxing environment for those seeking peace and quiet, with time to de-stress far from the twenty-first century's hustle and bustle. The village is a haven of well-being, the perfect setting for contemplation, mindful thinking, and creative reasoning. Those fortunate enough to be invited to Midwinter will find time spent in the village more than merely therapeutic. Today the village is a fount of inspiration and enrichment, enabling talented people to refresh their lives and explore new forms of imaginative play and creativity so as to discover life-changing perspectives. You may come here simply to recuperate and decompress, only to find that you are embarking on a change of direction that will transform your life forever.

I

Midwinter

'Youdunit, Bernadette,' Ethan said softly. 'So, have you committed the perfect murder? Or will one of our detectives solve the mystery?'

Bernadette Corrigan smiled as she sat down at the far end of the leather sofa. Keeping a safe distance, as always.

'We'll soon find out.'

'Care to give me a clue?'

'If I did,' she murmured. 'I'd have to kill you.'

'You don't approve of people who peek at the last page of a detective story?' She gave a brisk shake of the head. 'So the deed is done. No flowers, by request?'

'A holly wreath, perhaps.'

She waved at the Christmas decor. Midwinter's village hall had never looked so festive. Exquisitely crafted baubles, elegant lanterns, and a tinsel-festooned tree giving off a heady fragrance of pine. Mistletoe with snow-white berries and glossy evergreen leaves, looking so romantic that it was easy to forget the plant was parasitic. And poisonous.

The Midwinter Trust never does things by halves, Ethan thought.

Blood-red poinsettias lent a lurid splash of colour to half a dozen oak tables in the centre of the hall. At the far end, out of earshot, two of their colleagues were chatting across the bar counter. Bernadette glanced towards them for a moment, then looked away. A man in his fifties – a silver fox in Savile Row clothing – was chatting with the bartender. Twenty years his junior, she hung on his words as if committing them to memory. Maybe she was, Ethan thought. Maybe she was a good actor. Or, just possibly, a bad actor?

'You've earned the right to celebrate,' Ethan said as they clinked glasses. 'Murder obviously suits you.'

'I think so.' Bernadette inhaled the spicy aroma of the mulled wine. 'I'd better take care. I'd hate to give myself away to such a skilled mind-reader.'

Ethan grinned. 'You make me sound like a fairground act. A charlatan who plays deceitful mind games.'

'Sorry. An expert in psychiatry, I meant to say. I'm afraid you'll fathom my darkest secrets.'

'If only,' he murmured. 'Anyone would make the same diagnosis. For once in your life, you seem at ease. Not tearing around trying to get a hundred and one things done before some crazy self-imposed deadline.'

'You've written me off as a hopeless workaholic?'

'I'm glad to see you finally getting into the Christmas spirit.'

'Appearances are deceptive.'

'Isn't that always the way in Midwinter?'

She gave him a curious look. 'I'm on tenterhooks, waiting for our detectives to arrive. To find out how they'll play the game. If the puzzles I've concocted are too easy or too hard.'

'I bet you judged it to perfection.'

'Thanks for your confidence.' She smiled. 'And for

persuading me to come up with it. I'd never have managed to keep going without your constant encouragement.'

'You flatter me.'

Their eyes met for a moment, then she gave a light laugh.

'Not at all. That's why you're here, after all. You understand what makes people tick.'

He examined his fingernails. 'You know I haven't always got things right.'

'Don't be so hard on yourself.'

'Pot, meet kettle.' He savoured the tang of his mulled wine. 'You're turning the tables, trying to boost my morale.'

'I'm right. Admit it.'

He took a breath. 'Honestly, I can't believe this is actually happening. I never imagined coming back to Midwinter. If you'd told me five years ago that I'd ever want to set foot in this place again, let alone for a Christmas murder mystery game, I'd have said you were crazy.'

'The pandemic was such a strange time,' she murmured. 'Everyone in the world lived through a nightmare. So much uncertainty and fear for the future. We couldn't take anything for granted. Not even in Midwinter. A village like nowhere else.'

'You can say that again.'

'We pride ourselves on being different,' she said dreamily. 'This is such a special place. A refuge from the damaged world outside. Five years ago, things were so... very challenging.'

He nodded. 'I'm so grateful you gave me a second chance.'

'You know Midwinter inside out. You share our values, and you can keep a secret. Rare qualities, believe me.' She exhaled. 'Besides, it wasn't only my decision to offer you a new contract. Jeremy was strongly in favour. Chandra too.'

He said in a low voice, 'Believe me, I'm delighted to be back.'

For the first time in their acquaintance, she blushed. She hated any form of betrayal, most of all when it came to disclosing her own feelings. To cover her embarrassment, she looked away towards the two people at the bar. A shadow crossed her face.

Ethan followed her gaze. The bartender, attractive and vivacious, threw back her head and laughed at a bon mot from the silver fox. She rested a ringless hand on the snow globe which had pride of place on the bar counter. A superfluous ornament, given the Met Office's red weather warning. Outside, the wind was howling in fury. Within twenty-four hours, the snowstorm would cut them off from the outside world. Just like...

No, he mustn't dwell on the last time he was here. Not tonight. The game hadn't even begun.

Bernadette sipped her drink. 'I love the tang of cinnamon. Daisy mixes the ingredients perfectly. This is the best mulled wine I've ever tasted.'

'She's a woman of many talents.'

'Yes.' A pause. 'I wonder what she really makes of Midwinter. This place could hardly be more different from Maryland.'

Ethan said mischievously, 'Jeremy obviously approves.'

'So do I,' she said calmly.

Bernadette wasn't easy to tease. She had a lifetime's experience of keeping her emotions on a tight leash. Staying in control was part of her skill set. Time to get her talking about murder again.

'You cut it fine, getting things ready. Last night, you were still hard at work. This time tomorrow, and the game will be well and truly afoot.'

'Murder's a serious business,' she said. 'Takes a lot of planning.'

'So how do you go about weaving your plot?' He grinned. 'If you don't mind letting me into the tricks of your trade?'

'I simply asked myself who should kill whom and why. Motive is key, you know that better than anyone.'

He took a breath. 'Yes, the psychology of the murderer is crucial.'

'What drives one person to commit the ultimate crime, to end someone else's life?' She had a habit of avoiding his gaze, but for once she looked straight into his eyes. 'Even though we're indulging in make-believe, *whodunit* and *whydunit* need a credible explanation.'

'And *howdunit*?'

'If the method of murder is too outlandish, every last shred of plausibility flies out of the window. So my crime isn't committed with the help of wild animals or elaborate Heath Robinson-like contraptions or poisons unknown to medical science. This is like any game. We need to set out the rules and keep to them.'

He raised his eyebrows. 'You're playing fair?'

'Of course. Cheating can't be tolerated in a mystery game. That goes for the puzzle-maker too. All the clues must be laid out before the people who are hunting the truth. Misdirection is fine, but solving the puzzle mustn't be so arduous that the players find it impossible. Twists are part of the fun, but only if they make sense in the context of the mystery. My aim is to lose gracefully so the winner is pleased that they've done something smart. Figuring out the answer needs to reward you with a sense of fulfilment.'

'You sound positively evangelical.'

'The skill lies in diverting attention from what really matters. Seducing the players with red herrings.'

'Deception, in other words?'

She shrugged. 'Isn't that our stock-in-trade?'

'See yourself as a new Queen of Crime? Even a professional crime writer like Harry Crystal might look over his shoulder?'

A shake of the head. 'Poor old Harry. He's not so much a Prince of Puzzlers as a literary has-been.'

He flashed a grin. 'You think he's lost the plot?'

'You tell me.' She ran her fingers through her mass of thick chestnut hair. A habitual gesture, a sign she was choosing her words with special care. 'His career has fallen apart. Why else was he so desperate to come here?'

Ethan pursed his lips. 'A last throw of the dice. Unless, of course, he has another agenda. Something we're not aware of.'

'I don't believe it.'

'Who knows? He is a man of mystery, after all.'

'Thirty-two mysteries to be precise. His gimmick was coming up with titles that riff on masterpieces of the genre. Something he stumbled on by accident, then tried to turn to his advantage. Of course it was crazy to invite comparison with the classics.' She smiled. 'Weirdly enough, his books helped to inspire my own mystery.'

'Really?'

'Sort of. Not that I want to murder people for a living.'

He considered her. 'Just an occasional indulgence, then?'

She finished her drink. 'We call this a game, but Jeremy is deadly serious. He says the Midwinter Trust's future is at stake. Everything depends on what happens this Christmas.'

'No pressure, then.' Ethan shook his head. 'Is he right?'

'Yes. His passion for Midwinter never falters. Despite all the setbacks, he keeps the faith.'

'I admire his confidence,' he murmured. 'After all that's happened...'

'Jeremy is right. We must look forward, not back. Your evaluations of our guests are invaluable. So is having you on the spot to see how they cope once they start to play the game.'

'I wouldn't miss this for anything.' He put down his glass. 'The most important person in Midwinter is you. You make all the pieces of the jigsaw fit.'

'The first thing Jeremy told me when I arrived in Midwinter is that no one is indispensable.'

'He'd be lost without you.'

'No, he'd be fine,' she said. 'He's the ultimate survivor.'

'You think so?' he said wryly.

'Absolutely. Take this Christmas. The forecasters are predicting a snowmageddon. The worst weather since you-know-when, and Jeremy is jubilant. Reckons it will create the perfect atmosphere for what we want to do. Nothing fazes him.'

Ethan finished his drink. 'I'd better be off. An early night is called for before the fun begins. You're obviously not going to give me a clue about whodunit. Won't you at least tell me the name of the game?'

'It's spelled out in this invitation to our guests, but they need to decrypt a cipher in ancient Greek. A limbering-up puzzle to get them in the mood.'

She took an oblong card from her bag and pointed to the Greek letters and accompanying verse.

λ η ρ ρ   υ η μ σ γ π   η μ
σ ζ γ   κ η ω π ψ π χ
υ η σ ζ   ψ   ι μ η δ γ

if it's all greek to you,
then just clear your head
go two letters forward
and forget about z

He wrinkled his brow. 'The verse is a clue?'

'Yes, the verse is all written in lower case, with no capitals, a hint that the cipher is also in lower case. Turns out there are twenty-five lower case symbols in ancient Greek, though sigma has two symbols, which confused me, never mind anyone else.' She grinned. 'If only I'd had Jeremy's posh education. Just as well I never became a cryptographer, eh? Anyway, there is a symbol to represent each letter of our alphabet except one. Which is "z", according to the verse. It's a substitution cipher. The verse tells you to move forward, plus two. So "alpha", the first symbol in the Greek alphabet, becomes the third letter in our alphabet, "c". In the cipher, the single symbol is most likely to represent "a" and the three-letter word is likely to be "the". One symbol appears six times, so it's likely to be another vowel, either "i" or "u". In fact, it's "i".'

'I'll take your word for it.' He rolled his eyes. 'Go on, I'm hopeless at these things. What's the solution?'

She threw a theatrical glance over her shoulder before lowering her voice to a throaty whisper.

'*Miss Winter in the Library with a Knife.*'

He blinked. 'Don't you need a spoiler alert before revealing that? If Miss Winter is your murderer…'

'Miss Winter isn't a character in my mystery.'

His eyebrows lifted.

'There's no library, either.'

A pause. 'Dare I ask about the knife?'

'None of my characters has a knife.' She gave an enigmatic smile. 'Told you it was a mystery.'

What Shall I Read Now?

Books by Harry Crystal

British author
Mystery genre

Murder Isn't Easy
Innocent's Blood
Six Red Herrings
Why Didn't They Ask Evelyn?
No More Dying Today
Trent's Last Caper
Endless Fright
Strangers on a Plane
Rear View Mirror
In the Heat of the Moment
Intruder in the House
Nightmare Avenue
The Nine Gaolers
Have His Car Crash
End of Sentence
Last Seen Weeping
In a Lonely Daze
Bier Island
Rogue Males
And Then There Was Nothing

Red Heartburst
You Only Live Once
Which Body?
I, the Judge
The Blonde Wore Black
Hangover Street
After the Burial
Kiss the Girls Again
No or Maybe?
I Is for Investigation
Farewell, My Lorelei
Elephants Can Forget

2

Harry Crystal's Journal

It's not too late, I thought as the train slowed to a nervous crawl, apparently as reluctant to reach the station as I was. *You can still change your mind. Go home and forget about murder.*

Flecks of snow smeared the window, failing to obscure the gloom of the weather-beaten uplands. Why would anyone want to spend their Christmas playing a mysterious game with a bunch of strangers in this remote corner of England? There was a simple answer. I had nobody else to see, nowhere else to go.

The Midwinter Trust was offering a chance to put the disasters of the past behind me. An outside chance, to say the very least, given that five other people were competing to beat me to the ultimate prize.

A brand-new life.

When the Trust invited me to spend a few nights over Christmas at their expense in the obscure hamlet of Midwinter at the top of the Pennines – plus a cash bonus at the end simply for taking part – I could hardly say no. This was exactly the right moment to clutch at a straw.

As the train inched forward, I asked myself again the

question I'd wrestled with for so long before setting off on my journey. What if, by some outlandish fluke, I won the game? Everything would change in the blink of an eye.

Was that what I wanted? Or should I reconcile myself to being a born loser, cocooning myself in a comfort blanket of under-achievement?

Optimism doesn't come naturally to me. I've a flair for picturing worst-case scenarios. Jocasta, my ex-wife, used to jibe that a glimpse of me was enough to make any insurance salesman's heart soar. I'm easy meat, a sucker for peace of mind policies guarding against all manner of unlikely disasters. Was it brave or foolish to venture into the unknown, risking ridicule and humiliation in return for the dream of an unlikely metamorphosis?

Just so long, said a small mischievous voice inside my head, *as I don't suffer the same kind of transformation as that guy in the Kafka story who woke up one morning and found he'd turned into a gigantic insect...*

The train shuddered to a standstill, as if depressed by the wintry bleakness of the surroundings. I'd looked up Midwinter Halt on the internet and learned it was Britain's least frequented station. So insignificant that a quarter of the way through the twenty-first century, the powers-that-be had forgotten to close it.

Decision time.

'You've got nothing left to lose,' I said to myself.

Was that true?

And if so, why did I feel a shiver down my spine that was entirely unconnected with the weather outside?

Feel the fear and do it anyway. An empowering mantra, beloved by my ex-wife, which may explain why she married me. A life-affirming philosophy, guaranteed to lead to all kinds of trouble. But what alternative did I have but to carry on to Midwinter? The prospect of heading straight back to my rented garret in Manchester and spending the festive season scraping mould off the ceiling was scarcely alluring.

I heaved my bags down from the rack and gripped the door handle. The station was unstaffed and I couldn't see a soul. The dusting of white on the platform was unsullied by a single footprint.

As I got down, blinking snowflakes out of my eyes, a door in the rear compartment swung open. A tall woman stepped down to the platform. With her back half-turned to me, she manoeuvred her large suitcase with a vigour that put me to shame. In padded coat, leather boots, green bob hat, and matching mittens, she looked ready for an expedition to the North Cape, let alone the north Pennines.

As I moved forward, the crunch of suitcase wheels through the snow made her stop in her tracks and throw a suspicious glance over her shoulder. Anyone would think I was a potential killer rather than an obscure crime writer and wannabe detective.

She wore big fancy glasses with frames as red as the hair tumbling down to her shoulders. With a shock of recognition like a slap on the cheek, I realised who she was.

Carys Neville…

A woman I had never met.

And yet she was the woman who had, without a second thought, given my career the kiss of death.

Midwinter nestles in the remotest corner of the kingdom, close to where the ancient ceremonial counties of Cumberland, Yorkshire, and Northumberland meet. One of the highest villages in the country, Midwinter is also the coldest by virtue of its exposed location close to the summit of Midwinter Fell. It is said to be the least accessible settlement in England, reached by a single lane – frequently cut off by snow – which winds through fell country to connect Midwinter with an unstaffed station seven miles away, Midwinter Halt.

The village of Midwinter is privately owned by the Midwinter Trust, which manages the community in accordance with the guiding values laid down by Sir Maurice Midwinter:

- service
- integrity
- sanctuary

Midwinter provides a safe space for healing, reflection, and personal growth. There is a reading room and a village hall (with multi-faith room, small gym, and bar among other facilities) where activities including yoga and breathwork classes led by our Head of People, and creative writing and gameplay workshops conducted by our Deputy Director, are on <u>offer</u>. With almost zero light pollution, you couldn't <u>wish</u> for better <u>conditions</u> for stargazing. <u>If you</u> are easily disturbed by noise, don't worry, <u>you</u> will only hear birdsong. The village does not <u>have</u> a spa or swimming pool and services available include neither facials nor winter sports, although cold water therapy is available for those wishing to bathe in the fresh spring water of Midwinter Burn. Life in Midwinter is certainly not for everyone, which is as well, for vacancies are extremely limited and much sought after. For the lucky residents who fall under its magical spell, the village offers <u>something</u> far greater than a tranquil refuge from the outside world. Midwinter is a haven offering people from any background an opportunity to find a fresh passion and purpose, to build resilience, to <u>share</u> and <u>apply</u> their wisdom, and remake their lives.

3

Harry Crystal's Journal

My heart pounded. For all the needling cold, I felt clammy with apprehension. A trickle of sweat moistened my forehead.

Even though Carys and I had never come face to face before this moment, I'd stuck metaphorical pins in her online image so many times, I had no doubt about her identity.

Incredible... so the Midwinter Trust had offered her the same invitation as me. An astonishing coincidence.

Or was it?

The curse of a crime writer is a feverish imagination. Sometimes my head feels as though it could explode with ideas for absurd plot twists. Within moments, an explanation sprang to mind.

Carys and I did have something in common, namely connections with the world of crime writing. Was that why we'd been chosen to play a murder mystery game?

Grinding my teeth, I steeled myself to give nothing away. Far too early in the game to risk the slightest mistake. The moment would come when I had to gamble, but right now I didn't even know if the game had started. As for Carys Neville, her expression told me she'd taken our instructions to heart.

Trust no one.

Fixing on a bright, harmless smile, I said, 'Looks like we've landed in the back of beyond, doesn't it?'

'Wait till we get to Midwinter,' she said as the train set off again, gaining speed as if determined to escape as quickly as possible. 'The village will make this godforsaken dump look like the Eurostar terminal at St Pancras.'

'You're heading for Midwinter too?'

She considered me, sceptical as a border guard weighing up a traveller with a dodgy passport. I gave myself a mental kick up the backside. It hadn't taken me long to make my first mistake. Over-acting the part of a well-meaning idiot.

'Where else?'

Good question. The fell rose beyond the station, featureless but for a few trees bowed into submission by the unforgiving wind. Whichever way you looked, snow was drizzling. Nobody would come to Midwinter Halt without a very good reason. Not less than forty-eight hours before Christmas, with weather alarms as doom-laden as the ranting of a hell-fire preacher.

'You're quite the detective.' I experimented with jocularity. 'I'm out of my league already. Harry Crystal, pleased to meet you.'

I put out my hand. It was cold and ungloved, and she ignored it. Surely my name rang at least the faintest of bells? Her expression gave nothing away.

'Carys Neville.'

I feigned ignorance. Playing to my strength, as my ex, Jocasta, liked to say.

'Carys Neville?' I repeated vaguely. 'And what do you do?'

Did I detect a flicker of anger in the eyes behind those large, fashionable spectacles? I felt a jolt of satisfaction, like an amateur chess player spotting a flaw in a grandmaster's opening gambit. Was Carys so vain that she expected a stranger to bow and scrape on hearing her name? Whatever the reason, I'd struck a nerve.

'I'm a cultural commentator.'

Other descriptions sprang to mind, like *unqualified smartarse with the personality of a piranha and all the compassion of a boa constrictor*. I bit my tongue.

'Sounds fascinating!'

She shrugged. 'It pays the rent.'

Does it? I wondered.

'And what aspects of culture do you comment on?'

'This and that. Some people call me an influencer.'

'Goodness me. And who do you influence?'

'People of taste and discernment.' Her tone made it abundantly clear I didn't qualify in either category, but in case I hadn't got the message, she rubbed it in with a sidelong glance at my tweed trousers and Hush Puppies. 'Aspirational individuals. Sophisticates who care about fashion and style.'

'Hence the red spectacles?' I couldn't resist a retaliatory swipe.

'Madder.'

I blinked. So now she was questioning my sanity?

'What?'

She touched the spectacle frame. 'The shade is madder. Not red.'

I gritted my teeth, uneasily aware I was squandering the initiative. 'I'm intrigued, Carys. Okay to call you by your first name, I hope? No sense in being formal when we're spending Christmas together. Nice and cosy.'

Glancing around the deserted station, she waved away my bonhomie as if swatting a mosquito. 'Is that what you think?

You'll soon change your tune… *Harry*. There's nothing cosy about Midwinter.'

Her tone was as harsh as if I'd giggled during a funeral. I abandoned any pretence of sycophancy. 'Steady on. This is only a game we're playing, remember.'

'For high stakes,' she retorted.

Her jaw tightened and I could tell she was furious with herself. I'd provoked her into saying too much and she was remembering the instruction we'd been given.

Say nothing to *anyone* about the true purpose of the game. Do not discuss the prize on offer. Breach of this rule will result in your instant disqualification. The decision of the Director of the Midwinter Trust is final. There is no right of appeal.

She was quick to change the subject. 'So where is the driver? I was told I'd be met at the station.'

'Me too.' I chortled. 'I half expected to see someone brandishing a card with my name in block capitals. Like being greeted at an airport terminal.'

She couldn't even be bothered to roll her eyes. 'So you wouldn't miss them in the crowd? I don't think so.'

'Maybe this is part of the game. Sort of initiative test?'

'Forget it. If the driver has any sense, he'll be keeping snug in his car.'

A derelict waiting room stood in front of us, draped with cobwebs rather than Yuletide bunting. The windows were boarded and the door padlocked, condemning any passengers to freeze outside. I strolled along the platform and spotted a sleek black Mercedes parked in the pebbled yard behind the station. A sinewy figure in a dark suit and cap bent over the bonnet, clearing the snow off the windscreen with a microfiber cloth. A losing battle.

Quickening my pace, I called out, 'Our car is here.'

The driver turned round and I had another surprise. She was a youngish woman, strongly built. The temperature was below zero and she must have been chilled to the bone, but she seemed impervious to the elements. As we approached, she brushed flecks of snow off her jacket and stuffed the cloth in her pocket, her unremarkable features forming a professional veneer of welcome.

'Ms Neville? Mr Crystal? My name is Frankie, and I'm your chauffeur.' She spoke in a warm Geordie accent. 'So sorry I wasn't on the platform to greet you. May I see your IDs? And your invitations?'

I fished in my pocket for my passport and the card inviting me to spend Christmas at Midwinter. Carys Neville did likewise. During the online briefing, I'd done a theatrical double take when Chandra Masood told me to bring photographic identification. But although she gave the impression of being a naturally smiley person, Chandra wasn't joking.

'Feels like we're crossing the border into a foreign land,' I said.

'You've no idea how many people are dying to come to Midwinter to play the game,' Frankie said.

I said playfully, 'When you say *dying…*'

Frankie's expression was serious. 'I gather you've been carefully selected after a rigorous screening process. They tell me you're one of the lucky few. This is a once-in-a-lifetime opportunity. The Midwinter Trust needs to make sure nobody passes it on to a third party.'

I felt privileged and put in my place at one and the same time.

Although I'd expected the chauffeur to spare the documents no more than a cursory glance, she considered our passport photographs with as much care as if checking for telltale signs of cosmetic surgery. As usual I found myself wishing my picture didn't make me one of life's lost souls, weary and dissolute. If only I could use the author photo on the back of my books. But I'd be the first to admit, that black-and-white image made me look like a different person. Fifteen years younger, for a start.

'Thanks very much. It would never do to pick up the wrong people, would it?'

Carys cast a mocking glance at the deserted station. 'Fat chance of that.'

Frankie's response was a disarming smile. Obviously, she was as immune to sarcasm as the cold. Handing back the paperwork, she said, 'I'll take your bags.'

Fretting about the scruffiness of my old suitcase, I hovered behind Frankie as she opened the trunk lid with the flick of a remote fob. The boot-space was a cavern. I saw a zipped bag marked *First Aid Kit*, hi-vis vest, lantern, rope, snow shovel, and snow chain. A blanket was draped over a heap of fairy lights. There was even a large cool box, which the weather forecast surely rendered superfluous. Frankie was leaving nothing to chance. But even when she'd stowed our suitcases, there was still plenty of room.

The boot is big enough to hide a body. I tried to banish the thought, in vain. Once a crime writer, always a crime writer.

Frankie glanced over her shoulder at me and snapped the boot shut. 'Between you and me, this is my first contract for Midwinter Trust. A Very Important Client. I need to make sure I do everything by the book, one hundred per cent. My firm's good name depends on giving first-class service.'

'Going the extra mile?' I suggested.

'Very good, sir!' My quip earned a broader grin than it deserved. 'We're very discreet. No logos on the vehicles, y'know, but the company name is Karma Kars of Kielder. If you care to leave an online review...'

'Happy to help, Frankie. And do call me Harry. This,' I added, waving at my companion with a frisson of malicious pleasure, 'is my colleague... um... Carys?'

'Delighted to meet you both. Believe it or not, I did allow extra time to get here, but it wasn't enough. Conditions on the road through the fells are far worse than when I did the same trip earlier today. Absolute murder.'

'How appropriate,' Carys murmured.

Frankie gave her an uncertain glance. 'I do apologise.'

Carys shrugged. 'No worries. Nobody died.'

A momentary pause.

'Don't worry, Frankie,' I said. 'Your secret is safe with us.'

The chauffeur gave me a thoughtful look. 'Would you both like to sit in the back together? The seats are heated individually, you're free to choose the temperature you find most comfortable.'

'I'll go in the front,' Carys said quickly. 'I like to know where I'm going.'

Another illustration of the differences between us. I prefer to remain ignorant of what lies ahead. Saves a lot of worry and unhappiness.

Frankie held open the door for her while I did a quick search for the limo company on my phone. No joy. Our chauffeur wasn't joking when she said they were discreet. I guessed that if you needed to look them up, you couldn't afford them. She ushered me into the rear and I sank into the sensual embrace of the upholstery. A screen gleamed in front of me; a capacious holder contained biscuits, tumblers, a bottle of spring water, and a whisky miniature. Nothing but the best for the Midwinter Trust. They certainly knew how to look after their guests.

'Never mind the weather,' the chauffeur said, settling behind the steering wheel. 'The climate control system is state-of-the-art. You'll feel like you're travelling on a magic carpet ride.'

'Wonderful,' I said.

'Help yourselves to something to drink.' Frankie glanced at me over her shoulder. 'Fancy a winter warmer?'

'Not for me,' Carys said, as I reached for the whisky. 'I'd rather keep my wits about me.'

She was determined to colonise the moral high ground. Ironic, given her history, but I pulled my hand away from the neck of the miniature and surrendered to the back seat's embrace. Better not give anyone the wrong idea. What if this cab ride formed part of the game? Frankie was a hired hand, but that didn't mean she was on our side. The people from Midwinter Trust might have instructed her to put us to the test.

Much as it hurt me to admit, Carys was right. I needed to remain focused, even in the earliest stages of the game, as I fine-tuned my strategy. During my online briefing, Bernadette and Chandra had stressed the value of team-working, even though we were competing for a single prize. However, Carys was scarcely a natural collaborator and I'd burn in hell before I'd take her into my confidence. She was in it to win it, just like me. What's more, I had no doubt she was as ruthless as she was self-centred. If she spotted any chinks in the armour of her fellow players, she'd exploit them without mercy.

Everyone has secrets, Bernadette had said during the briefing. Knowledge is power. Right now, I wasn't even prepared to admit to knowing who Carys was, let alone that I wished she was dead.

MIDWINTER
A RETREAT THAT IS A RARE TREAT

HOME   ABOUT   HISTORY   PEOPLE   CONTACT

Midwinter was founded by Marcus Midwinter, a wealthy entrepreneur noted for his forward-thinking and social conscience. He resolved to make good use of the rich lead and silver deposits of the north Pennines first discovered by the Romans. His aim was to benefit local people, whose incomes were meagre and who had previously been reliant for their survival on farming in an unforgiving location and climate. He acquired the mining rights for the upland area known as Pagans' Fell together with a great deal of land in the vicinity.

Marcus Midwinter did not <u>have</u> any concern about making vast profits. He'd inherited great wealth from a distant relative, and dreamed of creating a small, highly collegiate community, with mine-workers and their families accommodated in well-designed and comfortable cottages in a wonderful situation on a small plateau just below the summit of the fell and looking out over beautiful, unspoiled countryside. The First World War interrupted the construction project before work could be completed on a chapel and school meant to stand a short distance from the houses. However, a village hall and reading room were built in the heart of Midwinter, looking out on a village green, <u>complete</u> with pond, so as to ensure that the miners and their families had ample opportunities for relaxation and recreation.

By the time war broke out, it was already evident that the deposits of silver, in particular, were less plentiful and more difficult to extract than Marcus used to <u>believe</u>. Anxious about the future, and determined <u>to</u> serve their country, the miners – with their employers' blessing – joined up to fight 'the war to end all wars' and the mines ceased to be worked. Tragically, few of the men returned. Today, the names of those who died are recorded on a memorial cross.

These disasters were compounded by personal misery when he lost his wife, Melissa, on Armistice Day, when their only son, Maurice, was born. Marcus's dream in its original <u>form</u> may have died, but Maurice was determined that his father's spirit should live on. The result was the creation of the Midwinter Trust.

4

Harry Crystal's Journal

'Are we nearly there yet?' I asked, after ten minutes of a silence broken only by the swish of the windscreen wipers.

Carys Neville was keeping her mouth shut, but I was tired of fretting about giving any hostages to fortune. By engaging the chauffeur in conversation, I might learn something useful. If I tempted my rival to loosen her tongue, that would be a bonus.

Frankie allowed herself a polite chuckle. 'As the crow flies, Midwinter isn't far from here. But this road gets more treacherous as we climb the fell. See that warning?'

We crossed a humpback bridge over a frozen stream and she gestured to a sign at the side of the road. I could barely make out the words.

DANGER – WINTER DRIVING CONDITIONS CAN BE
EXTREMELY HAZARDOUS.

'That's us told, eh?' Frankie chortled. 'They're not wrong, mind. This car has the best all-weather tyres on the market, but we need to take it steady. Don't want to finish up stuck in a burn, do we? Let alone flip over the edge of the fell-side.'

That was one thing I wasn't afraid of as she manoeuvred the car around one sharp bend after another with impressive confidence. The snowy moorland was beautiful yet unforgiving, like a lover taken for granted once too often. Every now and then our long and winding road passed a lonely farmhouse and a scattering of melancholy sheep. Buildings and dry-stone walls merged with the jagged landscape. Becks tumbled down from the crags, flurries of wind blew the snow this way and that. The road surface rising ahead of us was a virginal white. We hadn't passed another vehicle since leaving the station.

The rhythm of the wipers was hypnotic. I sat back in my seat, inhaling the smell of new leather.

'You're giving us a smooth ride, despite the rotten conditions,' I said.

'That's what I'm paid for, Harry. We pride ourselves on looking after our clients.'

'Are Carys and I the last to arrive?'

'Nope. Two people came this morning. Poppy and Baz, they're called. And I have one more pick-up scheduled for the last two guests.'

'What can you tell us about the others?' I paused. 'If you're able to say, that is.'

'Sorry,' she said. 'I'm only a hired hand. Best leave it to Bernadette and Chandra to make all the introductions this evening. To be honest, I know next to nothing about this Christmas party of yours.'

'Party?' Sarcasm dripped from Carys's voice, as irritating as raindrops from a leaky gutter.

'You've all come here to play a game, isn't that right? A deluxe murder mystery?'

'Sort of,' I said.

'Lovely. So it should be, mind. Christmas in Midwinter can't come cheap.'

I was tempted to brag that we hadn't paid a penny for our trip to the middle of nowhere and, win or lose, would be taking home a fat cash bonus. Caution held me back. My aim was to pick up information, not toss it around.

'You report to Chandra Masood?'

'Yup.'

'Did she brief you about us?'

Frankie shook her head. 'I suppose I don't need to know. Once I drop you both at the village, I'd best make a quick turnaround. Can't afford to be late again, not when the weather's worsening by the hour.'

'At least we have the road to ourselves,' I said. 'Full-time driving must be nightmarish when your passengers have deadlines to meet, planes to catch.'

'All in a day's work,' Frankie said. 'You need to take the rough with the smooth, like.'

'Even the gentlest of us can succumb to road rage every now and then.'

'I need to keep my temper. Don't want to drop dead of a heart attack.'

'I'm sure you needn't worry about that. You're obviously as fit as a fiddle.'

She laughed. 'You wouldn't think so to look at me, but I've got a heart condition. The medics tell me I could keel over at any moment.'

'Goodness.' I didn't know what else to say.

'No worries, Harry. I keep fit with plenty of exercise. No sense in letting it get me down. I was born this way and I've survived in good fettle so far.' She laughed. 'All I need is to keep calm and carry on.'

'Good philosophy,' I said. 'Wish I could apply it.'

'Luckily, I'm very patient.'

'You must be to work with the Midwinter Trust. Bernadette Corrigan strikes me as a real stickler. Keen to make sure everyone does the right thing.'

In the mirror, Frankie's lips curved in a faint smile. 'You reckon?'

Intriguing. Bernadette came across as a buttoned-up jobsworth, but as my late mother used to say darkly, the quiet ones are always the worst. Perhaps the woman let her hair down after a few drinks.

'Oh yes?'

Frankie gave a sorrowful shake of the head.

'First thing you learn in this job is to respect confidentiality.'

'Sorry, I understand.' I'd pushed my luck too far. Our chauffeur might not be a member of the tight-knit group responsible for organising the game, but they were important clients and she knew which side her bread was buttered. Frustrating, but I had to play it softly, softly. 'You need to be discreet.'

'I agreed to terms and conditions, Harry,' she said. 'You know how it is.'

'Absolutely. Same goes for Carys and me.'

Carys grunted. Like me, she must have signed a non-disclosure agreement as a pre-requisite of playing the game. Reams of small print drafted by lawyers who gave the impression of being paid by the word. The conditions even imposed legal penalties for breaking the rules, hefty 'liquidated damages' payable to the Trust if we stepped out of line. Anyone who didn't take care would wind up seriously out of pocket.

'Feels like I'm signing my life away,' I'd said to Bernadette during our online meeting. Her nod of confirmation was discouraging.

Should I reproach myself for not studying the documentation with more care? No regrets, I told myself. The jargon was wrapped up in a series of polysyllabic clauses and sub-paragraphs. If I tried to pick my way through the labyrinth of verbiage, my head would never stop spinning.

'I suppose you drive plenty of VIPs around? Celebrities? Famous faces?'

Frankie had developed a knack for rebuffing nosey parkers without giving offence. 'Me, I try to treat everyone the same. Not just the corporate clients and big shots. I respect the privacy of every single passenger.'

'What happens in the limo, stays in the limo?'

She laughed. 'Harry, you never said a truer word.'

The road crept upward, clinging neurotically to the edge of the fell. At a sharp bend, Carys shifted again in her seat. She couldn't be uncomfortable, not in this state-of-the-art sedan. Was she annoyed by my attempts to establish a rapport with Frankie? At present, I didn't know what mattered and what didn't. Bernadette had promised to give all six of us players an initial briefing about the game tonight. Until then, Carys was like me. Floundering in the dark.

No harm in continuing to pump Frankie for information. She'd signed an NDA, but everyone likes talking about themselves. Some people talk of little else. Anything was worth a try if it gave me an edge in the contest.

'How long have you been a chauffeur?'

'I always loved driving. Over the years, mind, I've done all sorts. Practical things, like. I was never a scholar.'

'University of life, eh?'

'Aye, school of hard knocks.' In the rearview mirror, she gave me a quick once-over before returning her attention to the road. 'That's why Midwinter Trust hired me.'

'Is that so?'

'Yup, they wanted an experienced driver. Even during a mild winter there's more chance of a white Christmas up here than anywhere else in the country. They needed someone who can handle a big car in bad weather. But there's more to it than that. The Trust only has a skeleton staff in Midwinter at this time of year. Everyone is expected to multitask. Me included. Shoulders to the wheel, no exceptions. Even the Director mucks in.'

Carys was no longer able to contain herself. 'Oh really?' she enquired with unvarnished hostility.

'Believe me,' Frankie said earnestly. 'He's even started helping out in the kitchen.'

Carys made a scornful noise.

'There's a new cook called Daisy Wu. Sweet lady. The Director has been showing her the ropes. She's American, but the Christmas menu is traditional English. Mrs Beaton would be proud.'

'That's all right, then.'

Carys's snide retort washed over the chauffeur, who seemed for a moment to be lost in thought.

'All I know is that Bernadette said she wants to make sure all you guests have an experience you'll never forget.'

She made it sound almost sinister.

'Do you live locally?' I asked.

'We'll be cheek by jowl in Midwinter over the next few days,' Frankie said. 'You go home the day after Boxing Day, isn't that right?'

I was beginning to realise that, for all her apparent openness, she had a knack for responding to a question in a way that was nothing like a direct answer.

'Uh-huh. So you're with us for the duration?'

'Yeah, the Trust employs a handyman to handle domestic jobs and do the driving. He had health problems, so at the last minute they needed someone to take his place. His bad luck did me a good turn.'

'You took over from him?' I asked.

'Yup. Not easy to find someone reliable with practical skills who is free over Christmas at short notice. Especially since the Trust are so picky about people they employ. That's why I was recommended. I can turn my hand to most things. After I left college, I worked in an engineer's for a bit. I've always loved cars, and fiddling about with electrics and what-not. Jill of all trades, that's what they call me.'

I laughed. 'Sounds as if you're looking forward to the next few days?'

'Can't wait. It's the chance of a lifetime. Even though I'm just a stand-in, the folk from Midwinter Trust have already made me feel at home. Just what you want at Christmas, isn't it? A luxury break. Makes a change from sitting at home, having far too much to eat and drink and falling asleep in front of the telly.'

'Your family don't mind you deserting them for the festive season?'

'I lost Mam and Dad when I was young, and I've not got any close relatives left,' she said quietly. 'So I live on my own. What about you?'

'Divorced,' I said. 'My ex ran off with someone else.'

'Sorry to hear that.'

'So was my bank manager. As for Saskia, our daughter,

she's nineteen, and an eco-activist. Obsessively concerned about the planet.'

'That's nice.'

'She hasn't spoken to me since I refused to sell my car and stop eating meat and fish. Says it isn't enough for me just to recycle my plots… or my jokes.'

'Ah.'

'If you've only just come here,' I said, 'I suppose you don't know much more than us about the Midwinter Trust?'

Carys finally succumbed to the urge to utter an exasperated groan. I pictured a speech bubble over her head: *Why does he keep banging his head against a brick wall? Surely he can't be as stupid as he looks?*

To my surprise, Frankie seemed to ponder my question rather than brush it aside. Encouraging. If I was any judge of people – admittedly, Jocasta and Saskia would find that idea laughable – our chauffeur was a potential ally. Totally different from Bernadette Corrigan, and even from a charming small-talker like Chandra Masood.

If I could somehow enlist the chauffeur's help, that would put me one step ahead of my rivals in the game. Always good to have a foot in the enemy's camp. Not that the Midwinter Trust was the enemy. That was the other five players.

So I persisted. 'I got an invitation to apply to come to Midwinter out of the blue. The Trust doesn't have much of an online presence. Obviously, I've looked at their website, which made the place sound wonderful. There was also something from a local history group which painted a less positive picture.'

Frankie glanced at me in her rearview mirror, her expression unreadable. 'Is that right?'

'Oddly enough, when I looked again a few days later, the

local history group's site had been taken down. Chandra told me the Trust's aim is to help to make the world a more peaceful place. What I don't understand is how you manage that from somewhere as remote as this?'

Frankie shook her head. 'You're asking the wrong person. All I can say is, they know what they're about. For such a tiny outfit, they're very well organised. There's even a medic on site. Name of Ethan Swift. Decent bloke.'

'What exactly is his role at Midwinter?'

'When you work for the Trust, even if you're a contractor like me, you have to see Ethan and undergo a medical. He checks out your physical health, but he's also a qualified psychiatrist. Wants to know all about your mental well-being. Something to do with the Trust's insurance, I guess. Red tape, like.'

'So by hiring Ethan, they kill two birds with one stone,' I said. 'Someone is on hand to deal with any basic medical issues. And the Trust can keep a close eye on the state of mind of the people playing the game. We had to complete a long questionnaire before we were invited. Some kind of evaluation, I suppose.'

Frankie nodded. 'Makes me wonder about this game of yours. Test of nerve, is it?'

I became provocative. 'It's a question of solving a murder mystery. No need for a psychiatrist, really. I mean, how stressful can this game really be? A few nights in a peaceful hamlet at Christmas, trying to make sense of a puzzle? What could possibly go wrong?'

'There's a lot at stake,' Carys muttered.

'Don't forget, there's every chance the village will get cut off because of the weather. It's happened before.' Frankie sounded sombre. 'And that could become... very stressful.'

'Is that right?' I said.

'So I hear,' she said quickly. 'Don't you fret. Health and safety's a big deal these days, isn't it? The Midwinter Trust don't want to leave anything to chance.'

I nodded. 'Who else is there? As part of the Trust?'

'Well, the big boss, obviously.'

'You mean Jeremy Vandervell?'

'The Director, that's right.'

He'd taken no part in the online briefing. I risked another question. 'What's he like?'

Frankie seemed uncharacteristically hesitant. 'Very... professional.'

Did I detect a hint of doubt, or was my imagination running away with me? If Frankie knew anything negative about Jeremy, she wasn't saying.

'Jeremy runs a tight ship,' I said. 'For such an influential organisation, the staff is very small.'

'The Trust's a not-for-profit, isn't it? I suppose they have to watch the pennies, same as everyone else.'

Carys was growing restive. I sensed that she was sick of keeping quiet while Frankie and I chatted. 'One thing's for sure,' she said. 'Midwinter Trust isn't strapped for cash.'

'I guess that's right,' Frankie said. 'Chandra told me the original endowment from the Midwinter family was huge. Back in the day, Marcus Midwinter owned this whole area. Imagine!'

'The Midwinter Mines,' I said. 'An underground treasure trove of precious metal.'

'Except that most of the ore was lead, not silver as the old man hoped.' Carys sounded like a teacher, correcting a dense pupil's lazy assumption. 'Mining soon became uneconomic.'

'Pity,' I said. 'The official website talks about the history of

Midwinter. Marcus built a model village for his workforce. The man was years ahead of his time.'

'Vain as peacock on an ego trip,' Carys said. 'Calling the place after himself.'

'I gather it used to be called Pagans' Fell,' I said.

Frankie said, 'Yup. In olden days it was a site of human sacrifice.'

I filled in the silence with a light laugh.

'No wicker men around these days, I hope?'

'You know what they say.' Frankie chuckled. 'No smoke without fire.'

'I'm not surprised Marcus changed the name. Especially when he was trying to create a sense of community and well-being for his workforce. Living conditions must have been far better than ordinary colliery workers could ever hope for.'

'Marcus didn't finish work on the village,' Carys snapped. 'The miners went off to fight in the so-called "war to end all wars" and never came back to Midwinter.'

There was a short silence.

'The old boy was a do-gooder, by all accounts,' Frankie said. 'So was his son – that's why he founded the Midwinter Trust.'

Carys stared moodily out at the wild landscape. Snow was now falling heavily.

'The climate is brutal,' she said. 'Life here must have been tough.'

'Any minute now, you'll see remnants of the mine workings. Quite ghostly. There isn't much left, mind. Mother Nature reclaims her land, but there are still traces of the old industry. Only now they're hidden by the snow.'

The car glided to a halt on a slender finger of land. On

either side, the ground fell away sharply. Ahead of us, a metal gate blocked the way. In front of it was a snow-encrusted sign.

PRIVATE PROPERTY OF THE MIDWINTER TRUST.
NO PUBLIC RIGHT OF WAY. TRESPASSERS ENTER
AT THEIR OWN RISK.

'This will only take a jiffy,' Frankie said.

She jumped out of the car and opened the gate. After driving us through, she closed it again.

'Not exactly high security,' Carys murmured.

'The gate keeps out the sheep,' Frankie said mildly. 'If the poor creatures got above this level, they'd risk getting buried in a snowdrift. The village lies on a shelf of land below the brow of the fell. This last stretch is the toughest part of the drive. As the snow gets fiercer, it will block the road.'

Carys sat up in her seat. 'So we won't be able to get out of here?'

Frankie chuckled. 'Don't let a bit of the white stuff bother you. With any luck, the snow will start melting before you're ready to leave. Even if it doesn't, there are worse places to find yourself stuck. Bernadette prides herself on being well prepared.'

As Carys and I digested the prospect of being trapped in a remote village with a motley collection of strangers, Frankie drove on in silence. I could see that she wasn't exaggerating. The road – now a rutted track without passing places – was narrower and the snow deeper than down in the valley. Visibility was wretched and the wind brutal.

Frankie waved towards a snow-coated arch of rough

masonry close to the track. 'The old entrance to the mines. Barred off. The Trust don't want anyone falling down the shaft and breaking their necks.'

We'd reached a small plateau of land, and I saw the remains of a tumbledown building. The walls were still standing but the roof had collapsed.

'That was meant to be the village school,' Frankie said. 'They hadn't finished it when the First World War began. Over there, they were supposed to build a chapel. Not much left now but the foundations. After the Armistice, there weren't enough families left for it to be worth finishing the construction work.'

The road rose again before levelling off. At last, the village proper came into view. A scattering of single-storey stone cottages and larger buildings were grouped around a frozen oval lake and a patch of open land. The village green had turned white. Lights shone from several windows as well as the cast-iron lamp-posts, illuminating a canopied drinking fountain and a memorial cross. A Christmas tree towered above us, with coloured lights sparkling defiance through the wintry murk.

I felt a prickling on my spine. Midwinter should be idyllic. A Christmas retreat, in the middle of nowhere. But this was no green and pleasant land. In the gloom, the atmosphere felt brooding and oppressive.

'Journey's end,' Frankie said.

'So this is it?' Carys murmured.

'Right. There's a rough path to the summit. If the weather wasn't so bad, you could see a cairn at the top. They used to call it Pagans' Peak.'

Even in the warmth of the car, I couldn't help shivering. Frankie eased the Mercedes to a halt in front of a double-fronted single-storey building. Above the main door was an old sign, carved into the stone and recently repainted: READING ROOM.

'Old Marcus wanted his workers and their families to get a decent education,' Frankie said. 'This is where you check in. Each of you has your own cottage. Don't fret about your bags. Chandra has given me duplicate keys, and before I set off again, I'll make sure your case is waiting for you inside the front door. Once it's been checked.'

I couldn't help myself. 'Checked?'

'Didn't they mention it? Security, you know.'

'The small print in the contract,' Carys murmured. 'Page five.'

'Chandra did explain what I was and wasn't allowed to bring here.' I felt foolish and under-prepared. 'Though I didn't quite realise…'

'No panic,' Frankie said brightly. 'I'm sure you haven't brought anything you shouldn't.'

I couldn't see Carys's face, but I felt sure she was indulging in a superior smile. Possibly a smirk of glee.

'They simply want to make sure you're all on a level playing field for this game of yours,' Frankie continued. 'No cheating is allowed, obviously. Not that anyone's accusing anyone. Just a precaution, see? So everyone knows where they stand.'

Except that we don't, I thought.

Frankie waved us towards the door of the reading room.

'You do know to hand in your smart phones, don't you? They'll be kept with your passports in the safe and returned to you when it's time to leave.'

'Seriously?' I asked.

'Don't worry. You won't run short of stuff to read. We don't have telly or radio in Midwinter, let alone access to the internet.'

49

'What if…?'

'You heard what she said,' Carys snapped. 'No cheating. You can't consult Google or phone a friend. We're on our own now. You wouldn't want to take a sneaky advantage over the rest of us, would you?'

She made no effort to soften the bite of her words. I was tempted to protest, but of course she'd got my measure. Sneaky advantages are fine in my book, as long as I'm the one taking them.

'Don't worry,' Frankie said. 'Even in the height of summer, the wi-fi connection here is lousy. It was out of action this morning and I guess it's kaput for the duration. So you're not missing out.'

'How refreshing.' I said quickly. 'We can talk to each other and lose ourselves in a good story, rather than endlessly scrolling through meaningless messages.'

'Too right.' Frankie laughed. 'If the power goes, the ice house is packed with everything we need. Including candles and matches.'

The blizzard outside sounded wilder by the minute, but here in the warmth, surrounded by books, I should have felt perfectly at home.

Instead, I felt clammy with unease.

'Seems like they have thought of everything,' I muttered.

Frankie beamed.

'Welcome to Midwinter!'

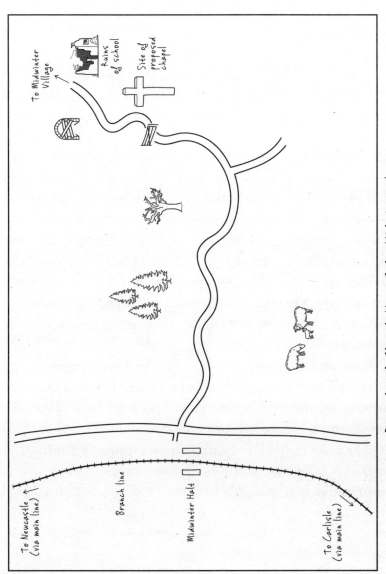

To Midwinter
Village

Ruins
of school

Site of
proposed
chapel

To Newcastle
(via main line)

Branch line

Midwinter Halt

To Carlisle
(via main line)

Bernadette's Sketch Map of the Midwinter Area

5

Harry Crystal's Journal

'So you're Harry Crystal?' The young woman's eyes opened wide. Her lips were slightly parted. 'The detective-story writer?'

'That's me.'

'Awesome!' Her beam showed a lot of perfect teeth, while a touch of la-di-da in her voice suggested an expensive education. 'I'm Poppy de Lisle, fantastic to meet you. Waiting for the key to your cottage?'

'That's right.'

The reading room was awash with bunting. A huge fir tree was laden with baubles. Tinsel was even draped over the iron doorstop. There was one window, an unmarked internal door, and two walls lined with shelves. Against the third wall towered a bookcase that almost touched the ceiling; it was free-standing and so tightly crammed with books that I feared one push would topple it over. The old bibliophile's joke sprang to mind: *There's no such thing as too many books. Just not enough bookshelves.*

The furniture was pleasantly old-fashioned: half a dozen comfortable chairs and two heavy mahogany desks equipped with posh stationery, fountain pens, and silver letter-openers, together with a stack of board games, jigsaw puzzles, and tables for chess and backgammon.

A few minutes earlier, Chandra Masood had handed me two simple sketch maps drawn by Bernadette. One showed the local area, the other featured the village in greater detail. We were welcome to play a game here after dinner this evening, Chandra said.

The first shock came when I glanced at the contents of the tall bookcase. Everything from the latest bestsellers to Dickens and Shakespeare. What I'd never anticipated was to see a *complete set* of my own novels, all thirty-two titles in hardback, neatly lined up in a row. All were first editions – admittedly, none of them had sold enough to merit a second edition. They weren't precisely in chronological order of publication – the fourth and sixth books were out of place – but never mind. Until now, I'd assumed that nowhere except my own study could you find a copy of every single one of my novels.

Wow. The days were long gone when I rushed into bookshops, eager to find copies of my latest, determined to relocate them in more prominent, face-out positions. Nowadays my books were mostly found in charity shops and car boot sales. Occasionally in builders' skips.

That wasn't all. On the shelf immediately below my collected works were the famous mystery novels referenced in each of my titles. This gimmick had begun by accident, when I called my first novel *Murder Isn't Easy*. A *cri de coeur*, given the long struggle I had writing the wretched thing, let alone finding someone willing to publish it. I went to a book festival (ah, those long-ago days when I was invited to talk about my writing!) and an earnest young man in the audience asked me if my aim was to create a metanarrative reimagining

Agatha Christie's *Murder is Easy*. When I said nothing was further from my mind, he looked disgusted.

But he gave me an idea. Perhaps readers who didn't look carefully might pick up mine by mistake. My next novel's title played on P. D. James's *Innocent Blood* and my agent was gleeful. People who buy books often do so on impulse, he said, especially in supermarkets. Book buyers might pick up my novels in the mistaken belief they were written by greats of the genre. Especially since my surname resembled Dame Agatha's.

Over the years, we tested this theory to destruction, but no supermarket ever stocked my books and my income never rose far above the breadline. Bram Stoker said in *Dracula* that we learn from failure, not success. On his logic, I should be the best-educated man in Britain. I fantasised about writing under a pseudonym, pretending to be a debut author freed of the ball and chain of a lousy sales record, hoping to fill columns of *Booktrader Magazine* with snippets about fifteen-way auctions and six-figure pre-emptive bids for my utterly immersive masterpiece. My agent poured cold water on these dreams, advising that my best hope lay in casual readers confusing me with Christie. Instead, casual acquaintances routinely asked me if I wrote under my own name. A polite way of saying they'd never heard of me.

So Midwinter's reading room made me think I'd walked into heaven. My novels were in pristine condition – presumably nobody in the village had read them, but who cared? A cynic would say it was better that way. I was trying to convince myself I wasn't hallucinating when the outer door had swung open and Poppy bounced in, a pink-cheeked picture of such indomitable enthusiasm that I half expected her to be wielding a hockey stick.

'Checking in here is more complicated than I expected,' I said. 'I should have seen the warning signs when Chandra talked about "onboarding".'

'I suppose they can't be too careful?' she said vaguely. 'Everything is very hush-hush, isn't it? So exciting! I absolutely adore mystery games. Love them so much, even if I never manage to win?'

The randomness with which she turned ordinary sentences into questions was baffling. A cunning tactic, perhaps, to confuse anyone she spoke to.

'Maybe your luck is about to change.'

'I wish! Sweet of you to say, though.'

'You arrived earlier today?'

'That's right, I've had a few hours to de-stress and reset. Adjust to my new surroundings?'

'Not to mention the prospect of being snowed in?'

'Wouldn't that be awesome?' Her eyes shone. 'When Frankie dropped us at the village hall, only a few flakes were falling. Now it's pelting down. Chandra says the forecast is positively apocalyptic?'

'She assured me the Midwinter Trust prepares for all eventualities.'

'Incredibly efficient, aren't they?'

'So far everything seems slickly organised. I suppose it helps if money is no object.'

She pouted. 'Aren't you being rather cynical?'

'That's what fifteen years as a full-time writer does to a man.' I sighed. 'Wrings the optimism out of you. Drains your faith in human nature.'

An uncertain laugh. 'So that's why...'

Her voice trailed away and a look of panic filled her eyes. I guessed it had dawned on her that she was flirting with disaster, in the form of instant disqualification from the game and expulsion from Midwinter within hours of her arrival. What if she'd asked about the real reason I was here? Suppose Chandra came in to fetch me and heard? Was it far-fetched to picture Bernadette listening at the door?

No, don't get carried away, I told myself, *that never ends well for you. This is only a game, when all's said and done. It's not as if we're investigating an* actual *murder*.

There was an innocence about Poppy – an *apparent* innocence, at any rate – that I found appealing. She might be – no, I reminded myself, she definitely *was* – an opponent, but I wanted to ease her discomfiture.

'You've come across my name?'

'Of course,' she said. 'And...'

She faltered. I knew what she was about to say. And your photograph. But I didn't look the way I used to do. Her cheeks turned crimson. I took pity on her.

'Delighted to hear it.'

'Oh yes!' She brightened. 'Your books were all the rage...'

Too late, she realised she'd used the past tense. No need to add *back in the day*. She put her hand to her mouth and I made another attempt to put her out of her misery.

'You're a crime fan, then?'

'I'm a publicist,' she said. 'I went into comms straight from uni. Later on, I gave the publishing business a try.'

'Which company?'

'So, I joined Paxton & Lightfoot.'

'P&L?' Their unaffectionate nickname in the trade reflected their ruthless focus on the bottom line.

A cloud passed over her face. 'These days, basically, I'm freelance.'

'Corporate culture too stifling? Can't blame you for deciding to go it alone. So much more freedom.'

'Tell you the truth,' she said. 'They decided for me.'

P&L were one of the Big Seven, but I was vaguely aware that in recent times they'd gone through a latest round of redundancies… or de-layering programme, to use their favourite euphemism. Apparently, they'd experienced a rough patch after paying big bucks for too many ghost-written novels purporting to be written by celebrities who could barely string two sentences together, and wannabe 'cult novels', aka incomprehensible garbage that nobody wanted to read. Not that I'm bitter.

'But you've enjoyed going solo?'

A hunted look crept into her blue eyes. 'So, I'm not a natural entrepreneur?'

I bet. Her satin jacket and leather trousers hadn't come from any market stall, but I diagnosed wealthy parents rather than a client list glittering like the gold bracelet on her wrist. Poppy's honesty was disarming, but I reminded myself of Bernadette's advice. *Trust no one.*

'You came here with one of the other players?' I asked.

'Baz Frederick, the podcaster?'

'Never heard of him.'

'*Black Death*?' she said patiently. 'His investigations were awesome.'

'Were?'

'Basically, everything went wrong because of one particular episode. He wanted to re-examine an unsolved case.'

'What was it about?'

'Not sure of the details, but at the end of the previous podcast, he mentioned it was going to be called *Evil under the Snow*. Great title, totally original. After that, total silence. No wonder he's...'

She stopped short as she realised she was talking too much. A habit to be encouraged.

'I arrived with a woman called Carys Neville,' I said.

'The influencer?'

'Or is it influenza? One way or another, I'm sure she's gone viral.'

Poppy giggled and I felt myself warming to her. I couldn't remember the last time Jocasta or Sasha had done anything other than pretend to throw up in response to my feeble jokes.

'You've come across her?' I asked.

'So, I know her by reputation? Just before I left P&L, Cancelo hired her as a consultant.'

'Is that right?'

Cancelo was the upmarket imprint in the P&L group, originally founded by a Spanish disciple of Borges and famed for producing obscure, highbrow fiction, typically described as a reimagined *bildungsroman*. The demented storylines were described as *personal and propulsive* or *subverting the form of the novel* and hailed, in extreme cases, as *in the most dazzling traditions of magic realism*. Beautifully produced, with tasselled bookmarks, they won innumerable prizes. Nobody ever opened them, let alone used the bookmarks, but it was a mark of refined taste to display them on your shelves.

'Her recommendations led to scores of authors being culled from Cancelo's list. Ever wonder why people talk about Cancelo culture? Carys Neville, that's why.' The corners of her mouth turned down. 'And then she was cancelled herself.'

I blinked. 'Really?'

'A colleague she'd snubbed leaked an early draft of her

report. The language she'd used about some of the authors was called out as highly inappropriate.'

I succeeded in choking back a snigger, but found it impossible not to smirk.

'How sad.' I couldn't restrain my incurable nosiness. 'What sort of thing?'

'Some of it I wouldn't like to repeat in mixed company.'

An odd phrase, I'd always assumed it was only used by men to patronise women. Then again, the age of equality...

'Oh go on,' I wheedled.

Poppy wavered before succumbing to temptation and allowing a conspiratorial smile to cross her face. She leaned forward, enabling me to catch a delicate whiff of floral perfume. Rich but not in the least raunchy, like Poppy herself.

'Even the mild stuff she wrote about their novels was a bit – sharp. You know the sort of thing?'

I tried not to look as though I was salivating for bad news.

'Where the final document said a book was *slow-burning*, the original said, "so mind-blowingly tedious it makes you want to shoot yourself". *Lacerating* meant "horrible", *profound* equalled "incomprehensible", and *multi-layered* was a euphemism for "a short story padded out into a novel". Get the picture?'

'Oh dear. How unfortunate for Carys.' Privately, I was ecstatic. Even her insults were derivative.

'Basically, she insisted it was all down to a computer glitch. The final document was squeaky clean. The denials did her no good. You know how things are these days? One false step, and you plunge into the abyss?'

'Never to climb out, huh?' A shiver of pleasure coursed down my spine. Nothing beats the misfortune of an enemy for improving your day. 'Oh dear, what a shame. But no smoke without fire, eh?'

Poppy's voice dropped to a whisper. 'I mean, nobody actually said she was sacked, but we all know what *long-term strategic furlough* means, don't we?'

'I guess we do.'

'I'm surprised you didn't know. The news was in the trade press.'

'Never read it.'

Far too depressing to be bombarded with never-ending updates about other writers' triumphs. Awards for this, auctions for that. That's why I'd sooner stick pins in my eyes than faff around with social media. How soul-destroying to feel morally obliged to keep liking and reposting the humblebrags of people who sell a hundred times as many books as me and own more houses than I've had five figure advances. Not that I approve of jealousy, obviously. All the same, sometimes it's hard not to be bitter, not to think, *Why them? Why not me?*

'Gosh.'

Poppy sounded shocked, as if being starved of industry gossip was beyond the reach of her imagination. I was equally nonplussed. I hadn't realised anyone still said *gosh*.

'Come to think of it,' I said, 'I've not heard anything about Carys lately. We didn't really chat in the car on the way here. She strikes me as a loner. What's she up to these days?'

'Nothing as far as I know.' Poppy paused so extravagantly that I could almost see the cogs whirring in her brain. 'Funny, isn't it?'

'What?'

'One way or another, the four of us seem to be involved with crime?'

'Is that so surprising? Given that we're here to solve a murder?'

Poppy hesitated. 'There's something else.'

'What do you mean?'

'It looks like we've all... well, had a bit of a blip in our careers?'

I considered her, weighing up what to say.

'Please don't take offence,' she said anxiously. 'You've had a run of rotten luck. It's never easy for writers in the midlist.'

'Midlist!' I groaned. 'The industry's ultimate euphemism. Meaning, the ninety-nine per cent of writers the great reading public never heard of.'

'You'll bounce back, trust me? With the right agent and the right editor. Not to mention the right publicity strategy!'

I felt a sharp stab of irritation. It is one thing to be politely self-deprecating about one's lack of critical and commercial success, quite another to have the dismal reality rubbed in, even by someone as apparently well-meaning as Poppy de Lisle. Luckily, she'd given me the chance to indulge in compensatory *schadenfreude*.

'I'd no idea Carys Neville had run into trouble with Cancelo.'

'The official announcement talked about her moving on to pursue other exciting opportunities?'

'Claiming benefits, for instance?' My waspish tone made Poppy blink. 'You know yourself that there are lies, damned lies, and press releases about departing staff. Well, well, who would have thought it? The biter bit, eh?'

Poppy contemplated her pink-painted fingernails. 'I hate to sound unkind, but I hear she isn't the easiest.'

'I'll let you into a secret,' I said in a conspiratorial whisper.

'That woman wrecked my career, such as it was. All it took was a few cruel, coruscating sentences online.'

Her eyes widened. 'Really?'

'According to Carys, when my publishers claimed my books were *in the tradition* of Agatha Christie, they really meant I was a brazen copycat. She said the aim was simply to put her name in huge type on the covers, so readers might think they were buying her latest. "Never mind the mis-selling," Carys said, "he has at least created a new sub-genre. Fiction to snooze through. *Dozy Crime*."'

Poppy winced. 'Oh dear.'

'It felt like a casual drive-by shooting… of my self-esteem. I'm sure she never read a word I wrote. I just happened to be a convenient target. A scapegoat. Probably a name she plucked out of a hat.'

'Gosh, must have been awkward for the two of you today, travelling together in the car?'

'She had no idea who I was.'

'Seriously?'

I hesitated. Was Carys even more devious than I realised? Suppose she had recognised me, despite the fact I hardly resemble the photograph on my book jackets. Did it suit her warped and malicious sense of humour to pretend she didn't know my name?

'I was dropped by my publisher. Carys's condemnation was the straw that broke the camel's back. My agent tried shopping my books elsewhere, but he told me my brand was tarnished beyond repair. I didn't even know I was a brand. I thought I was just a crime writer. Anyway, she dropped me too.'

'Oh goodness.'

'My fortunes never recovered. I try to follow the latest

market trends, so finally I published my most recent novel…
um, independently.'

'Self-publishing can be awesome,' Poppy said brightly.
'What's it all about, Harry?'

'*Elephants Can Forget* is set in a safari park. Aimed fair
and square at animal lovers. Loads of bestsellers feature cat
detectives and sleuthing dogs. I took the concept to the next
level. A mystery-solving menagerie.'

'Speaking directly to the end user? Wonderful!'

'I envisaged a series. Tag-line: *Zoos with Clues*.'

'Brill!'

I hung my head. 'So far, I've sold twenty-nine copies. Less
than the number of hate messages I received from animal
liberation activists.'

She rested a hand on my arm and gave a comforting
squeeze. 'A targeted marketing campaign can make all the
difference? Perhaps we should talk?'

I gave her a quizzical look.

'I mean… when the game is over?' she said hurriedly.

'You may be right,' I said.

It wouldn't do any harm to bring Poppy on side, but I told
myself not to make my usual mistake of getting carried away.
Unlike Frankie the chauffeur, this young woman had skin in
the game. We were competing against each other, after all.

The door opened and Chandra looked in.

'So you're getting to know each other. Lovely! Ready to
come along with me, Harry? Time to check in.'

'I feel as though I've signed my life over to you,' I grumbled,
as I scrawled my signature on the last dotted line.

'You must get bored with people asking for your autograph,' Chandra Masood said pleasantly. She had big eyes and shoulder-length black hair. Mid-thirties at a guess, but it was hard to tell.

'If only,' I grumbled. 'A dealer once told me my books are worth more unsigned. Is all this bureaucracy absolutely necessary? The stuff about confidentiality? It's like a code of silence. A vow of *omertà*.'

'We value your privacy,' she intoned.

I grunted. Surely that was the greatest lie of the twenty-first century? Along with *we use cookies to improve your experience* and *your call is important to us.*

Chandra was in charge of People at Midwinter Trust and she'd already said more than once that she was a 'people person'. Like any HR specialist, she had a way of dealing with disgruntled individuals. Flash a smile, insist that 'people are our most valuable resource', and pay no attention whatsoever to their latest pettifogging grievance.

'Here's hoping you have a wonderful Christmas with us!'

Things could only get better. But I reminded myself that people often say this just before the world collapses around them.

Checking in at Midwinter was like gaining access to a maximum-security prison. Not that I've ever been behind bars, but for the next few nights the village would resemble an upmarket jail, a sort of Hotel California with tinsel trimmings. I wasn't so much an honoured guest of Midwinter Trust as their captive.

What if I wanted to leave early, and for some unknown reason, they cut up rough? I'd be entirely dependent on Frankie's goodwill. In such appalling weather, there was no chance of getting back to the station on foot. Even if I could work out the route, I'd freeze to death before I was halfway there.

'Here are the keys to your cottage,' she said. 'Front door and back.'

I jangled the keys in my hand. 'Strange to see you still have good old-fashioned door-locks. With so much technology available.'

'Our resilience plan makes clear that we don't depend on high-tech systems.' Chandra smoothed her hair. 'At this time of year, there's always the danger that even the most sophisticated technology would fail. Given the climate, we've learned to expect the worst.'

'And which cottage am I in?'

She smiled. 'The name's on the key ring?'

I glanced at the cryptic legend.

{pp; Bore Vpyyshr

'Ah.' I blinked. 'Is this part of the game?'

'Just a simple key code. Like the cipher on your invitation. You did solve it, I hope?'

I hesitated, not sure whether to play dumb. She waited, and I caved in.

'The Greek alphabet cipher?' She nodded. 'I did come up with a phrase. But I wasn't sure if it made much sense.'

'Go on.'

'Miss Winter in the Library with a Knife?'

'Well done! Bernadette thought you'd enjoy another warm-up exercise to get those grey cells working.' She gave a sly smile. 'If you don't mind my saying so, you're the right type.'

Outside the wind screamed like a half-crazed vagrant begging for admittance to the warm and dry. I was in no rush to brave the outside, especially if I didn't know where I was heading.

'Sounds rough out there.'

'They call it a Pagan Wind. From the legends about this fell.'

'You mean the wind actually has a *name*? Like the Mistral or Chinook?'

'When it gusts in from the north-east, it knocks sheep off their feet and blows stone walls to pieces. I've heard tell of snowdrifts as deep as a cottage is high. Nobody can tell how long a Pagan Wind will blow. Two hours, two days, two weeks.'

'A fortnight? Are you serious? I hope you have plenty of provisions laid in. Just in case.'

She laughed. 'Take that worried look off your face, Harry. You won't starve. Daisy, our cook, is a marvel. She's made sure we have enough food stored to feed an army. I know you like an occasional tipple, so rest assured there's no shortage of drink, either – Jeremy insists on keeping a good cellar. As you'll discover at dinner.'

I felt a twinge of unease. *I know you like an occasional tipple.* An inconsequential pleasantry or a craftily barbed reference to my past misfortunes? How thoroughly did Midwinter Trust research its guests? I forced the semblance of a genial smile.

'You've thought of everything.'

'We do our best. The wine and our food reserves are kept in a big ice house behind the village hall. There's a massive amount of storage space and everything perishable can be shifted there if need be. If all else fails, we have candles, matches, and everything else you need to get by until the weather eases. Wind-up torches, you name it. Each cottage has its own first aid kit. Trust me, we'll be fine.'

'Sounds good,' I said, though I couldn't help remembering

that she and Bernadette had briefed me to trust *no one*, not even them.

She smiled. 'While you are here, we'll do our utmost to make sure you can play the game in comfort, whatever the elements throw at us.'

In person, Chandra was chattier than during the online briefings. Perhaps she hadn't wanted to tread on Bernadette's toes; there was no doubt which of the two women was in charge. I needed to find out as much as I could about this place and the people who ran it. Might Chandra be tempted into an indiscretion? Perhaps a glass or two of something from Jeremy's cellar would be in order. Yes, she might be wanting to assess how I handled the drink, but I needed a chance to get closer to her. Nothing ventured...

'So how long have you been with Midwinter Trust?'

A little laugh. 'Longer than I care to remember!'

Evasion was second nature with these people. I tried again. 'You must enjoy it, then?'

'Absolutely love it!' A radiant smile. 'The Director is totally committed to the cause. He's been here half his life, you know. Under his guidance, the Trust does such good work. So important in these troubled times.'

'Does the Director—?'

'Anyway, I shouldn't stand here gossiping. I must let you go. And there are things I need to do before this evening's briefing.'

'Seven o'clock in the village hall?'

'See you there.' She opened the door. 'Hey, one of your fellow guests has looked in. Baz, come and say hello to Harry Crystal!'

Baz Frederick was six inches taller, three stone heavier, and ten years younger than me. He was also far more debonair, in a three-piece suit and shiny black shoes. After crushing my fingers in a handshake, he wiped streaks of snow from his coat and treated me to a ferocious grin.

'Should have gone back to sunny Scarborough, shouldn't I? Spent Christmas with my family instead, huh?'

'It's probably not much warmer on the Yorkshire coast,' I said. 'Those gales coming in off the North Sea...'

He laughed uproariously and gave me a clap on the back that risked fracturing several vertebrae. 'Scarborough, Tobago, man. Four thousand miles away. My granny still lives there. Ma and Pa moved here before I was born, God rest their souls.'

I managed a weak grin while checking my spine was still intact. 'You've had time to settle into Midwinter?'

'Yeah, crazy set-up, don't you think?'

'I've only just arrived,' I said cautiously. 'Not even seen my cottage yet. I just pray the heating works.'

'If this snow keeps up...' He pretended to shiver. 'I don't know this part of England well.'

'You live down south?'

'Notting Hill, yeah.' He peered at me. 'So you're a crime novelist, huh?'

'I'm flattered that you recognise me.'

Chortling, he gave a decisive shake of the head. 'Chandra told me. I don't read made-up mysteries. Can't believe in them, yeah?'

'Uh-huh.' I had to restrain myself from pointing out that he'd come to Midwinter to solve just such a puzzle.

'True crime is my bag, not stuff that never happened. I mean, what's the point?'

I dug my fingernails into my palm, forcing myself not to rise to the bait. 'I gather you're a… podcaster.'

I made it sound like *lamplighter* or *telegram messenger*.

'Not right now.' He breathed out and I caught a pungent whiff of tobacco. 'Went through a rough patch, trod on too many toes, know what I mean? It was time to take a break.'

'So you decided to come to Midwinter and play the game?' I said carelessly, hoping to draw him out.

Baz put a finger to his lips. 'Not allowed to talk about that, man. They sure have a lot of rules here. I fell asleep reading all the crap they sent. Lord knows what I agreed to. Probably sold my soul to the Trust. Much good it'll do them.'

I gave a sympathetic nod. 'Do you know anything about the other people who are taking part?'

He ticked the names off on huge fingers stained with nicotine. 'You got here at the same time as a woman called Carys, right? I came with this sweet kid called Poppy, she's in publicity.'

'Yes, she seems lovely. Quite… innocent, I thought.'

'You reckon, Harry? This is Midwinter, remember? If you ask me, there's nothing innocent about this village. Or about any of us.'

I smiled. 'You make me feel like Josef K. Guilty of something, but I don't know what.'

'Josef K.?' he asked.

'The protagonist in *The Trial*.'

He shook his head. 'Courtroom dramas are so yesterday, man. True crime podcasts, they're the future – you heard it here first, yeah?'

'If you say so.'

'The last two guests are an agent and an editor, Chandra

said.' He eyed me thoughtfully. 'They work in crime fiction too. Pals of yours, maybe? Zack and Grace?'

I frowned. 'Not Zack Jardine and Grace Kinsella by any chance?'

'Right first time, Harry. So you do know them?'

'Only by reputation. I'm not a big enough fish to swim in the same pool.'

Baz laughed. 'Hey, don't run yourself down, man. A veteran like you must know this mystery world inside out.'

I winced at the dreaded word *veteran*, a publishing world euphemism for *past it*, but Baz breezed on.

'Experience counts, man. If you ask me, you're the favourite to win the game.'

I felt my shoulders sagging. This was exactly the opposite of the impression I hoped to create. I preferred to think of myself as a plucky outsider. Battling against the odds. Yet whatever I did, my age counted against me.

'I'm only forty-five,' I couldn't help saying.

Baz shook his head in sympathy, as if I'd announced that I was about to acquire a stairlift and a Zimmer frame in a two-for-one deal. I was so annoyed that I almost missed the look of calculation creeping into his eyes.

'So what do you know about Zack and Grace?'

I was taken aback by his persistence. He was clearly as determined to research his opponents as I was. But what if his real aim was to figure out how much I knew, and to work out whether – despite my advanced age – I represented serious competition? I resolved to stay on my guard.

'Only what everyone knows,' I said casually. 'Zack was a rising star as a literary agent, a hotshot with a flair for finding gems in the slush pile.'

'The slush pile?'

'The zillions of unsolicited manuscripts agents and publishers receive. That's how Zack discovered Ravenna Gray.'

'Wow, even I've heard of her.'

'Everyone knows her. The biggest sensation in fictional crime for ages. Fifty Shades of Success, as the headline writers loved to say. Zack's first mistake was to put all his eggs in one basket. When Spielberg begged Ravenna to let him film her first book, she fired Zack and signed up with one of the biggest agencies in the world. Zack's second mistake was to accuse Ravenna of breach of contract. She retaliated by suing him for sexual harassment. His other clients deserted him and his agency had to shut up shop.'

'Was Ravenna's editor Grace Kinsella?'

Again, that measuring gaze. Instinct told me that he already knew the answer, but was itching to find out how well-informed I was about our fellow guests. Why did it matter to him?

I shook my head. 'Uh-uh. Grace made a name for herself by talent-spotting unknown authors who wrote psychological thrillers full of charming sociopaths and unreliable narrators. *The Girl on the Plane* and *The Woman in the Witness Box* sold by the million and Netflix signed her to an exclusive consultancy deal. Critics said the books she edited made Patricia Highsmith look like Barbara Cartland.'

'Barbara who?'

I waved a hand. 'Doesn't matter. Just a lousy joke. I'm full of them, as my wife and daughter often pointed out.'

Baz stroked his jaw. 'Sounds like Grace doesn't fit the pattern.'

'The pattern?'

'If she's that successful, how come she's spending Christmas here, hanging out with a bunch of no-hopers who don't have two pennies to rub together?'

I cringed at this. 'Grace fell on hard times after someone ran a check on her authors' books. Seems they were mostly hacks who used artificial intelligence to plunder bestsellers for quotable lines and memorable situations. Grace's edits made them readable, but she'd failed to do her due diligence. Netflix cancelled and sued for their lost investment. Online platforms banned the books. Grace became a non-person.'

'And now she's turned up in Midwinter,' Baz said softly. 'Don't you wonder why?'

'One way or another, all six of us are involved with writing about crime.'

'Kind of makes sense. We're here to solve a mystery, don't forget.' Baz smiled grimly. 'And another thing.'

'What's that?'

'No easy way to say this, man. But we've got to face facts.'

I felt my heart sinking. Facing facts is my least favourite occupation. That's why I write novels. I yearn to create worlds of my own where harsh reality never intrudes.

'Go on.'

'We've all taken a wrong turn. Our lives have gone sour. We're desperate to start over.'

'I'm not sure *desperate* is quite the right—' I began.

'Hey man,' he interrupted, 'no need to put a brave face on it with me. We're all in this together.'

I frowned. I associated this phrase with people who hadn't the faintest desire to be in anything together with me.

'You think?'

Baz gave an impatient wave of the hand. I felt sure there was plenty he wanted to get off his chest, and that he was parcelling up bits and pieces of information to share with others while he familiarised himself with Midwinter.

'Don't you see, Harry? That's the reason we're spending Christmas in this crazy little village, trying to turn our lives around by solving a murder mystery. That's what the Midwinter Trust says they are trying to do – gather half a dozen failures and make one of us into a big-time winner. So ask yourself this.' He paused. '*Why?*'

MIDWINTER
A RETREAT THAT IS A RARE TREAT

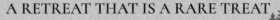

Midwinter is exclusive but not elitist, taking the traditions of village life a century ago and repackaging them for those who aspire to a better future in perfect harmony with the values of the Midwinter Trust, a not-for-profit organisation regulated under the <u>terms</u> of the Midwinter Trust Act 1946. Founded by Sir Maurice Midwinter, the Trust is currently chaired by Jeremy Vandervell, who also serves in an executive capacity. The other trustees are Bernadette Corrigan and Chandra Masood.

Jeremy Vandervell is the Director of the Midwinter Trust. He was educated at Westminster School <u>and</u> Trinity College, Cambridge, where he studied History. On graduating with First Class Honours, he joined the civil service, and during the course of his duties he met Sir Maurice Midwinter, who recruited him to join <u>the</u> Midwinter Trust. The rest, as he likes to say, is history…

Bernadette Corrigan is the Deputy Director of the Midwinter Trust. She comes originally from Belfast but her family moved to England when she was very young. She worked as a civil servant prior to joining the Trust. Her hobbies include creative writing and playing word games.

Chandra Masood is the Midwinter Trust's Head of People. Her parents came from Afghanistan to England to start a new life here shortly before she was born and she trained as a human resources manager in government for several years before accepting an invitation to develop and implement new people systems for the Trust. In her limited downtime, Chandra's passions include yoga and various forms of therapeutic mindfulness.

6

Harry Crystal's Journal

Thankfully it didn't take too much head-scratching to figure out the key code before I left the warmth of the village hall.

{pp; Bore Vpyyshr

'You're the right type,' Chandra had said, dropping the broadest of hints. This was a typewriter code, with each symbol representing a letter to its immediate right on a conventional keyboard, with capitals represented by upper case letters or the equivalent. I'd actually used something similar in *The Nine Gaolers*. So the answer was:

Pool View Cottage

I felt gratified. Bernadette's psychology was sound. She was getting us into the mood for the game with gentle confidence-boosters.

My billet was in a semi-detached, single-storey dwelling. The whitewashed walls matched the landscape. A holly wreath hung on the door of each cottage in the village. Although my new home was only a short distance from the reading room, I was covered in snow by the time I put my key in the lock.

Pool View Cottage was as well-appointed as anyone could hope for from a tiny stone house originally built for a miner's family early in the twentieth century. Central heating radiators tapped and clicked, but a log fire had been laid in the living room. Packets of matches lay on the table, and there was a scuttle full of logs for when the embers burned low. An open fire at Christmas – heavenly. All I needed now was a few chestnuts to roast.

No sign of those, but I had tea, coffee, and fluffy white towels, not to mention complimentary freebies including a fleecy white dressing gown. The Trust had also supplied a wind-up torch, candles, an ice axe, and a pair of sturdy trekking poles for getting about in the snow. A small bookcase had three packed shelves. There were even three or four paperback editions of my own efforts, as if some chambermaid with a sense of irony had thought I might like to reacquaint myself with the reasons for the implosion of my literary career.

There was a desk and chair, along with plenty of stationery and envelopes. On the desk were a nice new leather-bound journal, a spiral-bound notebook for jotting down information about the murder mystery game, and a silver rollerball pen in a gift box. They were accompanied by a small oblong card saying: *With the compliments of the Midwinter Trust*. I was amused by the unsubtle reminder that we were expected to write up our experiences. Already I've filled quite a few pages of the journal. A lot has happened in a short time.

True to her promise, Frankie had deposited my suitcase inside the front door. While unpacking, I examined the contents with care to make sure nothing was missing.

Not that I thought Chandra and her colleagues would have light fingers, but I was determined to take nothing for granted.

After I'd washed and changed, I reached inside my pocket from sheer force of habit, groping for my smartphone to check all my messages. It took a few moments to remember the phone was now locked away in a safe. My personal connection with the outside world had been severed. As the implications of this hit home, I felt anything but cosy. There was no escaping the cold reality.

I was at the mercy of the Midwinter Trust.

Good thing they were determined to make the world a better place, I thought. Imagine if their motives were questionable…

No, I told myself, I must break out of my habitually negative mindset and convince myself I was capable of winning the game. Right now I could do with some of Jocasta's positive thinking. What was that old quote from Henry Ford? *Whether you think you can, or think you can't, you're right.* I must convince myself my career, my whole life even, was *not* an abject failure. Merely a success-in-waiting.

As I watched the flames leap in the fireplace, listened to the crackle of the burning logs, I reminded myself that nobody had forced me to spend Christmas here. I was a volunteer, not a conscript. I knew exactly what I was getting myself into.

Except, of course, this was untrue. I had only the haziest notion of what lay ahead. Bernadette and Chandra had given no explanation of the murder mystery I was required to solve. Until the six of us were briefed this evening, I only had a few crumbs of information to go on.

The painful truth was that avoiding negative thoughts only took you so far. I hated admitting it, even to myself, but Baz was right. I was a has-been, desperate to start with a blank sheet of paper, to turn over a new page, begin a fresh chapter, and every other book-related cliché I could call to mind.

Had I been too complacent? I'd given little thought to my potential opponents, but I'd assumed they wouldn't be quite as ferociously driven to succeed as I was. What if their own misadventures had made them equally competitive? What if, in order to win, they were prepared to play dirty? Perhaps *very* dirty?

Leaning back in my armchair, I couldn't help wondering if I'd committed yet another blunder. The latest in a long line, and just possibly the biggest of my life.

I arrived at the village hall in good time to size up the new arrivals before the briefing began, only to find that Poppy had beaten me to it. Another reminder not to take my rivals for granted.

Poppy was already in animated conversation over mulled wine and nibbles with Zack Jardine, who hung on her every word with the attentiveness of a born Lothario. Through discreetly placed speakers, Perry Como was crooning 'It's Beginning to Look a Lot Like Christmas'.

As if determined to avoid infection by the festive spirit, Grace Kinsella sipped a gin and tonic and kept her own counsel. I was pretty sure she was listening to every word the other pair uttered. An opponent to keep a close eye on.

The hall was the largest building in Midwinter. Literally and metaphorically, it stood at the heart of the village. Marcus Midwinter's vision had been generations ahead of its time. Nowadays, you'd call the hall a community hub. The Trust had evidently spared no expense in modernising the building.

Above our heads was a mezzanine level, with a galleried walkway and the offices of Jeremy and his colleagues. The ground floor was dominated by a large dining area with half a dozen tables. A large noticeboard adorned the rear wall, in between doors to utility rooms and the kitchen. On the polished counter of the well-stocked bar stood a snow globe.

During the onboarding process, Chandra Masood had reminded me that guests had been invited on an all-inclusive basis. There was a free bar throughout our stay in the village. Full marks to Jeremy and the Midwinter Trust for neither stinting on drink nor fobbing the guests off with cheap supermarket plonk. But I wasn't going to go mad with the booze. Not this time. I was determined to prove to myself – and everyone else – that I could handle it. In moderation.

The woman behind the bar greeted me with a dazzling smile. Her teeth were so perfect that my own mouthful of ham-fisted British dentistry made my cheeks burn with embarrassment.

'Gotta get into the Christmas spirit, in weather like this.' She pretended to shiver before extending a small hand over the counter. 'I'm Daisy Wu. You're Harry Crystal, right? Fabulous to meet you.'

The tingle of pleasure at being recognised by a good-looking woman vanished when I realised she'd worked out my identity through a process of elimination. Not to worry, this was a chance to get her talking. According to our chauffeur, Daisy was relatively new to Midwinter. An outsider, almost. An American, too. Maybe Daisy was instinctively more open and chattier than her British colleagues in the senior management team.

'What can I get you? The mulled wine's delicious, if you're

looking to get into the festive mood. And do help yourself to a sausage roll or a falafel.'

We chatted as she poured, but my hopes were soon dashed. She proved adept at stonewalling whenever I tried to pump her for information about what lay in store for players of the game. Each question was met with a bright smile and a modest reminder that she was simply head cook and bottle washer, someone who loved music and was responsible for the Christmas playlist.

'One of my favourites,' she said, nodding to the speakers. Good old Brenda Lee, 'Rockin' Around the Christmas Tree'.

I adjusted my tactics. 'You sound like a native New Yorker.'

She clapped her hands. 'Got it in one! You sure are a detective. Yeah, I was born and raised on Roosevelt Island in the East River.'

'Sounds very swish.'

'Not in those days. The main landmarks were a lunatic asylum and a smallpox hospital. As I grew up, I'd gaze across the water to Manhattan. The UN building and all the other skyscrapers seemed so near and yet so far. As if they belonged to a different world. Later on, I moved to Frederick, Maryland. Very different, but not far from DC. Incredible city. I worked in a big office the other side of the Potomac.'

She eyed me up, as if encouraging a confidence, but I stuck to my plan not to say too much.

'Lived in Britain long?'

'Since the start of this year.'

'What did you do before you came here?'

'Practising your detective skills?' She laughed. 'Let's just say that over the years, I've done my share of roaming around.'

And that was as far as I got before Baz Frederick turned up.

Following him in was Carys Neville. Her arrival was greeted by Elvis Presley's 'Santa Claus Is Back In Town', as if Daisy's playlist was indulging in a touch of satire.

'Mulled wine?' Daisy asked. 'Sausage roll?'

Carys made a face. 'I'm a vegetarian and a teetotaller.'

Just like my ex-wife, I reflected. Not to mention Adolf Hitler.

As Daisy cheerfully ran through the vegetarian and non-alcoholic alternatives, I wandered off to join the others. Poppy asked Grace about the journey from the station, only to be rewarded with an exaggerated groan.

'Nightmare, absolute nightmare! I thought we were going to get stuck on the hill. If this storm keeps up, it will take a snow plough to get through.'

'At least you were in safe hands with Frankie. Awesome, isn't she?'

Grace gave a brisk nod. Her blonde hair was cut in a razor-sharp bob and she looked casually elegant in faux-leather black leggings, kitten heels, and a red top with an asymmetrical open shoulder revealing pale, flawless skin.

'I bet Frankie has some tales she can tell. Celebrities she's chauffeured around. I said to her, if she ever fancied writing about her experiences, she should get in touch and we could do lunch.'

'You editors, gosh, you're incorrigible,' Poppy said lightly. 'Always on the lookout for the next big thing?'

'I'm thinking of starting my own imprint. A curated list.' Grace sounded defensive. 'Besides, I always love coming back to this part of the world.'

Zack Jardine pricked up his ears. 'You've been here before?'

Grace shook her head, as if irritated that she'd let something slip. 'Not to Midwinter, no. In fact, I'd never even heard of the place until… What I mean is, I grew up on the north-east coast. By the seaside at Whitley Bay.'

Zack gave a thoughtful nod. 'Cool.'

'Chilly, actually,' Grace said in a wry tone. 'Or as we liked to say, bracing. Especially when the wind blew in from the North Sea. *Brrrr!*'

She gave a theatrical shiver, as if keen to distract attention from what she'd been about to say before stopping herself. When, and in what circumstances, did she first hear about Midwinter?

Poppy turned to me. 'Sorry, I'm forgetting my manners. Harry, have you met Zack and Grace? Guys, meet Harry Crystal, he writes detective stories. Awesome, huh? I mean, this is the man we all need to watch. He's the guru, the go-to guy. He's got a head start on the rest of us.'

I tried not to shudder as I shook hands. Poppy took no notice.

'Now all of us deadly rivals have arrived safely,' she said, 'I bet none of you can wait for the fun to begin. I know I'm counting the minutes!'

Ignoring her, Grace frowned at me. 'You're an author, then?'

'Mystery fiction, that's right.'

'Popular genre. Anything published?'

'Thirty-two novels. My first was longlisted for a Debut Dagger. Admittedly in a thin year.'

She laughed as she put down her empty wine glass. I suspected it hadn't been her first drink of the evening.

'Hope you didn't shove the Dagger in the winner's back. Do you write under your own name?'

'Yes.' I ground my teeth in frustration. 'Harry Crystal.'

She nodded sagely but nothing in her expression indicated

that she'd ever heard of me. Fifteen years as a published author, and even to professionals in my own field, my name meant nothing. Grace's career might also be on the rocks, but that was scant consolation.

In the background, Herb Alpert was treating us to 'The Bell That Couldn't Jingle', and I recalled that Tolstoy said music is the shorthand of emotion. Certainly, I was beginning to feel a lot like the biggest loser in Midwinter.

Time to push back. I mustered a smile and said, 'Of course your name is familiar, Grace. Didn't you have a great deal of success in the publishing world?'

She shrugged. 'Past tense is right.'

Her searching gaze made me feel like a sliver of DNA under a forensic scientist's microscope. This was someone else intent on giving nothing away. If I couldn't prise anything useful out of her, at least I could play a part. Portraying an amiable misfit, full of harmless bonhomie came all too naturally to me. I needed my opponents to see me as someone here to make up the numbers. Not somebody to worry about. Certainly not a threat.

'You're too modest! A journeyman like me can't help feeling a twitch of envy at all your successes. A *Sunday Times* bestseller here, a Richard and Judy pick of the year there. Rapturous reviews on Radio 4.' I mustered a cheesy grin as I got into my stride. 'Books that cram the supermarket shelves.'

'Like so many rotting vegetables,' she said. 'Trouble is, I passed my sell-by date too.'

I was saved from uttering hypocritical words of consolation by the arrival of Bernadette, who was clutching a slim folder, and Chandra Masood. They were accompanied by a tall, willowy man with shoulder-length hair that was dark and wild. This was the first time I'd set eyes on Ethan Swift.

I'd had a mental picture of a frowning ascetic, but he was unexpectedly handsome. Poppy gave him a long, measuring gaze. Even Grace stole a covert glance in his direction.

Like a warm-up act for the star of a concert, the trio were followed by Jeremy Vandervell, dapper in tailored jacket and old school tie. His every stride gave the impression of a man born to command. He glanced round at the assembled guests, oozing confidence and authority the way most people sweat. I almost broke out into a round of applause before thrusting my hands deeper into my pockets. Better not stand out from the crowd.

The four of them walked across to a low dais at the front of the hall. Half a dozen armchairs were arranged in a semicircle around a table with a jug of water and half a dozen glasses. Daisy emerged from behind the bar to do the pouring, her movements swift yet sinuous. Zack and Jeremy watched her with undisguised admiration, Bernadette with the disdain of a gardener contemplating blackspot on a once-lovely rose. At the same time, Frankie bustled through the main entrance, wiping snow from her jacket, and made her way to the front.

An encouraging nod from Chandra prompted Poppy to step forward. There were chairs for the guests, and we took our places one by one. Each of us had brought our notebooks. Everyone else flipped theirs open, revealing a blank first page. So I was the only one who had already begun to make any sort of record. Perhaps it was predictable. I was the professional author in the group.

I breathed out. The twelve of us were gathered together for the very first time. Like a jury, I thought. Except that six of us were on trial.

Let the game commence.

Winner takes all.

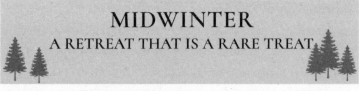
Would you like to apply to stay in Midwinter? If so, enter the code in the box below together with your full name, date of birth, address, email address, and personal mobile number:

Sorry, Midwinter is now fully booked for the foreseeable future.

7

Midwinter

Ethan nudged his chair further away from the others as he took his seat, making sure he had a good view of everyone. Before they'd come in, Bernadette had taken him aside and asked him to keep a close eye on the new arrivals.

'Tell me if you spot anything untoward. The slightest hint of potential trouble. If the weather deteriorates, everyone will be trapped in the village, with no way out. Perfect conditions for a murder mystery game, but some guests may feel uncomfortable. What if they're not as robust as we believe?'

Ethan took a breath. 'This is very different from last time. Everything has changed.'

'Of course,' she said quietly. 'We've put the past behind us. As for this group, I want to see how they react under pressure.'

'You've done your homework. You already know plenty about them.'

'With your help, yes. Background research and analysis is vital, but there's always something you don't know. Maybe something that makes the difference between... success and failure.'

'For a moment,' he said softly, 'I thought you were about to say, the difference between life and death.'

'Their whole future is on the line. Like ours.'

'You're not usually so melodramatic, Bernadette,' he'd said mildly. 'Don't forget, they're only here to play a game.'

A sharp look. 'You know how much is at stake.'

With that, she'd turned to look at Jeremy, waiting for the go-ahead so the briefing could begin.

From his vantage point on the dais, Ethan scanned the guests. A mixed bunch, yet chosen with the utmost care.

Carys Neville's languid yawn reinforced the impression of superiority tinged with ennui. An act? Unquestionably. The woman was hopelessly insecure and her attempts to cover this up with passive-aggressive snarkiness were as transparent as they were irksome. Baz Frederick, in contrast, was leaning forward in his chair, pen poised. Grace Kinsella's sharp chin jutted defiantly, as if she were gearing up for an argument.

The dress code was smart casual, although Baz was wearing a three-piece suit. Ethan wondered if Grace had tried to steal a march on her female rivals, seeking some kind of obscure psychological advantage, through her choice of outfit. The open-shoulder top and fake leather leggings displayed her figure to considerable advantage. Not that Ethan was in the least attracted, but it had only taken a nanosecond for her to attract an interested glance from the Director of the Midwinter Trust. Jeremy Vandervell was so utterly predictable.

Zack Jardine, in velvet jacket and cravat, had opted for a raffish look. Ethan noticed him nibbling at a hangnail, a giveaway clue to nervous energy beneath a façade of sophistication. Poppy de Lisle was chewing her pen. Ethan had caught her looking at him, but when his eyes met hers, a pink tinge came to her cheeks and she glanced away.

As for Harry Crystal, his expression of amiable bemusement suggested that he'd wandered inside to shelter from the storm and found himself mistaken for someone who understood what was going on.

Ethan wondered about Harry. Could anyone be quite so naïve? After all, he'd written a pile of mystery novels, even if few people read them. He wasn't entirely stupid.

Jeremy rapped on his glass. As if by magic, the music stopped.

'Good evening, ladies and gentlemen. A very warm welcome to our little village. Thank you so much for joining us here at this special time of year. I'm truly delighted to greet you all.'

A mellifluous voice. Ethan had noticed that Jeremy liked to remind people that he was North of England born and bred, but nobody would ever guess he came from the neighbourhood of the Tyneside shipyards. Anyone less like a horny-handed son of toil would be hard to imagine. He probably knew all the words to the 'Eton Boating Song'. Three years at Cambridge, followed by a spell in the diplomatic service had smoothed any rough provincial edges from his accent. To look at or listen to him, you'd never guess anything about his background, except that it hadn't lacked in privilege.

'One thing you'll have noticed already. Midwinter is determined to live up to its name.'

Jeremy paused to allow an appreciative murmur of amusement. His smile was positively beatific, although a shrewd observer might detect a touch of condescension lurking just beneath the surface.

'My name is Jeremy Vandervell, and I'm the Director of the Midwinter Trust. Not that you need me to tell you that. You are dedicated sleuths, after all.' A full-wattage beam prompted wary smiles from his audience. 'You've travelled here, from far-flung parts of the country, braving the fickle elements and the even less reliable rail network, to spend your Christmas with us. We are honoured.'

He lowered his voice, as if to suggest intimacy, a shared confidence. 'I won't insult your intelligence by harping on about the Midwinter Trust. You all have an idea of what we're about, in principle if not yet in rich full detail. In today's complicated world, some might regard our very existence as anachronistic. We see things differently. Our small size and aversion to bureaucracy makes us quick on our feet. Adaptable, innovative, forward-thinking.'

Daisy's expression struck Ethan as hard to interpret. Was she *amused*?

'Our mission statement is simplicity itself,' Jeremy said. 'We strive to make the world a better place. A noble cause. As for myself, I've been dedicated to the ideal of service since I first joined the Trust. Which was more years ago than I care to remember. Possibly before one or two of you were even born.'

His smile contrived to be self-deprecating yet smug at one and the same time. Quite a feat. But then, the Director of the Midwinter Trust was quite something. Ethan didn't need an in-depth psychological profile of Jeremy Vandervell to know what the man was capable of.

'We owe huge gratitude to the visionary thinking of Marcus Midwinter, and to his son, Sir Maurice, who turned the Midwinter Trust into a reality, laying the groundwork for what we do today. It was the privilege of my life to get to know Sir Maurice before he died.'

As if responding to stage directions, Bernadette and Chandra nodded thoughtfully. Daisy gazed at the Director. Her smile was admiring, but didn't extend to her eyes, which were scrutinising Jeremy Vandervell with care.

'The world moves on and the Midwinter Trust moves with it. We're acutely aware that we can't be set in our ways, we're eager to welcome fresh blood. Fresh thinking. Fresh imagination.'

Neat, Ethan thought. The man resembled a gangster's silver-tongued defence counsel, pre-empting potential lines of attack while contriving to sound like the voice of reason. His survival instincts were finely tuned. No wonder he'd lasted so long at Midwinter. Give him an inch of wriggle room, and he'd steal a mile. If anybody was capable of getting away with murder, it was Jeremy Vandervell.

The Director gave a little cough, his favourite conversational punctuation mark. 'All that is why, ladies and gentlemen – if I'm permitted to use such an old-fashioned term these days – you are here.'

A lordly wave encompassed his whole audience, but Ethan saw Jeremy looking directly at Poppy, rather than the more obviously glamorous Grace. What was the man up to? Trying to convey some sort of direct message beneath the guff?

'You've come through a rigorous selection process and now it's time for the fun to begin. Fun with a serious purpose, I hasten to add. We've invited you to Midwinter to play a game. To solve a mystery. Only one fortunate – and talented – individual in this room can be declared the victor. So let me start by wishing each and every one of you the very best of luck.'

Jeremy's demeanour as he considered the six faces in front of him suggested a benevolent patriarch. Not that Ethan was fooled for one moment. He knew Jeremy Vandervell's velvet glove concealed an iron fist.

'You might say that I am Midwinter's Master of the Revels, but let me assure you that this Christmas game is truly a team effort. I'm fortunate to be assisted by highly talented colleagues who share my passion for this village and everything the Midwinter Trust stands for. They share my determination to make sure that the Trust is and remains a beacon of excellence in an increasingly troubled and dangerous world.'

He paused to allow his words to sink in.

'Rest assured, we'll work night and day to make sure you all have an unforgettable time. So without more ado, I'd like you to meet each of my colleagues in turn. Please forgive me if I sound like a conductor introducing the principal players in his orchestra. You see, we aim to combine in perfect harmony.'

Ethan shifted in his chair. Typical Jeremy. Smooth as silk, but sometimes he overdid things. Went too far. A character flaw. Nobody remains lucky forever.

Jeremy indicated the chauffeur. 'First, someone you've all had the pleasure of meeting in person. We're so grateful to her for getting you here safely despite the dreadful weather. She is a local lass, and for the next few days, she has agreed to stay with us and serve as an honorary member of staff with the Midwinter Trust. Ms Frankie Rowland.'

As though embarrassed by the attention, Frankie made a gesture of acknowledgment with her hand. Poppy de Lisle seemed about to clap, before thinking better of it.

'Beside her, Ms Bernadette Corrigan, my deputy and the brains behind our Christmas contest.' He tossed her a breezy smile. 'You've already met her in your online briefings, and in a few moments, she'll give you some initial details about the puzzle you are here to solve.'

Bernadette gave a brisk nod.

'Next, another key decision-maker. Again, someone you met during the application process. Ms Chandra Masood is responsible for everything to do with People. If at any time you experience any difficulties at all, please speak to Chandra and she'll sort things out. Just as long as you don't expect her to be able to do anything to improve the weather!'

On cue, Chandra gave a rueful smile.

'I'm told we're about to be snowed in. There may even be a slight delay in getting you back to the station.' Jeremy paused. 'Not to worry. Personally, I believe the snow creates the perfect environment for the game you've come here to play.'

Ethan glanced at the guests. Their expressions gave no clue to what was going on in their minds.

'On my right,' Jeremy continued, 'is the most important person in Midwinter. Daisy Wu is in charge of food and drink. In a short time, she's already proved herself to be a superb cook as well as a first-rate mixologist.'

Daisy responded with a small wave. Despite everything, Ethan couldn't help being amused by Jeremy's encomium. The Director seized every possible opportunity to spend time in her company, passing it off as a mark of strong yet sensitive leadership. But Ethan noticed Chandra's expression tighten as she listened to her boss heaping praise on the American woman. As for Bernadette...

Jeremy turned to Ethan.

'Finally, another key member of the team. Ethan Swift can offer expert assistance in the exceptionally unlikely event that any of you experience a problem of any kind, physical or mental. As you're well aware, we've already spoken with you about your state of health and checked the details of any form of medication that you're taking. If you are wondering whether this is... well, a little fussy, you can be absolutely confident that your well-being and safety are things we take extremely seriously at Midwinter. This village is a haven, but we leave nothing to chance.'

Ethan glanced at his colleagues and caught Chandra frowning. Was she thinking, *better late than never*?

'Now that's more than enough from me,' Jeremy said. 'You want to hear about the game. So Bernadette will say a few words about the challenge she's set for you.'

His deputy smoothed down her hair before scrambling to her feet.

'Thanks so much, Jeremy, and good evening. I won't beat about the bush.'

Bernadette smiled and took a step forward to the edge of the dais. Her demeanour had an edge of challenge.

'Murder has been done in Midwinter and it's up to the six of you to work out the solution to the mystery. To do this, you'll need to make a variety of... deductions.'

She paused, allowing her final word to hang in the air.

'To begin with, another gentle practice exercise. Chandra tells me that you all solved the Greek cipher, even if none of you thought it made much sense. As it happens, you've worked out the name of the game you've come to play. *Miss Winter in the Library with a Knife.*'

Several of the guests frowned. Ethan could see that Bernadette was pleased by their uncertainty.

'My question for you is this: *What inspired me to come up with this particular name for our game?* Here is a hint. Miss Winter *doesn't* feature in the mystery you need to solve. In the spirit of transparency, I should tell you that Miss Winter happens to be the detective in Harry Crystal's long series of books, but that's nothing more than a pleasing coincidence, neither here nor there. Don't worry. In playing the game itself, you'll all receive the same information.'

Harry Crystal looked uncomfortable. *The term 'hangdog appearance'*, Ethan thought, *might have been coined specially for him.*

'There was never a library in Midwinter, not a public village library in the usual sense. However, Marcus Midwinter conceived our reading room as a place for quiet recreation. That's where I had the idea for the game.'

She folded her arms, like a teacher addressing a class of puzzled pupils.

'Tomorrow morning, those of you who figure out the answer – all six of you, I hope – should write it on a note, to be sealed in one of the envelopes you'll have found in your cottages. You can hand the solution to me during breakfast. Don't get too excited, there is no prize. Win or lose, it won't affect your chances of success in the game. But I'll explain the inspirations behind the answer and they will provide you with clues to the real mystery. All clear?'

There were one or two cautious nods from the heads in front of her.

'Excellent. This evening, let me explain the background to the puzzle and provide you with a sheet of supplementary information.'

Baz raised a hand. 'Will you take questions from the floor?'

'Remember what I said in the online briefing, Baz? We want to test your initiative right from the moment you set foot in Midwinter. So the answer is no, I'm afraid. Not tonight, at least.'

Her smile, firm and uncompromising, prompted Baz's brow to furrow. One or two giggles came from the other guests. *Nervous giggles*, Ethan thought. No wonder. These people had no idea what they were letting themselves in for.

'Further evidence,' she continued briskly, 'will come to

light as the game proceeds. Be warned, red herrings aplenty will jostle for your attention alongside the clues.'

She fiddled with her folder. Building tension like someone in a Hitchcock movie. All six contestants were paying close attention. On the platform, Chandra and Daisy exchanged quick glances. Even Frankie was leaning forward in her chair, seemingly agog.

Jeremy gave an imperceptible nod. Ethan was never sure precisely what thoughts were coursing through the man's brain. Maybe it was better not to know. The Trust hadn't invited him to conduct a psychological evaluation of either the Director or his Deputy. That, Bernadette made plain, would be above his pay grade. Yet he'd been asked to interview Chandra, Daisy, and even – hilariously enough – Frankie Rowland.

Bernadette cleared her throat. 'Kristy Winkelman is a rich and famous crime writer. Tag-line: *If you like Christie, you'll love Kristy!* She has achieved astonishing success as a prolific self-published author of cosy whodunits, which have been a huge hit on TV. She's earned fame and fortune and become a household name. Unfortunately, tact and self-awareness aren't her forte. Her personal life is as full of complications and melodrama as her plots. Over the years, she has made enemies.'

A moment's pause to allow that to sink in.

'Kristy has arranged to hold a party in the wilds of the north Pennines, despite a Met Office forecast that is truly horrendous. Sound familiar?'

She smiled at her audience.

'Not that my fictional Midwinter should be confused with this village, naturally. There's still a white Christmas, but the weather conditions aren't as severe as those we expect over the next seventy-two hours. Anyway, Kristy isn't the sort to be deterred by a few snowflakes. This is not just any old festive knees-up, but a *divorce* party.'

Bernadette allowed the phrase to hover in the air. 'That's right, Kristy has decided to spend Christmas celebrating the end of her marriage to a TV gardener called Mike Sherwin. Unfortunately, everyone doesn't get to live happily ever after.'

She took the plastic wallet out of the folder and put it down on the edge of the table.

'Kristy's break-up with Mike was acrimonious. It didn't help that she'd had a fling with Rishi Mehta, who stars in the screen adaptations of her books. Now the decree nisi has been signed, though, it's all water under the bridge. At least so far as Kristy is concerned. She's planning to marry a celebrity doctor called Tim Faber. To demonstrate there are no hard feelings now the legal formalities are progressing, Kristy has invited Mike along to join in the fun. He's accompanied by his new partner, Harriet Linaker. Who just happens to be Tim Faber's ex.'

Bernadette paused. 'Rishi is invited too, along with his co-star Bethan Kirtley, who got the role originally because she has a distant family connection to Kristy.'

She indulged in the luxury of a mischievous smile.

'So there you have it, ladies and gentlemen. Six people, each of them with hidden secrets, all cooped up together in Midwinter for Christmas.'

She's loving this, Ethan thought, as a dutiful ripple of amusement ran around the room. The Bernadette he knew kept her emotions under lock and key with a zeal bordering on the obsessive. Renowned for her efficiency as well as a love of order and method, she had a formidable memory for detail. She seemed a natural second-in-command rather than a born leader, under the spotlight at the centre of the stage.

Last time he and she had worked together, she was forever glancing over at Jeremy for approval or to check whether she was saying the right thing.

Inventing a murder mystery had liberated her creative instincts. Psychologically it made sense. She'd devised a game governed by clearly defined rules. As long as she was allowed to work within a structure, she could luxuriate in her comfort zone.

But what if events took an unpredictable and dangerous turn? What if, for some reason, she lost control? Never mind the guests she wanted to test... How strong was Bernadette Corrigan's own survival instinct?

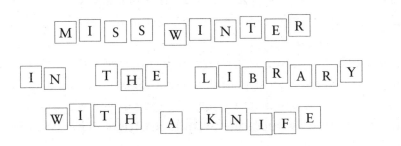

MISS WINTER IN THE LIBRARY WITH A KNIFE

Guests at the Christmas divorce party

KRISTY WINKELMAN
Writer

TIM FABER
Doctor

RISHI MEHTA
Actor

BETHAN KIRTLEY
Actor

HARRIET LINAKER
Jeweller

MIKE SHERWIN
Gardener

8

Poppy de Lisle's Journal

During my online briefing, Bernadette said all the players in the game ought to keep a diary. A private journal to note down their own thoughts and experiences while they were playing the game. Extremely useful, or so she said.

But useful to *whom*, Bernadette? That is the question.

In case anyone forgot her advice, a nice shiny notebook and pen have been put in every guest's cottage. So we have no excuse.

Obviously, there's a hidden agenda. What if someone from Midwinter Trust sneaks into our rooms to peek at our notes? Checking what we say about the village, the people from the Trust, and our rivals in the game? Preparing to use the information for their own purposes, whatever they may be? *Anything that you write down may be taken in evidence and used against you?* Is that their cunning plan?

So I'll be totally upfront. What I write here will be selective. *Highly* selective. Some or all of it may be untrue.

There, I've said it. You've been warned.

If you happen to be reading this, it's up to you to decide whether you want to believe all of it, some of it, or none. Your choice, I don't care. After all, I'm not on oath, am I? Not yet, at any rate. You ought to be keeping your grubby little nose out of my affairs, not prying in such a dishonourable way. What about personal privacy, and all that other data protection bollocks? Not to mention sportsmanship, playing the game, doing the right thing?

Now I've got that off my chest, I must admit Bernadette wasn't wholly disingenuous. It *is* useful to create a private record. I'm betting I'll be in a small minority. Grace Kinsella won't commit herself in black and white. Zack Jardine probably can't be bothered. Baz Frederick's first instinct would be to record voice memos. Not so easy without his smartphone.

Harry Crystal, on the other hand, is old school. The sort who orders his thoughts by jotting them down. He's a writer by trade, so he'll find loads to put in a journal. Carys Neville might have been tempted, too, especially if she thought it would help her to win. But once bitten, twice shy. She's found out the hard way that private documents can slither out into the public domain, with devastating consequences.

What if more than one of us solves Bernadette's mystery? It's got to be possible. I mean, how hard can this game be? What if everyone is smart enough to come up with the right answer? The Trust will need some kind of tie-breaker to decide who wins the ultimate prize.

I guess that's what Baz wanted to ask. The prize might simply go to whoever is first to solve the mystery of *Miss Winter in the Library with a Knife*. But what if the deciding factor involves analysing what we've said in our private journals? Is that why Bernadette is encouraging us to write them? I wouldn't put anything past the people from the Midwinter Trust. They are mavericks, loose cannons.

I enjoyed this evening's briefing, and not only because

Ethan Swift has a touch of Heathcliff about him. The moody expression enhances his Byronic charm. I bet some patients consult him simply for the pleasure of gazing into his dreamy eyes. Even buttoned-up Bernadette permitted herself one or two sly glances when she thought nobody was looking. Naughty lady, shouldn't she be concentrating on her guests, rather than ogling a toyboy? Anyway, he could do better. With me, for instance. I've always loved *Wuthering Heights*, even if Cathy's wayward behaviour sets my teeth on edge. You'd never catch me marrying boring old Edgar. I quite fancy myself as a romantic heroine. And you don't get anywhere much more wuthering than Midwinter in a snowstorm.

Several incidents I'd better jot down before I forget. First, when Jeremy was introducing Daisy, Chandra's mask slipped. She's always so smiley and upbeat, it was jarring to see her features harden in contempt. Chandra isn't a member of Daisy's fan club. Is her dislike down to jealousy or some subtler cause?

Second, Frankie the driver looked tense when Jeremy Vandervell was talking. What could she be worried about? Otherwise, she seems so unflappable, so completely in control.

Third, Baz Frederick strikes me as the life and soul of the party. But as the evening wore on, something seemed to get under his skin. He became quite twitchy.

Finally, and most significantly, something odd happened as Bernadette was coming to the end of her briefing. She'd brought notes in a plastic wallet, and when she'd finished outlining the scenario about Kristy Winkelman's divorce party, she said she'd give each of us an information sheet about Kristy and the people she invited to the divorce party.

As she slid the pieces of paper out of the wallet, her foot seemed to catch Frankie Rowlands' ankle. She managed to keep her balance, but a fumble sent the sheets scattering to the floor. I jumped to my feet and so did Baz Frederick. We gathered them up to hand back to her.

But she dropped more than just the information sheets. I counted three additional pieces of A4. Two of them I picked up. Baz pounced on the other one. Bernadette snatched them all back from us with a muttered word of thanks, but the incident obviously disconcerted her. As if she didn't recognise those extra sheets, didn't expect them to be there.

She took a few moments to regain her composure before thrusting the three extra sheets back in the wallet and carrying on as if nothing out of the ordinary had happened. A professional to her fingertips, that's Bernadette. But I'd had enough time to see what was written on the sheets. So, I think, did my opponents in the game.

One word was written in large capital letters on each of the sheets:

NO

ONE

WILL

Was this part of the game, a cunning test of our powers of observation? Did Bernadette drop the sheets deliberately, and if so, why?

Or was it pure chance? If so, had Bernadette put those sheets in the wallet herself? Or had someone else managed

to slip them into the wallet with a view to startling her? Or
giving her a warning?

No one will win the game?

Or, if I really wanted to let my imagination rip:

No one will get out of here alive?

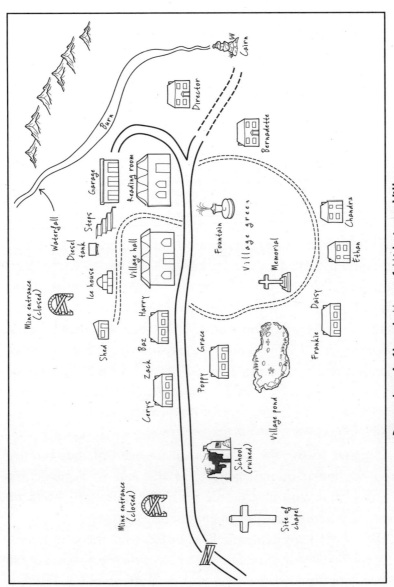

Bernadette's Sketch Map of Midwinter Village

9

Harry Crystal's Journal

*M*iss Winter in the Library with a Knife.

Why has Bernadette referenced my series character Miss Winter in her mystery game? Chewing it over, I decided the name appealed to her because it's similar to Midwinter. Of course, people who dream up murder mysteries draw inspiration from other puzzle-makers. That's how creative imaginations work. You know what they say: bad writers plagiarise, good writers borrow, great writers steal. If you're a genius, you're permitted to call it an homage. Just as my titles are hat-tips to famous crime novels, which they don't otherwise resemble in any way – especially when it comes to sales and reviews.

But that wasn't the only strange moment of the evening. What to make of the incident at the end of Bernadette's briefing, that curious charade with the fluttering sheets of paper apparently bearing an enigmatic message?

Did Bernadette deliberately stumble over the chauffeur's outstretched leg or foot? She gave poor Frankie a reproachful glance, but I'm betting that was a bluff. Possibly Frankie tripped her on purpose, for reasons I can't imagine, or maybe it was an accident. But Bernadette is so well organised there's a touch of compulsion lurking beneath that business-like exterior. I'd say we were meant to see those three words.

WILL

NO

ONE

It's like the start of a sentence that ends with a phrase like 'rid me of this turbulent priest'. But of course I may be wrong about the order of the words. How about:

ONE

WILL

NO

That might be the opening of a sentence along the following lines: 'One will not survive Christmas'. Something of the sort.

I can't make head or tail of it. I console myself by thinking that it's one of those red herrings Bernadette mentioned. I only hope it's not an essential ingredient of the mystery game.

After Bernadette handed us each a sheet to remind us of the six characters in the puzzle, Daisy placed a tray of mulled wine, soft drinks, and nuts on the bar counter and invited us to help ourselves while she put the finishing touches to our evening meal. Jeremy Vandervell accompanied her into the kitchen, closely followed by Bernadette and Chandra

Masood. For an instant I fancied the two women were acting as chaperones.

The music started up again. The Ronettes, warbling 'Frosty the Snowman'. As the players in the game wandered over to the bar, Frankie began to shift the table and chairs. Helped by Ethan Swift, she set about putting them together to form a single table with six places on each side. I made a half-hearted offer of assistance, only to be shooed away.

'This is your first night in Midwinter,' Ethan said. 'Why not relax after your journey? Take it easy, the game starts in earnest tomorrow and we want you all to feel refreshed and on top form.'

I left them to it and found myself standing next to Baz Frederick at the bar counter. Grace Kinsella had already helped herself to a glass of mulled wine before gliding away, as if determined to avoid getting embroiled in conversation. I felt like a holiday-maker on the first evening of a package tour, with everyone tiptoeing around each other, on their best behaviour – at least until they'd had a few drinks and their inhibitions melted away.

'So what do you make of the Kristy Winkelman mystery?' I asked.

Baz exhaled and again I caught the whiff of tobacco. A hardened smoker, for sure. The cottages were kitted out with smoke alarms and warning notices about the legal rules preventing people from lighting up inside and I guessed he was gasping for a cigarette. Perhaps that was why he seemed much less comfortable than he had been earlier. Deprived of his drug of choice.

'Not sure I'm ready to discuss it yet, man.'

'They said they encouraged team-working,' I said quickly.

'Yeah, but only one of us can win, right?'

'What happens if more than one person comes up with the right answer?'

A shrug of the massive shoulders. 'Exactly what I wanted to ask before she shut me up. I guess we'll find out soon enough, huh?'

He took a gulp of mulled wine. For a man who exuded confidence, he was clearly preoccupied and not in the mood for small talk. All the more reason to persist.

'You saw the sheets that Bernadette dropped? With one word written on each of them?'

He took a long stride away from the bar, as if pestered by a particularly irritating insect. As irritating insects do, I buzzed after him.

'Yeah, I picked up one of the sheets.'

'Any idea what those words mean?'

A pause. To my surprise, he seemed to be choosing his words with extreme care. During our first encounter he'd struck me as, along with Poppy de Lisle, the friendliest of my opponents. Maybe he wasn't simply suffering nicotine withdrawal symptoms. Had something happened to knock him off his stride? Or to make him – for some unaccountable reason – suspicious of me?

'What do you think?' he responded.

I drank some wine. 'Quite honestly, I haven't the foggiest.'

He peered at me, as if trying to detect telltale signs that I was lying. Given that I'm a natural fidget, my body language probably sent out all the wrong messages, so I decided to get on the front foot.

'What do you make of it? *Will no one?* Sounds as if something is missing. I've no idea whether it's a clue or a piece of rather clumsy misdirection.'

'Um.' For a fleeting instant Baz seemed on the brink of

sharing a confidence, only for something – probably my excessive eagerness – to hold him back. 'Hey, let's see if we find out anything else tonight, huh?'

With that, he knocked back the rest of his drink and strode away in search of the toilets.

'Was it something you said?' a voice murmured in my ear.

Turning, I found myself facing Zack Jardine. He was weighing me up with some care, like an art dealer checking a dusty portrait he suspected of being a forgery.

'When I met Baz earlier this evening,' I said, 'he came across as outgoing and talkative.'

'Yeah, I got the same impression.'

'Pitching a book idea to you, was he?' I said lightly.

Zack stared. 'What makes you say that?'

'Pure guesswork,' I said, taken aback.

Even though this was perfectly true, Zack's eyebrows shot up. 'Is that right?'

'Absolutely.'

'Cool.'

This was evidently Zack's default response when he didn't know what else to say. I smiled and waited for him to break the silence.

'I mean, you're quite the detective,' he said at last.

'Well,' I said, trying to sound self-deprecating. 'After writing all those novels, I suppose you get some kind of knack... Anyway, what sort of book is Baz hoping to write? True crime? Or does he fancy turning his hand to fiction?'

'I didn't enter into detailed discussions,' Zack said crisply. 'Always a mistake for a literary agent to show much interest. Do that, and you never shake off the wannabes and never-will-bes.'

He avoided my eye as he spoke. I didn't entirely believe

him, but why would he want to lie? This wasn't the moment for a direct challenge. The game had barely begun, and the six of us were simply sniffing around each other, like mongrels in a dog park.

Frankie and Ethan were laying the tables and putting out place cards. They were chatting nineteen to the dozen and gave every sign of enjoying their Christmas at least as much as any of us guests. The Midwinter Trust had fostered an ethos of team-working. With only six people to look after as many guests, everyone was pulling their weight.

'Baz seems bothered about something,' I said.

'Such as?' Zack asked.

'Your guess is as good as mine.'

'I doubt it, Henry.'

'Harry.'

'Cool.' He considered me. 'Surely you have a theory about what's worrying him? You're a detective novelist, a seasoned pro. I'm just a humble literary agent.'

A humble literary agent? I was about to retort that this was a contradiction in terms, but I reminded myself in the nick of time of the need for prudence. Crazy to antagonise anyone at this stage, even someone who couldn't remember my name.

'I've never heard any of his podcasts.'

'Right now, he's taking a break from podcasting.'

'Looking for a proper job?' Zack frowned at my little jest. 'Are you one of his listeners?'

Zack seemed taken aback. 'I... I may have listened to them once or twice.'

In other words, yes. Why be so coy? I sniffed a chance to press home my advantage. If I had an advantage.

'Has Baz ever written about the cases he discusses in his podcasts?' I asked.

To my surprise and – let's not beat about the bush – gratification, Zack's eyes widened in alarm. He swallowed some mulled wine, as if to steady his nerves, before muttering, 'You'd have to ask him.'

'Thanks. I will.'

Zack cleared his throat noisily. 'No worries,' he said, and hurried away.

Grace Kinsella drifted to my side. 'You look so harmless, Harry. Yet in the past few minutes I've seen you scare off two of our fellow guests with a few obviously well-chosen words.'

'I'll try not to make it three in a row.'

'Don't worry, I'm made of sterner stuff.'

She leaned towards me and I caught a whiff of perfume. It smelled delicate and expensive.

Emboldened, I said, 'Don't tell me you're keeping an eye on me?'

'You're a published mystery writer. So presumably the closest thing in Midwinter to a hotshot detective.'

I winced at the irony. The one time in my life when I was desperate for people to underestimate me, everyone was doing the exact opposite.

'I wish.'

'So what did you say to upset the other two?'

'Not a thing. We were only passing the time of day.' I hesitated. 'I asked about Baz's book.'

She frowned. 'So you know about his book?'

I tried to look mysterious. Probably I only succeeded in looking as though I had some kind of facial tic.

'I've heard whispers,' I said enigmatically.

'You have?'

'Strictly between you and me, of course.'

'Of course.' She hesitated. 'Whispers about...?'

I was determined not to let her pin me down, especially given that I didn't know what I was talking about.

'I'm pretty sure I haven't got the full picture. I bet you know more than me. After all, you're in the publishing business.'

Grace took a sip of her drink. '*Was* in the publishing business is closer to the truth.'

I murmured something vague and unintelligible, hoping she'd be tempted to keep talking. And she was.

'In case you're wondering, Baz was never one of the authors on my list. In the days when I had a list.'

'Ah,' I said meaningfully.

'It's not like he sent me a manuscript and spent six months waiting for me to dig it out of the slush pile.'

'No?'

'Absolutely not. We bumped into each other at a champagne reception for some overpaid celebrity author's debut novel.'

'Oh?'

I was beginning to persuade myself that I'd mastered the art of cross-examination, one syllable at a time. If all else failed, perhaps I could market the technique to aspiring barristers and people who interviewed slippery politicians.

'We had nothing more than a brief conversation. Barely ten minutes. Perhaps five. He mentioned the book in passing. No detail. And he said he'd talked to Zack, who might be willing to take him on as a client.'

'Yeah?'

She shifted from one foot to another, apparently discerning a touch of scepticism in my latest, carefully crafted syllable.

'I'm not pretending I wasn't interested, but there were so many obstacles to getting his book into print. Including a possible injunction.'

'Really?'

'Yes, he downplayed it, said the people suing him didn't have a leg to stand on, but it was a red flag. I said he needed to get his ducks in a row before taking things further. Frankly, I didn't have an opportunity to give the matter serious thought. Everything came to a halt the moment my career fell apart.'

'So...?'

'So I never talked to Baz Frederick again until today. I had no idea that he or Zack would be here. We could hardly discuss it on the way from the station, in the chauffeur's hearing. Probably Zack's conversation with Baz was as vague as mine.'

'Vague?' I experimented with a derisive tone, provoking an immediate reaction.

'Yes, vague! Like I say, we never talked terms.' She paused, as if to reflect on whatever was troubling her. 'Between you and me, I'm having second thoughts about this whole charade. How about you?'

'Me?'

My question seemed to give her an idea. Our surreal conversation was making me feel like Chance the gardener in *Being There*, the simple-minded fellow whose Delphic utterances are treated as statements of the utmost profundity.

'I mean, Baz didn't approach you with a view to ghost-writing his book, did he?'

'No.'

She sighed. 'This whole business is mystifying.'

You can say that again, I was tempted to reply, in a burst of loquacity. *Imagine how I feel, not knowing what the hell is going on.*

'And then there was that stuff with those sheets of paper. Bizarre.'

'Will,' I said. For a moment she looked confused, so I added in a positive gabble, 'No. One.'

'Yes! Exactly! Someone is up to something, without a doubt. What I don't know is this: Was Bernadette taunting us? Or is someone taunting her? And is this deeply serious, or simply a joke in the worst possible taste?'

'Ha!'

She gave me a curious look. 'You're a cagey fellow, Harry. Adept at keeping your cards close to your chest.'

I was tempted to reply that it's so much easier when you don't actually possess any cards, but somehow, I managed to bite my tongue.

'Um.'

The snag with my ingenious m.o., I'd discovered, was that it didn't take long to run short of suitable syllables.

'Off the record,' Grace said. 'I'm not sure I care who wins this bloody game. So if you fancy sharing information with me to mutual benefit, fine. We'd need to be discreet, obviously. The walls of Midwinter have plenty of ears.'

'Sure,' I said.

She patted my hand and murmured, 'Look at Baz. Not a happy bunny, is he?'

The big man was knocking back his latest glass of mulled wine and his brow was furrowed, as if he were trying to solve a complex equation in his head. As Grace and I watched, Zack Jardine spoke to him while picking up another glass from the tray. The muttered reply provoked a so-what shrug and Zack turned on his heel to resume his attempts to chat up Poppy de Lisle. She was sticking to diet Coke. So was Carys Neville, who stood on her own at the back of the hall, watching the rest of us with a sardonic smirk on her face.

'What do you make of Carys?' Grace asked.

Before I could conjure up an appropriate syllable that wasn't deeply offensive, the kitchen door swung open and Chandra sashayed out.

'Hello again, everyone. Hope you've enjoyed getting to know each other! Would you like to take your seats? Dinner is served.'

A HISTORY OF MIDWINTER, BY J. DOE OF THE NORTH PENNINE HISTORICAL SOCIETY

Part One: The Curse

The tiny village of Midwinter may be the most curious place in the country. Undoubtedly it is the most remote. The Midwinter Trust owns the whole village, built on a remote and mysterious peak known since time immemorial as Pagans' Fell. Public records give few clues to the origin of the name, or the fell's history, but local folklore suggests that in pre-Roman times it was home to a small cult of pagans who sacrificed fellow humans. The Romans were attracted to the area by the prospect of exploiting the rich mineral resources of the land – notably silver, and also lead – but they did not stay long. For more than a millennium thereafter, the fell was regarded with fear and hostility by people who lived nearby. Inevitably, fanciful legends grew up, most notably a story about a curse placed by the pagans on the fell that had caused the Romans to flee for their lives. The ground was so poor that it was impossible to farm and nobody occupied or worked on the fell.

Everything changed with the arrival of Marcus Midwinter, an idealistic and extraordinarily rich young man with the willl to create a new community under his leadership. He convinced himself that building a mine to extract silver would provide jobs annd wealth for a select few workers who would live together harmoniously. Unlike the founders of more famous 'model villages' such as Port Sunlight, Bournville, and Saltaire, Midwinter was less concerned with profit than power. In effect, Marcus was founding his own cult.

At first, building work progressed smoothly but it soon became clear that the mine was uneconomic. Worse still, some of the workings collapsed, causing serious casualties. Workers – mostly imported from the slums of Penrith and Carlisle – learned that their houses were built on land with a pagan history and rumours that Midwinter was cursed took hold. When war broke out, almost every man of age joined the army, only for most of them to be killed in France. The community was devastated beyond repair.

Marcus Midwinter's son, Maurice, was born at the end of the war, but his wife died in childbirth. This bereavement coupled with the destruction of his dream mustt have caused a severe nervous breakdown from which Marcus never fully recovered. He refused to leave the village, but his vast wealth more than sufficed to provide for his care as well as for his son's education.

10

Midwinter

'Congratulations, everyone, that seemed to go extremely well,' Jeremy Vandervell said with a beam that Ethan thought radiated complacency.

Dinner was over, and the six detectives had left the village hall. The Director was relaxing in an armchair on the dais in the company of Bernadette, Chandra, and Ethan. Daisy, wearing an apron that said *A chef is someone who turns food into happiness* hurried to and fro, readying everything for breakfast in the morning.

Bernadette took a breath. 'Except for that incident with the extra sheets of paper.'

Jeremy pursed his lips. 'Mmmm, yes. Very odd.'

'You can say that again,' Ethan murmured.

Reaching into her bag, Bernadette retrieved the folder and slid out the three sheets of paper, now badly crumpled.

NO

WILL

ONE

Ethan picked up the sheets and studied them intently, as if wondering if something had been written in addition, presumably in invisible ink.

'Any idea how this stuff got into your folder?' Jeremy asked.

'None whatsoever.' A rare touch of colour came to Bernadette's cheeks. 'I mean, I did leave the folder out when I nipped to the loo. I was only away for a couple of minutes but I suppose someone must have seized the opportunity...'

'You left it where, exactly?'

Jeremy's charm was legendary and his demeanour seldom less than suave, even as he delivered his most scathing put-downs. Ethan sometimes wondered if private education in Britain was geared primarily towards cultivating self-confidence and surface bonhomie. In truth, he despised Jeremy, yet he couldn't quite suppress a grudging respect for the way the Director invariably kept his cool. Even in the face of disaster five years ago, he hadn't once lost his temper, let alone his unflinching sense of purpose. For all his idealistic faith in the Midwinter Trust, he was a pragmatist to his bones, not a flaky lightweight who lost the plot or ranted and raved. A minor mishap like the superfluous sheets in the folder would never knock a man like Jeremy off course. Even so, it had touched a nerve.

Pointing to the small table, Bernadette cleared her throat. 'Here.'

'In full view of all the guests?'

A pause.

'Well, yes.'

'I see.' He adjusted his tie as he allowed the others to reflect on the scale of her faux-pas. 'So anyone could have interfered with it?'

'I'm dreadfully sorry, Jeremy. I thought... well, the folder didn't contain any sensitive material. On the contrary. There was nothing but the information sheets that were due to be handed out to everyone a few minutes later.'

What was it about Jeremy Vandervell, Ethan wondered, that reduced a woman as formidable as Bernadette to embarrassing self-justification? Despite everything, he felt he should intervene. Say something to support her.

'Fair enough,' he said mildly. 'Certainly not a breach of confidentiality.'

'I didn't suggest otherwise,' Jeremy said. 'I simply wanted to establish what had happened.'

'I wondered if you'd put those extra sheets in the folder yourself,' Chandra said.

Bernadette's head jerked in her direction. 'Why on earth would I do that?'

Chandra spread her arms. 'Some kind of red herring?'

'*A red herring?*' Bernadette might have been impersonating Lady Bracknell.

'You're our Mistress of Mystery. I wondered if you were… I don't know, setting a test, laying down a challenge of some kind.'

'You must be joking. Why in God's name would I rake up what happened five years ago, just when we've finally managed to put it behind us?'

Chandra said with exaggerated patience, 'Please don't put words into my mouth. Ethan's right, it's not that what you did was *really* careless. No need for anyone to get overwrought.'

'I'm not overwrought. Just perplexed.'

'Aren't we all?' Jeremy said, easing into chairman mode. 'It's very strange. And, to speak bluntly, subversive. A malicious attempt to mar an otherwise successful start to Christmas.'

'I suppose,' Bernadette said tentatively, 'this does mean what we think it means?'

'What else?' Jeremy demanded. 'A sly and tasteless reference to a terrible calamity we all wish had never occurred.'

Chandra nodded. 'An utter nightmare. Speaking personally, I'd be happy never to think about it again.'

'Except that it's impossible to forget,' Ethan said sotto voce.

'We've always accepted,' Jeremy said judicially, 'that we must learn lessons from the past. So as to embed good practice in everything we do, and make sure that any mistakes, are never repeated.'

They were interrupted by the return of Frankie Rowland. The village had a solitary garage, which stood behind the reading room. Originally built to house Marcus Midwinter's Daimler, it was large enough to accommodate three vehicles, including Jeremy's BMW and Bernadette's Volvo. Frankie had put her limousine away for the night before coming into the hall to say goodnight.

'Thank goodness all your guests got here,' she said cheerily. 'There were moments on that last trip when I wondered if the snow would be too deep for us to make it. Another hour, and the road would have been impassable.'

'What would we do without you?' Jeremy said.

Frankie beamed at him. 'Isn't this a fun way to celebrate Christmas? I hope you aren't going to stay up working all night.'

'Just chewing the fat,' he said. 'Goodnight.'

The most courteous of dismissals, Ethan thought.

Taking the hint, Frankie glanced at her wrist-watch. 'Right, that's me. Hey, it's almost Christmas Eve. Night, everyone. See you all bright and early in the morning.'

As the main door closed behind her, Ethan said, 'If nobody from the Trust put those sheets in the folder, who did?'

'One of the guests,' Chandra said. 'Must be.'

'Any ideas?' Jeremy asked.

'There's one obvious suspect, isn't there?'

'Baz Frederick?' Ethan asked.

'Got it in one,' Chandra said. 'He simply won't give up. Poking his nose in where it isn't wanted.'

Bernadette said, 'I don't know. He looked as surprised as anyone when he picked up the sheet. And he isn't the only one who knows something about what happened. What about Grace Kinsella, Zack Jardine, Carys Neville...'

'We can't rule any of them out, but Baz Frederick is full of bravado and defiance. I wouldn't put it past him to slip those sheets into the folder.'

'Why?' Bernadette asked. 'He's hardly going to endear himself to anyone by behaving like that.'

'He didn't take much of a risk, given that we can't prove he was responsible,' Chandra retorted. 'Unless you're suggesting we fingerprint the folder?'

'Now you're being...' Bernadette gave a weary shake of the head. 'Never mind. All I'm saying is, the case is closed. What does anyone have to gain from raking up the past?'

'You don't think it's a kind of warning?' Chandra asked.

'Warning of what?' Ethan said.

'Who knows? Baz is the sort who enjoys putting the cat among the pigeons. He has a taste for controversy. Is he putting us on notice? Telling us to take the utmost care to make sure that Bernadette's game doesn't result in... another tragedy?'

'Why make a nuisance of himself?' Ethan said. 'If he wants to win the game, he has a lot to lose if...'

'Perhaps he doesn't care about the game,' Chandra said quietly. 'He went to great lengths to investigate what happened in Midwinter five years ago. To describe his behaviour as a nuisance is an understatement. Thank goodness it fizzled out, but that doesn't mean he's lost all hope of writing about it. Suppose he's treating this whole exercise as research for another exposé?'

'He signed up to the terms and conditions,' Bernadette said. 'The lawyers are confident the wording is watertight. We've got him where we want him. If he or anyone else steps out of line, we'll be down on them like…'

'A ton of bricks?' Ethan suggested.

She gestured towards the hall's curtained windows. The wind was roaring, louder than ever.

'*Avalanche* is the word that comes to mind. Especially with the snow drifting deeper by the minute.'

Jeremy scanned his colleagues. 'Remember this, everyone. Over the past eighty years, the Midwinter Trust hasn't done such a bad job. Yes, there was a blemish, but nobody gets it right all the time. We did nothing wrong.'

'That's not quite—' Ethan began.

'We were exonerated,' Jeremy snapped. 'It's a matter of record. Never mind the caveats and weasel words. There was no question of criminal guilt. Besides, this Christmas is entirely different. We've simply invited six people here to play a game. What could be less threatening than that? There's no need for anyone – colleague or guest – to feel the slightest anxiety.'

The smack of firm leadership, administered by the velvet glove, Ethan thought, as the two women nodded with unmistakeable relief. Jeremy should have been a minister of the Crown. He had an unrivalled gift for telling people what they wanted to hear.

The kitchen door opened and Daisy shimmied out. As usual, a diffident smile brightened her lovely features. For the hundredth time, Ethan wondered what was really going on inside her head.

'Everything's ready for breakfast,' she announced. 'I'm off to bed. Goodnight, everyone.'

'Thanks very much, Daisy,' Jeremy and Chandra said in unison.

'My pleasure. See you in the morning!'

As she put on her coat, Jeremy turned to his colleagues. 'Right, I think we've taken things as far as we can for the moment. As for that incident with the sheets, chances are, it's nothing more than a childish prank. Bernadette, will you tell our guests more about the game after breakfast?'

She forced a smile.

'Don't worry. I'll keep tight hold of the folder this time.'

A HISTORY OF MIDWINTER, BY J. DOE OF THE NORTH PENNINE HISTORICAL SOCIETY

Part Two: The Trust

Maurice Midwinter graduated a fortnight after his father's death in 1939. He joined up as soon as war was declared, only to bee seconded to an office-based role, first in Whitehall, then in Buckinghamshire, and finally in the Scottish Highlands. Although he never saw active service, he received a knighthood, allegedly in recompense for the war-time requisitioning of Midwinter, after which it was left a semi-derelict ghost village. Not needing to work for a living, Maurice devoted many years to rebuilding and reinventing the village, drawing on his war-time exploits to found the Midwinter Trust, whose self-appointed mission was 'to serve the greater good'.

A sophisticated networker with unrivalled establishment connections, Maurice secured the passage of a piece of legislation making the Trust answerable only to the government of the day. Since ministers have more to do than oversee the operations of a small not-for-profit organisation with custodianship of an obscure northern hamlet, Maurice effectively had carte blanche to run Midwinter without being heldtoaccount. His influence meant the rarely used Midwinter Halt miraculously avoided repeated culls of the railway network.

The Trust allowed visitors to stay in the rebuilt cottages, no doubt charging them a handsome price to recharge their batteries. Mindful of the dark history of Pagans' Fell, local people kept their distance, not least because Maurice's obsession for preserving his privacy verged on paranoia. Perhaps the misery of having a mother he never knew and a father who had lost his mind were the root cause. His love of secrecy contrasted oddly with the Trust's stated aims and he was quick to resort to litigation if he felt the village's seclusion was in any way at risk. There is no public right of way up to Midwinter, and ramblers and sightseers were fiercely discouraged. Small wonder that the Trust was nicknamed locally the Mistrust.

11

Harry Crystal's Journal

Conversation over dinner was in the commonplace 'have you travelled far?' vein. None of us guests lived in the north Pennines, although by the end of the evening, Frankie had announced with delight her discovery that no fewer than three of us – Grace, Zack, and Carys – had also grown up in the north-east of England.

The six representatives of the Midwinter Trust sat among us, which may be why everybody seemed so keen to give little away. The other guests were probably as anxious as I was about being monitored by our hosts. The people from the Trust were unfailingly pleasant but intent on giving no hints about the mystery. Bernadette Corrigan was maddeningly vague about the game, meeting every attempt to prise out information with variations on the theme of 'all in good time'.

Like Ethan Swift, who quietly kept an eye on everyone during the meal, I devoted myself mainly to people-watching. Which of my fellow guests was my most formidable rival?

Should I discount Poppy de Lisle? Until I met her, I'd never come across anyone who genuinely believed that schooldays are the happiest of your life, but she seems to regard coming to Midwinter as a chance to relive her youth and indulge her taste for playing 'jolly games'. Perhaps being trapped in the village reminded her of long years of imprisonment in a high-class girls' boarding school in the Home Counties. But she's not quite as innocent as she seems. The way her gaze kept returning to Ethan left me in no doubt that she fancies him.

Zack Jardine spotted this as well. He seemed put out by the attention she paid to Ethan. I noticed the way his gaze kept lingering on the women in the room, especially Daisy Wu. I remembered the story that he'd been accused of sexual harassment. Maybe that hadn't simply been a ruse to kill off his legal claims against his former client. No smoke without fire? Too soon to tell. Best not to allow my prejudice against literary agents to influence my judgment.

As for Grace Kinsella, does she have a vulnerable side? Some editors are failed writers. Mind you, as T.S. Eliot once said, so are most writers. The dreadful Carys Neville was, thankfully, placed at the far end of the table, opposite Frankie the driver. Next to Frankie was Baz Frederick, who started the meal by explaining loudly why podcasts are so much more worthwhile than books. He spent the rest of the meal chatting with Frankie. I noticed that he had plenty to drink. My own intake was relatively modest. Does Baz have a problem with alcohol? It takes one to know one, and I suspected the answer was yes.

Daisy sat at the end of the table, on my left, with Jeremy Vandervell on my right. I felt flattered that he'd chosen to sit beside me. A promising sign? I warned myself not to get my hopes up prematurely. Poppy de Lisle sat opposite me, with Chandra Masood in between her and Grace.

Jeremy paid Daisy plenty of attention, talking to her across me more than once. Poppy may have been oblivious to this, but Chandra wasn't. I saw her lips compressing in disapproval. Had her own nose been put out of joint?

Hard though I tried to pump Jeremy, I got precisely nowhere. He spent most of the time talking about Marcus Midwinter and his son Maurice.

'Marcus was a man with a marvellous dream,' he told me. 'He had great ambitions for this village, but the geology of the fell slowed down construction work. To make matters worse, most of the miners were lost during the Great War. You may have seen the memorial outside, a tribute to their sacrifice *pro patria*. Marcus lost his wife after she gave birth. The mines became unprofitable and Marcus suffered wretched health for the next twenty years. Midwinter became as quiet as the grave.'

'Spooky,' Poppy said, with a bright smile. Jeremy winced. Too thick-skinned to notice, she carried on regardless. 'I mean, is Midwinter haunted by a resident ghost, do you know?'

'Absolutely not,' Jeremy retorted, although his terse response failed to wipe the smile off Poppy's face. Had she provoked him deliberately? I couldn't imagine why she'd wish to do so. Unlike Carys Neville and, no doubt, Grace Kinsella, she's not the provocative type, if I am any judge.

But you're not such a great judge, are you? whispered a small voice inside my head. *You thought the sun shone out of Jocasta's backside right up until the moment she told you she was moving in with the lover she'd been sleeping with for the past eighteen months.*

That lover just happened to be my agent's foreign rights associate, who should have devoted every waking moment to getting my novels translated across the globe. When she referred to making a 'passion pitch', I thought she meant extolling my virtues to overseas publishers. Not seducing Jocasta.

Snap out of it, I told myself. Poppy was nothing like my ex, thank God.

Jeremy droned on about the Midwinters. 'Sir Maurice was another visionary, and a firm believer in *noblesse oblige*. Not that they were actually members of the nobility, of course. They saw themselves as ordinary people, even though Maurice was knighted after the Second World War for services to his country.'

'Dashing fighter, was he?' I asked, hoping to curry favour by showing an interest.

'The knighthood recognised his selfless work, as well as his willingness to allow this village to be requisitioned by the government,' Jeremy said curtly. Gongs for the boys, in other words, but I kept my mouth shut. 'He inherited Midwinter when he was still a young man. Once the war was over, he founded the Trust and came back here with a view to rebuilding the village.'

'Fancied himself as a sort of lord of the manor, did he?'

Jeremy's brows knitted. 'There was nothing stuffy or snobbish about Sir Maurice. It's been the honour of my life to follow in the footsteps of such a great man. As well as to carry on the good work of the Trust.'

'Gosh, how wonderful.' Poppy beamed. 'And how would you describe that good work, Mr Vandervell?'

'Jeremy, please! We don't stand on ceremony in Midwinter. We're all on first name terms, Frankie included.'

He turned his attention to his food and a few moments passed before I realised that he hadn't answered her question.

Again, I found myself wondering about the Midwinter

Trust. Bernadette and Chandra had promised to tell me more about its activities once I was here. Which was absolutely vital since a handsome cash payment wasn't the only prize for winning the murder mystery game. There was also the possibility of signing up for long-term membership of the Midwinter Trust.

At the moment, I still had no idea about what, if I did manage to win, I might be getting myself into.

After dinner, all six guests clomped through the snow to the reading room. I assumed everyone fancied whiling away an hour or so by playing a board game, prior to retiring to bed. When I asked if anyone fancied a game of Scrabble or Monopoly or backgammon, I was rewarded with expressions that ranged from disdain (Carys), through disinterest (or do I mean uninterest? This is where editors come in handy) on the part of Baz and Zack, to sardonic disbelief (Grace). Poppy came to my rescue, saying that she'd always enjoyed draughts. So while the others scanned the bookshelves, she and I sat down to play.

Baz was quick to drift away. His thoughts were clearly elsewhere, and he gave the books in the room no more than a cursory glance before muttering goodnight. Carys followed shortly afterwards. Zack and Grace took their time and each of them picked up several of my own novels with undisguised curiosity, only to put them down again with an alacrity I couldn't help but find crushing. After a while, something suddenly occurred to Grace as she scanned the titles, and she wasted no time in leaving us to it. Within a minute, Zack also saw whatever she'd seen. He left the reading room without another word, but with a distinct spring in his step.

As the door closed behind him, Poppy took my last piece almost apologetically. 'So that makes three games each, doesn't it? An honourable draw? Thanks so much for playing.'

'My pleasure.'

'Looks like we're very well matched?'

'Except that I've concentrated on the board and you've peered around at the books after every move.'

'Sorry, I didn't mean to be rude. Hope I didn't put you off?'

'Not at all. Seen anything you want to read? Plenty to choose from, quite apart from my own humble efforts. I'm surprised none of the others stayed long. I'm not sure why they bothered to come here if they didn't want to play a game.'

She grinned. 'Trying to solve Bernadette's riddle?'

'By looking at the books?'

'Yes, don't you recall? She came up with the name of this game when she was here, she told us. A hint that something in this room inspired it.'

'Ah.'

'Of course, you – of all people – are already ahead of me.'

'Sorry, I'm lagging miles behind.'

She wagged her finger. 'Naughty, naughty. I may not have the sharpest brain in Midwinter, but I'm not completely naïve?'

I was abashed. 'Forgive me. I didn't intend...'

'No worries, Harry. I simply didn't expect you to make heavy weather of it.'

I cupped my hand to my ear, as if listening to the storm outside. 'Seems appropriate in these conditions, don't you agree?'

She laughed. 'Are you honestly saying you haven't worked out the answer to the riddle?'

I felt myself blushing. Feigning ineptitude suited me fine. It lessened the pressure I felt to succeed. But I was uneasily conscious that it wasn't merely pretence.

'I hope this doesn't turn into the sort of Christmas we had during my marriage,' I blurted out. 'My ex-wife and daughter constantly pointing out anything I got wrong. In other words, everything from making a hash of carving the turkey to scoffing too many mince pies before dinner.'

Now it was her turn to go pink. 'Oh, Harry. I'm so sorry. I never meant to poke fun at you.'

'No problem.' I forced a grin. 'I'm used to it. I always longed to find something I excelled at, and when my first book was published, I thought I'd cracked it. But that was as good as it ever got. Eventually it dawned on me that I was a one-hit wonder. The reviewers called my debut novel a playful tribute to the classics of crime. Later on, they weren't so kind. The stories were derivative and I was a hack writer, churning out stories that other people told better. What I thought of as tropes, the critics called clichés.'

'You're far too hard on yourself.' She pointed to the shelf of my books. 'Thirty-two titles, that's a real achievement.'

Something in her tone suddenly made me feel abashed. 'Sorry, I didn't mean to sound maudlin. I've knocked back too much of Daisy's mulled wine.'

She laughed. 'Me too.'

'Forget what I said. I don't want to be a party pooper. Specially not at Christmas.'

'Believe me, I know how you feel?' She swallowed. 'When I was young, this was a time of year I dreaded. Daddy was an absolute stickler, you see. He was very senior in the civil service, and very proper. Christmas at home was like a fortnight in a punishment cell. Mummy and I were always getting into trouble for putting the baubles on the wrong branches of the tree, that sort of thing.'

'They say it's a time for families to come together,' I said. 'Nothing could be further from the truth. No wonder divorce lawyers are at their busiest during the first week in January.'

She nodded. 'Going to school was such a relief. An escape. I never wanted to come home in the holidays. Especially at Christmas. It does seem to bring out the worst in some people.'

'Too right.'

'What are your family doing this Christmas?'

'Jocasta, my ex, has swanned off to the Maldives with her new wife.'

Poppy's eyes widened. 'So...?'

'Yes, second time around, she married a woman. She once said that at least I'd achieved one good thing. Our life together made her realise how little she cared for men. My daughter will be searching the country for some infrastructure project financed by a hedge fund, so she can hold a candle-lit protest right outside.'

'So she's passionate about the environment?' Poppy said. 'Saving the planet! How wonderful.'

'Yeah, I suppose it's best to look on the bright side. What about your people?'

Poppy paused before answering. 'My parents are dead.'

'Oh, I'm sorry.'

'It's all right. They weren't my real parents. I was adopted.'

'Are you in touch with your birth parents?'

She shook her head. 'I never knew them.'

'Thought about trying to make contact?'

A shrug. 'There are some things it's better not to know. And some people are better remaining a mystery.'

There was a silence. Trying to lighten the mood, I said, 'I rather hope the same is true of the answer to Bernadette's riddle.'

She sprang to her feet. All of a sudden, she seemed anxious to leave.

'Just keep looking, and you'll see the solution staring you right in the face. Goodnight, Harry.'

A HISTORY OF MIDWINTER,
BY J. DOE OF THE NORTH PENNINE
HISTORICAL SOCIETY

Part Three: The Trust Today

Sir Maurice Midwinter died in 2010 and many assumed the Midwinter Trust would die with him. Perhaps that is also what people hoped. The ancient pagan history of the village has continued to hang in the cold air.

However, Jeremy Vandervell, a protégé of Sir Maurice who became Director of the Trust in 2000, has (so far, and contrary to rumours of its imminent demise that gained fresh strength during the pandemic) kept the village going as a sort of trendy and exclusive 'wellness centre'.

Today the Trust is Janus-faced. It remains unremittingly hostile towards researchers, historians, and online reviewers while continuing to proclaim its supposed commitment to making the world a better place.

12

Poppy de Lisle's Journal

M e and my big mouth. Sometimes, I think I don't deserve to
have got where I am today.

Things were going so well, and then I get lured into talking
about my personal life and my past. How could I be so
careless? I'm struggling to keep up my façade.

I blame Harry Crystal. The man is intent on presenting
himself as naïve and he has an inbuilt advantage, because –
whatever his ulterior motives, and I'm not yet clear what they
are, or even if they exist – the poor guy is so ingenuous, it's
utterly disarming. Did he lull me into a false sense of security
on purpose, by playing draughts so recklessly that I struggled
to let him win a few matches? Is he nursing a terrible secret?

Or is what you get precisely what you see, a vaguely
amiable and essentially harmless has-been who has made
such a mess of his career, his marriage, and his relationship
with his daughter that he regards Christmas at Midwinter as
his own personal last chance saloon?

The jury is out.

As for Bernadette's introductory riddle, I'm sure Grace and
Zack spotted the answer. I followed their eyes as they studied

the books on the shelves and each of them had a lightbulb moment then immediately made themselves scarce.

The riddle is another limbering-up exercise, like the typewriter code on the key ring for the cottage. But is it also a way of testing our competitive instincts? I'm intrigued that Bernadette Corrigan found inspiration in the writings of Harry Crystal. Surely that must be a first?

How humiliating if he doesn't work out the answer. Perhaps too humiliating to be credible?

Miss Winter in the Library is an acrostic based on his collected literary oeuvre.

Cool, as Zack would say.

The solution to Bernadette's riddle

Murder Isn't Easy

Innocent's Blood

Six Red Herrings

Strangers on a Plane

Why Didn't They Ask Evelyn?

In the Heat of the Moment

No More Dying Today

Trent's Last Caper

Endless Fright

Rear View Mirror

Intruder in the House

Nightmare Avenue

The Nine Gaolers

Have His Car Crash

End of Sentence

Last Seen Weeping

In a Lonely Daze

Bier Island

Rogue Males

And Then There Was Nothing

Red Heartburst

You Only Live Once

Which Body?

I, the Judge
The Blonde Wore Black
Hangover Street
After the Burial
Kiss the Girls Again
No or Maybe?
I is for Investigation
Farewell, My Lorelei
Elephants Can Forget

13

Midwinter

Ethan watched as his colleagues fetched their coats from the cloakroom. Jeremy was first to leave the hall, with Chandra close on his heels. Bernadette fiddled clumsily with the zip of her sheepskin coat and Ethan didn't need to rely on his psychiatric know-how to realise she was playing for time. When the two of them were alone, she smiled at him.

'Thanks for your support after I messed up with the folder. I'm very grateful.'

'Don't mention it.' He clicked his tongue. 'I hate to see him riding roughshod over you.'

'Roughshod?' A glimmer of a smile as she made her way back to the dais and sat down beside him. 'There's nothing rough about Jeremy. He's smooth as silk.'

'He's made a career out of patrician charm. I call it patronising.'

'Ouch.' This time she was genuinely amused. 'Not like you, Ethan. You're usually so considered. I've hardly ever heard you utter a bitchy word about anyone else before.'

He contemplated his fingernails. 'Sorry. I just felt he overstepped the mark. It's bad enough watching him fawn over Daisy...'

'Ah,' she said. 'You've noticed?'

'Noticed? Anyone with two eyes in their head can see what's going on. After everything he's said about the need for the Midwinter Trust to observe the highest ethical standards, to see him behaving like a love-struck teenager is pathetic.'

'Goodness me,' she said quietly. 'You are in a fierce mood tonight.'

'Not fierce, just frustrated. I'm not being pious. Jeremy is long since divorced and he's free to play around as he pleases. Including with younger women, as long as he doesn't hurt anyone. But the way he's treated you and Chandra... well, it sticks in my craw.'

'I never knew you cared,' she said lightly.

He didn't smile. 'It's simply not right.'

'Chandra and I are grown women. We've both been around the block a time or two. We're perfectly capable of looking after ourselves.'

'Of course, but the pair of you work so hard, and you're so loyal to Midwinter, and to Jeremy himself. To watch him messing the two of you about isn't my idea of good fun.'

She gave him a mischievous smile. 'So what is your idea of good fun?'

He avoided her eyes. 'Sorry, I ought to shut up. I've drunk too much mulled wine.'

'That's not like you, Ethan. You always strike me as someone who is very much in control.'

'An illusion, trust me,' he said. 'I'm one of life's marionettes, not a puppeteer. Any shrink would have a field day with Ethan Swift. Lucky I've cornered the market for psychiatric expertise in Midwinter, huh?'

She laughed. 'I appreciate your kindness.'

'Don't mention it. All you did was leave that folder out for a moment or two. Not a hanging offence.'

'Lax security. It's not as if I don't know better. I've been trained until I've got safety protocols coming out of my ears. Serve me right if Jeremy made me go on a refresher course.'

'Don't be silly. If Baz Frederick was so desperate to make a stir, he'd have found some other way.'

She leaned closer to him. 'Are we right to assume Baz Frederick is the person responsible for that memento mori or whatever it was?'

'Who else?' he snapped. 'Grace or Zack? Don't tell me you suspect Carys Neville? The woman is far too much of a narcissist to care about anyone but herself. Poppy de Lisle? I don't think so. As for poor old Harry Crystal…'

She put her hands up in feigned surrender. 'Okay, okay. Baz is the obvious culprit. But we can't rule out the possibility it was someone else.'

'I suppose you're right.'

'Zack and Grace have talked with Baz. How much he told them about what happened five years ago, we don't know. Baz was also in touch with Carys. Like any good investigator, he doesn't seem to have given much away, but we don't know how much they found out for themselves. Any of them might have slipped those sheets into my folder.'

He closed his eyes for a moment. 'Is Jeremy too clever for his own good? Was it really such a brilliant idea to invite them all here?'

A rueful smile. 'Chandra and I agonised over the pros and cons endlessly. At first, we both told him it was crazy. Far too risky. But the more he talked us through it, the more everything started to make sense.'

'He's extremely persuasive.'

'Don't I know it?' She gritted her teeth. 'Eventually we agreed it was right to be bold. We make our own rules at Midwinter, and we have to play by them.'

'Too late for second thoughts?'

'Far too late. Even if we weren't all snowed in.'

He sighed. 'Fancy a nightcap? Might cheer us both up.'

'I'm tempted,' she said. 'Better not, though. There's a lot to do tomorrow. I need my beauty sleep.'

'No you don't,' he said in a low voice.

She shifted under the intensity of his gaze. 'You're good for my morale, Ethan.'

'I hope so,' he said. 'All I want is for you to have confidence in yourself.'

'You think I lack confidence?'

'Not as far as your work is concerned. I've never met anyone as efficient. On a personal level…'

She stretched her arms and yawned. 'A bit late to be getting personal.'

'You think so?' he asked softly.

'Yes. Really. I must get off to bed. Thanks again, Ethan. You've cheered me up no end.'

'I'm glad,' he said.

'And now,' she said, 'I'd best be on my way before I change my mind about that nightcap.'

He glanced at his watch and seemed about to say something. Suddenly he froze.

'What's wrong?' she asked.

'Did you hear something?'

'Only the storm.'

'I'm probably mistaken,' he said slowly. 'Letting my imagination run away with me.'

'About what?'

He hesitated. 'For my sins, I've got unusually acute hearing. It's by far my strongest sense. I'm pretty certain I heard a strange sound. Though with the storm raging, it's impossible to tell.'

'What sort of sound?'

In answer, he shut his eyes, as if trying to recapture something in his memory.

'Difficult to describe.'

'Surely it wasn't the hoot of an owl. Or the scream of a fox. Even the hardiest creatures will be lying low tonight.'

Scrambling to his feet, he said, 'Even so, I ought to check it out. Satisfy my curiosity. Otherwise, I won't get a wink of sleep.'

'Curiosity about what?'

He wavered. 'I mean… I'm probably way off beam, but I thought it sounded like a human voice. A person crying out.'

'Crying out?'

'In pain or fear. Or both.'

'You're quite sure your imagination isn't working overtime?'

He gave a nervous smile. 'No, I'm not. All the same, I'd better look around.'

'In a snowstorm? Seriously?'

'I won't be long. I'd just like to satisfy myself. I mean, I couldn't bear a repeat of…'

He let out a low groan.

'This Christmas is totally different,' she said urgently. 'There's nobody here like…'

'Yes, yes, I know. But I just need to make sure. Either I

imagined the noise or... well, if you'd like to stay here, I'll only be two minutes. And then perhaps I can walk you back to your cottage, just in case.'

'Just in case of what?'

'I dunno,' he said helplessly.

'Listen, I've got a better idea,' she said. 'Let me come with you.'

'I'm not sure—' he began.

'I am,' she said bluntly. 'Come on, let's find out if your mind's playing tricks. I hope not. Far too late for us to bring in another psychiatrist in time for Christmas.'

He pulled on his coat and boots. Each of them took torches out of their pockets.

'So the sound came from this direction?' she asked, gripping the handle of the back door.

Ethan nodded.

'Makes sense, given that we were sitting on this side of the hall,' she said. 'I can't believe you could have heard anything from out the front. Is it possible someone was out by the ice house?'

'I suppose so. But at this time of night? What on earth could they be up to?'

Outside, the storm was still raging. The wind was savage, the snow crisp underfoot.

Not a living soul was in sight. All they could see was the snow-covered bulk of the ice house, its entrance looming in front of them. The large brick building had served the whole village in the pre-refrigerator age and was said to be one of the last of its kind. Occupying a hollow, close to a shed, the diesel tank, and a barred entrance to a disused mineshaft, the underground storage space extended for some distance below the surface. Ethan had explored the subterranean alcoves when he'd first arrived in Midwinter. He'd discovered that, in addition to a drain to take away the meltwater, a passage connected with the old mine workings further down the slope, a sort of ancient subway for village workers to use in bad weather. Beyond the ice house, a burn wove its way down from the heights of the fell. The water was frozen.

Bernadette pointed a gloved hand towards the ice house door. The padlock was crusted with snow.

'Nobody's opened that in the past few hours!' She had to shout to make herself heard.

'Let's go round the back!' he yelled.

They clumped through the snow to the other side of the building. The burn ran through a narrow channel which deepened as the ground dipped. Further on, it formed a waterfall that tumbled down the side of the fell.

Ethan came to a halt and shone a beam of light on the snow to reveal a torch lying on the ground.

He bent down and uttered a strangled cry.

'Look!'

Bernadette waved her torch in the direction he was pointing.

The ice on the surface of the burn had been smashed by the weight of a body which lay face down, four feet below the bank. It was motionless.

No need to check a pulse. The shock of the fall and immersion in freezing water would have been enough to kill anyone.

'Who is it?' Ethan shouted.

But he already knew the answer. Only one person in Midwinter was so tall and broad-shouldered.

For a moment he thought Bernadette was going to throw up. But she gathered her strength to answer his question.

'Baz Frederick.'

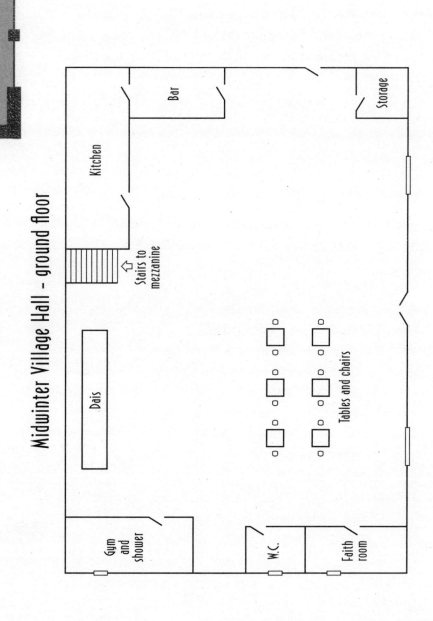

Midwinter Village Hall – ground floor

Kitchen

Bar

Storage

Stairs to mezzanine

Dais

Tables and chairs

Gym and shower

W.C.

Faith room

14

Harry Crystal's Journal

A bad sleeper at the best of times, I spent much of my first night in Midwinter tossing and turning. The bed was comfortable, and after making the short walk through the raging storm, I found the cottage warm and welcoming, but despite (or because of?) the effects of Daisy's mulled wine, which caused me to slump into a torpor as soon as I slid under the duvet, I soon found myself awake again. Had a noise roused me? I couldn't be certain.

I heaved myself out of bed and looked out of the window. Of course there was nothing to see but falling snow and darkness. The skies here are said to be the clearest in northern Europe, but that counts for nothing when you're in the middle of the worst snowstorm the area has seen for years.

I tried to get back to sleep, to no avail, and after a while I got up again. To occupy my mind, I set about writing up my journal. As I recorded my conversation with Poppy in the reading room, an idea jumped into my mind.

Too cold and too late to go back to the reading room to check my theory. I needed to work it out in my head.

Not that it took long. The list of my complete works was engraved on my memory, if nobody else's. And now

I understood why my books had been shelved with a slight deviation from chronological order.

Miss Winter in the Library with a Knife. Thirty-two letters. And I've produced thirty-two novels. The initial letters from their titles, with only minimal rearrangement, had supplied Bernadette with a name for her mystery. Should I be flattered? Or wary?

What had she said?

I'll explain the inspirations behind the answer and they will provide you with clues to the real mystery.

A Delphic utterance, but it dawned on me that I knew, better than anyone, what she meant.

She was referring to the classic crime novels which had inspired the titles for my own books.

The Key to Harry Crystal's Crime Novels

Murder Isn't Easy	Murder Is Easy	Agatha Christie
Innocent's Blood	Innocent Blood	P. D. James
Six Red Herrings	Five Red Herrings	Dorothy L. Sayers
Strangers on a Plane	Strangers on a Train	Patricia Highsmith
Why Didn't They Ask Evelyn?	Why Didn't They Ask Evans?	Agatha Christie
In the Heat of the Moment	In the Heat of the Night	John Ball
No More Dying Today	No More Dying Then	Ruth Rendell
Trent's Last Caper	Trent's Last Case	E. C. Bentley
Endless Fright	Endless Night	Agatha Christie
Rear View Mirror	Rear Window	Cornell Woolrich
Intruder in the House	Intruder in the Dust	William Faulkner

Nightmare Avenue	Nightmare Alley	William Lindsay Gresham
The Nine Gaolers	The Nine Tailors	Dorothy L. Sayers
Have His Car Crash	Have His Carcase	Dorothy L. Sayers
End of Sentence	End of Chapter	Nicholas Blake
Last Seen Weeping	Last Seen Wearing	Colin Dexter
In a Lonely Daze	In a Lonely Place	Dorothy B. Hughes
Bier Island	Bear Island	Alistair MacLean
Rogue Males	Rogue Male	Geoffrey Household
And Then There Was Nothing	And Then There Were None	Agatha Christie
Red Heartburst	Red Harvest	Dashiell Hammett
You Only Live Once	You Only Live Twice	Ian Fleming
Which Body?	Whose Body?	Dorothy L. Sayers
I, the Judge	I, the Jury	Mickey Spillane

The Blonde Wore Black	The Bride Wore Black	Cornell Woolrich
Hangover Street	Hangover Square	Patrick Hamilton
After the Burial	After the Funeral	Agatha Christie
Kiss the Girls Again	Kiss the Girls	James Patterson
No or Maybe?	N or M?	Agatha Christie
I is for Investigation	I is for Innocent	Sue Grafton
Farewell, My Lorelei	Farewell, My Lovely	Raymond Chandler
Elephants Can Forget	Elephants Can Remember	Agatha Christie

15

Midwinter

'I can't believe this is happening.'

Bernadette sat hunched up in her chair muttering to nobody in particular. Her face was as white as the landscape outside. Trying to process what had happened, and not doing a good job of it.

'You can say that again,' Ethan said with feeling.

'It's a nightmare, an absolute bloody nightmare'

'Yes.'

His mind was working furiously, trying to make sense of what had happened.

The four members of the senior management team had convened in Chandra's office on the mezzanine floor. She'd made everyone a hot drink and Ethan drained his mug with one last gulp. Baz's death had shocked him to the core. It wasn't in the script. Was it?

His limbs ached and his head buzzed with nervous tension. It was a miracle that neither he nor Jeremy had succumbed to hypothermia during their nocturnal exertions.

The Director was conferring with Chandra in low, urgent tones. Every now and then, he massaged his right shoulder. He'd tweaked a muscle but showed no other sign of strain following his close encounter with the dead weight of Baz Frederick's body. He and Ethan had spent what seemed like an eternity in the bitter cold and dark, manhandling the podcaster's remains out of the burn. Although the storm was beginning to ease, the task was exhausting and emotionally draining, a horrific trial of strength and will.

They'd managed to heave the corpse into the ice house. The women had cleared a deep alcove close to the door of the old building that had three broad shelves, and Ethan had taken out of the stores a winter sleeping bag in which the body could be preserved with at least a little dignity. At the first time of asking, the bag he chose wasn't quite big enough to accommodate Baz, but he'd found another that did the job. The stone building would serve as a temporary morgue until they figured out what to do.

Bernadette had messaged Jeremy and Chandra as soon as she'd recovered her composure following the discovery that Baz was dead. Jeremy said the four of them should meet in the hall in five minutes' time. The moment he arrived, he took command of the situation, insisting that they recover the body without delay. With that done, the next step was to decide how much to tell their guests, and what impact Baz's death would have on the game.

Ethan had a shrewd suspicion that, when he received Bernadette's message, the Director hadn't been asleep and hadn't been alone. For a man in such a senior and sensitive position, Jeremy Vandervell occasionally took absurd risks. Then again, leaders in many walks of life often played with fire. They persuaded themselves they were untouchable. How tempting to believe they could get away with anything. But that wasn't true, Ethan reflected. More, it was dangerous. Destructive.

Jeremy and Chandra joined them, and Bernadette straightened up at once. She hated showing any hint of weakness, seeing it as a form of betrayal.

'What do you make of it, Ethan?' Jeremy said. 'How did he die?'

'I'm no pathologist,' he said with a shrug. 'You'll need an autopsy to confirm whether there was water in his stomach and lungs. I've only taken a cursory look at the state of the body. Forensic science isn't my field of expertise. I'm no different from the rest of you. Most of what I know comes from watching programmes like *CSI*.'

'Nevertheless, you're medically qualified,' Jeremy said pleasantly. He seldom displayed impatience, even in the most testing circumstances. 'What is your view?'

'Speculation, more like.'

'Please. I'd value your opinion.'

Ethan sighed. 'My hunch is that he tripped into the burn and died within a few moments. It's well-established that if someone falls into a river in the depths of winter, their chances of survival tend to be poor. The burn is shallow, but immersion in freezing water is enough to kill even the healthiest person. Heart rate and blood pressure go through the roof within seconds.'

'Even if you're a good swimmer?'

'Makes very little difference. Your heart may give out at once, but even if you don't lose consciousness in the first few seconds, your first instinct on hitting the water is to gasp. It's an overwhelming urge, impossible to resist, but the gasp response means you take in water. If your head is fully underwater, that first gasp alone can be fatal.'

Jeremy rubbed his chin. 'Let me play devil's advocate. The burn is quite narrow. Yes, the channel at that point, behind the ice house, is a relatively deep V-shape, but there can't have been much water beneath the ice.'

'But more than enough to do serious damage to anyone unlucky enough to fall in,' Ethan said. 'Even if someone slips into a canal and in theory should be able to stand up on the bottom, they're often incapable of saving themselves. Your muscles seize up, and to all intents and purposes you're helpless. Even when the temperature is maybe fifteen degrees warmer than it is tonight, I'd expect someone to be rendered unconscious within thirty seconds, if not at the moment of impact.'

'Baz Frederick was wearing a bulky jacket. Would that make a significant difference?'

'Doubtful. As I say, hitting the cold water like that...'

Jeremy steepled his fingers. 'So no evidence of... third party involvement?'

'None whatsoever,' Ethan said quickly.

'But we weren't able to check the scene,' Bernadette interrupted.

'Inevitably.' Ethan sounded defensive. 'Much as I wanted to get the body under cover, my first priority was to make sure we didn't make matters worse by getting frostbite.'

'Quite right too,' she said. 'Sorry, Ethan, I didn't mean to criticise. If you hadn't heard Baz crying out, we wouldn't have found him until morning. In a worst-case scenario, one of the guests might have stumbled across the body, which scarcely bears thinking about. Our difficulty is, we have no idea how he ended up face down in the burn.'

Jeremy nodded. 'With the snow still coming down, we can't be certain he was alone.'

Ethan stared. 'What?'

'Even if there were footprints, they'd soon be covered.'

Ethan felt his cheeks burning. 'Do you seriously believe that Baz's death wasn't an accident?'

'Keep your voice down!' Chandra hissed. 'This office isn't soundproofed like Jeremy's. The walls are paper-thin.'

'Don't worry,' Bernadette said. 'Nobody will be eavesdropping in the middle of the night. My room is locked and the loos are on the other side. Nothing to get upset about.'

'Sorry,' Ethan said. 'It's just that… what happened came as a huge shock.'

'We understand.' She patted his hand in reassurance. 'You did a great job. If not for you, Baz would still be out there.'

'All I was saying,' the Director said pacifically, 'is that, at this early stage, we can't rule anything out.'

Chandra nodded. 'If there's no proof that a third party wasn't present at the scene, it's equally true there's nothing to suggest anyone else was with Baz, let alone that they had a hand in his death.'

'Suppose someone else was out there,' Bernadette said. 'Surely they'd have raised the alarm when he fell into the burn?'

Jeremy's face was a mask. *Computing possibilities*, Ethan thought. *Hoping to come up with a satisfactory calculation.*

'Unless they'd given him a helping hand.' Jeremy paused. 'Not that I believe that, of course. But it's only right to test the hypothesis.'

'Baz was hefty,' Chandra said. 'Stronger than anyone else in Midwinter, without a doubt. Wouldn't it be hard to give such a big man a shove that knocked him off his feet?'

'Not if someone crept up behind his back and took him unawares. He hadn't bothered to take his trekking poles or ice axe. He was the macho sort who reckoned he didn't need them. In a blizzard, he might have no idea that he wasn't on his own. Easy to lose your footing in these conditions.'

Chandra made a face. 'Isn't it more likely he simply stumbled over something without any outside help?'

'That's my guess,' Ethan said.

Jeremy looked thoughtful. 'So your conclusion about the likeliest cause of death is…?'

'I'd plump for an accident, every time. Ultimately, of course, it's a matter for the coroner. Here and now, it's impossible to know for sure.'

Bernadette leaned forward. 'Why would Baz go out there on his own in the dead of night?'

'You think he was looking for something?' Jeremy asked.

'In the middle of the worst blizzard for five years? What on earth could he have hoped to find?'

'He hadn't held back with the booze,' Ethan said. 'Harry Crystal's intake was modest by comparison.'

Bernadette nodded. 'Daisy's mulled wine carries a kick. I asked her to make sure of that. To give us a chance to see if it caused any of our guests… to lose their inhibitions. At least, those who aren't teetotal.'

'Baz probably went out for a few minutes to clear his head. If he was staggering about in minimal visibility, it would be so easy to trip over.'

'Was he carrying a torch?' Chandra asked.

Jeremy nodded. 'Perhaps he was trying to get the lie of the land when nobody else was around. If he thought it would give him an advantage in the game…'

'Why not wait until morning?' Bernadette asked.

'Because he didn't want anyone to know what he was doing.'

'There's another possible explanation,' Chandra said. 'Baz

Frederick was a heavy smoker. You could smell it on him. And he had nicotine-stained fingers. We don't allow smoking in any of the buildings in the village. So by the end of the night, he must have been gasping.'

'You think he went outside for a crafty fag?' Bernadette said. 'At dead of night, in the middle of a snowstorm? Seriously?'

Chandra folded her arms. 'It's as good an explanation as any I've heard.'

'Smoking is an addiction,' Ethan murmured. 'Sounds to me like you've hit the nail on the head, Chandra.'

Bernadette sighed. 'I'm not so sure. But if you think it makes psychological sense, Ethan…'

He shot her a glance, intended to signal gratitude for moral support. For all her professional standards, Bernadette didn't always manage to hide her reservations about Chandra.

Jeremy Vandervell was to blame for the tension between the two women, as he was to blame for so much else. When Ethan had first arrived in Midwinter more than five years ago, it hadn't taken long for him to realise that Chandra had recently supplanted Bernadette in Jeremy's affections. But the two rivals had worked out a modus vivendi. And now Chandra's own nose had been put out of joint, and finally she and Bernadette had found they had something in common. A shared antipathy, not directed at the Director for some reason, but towards his latest conquest, Daisy Wu.

Jeremy cupped his chin in his hands. 'A plausible theory, I suppose.'

'You sound sceptical,' Bernadette said.

'It's my duty to consider all the angles,' he said. 'Including whether we can rule out the possibility that Baz Frederick was murdered.'

Ethan winced. 'You think someone killed him?'

'No,' Jeremy said, 'I'm certainly not saying that. Simply running through the options.'

'Doesn't that raise the question of *why* anyone would want him dead?' Bernadette said.

There was a pause. Ethan started scribbling on a notepad.

'Nobody here needs reminding that Baz Frederick poked his nose into what happened here five years ago,' Jeremy said.

Chandra made an impatient noise. 'Do you really think that's relevant?'

'If he was murdered,' Bernadette said, weary as a parent explaining the obvious to a slow-on-the-uptake offspring, 'the killer must have a motive. Baz Frederick liked to make a song and dance about his investigative skills. We know he was fascinated by Midwinter and that... wretched business we'd all rather forget about. If someone was afraid...?'

'In theory, that's correct,' Jeremy interrupted. 'Thankfully, his inquiries were nipped in the bud.'

'If inquisitiveness wasn't the reason for his death, what was?'

Jeremy folded his arms. 'Consider the implications of what you're suggesting. All four of us were here five years ago. What all four of us want is to move on and leave the past behind us.'

'Doesn't that force us to ask ourselves an uncomfortable question,' Ethan said. 'Was it wise to invite him here? Or one gamble too many?'

This earned him a furious glare from Jeremy. Ethan tried to suppress a surge of elation. He'd never managed to provoke the Director before.

'We debated this at inordinate length. Not only before you came back to Midwinter, but afterwards. You know the plan. What's more, you agreed to it. No reservations. This isn't a moment to indulge in hindsight. We have a situation on our hands and we need to deal with it.'

'Of course, you're right,' Ethan said hurriedly. He'd gone too far. Baz's death had shaken him to the core, and as a result he'd allowed himself to get carried away. This was the wrong moment to antagonise the Director. 'I apologise.'

'Accepted,' Jeremy said crisply. 'Let's be clear, Daisy Wu and Frankie Rowland weren't around last time, so they don't enter into the equation. So if Baz's investigations into Midwinter's darkest hour provoked someone to murder him, the obvious suspect is sitting around this table.'

There was a short silence.

Ethan said lightly, 'Well, that lets Bernadette and me off. We sat here talking after you two left and were just about to head for our beds when I heard a faint noise. I can only presume that was Baz crying out as he fell into the burn.' He pointed to the sketch he'd drawn in his notepad. 'I've sketched the place where we found Baz. In case anyone gets curious. We don't want them tramping around the burn. The last thing we need is another accident.'

'Good thinking,' Jeremy said vaguely.

Chandra said, 'When the accident happened, I was already fast asleep. On my own, of course, so I can't prove it.'

Bernadette turned to her superior. 'Same with you, Jeremy?'

Ethan felt compelled, even if with the utmost reluctance, to admire the man's composure. Nothing fazed him. Not even the irony sharpening Bernadette's voice, or the scepticism glinting in Chandra's eyes as she watched his every move. Of course, none of them doubted that at the time of Baz Frederick's death, Jeremy had been with Daisy. If absolutely necessary, Daisy would alibi the Director. But none of them had a reason to back Jeremy Vandervell into a corner. At least, not right now.

'The point I'm making is this.' Jeremy contrived to evade the question while sounding as forthright as a judge who has tired of squabbling between learned counsel. 'It's vanishingly unlikely that any of us were involved with Baz Frederick's demise. We've spent years trying to make sure everyone accepts that what happened before was a tragic accident. No more, no less.'

'Exactly,' Chandra said. 'We've laid the rumour and innuendo to rest, thank goodness.'

'What has happened to Baz is a dreadful blow,' Jeremy said.

You can say that again, Ethan thought. What in God's name had gone wrong? He'd never expected Baz to be killed.

'Nevertheless, we mustn't overreact, let alone panic.'

Jeremy subjected them to a penetrating stare. The Director had a reputation, Ethan knew, for being a good man in a crisis. Although Chandra often joked that if you can keep your head when all around are losing theirs, maybe you simply don't appreciate the gravity of the situation?

'Guessing games will get us nowhere,' Jeremy continued. 'We mustn't turn on each other. There's no reason to believe that Baz was the victim of foul play.'

'No?' Bernadette asked.

'No. There doesn't seem to be a potential suspect, let alone a credible motive. None of us benefit from Baz's death. Quite the opposite. All of which lends strong support to the view that Baz died as a result of an unfortunate accident. So how do we handle it?'

'We must tell everyone else in the village that Baz has died,' Chandra said. 'We can't possibly hide the truth.'

'Not that we'd want to,' Jeremy said quickly.

'Of course not,' Chandra said.

'We're agreed that our guests must be told. That said, I don't think we need to raise the alarm… further afield just yet. That would be premature.'

Choosing his words carefully, Ethan thought. It hadn't taken the Director long to turn his mind to how best to avoid being held responsible for the occurrence of yet another tragedy on his watch.

Bernadette raised her eyebrows. 'Really?'

'Really. Let's face it, nothing can be done for the next forty-eight hours or however long it takes for the road to become passable again. In any event, tomorrow is Christmas Eve. Everything grinds to a halt in the outside world, even if not in Midwinter.'

Ethan forced himself to suppress a cynical smile. How easily his colleagues persuaded themselves that their rightful place was on the moral high ground.

'What about informing Baz's next of kin?' he asked.

'There are no close relatives,' Chandra said. 'We did a thorough background check on everyone during the recruitment process, don't forget. Baz lived on his own. No siblings, no surviving parents. Like all the other guests.'

'Yes, of course, you're right.'

'When I told him we must have something on record for the paperwork, he put down the name of some distant cousin as next of kin, but he told me they'd not had any contact for years.'

'This is all about managing communications,' Jeremy continued smoothly. 'We need to measure how much information we provide to people, and how and when we provide it. Remember this. The next few days are crucial for the Midwinter Trust. To be blunt, this Christmas is make or break.'

Bernadette nodded slowly. 'Agreed. We can't afford another catastrophe.'

'Baz Frederick's death is a human tragedy. We're all devastated, that goes without saying. But what's done is done. We need to focus on next steps with laser-like intensity.'

Why hadn't the man pursued a career in politics? Ethan wondered. His ability to obfuscate was matched only by a genius for dodging personal blame while sounding like the voice of sweet reason.

'In other words…?' Chandra murmured.

'First, we must brief Daisy and Frankie about Baz's death. Both women are robust individuals. I don't anticipate they will have any qualms, especially when I point out that it's overwhelmingly likely that the poor fellow died because of his acute craving for cigarettes. After breakfast, I'll address our guests. I'll explain that Baz has suffered a freak accident but that we intend to proceed as planned after allowing a brief period for people to come to terms with his death. It's not as if anyone in the village was personally close to him. Candidly, there's no reasonable alternative. It's not as if anyone will be able to leave Midwinter in the next forty-eight hours.'

'The guests will be suspicious,' Bernadette said. 'You'll face plenty of cross-examination.'

Jeremy shrugged. 'Not for the first time. I'll handle it.'

'It won't be easy,' Chandra said. 'One or two of them will be nervy. Don't you agree, Ethan?'

Ethan nodded. 'Harry Crystal, in particular, yes. But I think human nature will prevail. They came here to play a game. The stakes are high, and the brutal reality is this: Baz's death increases their odds of winning.'

'So each of the survivors had a motive for disposing of him,' Chandra said.

'As you've gathered,' Jeremy said, 'I don't believe this is a case of foul play. But you're right. If someone did have a reason to murder Baz, it wasn't one of us. It was one of our guests.'

Ethan nodded. 'Agreed.'

'And then there were five,' Bernadette said.

As they looked at each other, all the lights went out.

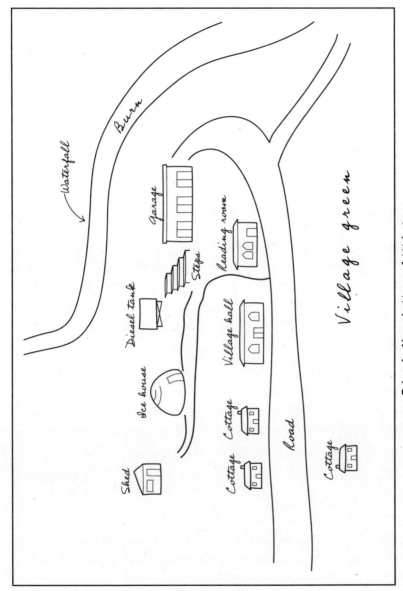

Ethan's Sketch Map of Midwinter

Waterfall
Burn
Garage
Reading room
Diesel tank
Steps
Village hall
Ice house
Cottage
Village green
Shed
Cottage
Road
Cottage

16

Midwinter

'At the risk of stating the obvious as we sit here in pitch darkness,' Jeremy Vandervell said calmly, 'the overhead lines must have gone down.'

The village hall was still agreeably warm, but Ethan found himself shivering with apprehension. To say that this evening hadn't gone exactly as planned, despite the fact he'd given everything so much thought in advance, was the ultimate understatement.

'Isn't the emergency generator supposed to kick in if there's a power cut?' he asked.

'Absolutely,' Jeremy murmured. 'No need for manual intervention.'

'Then why…?'

'Let there be light,' Jeremy interrupted. He'd been counting under his breath.

As if by magic, the lights came on again.

Bernadette and Chandra burst into spontaneous applause. Relief was etched all over their faces. Ethan leaned back in his chair. The Director beamed.

'The backup works automatically in the event of a mains

failure.' Jeremy failed to keep a trace of smugness out of his voice. 'Naturally, there's no chance of any further deliveries of fuel until the road is cleared. Fortunately, I asked for the diesel tank to be filled to the brim last week.'

'Can we keep the electric supply going throughout the whole village?' Chandra asked.

'Not everyone in Midwinter will use electricity at the same time, so as long as people are not unduly wasteful, we'll be fine. Apparently, it's called the principle of diversity. Of course, I had the generator tested as well. Best not to leave anything to chance.'

Except for the occasional sudden death, Ethan reflected.

'So nothing more can go wrong?' Chandra demanded.

Jeremy shrugged. 'Life can never be free of risk.'

'A point you made to the Commission of Inquiry,' Bernadette murmured.

'Precisely. There are no guarantees, unfortunately. Thank goodness that, at the end of the day, the Commission was prepared to take a realistic view.'

'So...?' Chandra persisted.

'Worrying about worst-case scenarios?' His paternal smile reminded Ethan of a father reassuring a child frightened by the dark. 'In theory, the diesel might get contaminated, or the emergency generator might suffer some kind of catastrophic failure out of the blue. It's not unknown, but we're talking about a hundred to one chance. I'm satisfied we've taken all reasonable precautions to make sure that this Christmas goes... much more smoothly than it did five years ago.'

'Except for Baz Frederick,' Chandra muttered.

'I've said my piece on that subject,' Jeremy said.

'Let's pray that things move smoothly from now on,' Bernadette said. 'We all deserve a truly peaceful Christmas.'

Ethan shifted in his chair, taking care not to voice the retort that sprang to mind.

You'll be lucky.

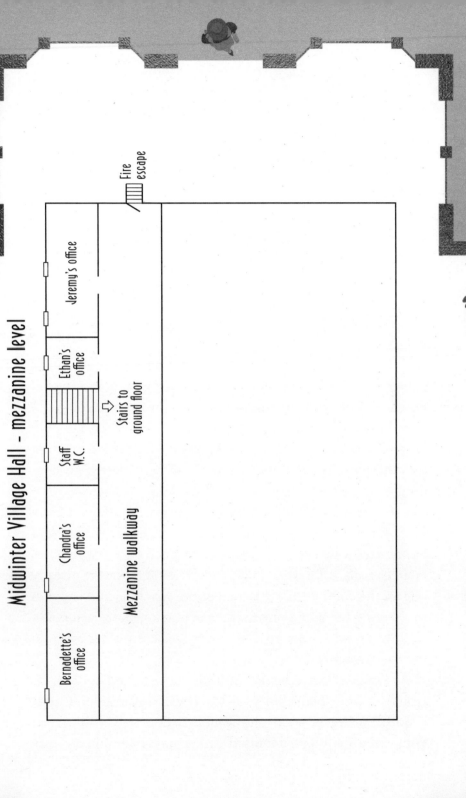

Midwinter Village Hall - mezzanine level

Bernadette's office

Chandra's office

Staff W.C.

Ethan's office

Jeremy's office

Mezzanine walkway

Stairs to ground floor

Fire escape

17

Harry Crystal's Journal

Christmas Eve.

After hours of fitful dozing, I woke at half seven. A glance through the curtains revealed that the snow was still falling, if not with the intensity of the previous evening. I'd been hopelessly slow in solving the riddle based on my own books. Time to up my game. So I mulled over the information we'd been given about the characters in Bernadette's mystery until breakfast time approached.

I set off for the village hall in the hope of being an early bird, but once again, I'd been beaten to it. Carys, Grace, and Poppy were already there, and Zack turned up a few minutes later. Cereals, croissants, juice, fruit and yogurts were already out on the counter, along with a coffee machine and supplies for making tea. Only one thing was missing as far as I could tell. Today there was no Christmas music burbling away in the background.

As Frankie busied herself putting out cups and cutlery, the women made their choice of tea bags. Ginseng for Carys, lemon for Grace, good old-fashioned English breakfast for Poppy. Zack contented himself with a glass of cranberry juice while I opted for the stimulus of strong coffee. I needed to be on my mettle.

At first the conversation was devoted to the weather. Frankie told us she'd been up since the crack of dawn. She'd made her way as far as the school that never was to see how the land lay. Under several feet of snow was the short answer.

'So we're trapped?' Carys Neville asked.

'Aye.' Frankie's eyes gleamed. I was pretty sure she was enjoying herself at the dreadful woman's expense. 'You're at the mercy of the Midwinter Trust, I'm afraid. There's no way out.'

Carys groaned. 'This is like being under house arrest. So how long will it take to clear the snow?'

'Once it stops falling? Two to three days, minimum.'

'*Minimum*?'

'Just as well you're all booked in until the twenty-seventh, eh?' Frankie said cheerfully. 'With any luck, you may get an extra day or two for free.'

'Awesome!' Poppy exclaimed. 'I so love Midwinter! It's everything I hoped it would be?'

'Viciously cold and cut off from the rest of the world?' Carys snapped.

'Well, if you put it like that… yes. To be perfectly honest, the rest of the world can be a bit too much sometimes, don't you think? Besides, what could be better than spending Christmas in good company, playing a mystery game specially created for us?'

Carys tossed a sceptical glance at our surroundings, as if searching in vain for good company. 'What about your family? Wouldn't you have preferred to spend the time with them?'

In a small voice, Poppy said, 'I lost my parents.'

'I don't expect any of us are blessed with too many loved ones,' Grace said. 'Isn't that why we're here?'

'One of the reasons, anyway,' I chipped in. 'You don't have any family either, Grace?'

She shook her head. 'Same as Poppy. My mum and dad died years ago, so did my elder brother. And I'm trying to forget my bastard of an ex-husband. What about you, Carys?'

'I'm not married. What's more, I never knew my father.'

'Oh?'

Carys looked torn between reticence and a desire to play for sympathy. 'My mother was a single parent. She's still alive, but in a care home. Early-onset Alzheimer's.'

'Sorry to hear that.'

Carys shrugged. 'Shit happens.'

'Too right.' Grace turned to me. 'Harry?'

'Broken home, broken marriage. Ex-wife living it up in the Maldives, daughter fully occupied with environmental activism. The only thing the two of them have got in common is that neither of them have spoken to me for ages.'

Grace gave a brisk nod. If I were paranoid, I might have interpreted it as a gesture indicating she saw why they'd cast me adrift. She switched her penetrating gaze to Zack, as if he were a culprit lined up in an identity parade.

'I'm an only child,' he said. 'Lost my parents ages ago.'

'In other words,' Grace said thoughtfully. 'Nobody will miss any of us if we don't get out of here.'

As we were digesting this, Daisy put her head round the kitchen door.

'Anyone for a full English?'

I was the only taker. My arteries could cope for a day or two, I assured myself as I tucked into my bacon, fried eggs, and monstrous Cumberland sausage, washed down with marmalade-covered toast and a couple of mugs of steaming coffee. I inhaled the smell of fat as if it were nectar. This was Christmas. An opportunity to indulge myself. Excess at someone else's expense. The best kind.

'Where's Baz?' Poppy asked suddenly. 'Don't tell me he's sleeping in on our first morning here?'

'Cool,' Zack murmured.

'If he's not careful, he'll miss all the fun!'

'Fun?' Carys said derisively.

Grace checked her wrist-watch. 'Cutting it fine, isn't he?'

'You haven't seen him, Frankie?' Poppy asked.

The chauffeur shifted in her seat. 'Uh-uh.'

She wasn't usually so monosyllabic. Mention of Baz's absence had prompted a frown. Was she anxious, and if so, why? I felt a tug of curiosity. Frankie Rowland didn't strike me as a born worrier.

Before anyone could interrogate her further, we were joined at the table by Chandra, Ethan, and Bernadette. They arrived together and greeted us cordially, but their mood seemed sombre.

Grace didn't waste time getting to the point. 'Bernadette, any idea where Baz might be?'

Bernadette responded with a perfunctory smile. 'Just give us a few moments, please. Jeremy will join us shortly.'

Grace frowned. 'It's Baz who's missing!'

'The Director would like to have a word with everyone,' Bernadette said.

'Don't tell me old Baz has done a runner,' Carys scoffed.

'Frankie's already told us that the road is blocked,' Grace said.

'Maybe he brought skis,' I suggested.

'I do hope he's all right?' Poppy said. 'I haven't had much chance to speak to him yet, but I've heard his podcast. It's really...'

'Awesome?' I suggested.

Her eyes sparkled with delight. 'You took the word right out of my mouth!'

'Last night, Baz was bothered about something,' Grace said.

'Didn't stop him knocking back the booze, did it?' Carys snapped. 'I bet he had a skinful. He's probably in his cottage right now, sleeping it off. Or nursing a hangover.'

Grace put her hands on her hips. 'Maybe he had a drink *because* something was bothering him.'

'Here's the Director now,' Bernadette said hurriedly as the door opened and Jeremy strode in.

I drained my mug as Jeremy marched to the dais. The caffeine had given me a pleasurable jolt. Jeremy had a whispered conversation with Bernadette and Chandra. Ethan Swift, sitting to one side, looked tense and ill at ease. Frankie pulled up a chair and sat next to him, her expression unreadable.

Jeremy bestowed on us a genial smile as he gave a pay-attention cough.

'Morning, everyone. Hope you all slept well.'

His gaze settled, rather randomly, I thought, on Zack, who murmured, 'No worries.'

'I have a couple of announcements to make. First, you may have noticed the lights flickering a few times this morning.

Let me assure you, there is nothing to be concerned about. It's the result of an overnight power cut.'

'Power cut?' Carys hissed. 'That's all we need.'

Jeremy brushed aside the interruption. 'As you saw on your way here, there is only one set of lines and poles to Midwinter. Not surprisingly, given the intensity of the storm, they came down in the small hours. I must reiterate, there's no cause for alarm. As soon as the fault occurred, our backup generator sprang into action exactly as planned.'

Carys grunted, but settled back in her chair. Jeremy beamed.

'Unfortunately, the climate here in Midwinter means this kind of mishap is far from rare. Isolation is the price we pay for living in such a gloriously peaceful part of the world. What's different this time is that our village isn't the only place affected. Or the first. Yesterday this rotten weather was responsible for a large-scale power outage in the north of England. We're far from alone, but I think I can claim that we are as well prepared as anyone for a challenge of this kind. Probably better.'

Poppy put up a hand. 'Will the power cut affect the game?'

'I'll talk about the game shortly. Suffice to say, the power cut should have minimal effect on us. Of course, the generator needs to serve the whole village, so please conserve energy as best you can. But I can promise you that we have ample supplies of fuel and there's nothing for you to worry about. You will be aware that the road to the station is now completely blocked by snow, but our stores are overflowing with food and other necessaries, so your comfort will not be affected during the course of your stay in Midwinter.'

Carys sniffed audibly, prompting a glare from Grace Kinsella.

Jeremy took a breath. 'The second matter I need to mention is most unfortunate. You will have noticed that your colleague, Baz Frederick, is not here this morning.'

The hall was quiet. Even Carys stopped fidgeting. Everyone's eyes were upon the Director of the Midwinter Trust. I had a sick feeling in the pit of my stomach. Jeremy's 'most unfortunate' was, I guessed, other people's 'catastrophic'.

'I very much regret to tell you that Baz has met with an extremely regrettable accident.'

I heard a small gasp. *Poppy*, I thought.

'What's the matter with the man?' Carys demanded.

Jeremy fixed his gaze on her. I doubt that Carys Neville had quailed often in her life, but she did now when faced with the patrician disdain in his chilly grey eyes.

'There is no easy way of saying this, I'm afraid.' His expression was sombre. 'I'm sorry to tell you that Baz Frederick died last night.'

My temples pounded as Jeremy's announcement sank in. I looked around to see how my fellow guests were reacting to the death of a man they'd dined with less than twelve hours earlier. A man who had been alive and well and looking forward to Christmas.

The colour had drained from Poppy's face. Zack's eyes had widened while Carys stared at Jeremy in apparent disbelief. We sat there for a few moments in shocked silence, finally broken by an exclamation from Grace.

'My God! Baz is dead?'

'Yes, Grace.' Jeremy bowed his head. 'Much as I hate to bear such dreadful tidings, I have no choice.'

'But how…?'

'Last night, he tripped in the darkness and fell head first into the burn,' Jeremy said. 'By the time we reached him, only a few minutes later, he was beyond help.'

'How could that happen?' Grace demanded.

'More easily than you might suppose,' Jeremy said in a sorrowful tone. 'Some of you may have noticed that Baz… I don't wish to sound critical in any way, Heaven forbid… drank quite a lot of mulled wine last night.'

'Why would anyone in their right mind potter around outside in weather like that, in the dead of night?'

'Good question,' Zack said. 'He was in the reading room last night with the rest of us.'

'Is that so?' Jeremy took a step forward. 'We need to piece together his precise movements after dinner. Could you tell us what happened?'

'Not a lot is the short answer. The guy was the first to leave.'

'Did the rest of you play board games yesterday evening?' Bernadette asked.

Grace brandished an envelope. 'Most of us were more concerned with finding the answer to the riddle you set us. I brought the answer along.'

'Me too,' Zack said.

'Thanks,' Bernadette replied. 'All in good time.'

Jeremy said, 'Let me ask again. What exactly went on in the reading room?'

'As Zack said, not a lot,' Grace replied. 'Baz had a cursory look around. I doubt he was in there for more than three minutes.'

'Did he speak to anyone else?'

'No.'

'Where did he go then?'

'Back to his cottage, presumably.'

'Did anyone see him after that?'

Along with everyone else, I shook my head.

Carys Neville cleared her throat. 'I didn't stay there long, either. I had a headache and I wasn't in the mood to play games. I gave up on the riddle and went off to bed.'

'I was there for another ten to fifteen minutes until I worked out the answer to Bernadette's question,' Grace said. 'Zack wasn't far behind me. I looked over my shoulder as I was heading off to my cottage, and I glimpsed him through the snow. That was the last I saw of anyone.'

Zack nodded. 'Same here. Fell asleep the moment my head hit the pillow. It had been a long day.'

Jeremy looked at Poppy. 'And you?'

'Harry and I played half a dozen games of draughts. I managed to solve the riddle in between moves.' She pointed to the sealed envelope on the table in front of her. 'The two of us chatted for a while after Grace and Zack left, and then I said goodnight.'

'So, Harry, you were the last to leave the reading room?'

'That's right,' I said sheepishly. 'I'm afraid it took far too long before the answer dawned on me.'

'Would any of you say Baz was the worse for wear when you last saw him?'

Zack hesitated. 'Baz was a big man who could hold his liquor. I wouldn't say he was drunk.'

Jeremy gave his customary judicial nod, as if a witness had made a vital concession that would feature prominently in his summing-up.

'How was he?'

'Subdued, compared to his manner earlier in the evening. Perhaps he had drunk a lot, but his speech wasn't slurred. Nothing like that.'

Jeremy inclined his head again. 'Thank you. What you've all said confirms our impression. Baz certainly wasn't incapacitated by drink last night.'

'Then why...?' Grace began.

'At present our investigation is not complete.' He slid in his disclaimer with such a combination of finesse and alacrity that I was lost in admiration. 'One possible explanation is that Baz went outside in the hope of clearing his head.'

'In a blizzard?' Grace scoffed.

'Even if he wasn't drunk, a few glasses of mulled wine might have affected his judgment.'

To everyone's surprise, Daisy Wu piped up.

'I may have overdone the alcohol. Made it stronger than I intended. I feel terrible about that.'

'You can't be blamed in any way, Daisy,' Jeremy said hurriedly. 'We're all adults here. Responsible for our own actions. In any event, we think it most likely that he went out to smoke a cigarette before retiring for the night. As you know, smoking isn't permitted in any building in the village, and I'm afraid Baz was a heavy smoker.'

'You're suggesting he went out in that weather, just for a crafty fag?' Grace demanded.

'If you put it like that,' Jeremy said, 'the answer is yes. Of course, the weather last night was appalling, but he didn't venture far. The burn is only on the other side of the ice house. That, as you will know from Bernadette's sketch map of the village, is just at the back of this building. A very short distance from where I'm standing now, especially if you're a big man who took long strides as Baz did. Even in poor weather, it would take him no more than two or three minutes to reach the burn.'

'Why would he bother to go even that far in the snow?'

'That area is not overlooked.'

Midwinter's equivalent of the school bike sheds, I thought, *where kids hung around smoking out of sight of their teachers.*

'Was Baz out there on his own?' Grace asked.

'We believe so. Nobody from the Midwinter Trust smokes, and as far as I'm aware, the only other smoker in the village is Zack.'

The agent flushed. 'Yeah, I'm trying to give them up.'

'So you didn't go out there with Baz last night?' Grace had appointed herself inquisitor-in-chief.

'No!' Zack sounded rattled. 'Like I said, I went straight back to my cottage and stayed there until I came out here for breakfast this morning.'

'Didn't I hear that he was a client of yours?'

'No way!'

'Sure about that?'

'Too right. He got in touch with me a while back about… a project he was working on. The discussions never came to anything.'

Grace turned her attention back to Jeremy. 'How was the body discovered? You say it was only a matter of minutes after he fell into the burn, but—'

'Thankfully,' Jeremy interrupted. 'My team is alert to anything in the least untoward. Your safety is a priority for us at all times. Ethan and Bernadette were still here in the village hall, discussing arrangements for today when Ethan heard a cry.'

'What sort of cry?' Grace wanted to know.

Ethan wriggled in his chair. 'Hard to describe. It was actually so faint that I wondered if I'd imagined it. Especially when Bernadette didn't notice it.'

Grace looked at the Deputy Director. 'You didn't?'

Bernadette's face was a blank. 'My ears aren't as sharp as Ethan's.'

There was a pause. I could guess what Grace was thinking. *Or maybe you just didn't want to hear anything.*

'Even though my hearing is unusually keen,' Ethan said, 'I wasn't sure about the sound I'd heard. Whether it was someone calling out or just a noise made by the storm. It was only for a split second. I couldn't tell whether the voice belonged to a man or a woman. I might have been completely mistaken.'

'So what did you do?' Grace seemed to be relishing her role as inquisitor-in-chief.

'I said to Bernadette that I'd like to go outside, just to make sure nothing was wrong. Even though she'd heard nothing, she insisted on accompanying me. Just in case.'

Grace's arched eyebrows expressed scepticism, and I found myself wondering whether Bernadette was lying. What if she'd heard the same noise but pretended otherwise?

Jeremy was growing restive, as if he'd had second thoughts about allowing guests to hijack the discussion. He gave a loud cough.

'So Ethan and Bernadette went out together to investigate. Despite the dreadful conditions, they found the body almost immediately. Such a terrible experience for both of them. Sadly, Baz was beyond help. There was nothing either of them could do to revive him. As you know, Ethan is medically qualified, and he conducted a brief examination. He is satisfied about the cause of death. The shock of immersion in freezing water killed Baz more or less instantly.' He paused. 'Desperately rotten luck.'

A *masterpiece of understatement*, I thought.

Grace folded her arms. 'How did he get in the water?'

'The evidence suggests he slipped and crashed head first through the ice. In the dark, and in such awful weather, entirely understandable.'

'And so tragic for poor Baz,' Bernadette said quickly.

Did she feel Jeremy wasn't showing quite enough empathy? There's a time and a place for the stiff upper lip, but this definitely wasn't it.

'Absolutely, Bernadette, thank you.' Yes, he'd got the message. 'A young man in his prime, with the world at his feet.'

'Tough to take it in.' Zack seemed to be in a daze. Much like the rest of us.

'It's a chance in a thousand, the sort of misfortune that might befall someone who was stone cold sober. Let alone a man who'd had a long journey up from London, and then had a few drinks.' He paused. 'Just to be sociable, of course.'

'This burn,' Grace asked, 'is it deep?'

'No, but Baz was a heavily built fellow, as you all know, and he would have fallen with considerable force.' He turned to Ethan. 'Isn't that right?'

Ethan nodded. 'I'm afraid the Director is spot on. It's so easy to fall in conditions like these. Which brings me on to another point. You're bound to be curious, it's only natural. I've done a little sketch of the area where the body was found, to give you a rough idea. We really don't want you tramping around there. Please, do take special care whenever you go outside at the moment. Use your trekking poles or ice axe to help you get about in the snow. Watch your steps and make sure you skirt round the village pool. Don't risk breaking bones. Or worse.'

He got to his feet and put the sketch map on the noticeboard.

'Excellent advice, ladies and gentlemen.' Jeremy heaved a sigh. 'Please don't forget that the village is honeycombed with disused mine workings. Over the years, several old tunnels have collapsed, which is why the main entrance to the shaft is barred and out of bounds. One or two of the old passageways built for miners run close to the heart of the village. After the storm, there may be further slippage of the land. For the time being, it's safest to stay inside as much as you can.'

Chandra had been keeping very quiet. Now she made a performance of clearing her throat before speaking.

'We're very much aware of the potential impact this sad news may have on you all, so please remember that Ethan will be available at any time to give one-to-one counselling to anyone affected.'

Poppy leaned forward. Unkindly, I wondered if she was entranced by the prospect of a one-to-one session with Ethan Swift, regardless of any feelings she had about the death of a man she hardly knew. She thrust her hand into the air like an over-excited schoolgirl itching to call out, 'Pick me! Pick me!' She was rewarded by Jeremy's headmasterly beam of encouragement.

'You have a question, Poppy. Go ahead, the floor is yours.'

'Does this mean that you don't intend to continue with the—' she began.

'The game?'

She nodded meekly, as if embarrassed by her own temerity. Privately, I was certain that all five of us were itching to know the answer to her question. And I guessed that everyone wanted to carry on as planned.

'Rest assured, we haven't forgotten why you all came here in the first place.' He glanced at his colleagues. 'The game will proceed. We believe that is what Baz would have wished. The last thing he'd have wanted was for this appalling accident to ruin everyone's Christmas by robbing you of the chance to play.'

Heads nodded in agreement, though I felt Jeremy's mind-reading was convenient rather than convincing. Personally, I didn't have the faintest notion of what Baz might actually have wished.

Bernadette said, 'In the circumstances, however, we've decided that it is appropriate to defer further discussion of the game. Please hand in your envelopes to me now, and I'll give you all a further briefing at lunchtime.'

I looked around the room, trying in vain to read the minds of my fellow players. When the shock subsided, would human nature assert itself, would people brighten as it dawned on them that Baz's death meant our chances of winning had suddenly improved?

Jeremy looked up. 'Once again, everyone, I'm so sorry to start the day by giving you such dreadful news. We will meet again for lunch at twelve noon. For the moment, I'd ask you to join me in a minute's silence. An opportunity for private reflection about the colleague we've lost.'

You have to hand it to the Director, I thought, as everyone stared at the floor. He hadn't tried to bury bad news, but he'd handled a very difficult announcement as slickly as possible.

Baz's death wasn't so much a disaster, as far as Jeremy Vandervell was concerned, as an obstacle to be overcome.

Meanwhile, life in Midwinter hadn't come to a full stop. A few hours' delay was neither here nor there.

The game must go on.

404

Page Not Found

The page you are looking for is no longer available.

18

Poppy de Lisle's Journal

So Baz Frederick is dead.

I'm sorely tempted to write: *this changes everything.*

You can't beat a touch of melodrama, especially not here in Midwinter. But is it true? Has anything *really* changed? Possibly not. Except for the dead guy, obviously.

I thought something was wrong as soon as I realised Baz hadn't made it to breakfast. He'd had a few drinks last night and he might have still been in his cottage, hungover and feeling sorry for himself. But he looked to me like a man who could take a hangover in his stride.

Sitting here in my cottage with only this notebook for company, I feel inclined to beat myself up. I know, I know – dwelling on what might have been is always a waste of time and energy. Trouble is, the temptation is so hard to resist.

If only I'd talked to him at greater length last night. Who knows what I might have discovered? I was trying to be careful, not to draw too much attention to myself. An own goal: in hindsight, that's screamingly obvious. In this life, we seldom get second chances. Jeremy Vandervell is an exception who proves the rule. Not to mention Bernadette Corrigan, Chandra Masood, and the gorgeous Ethan Swift.

I've made a determined effort to snap out of it. No sense in crying over spilt milk. What I need to figure out is this: is Baz's death significant in the greater scheme of things, or simply – not to put too fine a point on it – a red herring?

His podcast was very good, actually. I was a regular listener. True crime stuff is everywhere nowadays, a sort of audio equivalent of Japanese knotweed, but *Black Death* stood out from zillions of rival podcasts because it was neither a cut-and-paste exercise nor an exercise in vanity. Baz actually undertook his own original research. Persistent to a fault, he'd question witnesses, however reluctant, refusing to take no for an answer.

I admired his determination. The question is: was it to blame for his death?

The Midwinter Trust have survived one major scandal by the skin of their teeth, after years of playing cat and mouse with those who – let's make no bones about it – would love to see the Trust wound up and consigned to a footnote in some book about rural history. Another calamity could destroy the Trust and everything Jeremy has spent his life working for.

And yet. All is not lost, far from it. Jeremy is no fool. He and his colleagues have got their act together. They are all five years older and apparently wiser.

I've got to hand it to them. In extremely testing circumstances, they presented Baz's death in the best possible manner this morning. There was a ring of truth about what they said. Or at least plausibility.

Yes, Baz drank more than was wise. Yes, his initial bonhomie faded and he seemed twitchy about something. Perfectly reasonable to blame that on his craving for a smoke. Nicotine addiction might explain why he did something so stupid and dangerous as to creep around in a wild storm at dead of night.

Maybe Baz died in precisely the manner they described. But I wasn't willing to be fobbed off with lovely Ethan's sketch map. I couldn't take their word without checking for myself.

After breakfast, the five remaining players in the game sat around for a while, expressing our dismay at what we'd been told. But everyone was cagey about how much they said, taking refuge in clichés and platitudes. I didn't learn anything new. Eventually, I drifted out of the village hall in a seemingly aimless manner. I hurried round the back to get the lie of the land.

The snowflakes were falling gently now, almost caressing the ground, and several sets of footprints were faintly visible. No doubt there'd been a lot of activity there since Baz's corpse was discovered. The holly wreath had been removed from the door of his cottage. Chandra had told us it had been placed with his body in the ice house, as a mark of respect.

Sneaking around the back of the village hall, I found that the land fell away sharply as I approached the burn. Yes, in the dark and in a storm, even a fit and sure-footed man with a torch risked taking a tumble. What on earth had possessed Baz to come here? Was he really so hooked on his fags? Maybe he was, but why not simply go around the back of his own cottage for a quick drag? Admittedly he might be easier to spot there if anyone happened to look out of their window, but would that matter? Smoking outside isn't a crime, even in Midwinter.

Soon I discovered I wasn't the only one indulging in a bit of detective work. Carys Neville appeared a minute later. Evidently, she too was keen to see where Baz had died and decide for herself whether everything Jeremy had told us was to be believed.

'Poor chap,' I ventured, for want of anything better to say.

Carys sniffed. 'If you stagger out into a snowstorm when you're already the worse for wear, what do you expect? He only had himself to blame.'

I stared at her, but those big glasses were an effective disguise. I couldn't tell what was in her head.

'You think I'm callous?' She sounded scornful.

I gave a helpless shrug.

'At least I'm not a hypocrite.' She gestured towards the village hall. 'Not like some I could mention.'

Actually, her career as an influencer imploded because she *is* a hypocrite, but this was hardly the moment to point out that inconvenient truth. Anyway, it isn't in the nature of someone as sweet-natured as Poppy de Lisle to be provoked into such a snidey response.

Dear Poppy. I've come to realise that I enjoy pretending to be my ideal self. The guileless ingénue I'd love to have been, had my life not taken a very different turn.

I returned to my cottage without another word and tried to make sense of what happened to Baz.

Was it possible that his death was a blessing in disguise for Jeremy and the Midwinter Trust? He could buzz around as much as he liked, but he couldn't do the Midwinter Trust much harm, surely? Certainly not enough to justify...

Even in the privacy of my cottage, I hesitate, reluctant to articulate the possibility that had leaped into my mind during that minute of silence while we were supposedly paying our respects.

... murdering him.

19

Midwinter

'Well, I must say that went as well as we could have hoped,' Jeremy pronounced after the guests had finally drifted away from the village hall. 'Don't you agree?'

This question was his version of consultation, Ethan knew. The Director's blend of charm and confidence meant people found it hard to say no to him.

Jeremy looked around the table at his three senior colleagues. Daisy Wu was clearing up in the kitchen while Frankie Rowland was over at Baz Frederick's cottage, tidying up. Last night, Bernadette and Chandra had searched through Baz's possessions, making sure there was nothing that might cause any embarrassment which hadn't been picked up by the scanner at check-in. But the dead man hadn't written a single word in his complimentary journal and the pen was still in its gift box.

'We need to keep a close eye on Grace,' Chandra said. 'She's in the mood to stir up trouble.'

'Not to mention Carys,' Bernadette said. 'Tricky customer, that one.'

'We can't take anything or anybody for granted,' Jeremy said. 'But that's nothing new, is it? We discussed the challenges we faced with this bunch of people ad nauseam before any of them ever set foot in Midwinter.'

'Remember the sheets that were put in Bernadette's folder,' Chandra said. 'What was that all about?'

'In my view, Baz Frederick put them there in a crude attempt to rattle us. Or possibly some kind of sick joke.' Jeremy turned to Ethan. 'What's your professional judgment?'

Ethan nodded. 'Pure opportunism, in my opinion. Quite in keeping with his psychological profile. He liked to stir up trouble. Couldn't let well alone.'

'Understanding his personality helps us to understand why he died.' Jeremy became sententious. 'The craving for pleasure – alcohol and cigarettes – was his undoing.'

'Coupled with a touch of bravado,' Ethan said. 'Going out in the middle of a storm was reckless in the extreme. If he wasn't so rash, he'd be alive today.'

Chandra looked at him. 'You seem calmer about the situation than you were last night.'

Ethan scratched his chin. 'His death came as a bolt from the blue. Finding the body knocked me off balance, I don't mind admitting. I may be a medic with psychiatric training, but I'm only human.'

'Of course you are.' Bernadette gave Chandra a sharp look. 'It was quite horrible. Nothing prepares you for something like that.'

'Not even previous experience?' Chandra murmured.

'Do you want to explain what you mean?' Bernadette retorted.

Chandra covered her mouth, instantly contrite. 'Sorry, Bernadette. I shouldn't have said that.'

'Nerves are bound to fray after such a shock,' Jeremy said. 'Perfectly understandable. Baz Frederick's death wasn't in anyone's script.'

'Let's hope not,' Chandra said.

The Director declined to rise to the bait. 'We must keep our eye on the ball. The game hasn't begun properly, but it will soon be over. By Boxing Day, give or take, we should have done everything we set out to do. We have a plan, remember, and though I say it myself, it's a good one. All we have to do is concentrate on our agreed objective and keep our heads. And our tempers.'

He slid a glance at Chandra, who nodded vigorously.

'Absolutely. And once again, apologies. I spoke out of turn.'

Bernadette, with only the faintest reluctance, gave a smile of acknowledgment. 'It's all right, Chandra. No harm done.'

Daisy put her head around the door. 'Anyone for elevenses?'

Jeremy rubbed his hands. 'Thank you, Daisy. Another of your good ideas. You really are full of them.'

Chandra and Bernadette looked at each other. It was as if the row that had briefly threatened to flare up between them was already forgotten. They were ready to make common cause against the American woman who had supplanted them in the Director's affections.

Two women scorned, Ethan reflected. Never mind whatever mistakes Baz Frederick had made. Jeremy himself was getting careless in his old age.

Next time he put a foot wrong, it might prove fatal.

20

Harry Crystal's Journal

I hate to say it, but Carys Neville's jibe about house arrest wasn't so far from the truth. Jeremy Vandervell obviously didn't want any of us traipsing around outside. Yes, we needed to make sure we didn't suffer the same fate as poor old Baz, but his words of warning struck me as over the top. Was this strange little village really a death trap? How likely was it that old mine workings would collapse? Or did they simply provide a useful excuse for discouraging inquisitive guests who were inclined to snoop around where they weren't wanted?

I whiled away the time by pondering the information we'd been given about the characters in *Miss Winter in the Library with a Knife*. Bernadette had set things up so there were motives aplenty, in the tradition of the classic whodunit. But she'd also realised that it was a mistake to dole out too much information too soon. For all my experience at dreaming up convoluted mystery plots, I couldn't be sure which way this one was heading.

I got up to stretch my legs and peered through a chink in the curtains of the front room. Snow swirled around, but much less violently than before. In the distance I caught sight of a small, hooded figure bustling from the direction of the village hall towards the cluster of houses occupied by the people from the Midwinter Trust. Daisy Wu, presumably, the shortest person in the village. She took a circuitous route, skirting the village green and passing the war memorial before rejoining the route to her front door.

No sooner had she slipped from sight than my neighbour emerged from next door. Zack Jardine mooched around the village green aimlessly, or so it seemed. Perhaps he was simply bored with waiting for the game to begin in earnest.

To my surprise, Zack stopped at the memorial which stood at the far end of the snow-covered green. Something about it seemed to take him aback.

He lingered there for half a minute, simply gazing at the stone cross, before resuming his perambulation and finally heading back towards his home.

Hastily, I stepped away from the window. Even though we were opponents in a game – every detective for himself, so to speak – I was reluctant to embarrass myself by being caught spying on any of the others.

I threw on my coat and gloves and hurried out into the snow in the hope that I might undertake a bit of detective work before anyone else came along. The snow was deep underfoot as I crunched my way towards the village green and the cross that Zack had found so intriguing. Luck was on my side. There was nobody else about. Although why I should feel guilty about wandering outside my cottage, I found hard to explain, even to myself. We still live in a free country, don't we?

When I reached the cross, the first thing that struck me – as it had undoubtedly struck Zack – was that someone had been here earlier. The side of the memorial which bore the names of the dead had been wiped clean of snow. Yes, a few flakes now smeared it. But whereas the other side of the stone cross was completely covered by snow, this was not the case with the long list of names beneath the inscription:

TO THE GLORY OF GOD
THIS MONUMENT STANDS
IN PROUD AND LOVING MEMORY
OF THE MEN FROM THIS PARISH
WHO FELL IN THE SERVICE
OF THEIR BELOVED COUNTRY

Someone here was determined to remember the dead.

But why, exactly?

I looked at the list of names and counted them. Twenty-eight.

There was a gap between the first twenty-seven and the final name. On close inspection, the style of engraving was marginally different as well. On the face of things, it seemed as if all but one of the names had been engraved at the same time.

I stared at the final name, trying to summon some kind of inspiration.

William "Will" Noone

Why did that ring some kind of bell?

Was it... yes!

The explanation hit me like a punch in the stomach. It's a wonder I didn't keel over on the spot in amazement.

WILL NO ONE

WILL NOONE

The sheets that had fluttered from Bernadette Corrigan's folder yesterday evening bore the name of a dead man.

A message from the grave. But to whom? And for what reason?

21

Midwinter

'You need to know something,' Daisy Wu said after Jeremy Vandervell came into the kitchen.

A note of urgency in her words wiped away his smile of greeting. He glanced over his shoulder and realised he hadn't shut the door properly. Ethan was just outside, studying a notice that Bernadette had pinned to the board, within earshot.

He shot her a warning glance before lowering his voice. 'Something the matter?'

'Someone wiped the snow from the memorial,' Daisy said. 'So the list of names is plainly visible.'

Jeremy frowned. 'You mean…?'

'Zack Jardine has already picked up on it. Not too significant, given that he already knows about Will Noone. But I saw Harry Crystal staring at the names as well. The guy is so transparent, you can see through him. He clenched his fists in a sort of eureka moment as he put two and two together.'

'Meaning what?'

'He connected Will Noone's name with the sheets of paper that Baz Frederick – or whoever – slipped into Bernadette's folder last night.'

Jeremy groaned. 'That's all we need. An innocent becoming suspicious.'

The door opened again and Ethan appeared. 'Everything okay? You don't look happy, Jeremy.'

'Tell him, Daisy.'

Before Daisy could utter a word, they were joined by Bernadette.

'In conference?' she asked.

As the words left her mouth, the door swung open again and in walked Chandra.

'Hail, hail, the gang's all here,' Daisy said drily.

'What?' Chandra asked.

'An old American song. All right, let me explain what I saw just now.'

The moment she'd finished speaking, Bernadette made a dismissive gesture.

'Nothing to worry about,' she said. 'Almost everyone else in the village is in the picture to some extent regarding Will Noone. What difference will it make if Harry Crystal knows about him as well?'

'Harry is nosey,' Chandra said. 'If he starts poking under stones...'

'He's not very bright,' Bernadette said.

'The man has written lots of detective novels.'

'Thirty-two, to be exact.'

'He can't be entirely stupid.'

'No?' Bernadette invested the word with more irony than most syllables can bear.

'What do you think Harry will find?' Daisy asked quickly.

'Good question,' Bernadette said. 'Let's face it, the death of Will Noone has been investigated at enormous length and at no small cost to the public purse. The Midwinter Trust was given a clean bill of health.'

'Well,' Daisy demurred, 'that's putting it rather high, isn't it?'

'Innocent till proved guilty,' Bernadette replied. 'A fundamental principle of British law, Daisy. If you're in any doubt, I'm sure Jeremy will explain it to you. One-to-one, naturally.'

This was enough to provoke Jeremy into a response. Until now, he'd seemed nothing more than an interested spectator, like someone watching a football kickabout.

'Steady on, all of you. Aren't we in danger of letting the conversation get unnecessarily heated? Daisy's sole aim was to bring this little incident to our attention. No need for anyone to become argumentative.'

'And probably no need for you all to be in my kitchen,' Daisy said. 'Too many cooks, and all that?'

They took the hint. Even Jeremy looked sheepish as he led the way back into the main hall. *Bernadette had*, Ethan thought, *achieved the outcome she desired*. She was aiming to keep Daisy and Jeremy apart as far as possible, and he was glad about that. Jeremy's pursuit of the American cook was an unwanted complication. Things were tricky enough already, especially given Baz's death. He'd said as much to Frankie when they'd had a conversation earlier.

Lunch, a light buffet, didn't take long, either to prepare or to consume. Daisy had finally got the music going, but not even 'Rudolph the Red-Nosed Reindeer' did much to lift people's spirits. Conversation was stilted and sporadic and Ethan sensed that the guests were acutely conscious of Baz's absence. Harry Crystal seemed more withdrawn than usual, as if trying to make sense of the connection between the sheets scattered on the village hall floor yesterday evening and the memorial to the village's dead, both of which bore Will Noone's name.

Without ceremony, Bernadette opened the envelopes given to her by the guests and announced that four people had solved her riddle. *All the survivors except for Carys*, Ethan presumed, though Bernadette didn't name or shame.

'Well done to everyone who got the right answer. I hope this little exercise helped to get you thinking. *Miss Winter in the Library with a Knife* happens to be what you come up with when you take the initial letter from the titles of Harry Crystal's books in the order they were shelved in the reading room. Since we are lucky enough to have a detective writer with us over Christmas, I thought we should pay our respects to his work by referencing it in our game.'

Harry crossed his legs. *Trying to look nonchalant*, Ethan thought. A seasoned author, accustomed to admiration.

'Once again, let me emphasise that this doesn't give him any advantage over the rest of you. You'll all have access to the same information and clues. For instance, one or two of you may already have spotted the notice I've put up, listing all the titles and authors of the crime novels and thrillers to which Harry doffs his cap, so to speak, in the titles of his books.'

Everyone looked towards the board. Ethan noticed that Harry's cheeks had turned pink. He wasn't accustomed to anyone paying his books so much attention. And Bernadette's approach to the game certainly didn't sit well with his strategy of encouraging his competitors to underestimate him.

From the folder which she'd dropped the previous evening, she slid out five sheets of paper. One for each of the remaining guests. Looking over her shoulder, Ethan saw it was a list of books and authors, headed:

Murder at Midwinter – What Happened?

'Now,' she said. 'You need to do your utmost to put aside the dreadful news you've received today. Time to get down to the mystery. It should, at the very least, be a welcome distraction after what has happened. Here are the first important clues to the puzzle you have to solve. There's a sheet for each of you. Take it away and see what you make of it.'

She handed out a sheet to each guest. Harry gave it only a cursory glance. So, less predictably, did Carys Neville. She was the only person who hadn't bothered to guess the answer to Bernadette's conundrum, an indifference in keeping with her manner since she'd set foot in Midwinter.

Ethan had been tasked with studying the guests' personalities prior to their arrival and despite the limitations of remote assessment – there was no substitute for interacting with people at first hand – he could make a shrewd guess about what was going on.

Poppy and Harry's attempts to pretend that they were hapless no-hopers with negligible prospects of winning the game were far from sophisticated. Carys's approach was subtler. By nature, she was anti-social, a characteristic Ethan had noticed in others who lived their lives through social media. Undoubtedly, she was a narcissist. Her online profiles contained repeated injunctions to *be kind*, although even prior to her defenestration by equally kind souls on social media, she'd never been conspicuous for practising what she preached. Her behaviour in Midwinter was in keeping with the impression he'd already formed. Tempting to write her off as someone whose sole pleasure in life was making trouble. Did she care about winning the prize?

After giving the sheet a quick glance, Grace scowled. 'More stuff about detective stories. So these are the books that Harry took for so-called inspiration? Forgive my bluntness, but it does look like you're rigging the game in his favour. Whatever happened to playing fair?'

Ethan raised his eyebrows. This outright attack caused Poppy to gulp, while Zack winced. Carys allowed herself the semblance of a smug smile, the first time she'd shown signs of amusement since arriving in Midwinter.

Not that Bernadette was flustered. She'd expected a challenge, if not quite so soon or so ferocious. Looking Grace in the eye, she said calmly. 'I can assure you, along with everyone else, that Harry knows no more about the game than any of you. His only possible advantage is experience of concocting mysteries for his detective fiction. The other four of you are well versed in the genre. My advice to you is simply this: concentrate on the information supplied and see what you make of it. Answers by teatime, please. In sealed envelopes – you know the drill.'

Grace's response was a dissatisfied grunt.

Harry said meekly, 'Believe it or not, I don't have any inside information.'

Chandra gave an emphatic nod. 'For what it's worth, even I don't know the solution.'

'Nor me,' Jeremy said. 'Bernadette came up with *Miss Winter in the Library with a Knife* entirely on her own. She hasn't confided in any of us.'

'Perhaps I'm a mystery writer manqué.' Bernadette smiled

at Grace. 'We do understand that Baz's accident has come as a great shock to everyone. Nerves are bound to be strained. But we're less than twelve hours from Christmas Day. Let's do our utmost to kindle lots of festive spirit.'

Admirable sentiments, Ethan thought.

But it's never going to happen.

Murder at Midwinter - What Happened?

Murder Is Easy
Innocent Blood
Five Red Herrings
Strangers on a Train
Why Didn't They Ask Evans?
In the Heat of the Night
No More Dying Then
Trent's Last Case
Endless Night
Rear Window
Intruder in the Dust
Nightmare Alley
The Nine Tailors
Have His Carcase
End of Chapter
Last Seen Wearing
In a Lonely Place
Bear Island
Rogue Male
And Then There Were None
Red Harvest
You Only Live Twice
Whose Body?

I, the Jur**y**
The **B**ride Wore Bl**ack**
Hangover Square
After the Funeral
Kis**s** the Girls
N or M?
I is for Innocent
Fa**rew**ell, My Lovely
Elephants Can Remember

22

Harry Crystal's Journal

At the end of the briefing, I noticed Frankie Rowland slipping out of the village hall and hurried after her. Of all the people in Midwinter, she was the one with whom I felt I might be able to discuss what had happened. Unlike the other guests and the staff of the Trust, she didn't have a hidden agenda. But there were bound to be limits to her candour. The Trust was a valuable customer and she was too sensible to do anything to jeopardise the business relationship.

'Spare me a minute?' I called.

She turned to face me. 'Yes, Harry?'

'Can I ask you a question?'

'Sure, fire away.' She allowed herself a faint smile. 'Not that I can promise I'll know the answer. If you're hoping for a clue to solve the mystery, you're wasting your time. You heard what the Director said. Bernadette doesn't confide in him, let alone the likes of me. I may work for the Trust, but I'm not part of the inner circle.'

'This is nothing to do with the game.' I hesitated. 'At least, not as far as I know. I wondered if you'd come across the name Will Noone?'

She wrinkled her brow, as if racking her brains. 'Will Noone? Yes, it sounds vaguely familiar. Why do you ask?'

'His name is over there.' I waved towards the war memorial, which stood a few yards away. 'On the cross, right at the bottom. Looks as though it was added after all the others.'

'That's where I've seen it! I noticed it this morning.'

As if by tacit agreement, we trudged towards the memorial.

'Strange, don't you think?' I pointed. 'Looks like someone wiped snow off the memorial specially, just so the names are visible.'

She considered this. 'Now you come to mention it, I suppose that's true.'

'It's odd. And there's something else. Those sheets that Bernadette dropped yesterday evening, remember?'

'Uh, yes... I think so. When she tripped over me?'

I had no doubt she remembered the incident involving the sheets. She was temporising to give herself time to figure out how much to say.

'Put them together and they spell the name Will Noone.'

Her eyes widened. 'Oh!'

'Quite a coincidence.'

'Why would Baz Frederick...?'

She stopped herself mid-sentence.

'Yes?'

'Nothing.' She shook her head. 'I talk too much, that's my trouble.'

'Are you suggesting Baz put the sheets in Bernadette's folder?'

'I've no idea,' she said quickly. 'I'm only going on what someone else said.'

'Someone said that Baz was responsible? Who was it?'

'Look, I'm not naming names. It wouldn't be fair.' Frankie seemed uncharacteristically flustered. 'I mean, I've never been one for telling tales out of school. Let alone speaking ill of the dead. Poor man, what happened to him was awful. Bad enough to fall over and die. If Ethan hadn't heard him call out, his corpse would've been a slab of frozen ice by the time it was discovered. A small mercy, but at least it's something. Best to leave him to rest in peace, eh?'

'Absolutely. But I'm curious. Why did someone believe that Baz—?'

She took a step towards me. Her voice was low and urgent. 'Please, Harry. I'm only the hired help. The driver, the odd job person. I don't want to get dragged into anything I shouldn't. That's not why I'm here. I told you when we were in the car. I've signed papers. Terms and conditions.'

'Of course, I understand. This is strictly between you and me. Who was Will Noone and why would anyone suspect Baz of—?'

'Sorry, Harry, but I've said more than enough. I'm not meant to gossip with the guests. Bernadette and Chandra gave me firm orders.'

She looked over my shoulder and I guessed someone else was leaving the village hall. Raising her voice, she said, 'No hope of getting back to the station any time soon, sorry! I'll keep everyone posted as and when the conditions improve. The weather will start to clear soon enough, don't you fret.'

With that, she bustled away. As I began to trudge back towards my cottage, I glanced up and saw Grace and Poppy coming towards me.

Grace was as direct as ever. 'Trying to tap up poor Frankie

for clues? It's more than her job's worth. You're putting her in an impossible position.'

I mustered a weak smile. 'Why would I do that if I've already got an unfair advantage over the rest of you?'

She made an exasperated noise. 'Okay, I did let off steam in there. I can't really imagine why they'd want to indulge in favouritism where you're concerned.'

I doubted this was a compliment, and it certainly wasn't an apology, but it was probably as close to an olive branch as I was going to get.

'I don't think Frankie has any inside information,' I said. 'We were merely passing the time of day. She said how lucky it was that Ethan found Baz when he did. Otherwise, his corpse would have frozen into a slab of ice.'

Poppy shivered extravagantly. 'Such a terrible tragedy. He seemed such a nice man, too. How I wish I'd had the chance to talk to him properly. We only exchanged a few words.'

'He devoted his last evening on earth to knocking back the mulled wine.' Grace didn't have a sentimental bone in her body. 'Not such a bad way to go, I suppose.'

'Did you and he chat together?'

'For two or three minutes. No longer.'

Her tone struck me as defensive, prompting me to ask, 'What did he have to say for himself?'

'He was guarded. I had the impression that...'

Her voice trailed away. For the first time in our acquaintance, she seemed torn by indecision.

'Remember,' Poppy said brightly, 'Bernadette told us that, even though we're competing against each other, we need to show we are capable of team-working.'

'Exactly,' I said. 'We've all been keeping our cards close to our chests. After Baz's death, surely it's time to put a few of them on the table.'

'I suppose you're right,' Grace said grudgingly. 'Keeping his own counsel didn't do Baz much good, did it? My feeling was that he'd stumbled on some new information about the events of five years ago.'

'Really?'

I didn't have the faintest clue of what she was talking about, but tried to corral my features into a suitable expression. Knowing, sympathetic, yet anxious to learn more, all at the same time.

'Of course,' she said, dashing my hopes with a casual wave of her slim hand, 'we're forbidden from discussing the past.'

'The small print we signed?' Poppy asked.

Grace nodded. 'Clause thirty is worded very widely.'

I wanted to know more about what happened five years ago, but it didn't look as if now was the right moment to ask, so I allowed myself to be side-tracked.

'Clause thirty?' I asked.

'Yes, the paragraph requiring us not to communicate anything about the Midwinter Trust or its activities to any third party. We're bound to comply with the Midwinter Trust Act.'

'Which is what, exactly?'

'An obscure statute designed to shroud the Trust in secrecy. From what I can I make out, it exempts them from the usual statutory regime governing charities and not-for-profits. Among other things, that means we're prevented from talking about Will Noone.'

'Or else we'll be sued?'

'Worse than that. There's even a risk of criminal sanctions.'

I made an exasperated noise. 'Absurd. The Trust may have a lot of money, and perhaps a bit of influence, friends in high places and all that. But they aren't a law unto themselves.'

'You think not?' Grace exhaled. 'The rich are different, Harry.'

'They have more money?' Poppy said brightly, trying to ease the tension.

Grace shook her head. 'Power. That's the true difference. We daren't underestimate them.'

Poppy looked over her shoulder, rather theatrically I thought.

'But there's nobody else around. We can't be overheard.'

Grace's expression hardened. 'Someone will be watching us, though.'

'Are you serious?' I blurted out.

'Too bloody right I'm serious, Harry. What do you think this is, a sub-zero holiday resort?'

'Well…'

'There aren't any CCTV cameras,' Poppy said.

'And no bugging devices out here in the snow,' I added.

Grace gave an impatient snort. 'You're both missing the point. Remember, they take care not to rely on technology in Midwinter. Makes sense, seeing how unreliable power supplies seem to be. If you ask me, the Midwinter Trust relies on good old-fashioned methods of snooping.'

'Really?'

'Yes, really. Want a bit of free advice? Watch for twitching curtains, take a look round for eavesdroppers before you say anything you wouldn't want them to hear.'

'Gosh,' Poppy said lightly, brushing intrusive snowflakes out of her eyes. 'It sounds very cloak and dagger.'

Grace heaved a sigh in frustration. As if giving up on Poppy, she turned to me. 'How much do you remember about the contract we signed?'

'Well…' It wasn't easy to know what to say without putting my foot in my mouth.

'Has it crossed your mind that most if not all of us might solve Bernadette's mystery game? In which case, how do they decide who wins? My guess is, they're waiting for people to step out of line, so as to disqualify them.'

I tutted. 'I'd hate to think the Trust is so cynical.'

Her groan mixed irritation with sheer disbelief. That didn't concern me. If Grace regarded me as an idiot, fine. Anything that might encourage her to loosen her tongue was worth a try.

'Nothing would surprise me about the Midwinter Trust,' she said.

'Aren't you being a little…?'

'Paranoid?' She glared at me.

'I didn't say that,' I murmured. 'Besides, even if you are paranoid, it doesn't mean someone isn't out to get you.'

'Very funny. The simple truth is, I don't trust Jeremy Vandervell and his cronies an inch, but I'm afraid my lack of faith extends to everyone in the village.' She swivelled to face Poppy. 'How can I be sure that one of you hasn't been planted among us, to report back about any breach of the rules?'

As her eyes narrowed, Poppy's widened in a weird sort of ocular choreography.

'Gosh!'

Grace looked as though she wanted to scream. Did her hostility present me with an opportunity? *Carpe diem*, I told myself.

'You baffle me,' I said. 'Nobody forced you to spend Christmas in Midwinter. If you're so negative about the village and everyone in it, why did you come here?'

She gazed at me, and for a moment, I glimpsed behind the proud mask an unexpected hint of vulnerability. Yet in an instant it had vanished, and when she spoke, her voice had a touch of steel.

'Why do you imagine? Because I want to win the prize. I need the money.'

Grace was full of contradictions. A cynic who cared. A strong woman with, I felt increasingly convinced, a vulnerable streak that she tried so hard to hide that sometimes she went too far.

'So the game really matters to you?' I paused.

Poppy was watching Grace as closely as I was, trying to figure out what was going on inside this woman's head.

'Duh! Of course it does.'

'Why?'

'Isn't it obvious?' she retorted. 'I'm the same as the rest of you. No better, no worse. Just desperate to change my life.'

There was a short silence as Poppy and I digested this. Grace allowed herself a weary attempt at a smile.

'Then again, after Baz's death, maybe I'll settle for just staying alive.'

23

Poppy de Lisle's Journal

I wonder about Harry Crystal. I'm tempted to say I can read him like one of his books, but when I did once glance at one of his novels, I didn't get past chapter two. He has an unfortunate knack of remaining predictable even when he's slyly trying to steal a march, like ingratiating himself with the chauffeur. Not that his strategy is wrong-headed. Since coming to Midwinter, Frankie must have picked up bits and pieces of information, without necessarily putting them together to form a complete picture. At lunchtime, she seemed uncharacteristically distracted, as if something was preying on her mind. Mind you, the sudden death of someone as full of life as Baz Frederick is enough to give anyone pause.

Baz's accident is, quite literally, a game-changer. Whether his death was accidental, as Jeremy and his colleagues would have us believe, or something more sinister, it's a serious development. Even if it was just a case of rotten luck, a man losing his footing in the wrong place at the wrong time, it's bad news for the Midwinter Trust. Barely have they put the death of Will Noone behind them than someone else comes to grief on their patch.

So – was Baz's death just a freak misfortune? I'm keeping

an open mind. The explanation we've been given is plausible: Baz smoked like a chimney and could easily have slipped in vile weather after one drink too many. On the other hand, it's equally possible that someone wanted him dead.

If he was murdered, the logical suspects are Jeremy and his team. Baz's persistent probing into Will Noone's demise may have unnerved them. I can see that silencing him permanently might seem very tempting, although whether it would justify the risk of killing him during a Christmas game at Midwinter is a very different question. Did they panic? Did he force their hand? I can't be sure.

Might one of the guests have murdered him? Zack and Grace definitely had dealings with him. Probably Carys too.

Is Grace really as desperate as she says? Or indulging in some kind of intricate double bluff? That debacle with artificial intelligence suggests she's too clever for her own good. But does she have a credible motive to murder Baz? Surely it would have suited her to keep him alive if she still entertained hopes of publishing a book by him about Will Noone. If she's given up on that idea, other factors come into play.

The same goes for Zack Jardine. What if he did sign a formal agreement to act as Baz's agent? If so, he too had every reason to keep his client alive. I suppose agents do get sick of their clients, rather like lawyers and accountants. But killing them is a bit extreme. A prolonged failure to reply to emails and calls is the customary solution, and much less hassle.

I read some of Carys's outpourings online before I came here, and I've got no doubt that she is utterly selfish, dedicated only to doing what serves her own interests best. Did she know Baz before coming to Midwinter? Nothing would surprise me. She's keeping the rest of us at a distance and those fancy tinted glasses help her to hide what's going on in her mind.

Harry is the least likely culprit. Apart from any other consideration, I can't picture him killing Baz. He'd be much more likely to mess up. And if he knows the truth about Will Noone's fate, he's a far better liar than I give him credit for. I'm tempted to form an alliance with the man.

In the kind of books Harry writes, of course, the least likely person usually turns out to be the villain. But Harry has a kind of reverse Midas touch. He's lost his wife, daughter, publisher, and agent. Despite his advantages as a professional crime writer, I can't imagine him triumphing in Bernadette's game. I bet he dreams of being a slick poker player, winning big in Vegas, but he's more like a timid pensioner stuffing change into a one-armed bandit on the pier at Skegness and losing every penny.

Increasingly, I feel ready to take a calculated risk. Baz's death has shaken me, even if it was just a tragic mishap. And if it wasn't...

I bumped into Zack on the way back to my cottage after leaving Harry and Grace. He gave nothing away when I tried to chat him up. Despite his reputation, he couldn't even be bothered to flirt with me. Is his vagueness simply an act? I guess it's a skill he's cultivated, to keep authors quiet when they pester him for news about the fate of their latest manuscript, but to such an extent that it's now second nature.

'So sad about Baz!' I said, cutting to the chase.

For once, he didn't say *cool* or *no worries*. Instead, he gave me a melancholy look and inclined his head.

'Did you know him well?'

His expression was pensive. Borderline philosophical. After

much ruminating, he said, 'How well do any of us know each other?'

Stifling the urge to poke him in the eye, I tried again. 'You've met him in the past?'

'Why do you ask?'

'I'm curious, that's all. I hardly got the chance to speak to him last night. And yet his podcasts were so interesting.'

'You were one of his regular listeners?'

He'd taken the initiative in the conversation quite cleverly. Could there be more to Zack Jardine than met the eye?

'I wouldn't say regular,' I admitted. 'What about you?'

'I only heard his show once or twice.'

'Such a brilliant investigator, wasn't he? So relentless. Doggedly determined to get at the truth.' I paused. 'Whatever the cost.'

'Pity he didn't watch his step.'

'You mean literally?' I asked. 'Or metaphorically?'

'Either.' Zack shrugged. 'Or both.'

'You think his death was an accident?'

For once, there was nothing vague about his response. Leaning towards me, he said sharply, 'Why? Don't you?'

Finally, I'd managed to provoke a reaction, but he'd still contrived to turn the tables on me. I was coming round to the view that there *was* more to Zack Jardine than met the eye. After all, he'd enjoyed plenty of success before his career imploded.

'I don't know what to think.'

This had the advantage of being both true and suitable retaliation for Zack's own evasiveness. He scanned my expression for clues to what was in my mind and seemed less than gruntled about what he saw.

'Uh-huh.'

Time to change the subject. 'So what do you make of the latest puzzle?'

He pulled a crumpled sheet out of his pocket.

'Haven't given it any thought yet. What about you?'

'I'm going to study it back in my cottage.'

'Same here.'

With that, he sloped off and I came back here, to write this and try to make sense of the challenge Bernadette had set.

The most notable feature of the list of books and authors was that some letters were printed in a different typeface from the rest of the sheet. I jotted them down.

e
o
n
d
a
i
d
y
C
n
s
t
i
s
p
e
o
y
i
y

B

a

k

s

r

w

The ingredients of an anagram, for sure. Were capitals relevant or should they be ignored? Probably the latter, but I needed to consider both possibilities.

Within half an hour, I had my answer. Capitalisation of the clues proved to be immaterial.

I'd figured out who had died, and how.

24

Harry Crystal's Journal

After Poppy left us, saying she needed to wrap a cold towel around her head and solve the puzzle, Grace and I trudged back towards our own cottages. I decided to make another attempt to prise some information out of her. Nothing ventured, et cetera. There's one great advantage to being a professional writer. You become accustomed to rejection.

'I'm still hoping you'll tell me something about the events of five years ago.'

Her eyes narrowed. 'Are you indeed?'

'Yes,' I said, more sharply than I intended. 'It's about time I was let in on the secret. So what did happen, and how does it concern Will Noone?'

She stared at me. 'You really don't know?'

'I'd never come across the name Will Noone until I saw it on the memorial.'

For a few moments she weighed me up. Was this how it felt to be in a beauty parade, to be measured by sceptical eyes and found wanting? I forced a feeble smile, hoping against hope for a sympathy vote.

'We're both bound by clause thirty,' she said.

'I don't give a toss about clause thirty.'

A long pause.

'Goodness, Harry, that's fighting talk.'

I gritted my teeth. 'I get the feeling I'm the only person in Midwinter who doesn't have a clue what's going on. You talked about my having an unfair advantage in the game. Actually, it's the other way round. I'm trailing behind the rest of you.'

'Will Noone's death has nothing to do with the game,' she said. 'At least, not as far as I know.'

'Then why not tell me what you do know?'

Another pause.

'We can't talk here,' she said.

'How about my cottage?'

In my eagerness, the words tumbled out of my mouth before I could stop them. She shook her head. Not so much, perhaps, because I sounded like a cheap Casanova, more because of my thoughtlessness.

'Have you forgotten, Harry? We're not supposed to visit each other's cottages. It's in the rules. How many do you want to break?'

'Of course. I'm sorry,' I muttered.

She glanced around. There was no one to be seen.

'All right, I'll take a chance. Two minutes, I'll give you. Any longer, and people will think we're having an affair. It's bad enough being mentally undressed by Zack Jardine. I don't want anyone getting the wrong idea about me.'

I didn't know what to say to that, so I kept my mouth shut.

'What exactly do you want to know?' she demanded.

'Is whatever happened to Will Noone linked to the game we're playing?'

'Not as far as I can see.' She considered. 'Or at least, not directly.'

'Go on.'

'I'll give you the headlines,' she said. 'A quick summary of what Baz Frederick told me. He devoted himself to looking into the case.'

'Is that so?'

'Will Noone came to Midwinter five years ago. The Trust was responsible for his welfare.'

'Who was he?'

She gave me a stern look. 'We'll get on better if you don't interrupt with too many questions. Especially questions to which I don't know the answers.'

'Sorry. Please go on.'

'The weather was as bad then as it is now. Snowdrifts, village cut off... Will Noone was a fragile individual. He'd suffered a breakdown, so he came here to recuperate. It wasn't a success. He found Midwinter claustrophobic and stressful and simply couldn't cope. In the end, he lost it completely and escaped from the village on foot.'

'Risky.'

'Fatal. Jeremy and Bernadette dashed off after him as soon as the alarm was raised, but they were too late. They found his body under the snow. He'd frozen to death. The way Baz put it to me, the Midwinter Trust had one job to do, and they messed it up. Big style.'

'But his death was a tragic accident?'

'Yes, but that wasn't the point. He should never have been given the opportunity to risk his life. It was tantamount to letting him kill himself. The Midwinter Trust was supposed to be a safe haven. They had a duty of care towards the man and they let him down.'

'So?'

'So there was a huge fuss.'

I shook my head. 'How come I never heard anything about it?'

She grimaced at my naïveté. 'This was all behind closed doors. Jeremy Vandervell is a seasoned networker and very well connected. By whatever means necessary he made sure there was a publicity blackout. According to Baz, there was every chance that the Midwinter Trust and the people in charge might all be convicted of corporate manslaughter. A subject close to his heart. Several of his podcasts concerned investigations into malpractice by the high-and-mighty. He thought big organisations were too quick to sacrifice little people if it suited their business interests.'

'But the Midwinter Trust is tiny and it isn't a business.'

'Maybe, but it's rich and powerful. Baz saw it as a kind of metaphor for the establishment. The old way of doing things. Not remotely open or transparent. Just remote.'

'Was the Midwinter Trust ever charged with an offence?'

'No, it never came to that. There was some kind of inquiry that dragged on endlessly and eventually came up with a fudged conclusion. Jeremy and the Trust had their wrists slapped but their names were cleared.'

'End of story?'

'Not for Baz. Someone – not sure who, given how secretive this place is – told him about the case and begged him to investigate. Baz was like a dog with a bone, refusing to accept the official verdict. He'd begun work on a podcast about Will Noone's death and had big ideas about turning the whole case into a book. That's how I became involved. Zack too.'

'Zack?'

'That's right,' she said with exaggerated patience. 'Zack Jardine. Baz wanted an agent as well as a publisher. I'm guessing he also spoke to Carys, hoping to get an influencer on his side.'

'And Poppy? She is a publicist.'

'I'm not so sure about her. There's more to that girl than meets the eye, but what it is, I've no idea.'

'What did Baz tell you?'

'He reckoned the Midwinter Trust was not only responsible for Will Noone's death but was guilty of a cover-up. They knew he was flaky and they were guilty of gross negligence. Some of their records went missing. Supposedly deleted or destroyed by mistake. The usual sort of thing in this kind of scandal. Baz didn't give me chapter and verse. He didn't want to say too much before he'd completed his investigations. You have to remember, he wasn't really a radical, let alone an anarchist. He was – God rest his soul – a born conspiracy theorist. The sort who reckons Jack the Ripper was a Freemason and JFK was shot by the Mafia. He was convinced there was something fishy about Will Noone's death. Something that Jeremy Vandervell and his cronies concealed from the authorities throughout the investigation.'

'Namely?'

Grace spread her arms. 'If he knew, he didn't tell me.'

'Baz didn't accuse Jeremy of burying Will Noone in the snow?'

'No, like I said, the poor man froze to death. Even so, Baz

believed Jeremy was culpable. So were his colleagues at the Trust. They were supposed to take good care of Will, and they made a complete bollocks of it.'

'Wasn't that rather harsh? If Will Noone was determined to get away, they could hardly chain him to a dungeon wall.'

She shrugged. 'They could have kept him under constant watch. He was believed to be a suicide risk. Baz said Jeremy had become complacent. Admittedly, Will wasn't easy to handle. Like most people who finish up at Midwinter. He was a smart guy, a high achiever, but his nerves were in shreds, and he was utterly disillusioned with life. So he came here for a break over Christmas. The theory was that the crisp winter air would do him good. The Midwinter Trust was to take the best care of him for an unlimited period of time, and eventually he'd recover his health and get back to his desk. In practice, the exact opposite proved to be the case.'

'Oh?'

'He already had a track record of going AWOL. Once before, he'd run away at a time of extreme stress. And when no one was looking, he vanished again into the snow. Utter madness in a blizzard. He never stood a chance of making it to the station, but it gives you an idea of his state of mind. That's why Baz blamed the Trust for Will's death.'

I was curious. 'Bernadette was here at the relevant time, presumably?'

'Of course. Chandra and Ethan, too.'

'So, the current senior management team?'

'Correct. In those days, a local widow did the cooking, and the handyman was an old bloke who had worked at Midwinter for donkey's years. Unfortunately, by the time the alarm was raised, Will Noone was dead.'

The door of the village hall opened and Daisy Wu emerged.

She averted her gaze, as if embarrassed to have caught the two of us in flagrante, but without more ado, Grace hurried away, waving goodbye to me in the most ostentatious fashion imaginable.

'Good luck with the puzzle!'

I was left on my own in the snow, wondering what to make of what she'd told me. There was a connection between at least three of my original opponents – Baz, Zack, Grace – and Will Noone. The incidents with the A4 sheets and the memorial cross indicated that someone here was determined to keep the memory of Will Noone alive. But who? And why?

The paradox was this. Thanks to Grace, I'd learned a good deal. Unfortunately, what she'd told me gave rise to more questions than answers. I couldn't even be confident that all this stuff about Will Noone wasn't a gigantic red herring. What did it have to do with *Miss Winter in the Library with a Knife*?

One fact remained indisputable. Baz Frederick had been fascinated by Will Noone's fate. And now Baz was also dead. Again, at Christmas; again, at Midwinter in the snow. History was repeating itself.

I turned on my heel and headed for the reading room. An idea had occurred to me. Among the board games was a Scrabble set and I decided to use the lettered tiles to help me make sense of the puzzle Bernadette had posed.

Nobody else was around, so I was able to indulge in trial and error to my heart's content. I tried the letters in endless combinations before it dawned on me that the best starting point was to pick the name of one of the characters in the mystery.

The obvious victim was Kristy Winkelman herself, given the plethora of motives for her murder. I started by taking the letters from her first name from those available to me and proceeded from there. Within half an hour the answer was staring me in the face.

Kristy was poisoned by cyanide

HIYA!

October Yuletide shopping special pull-out

All I Want for Christmas...

Celebrity couples tell HIYA! what they'd really love to find under the Christmas tree...

MIKE SHERWIN
Celebrity gardener

You can't beat a gardening kit with a wide variety of really interesting seeds, something to brighten up the borders at any time of year.

KRISTY WINKELMAN
Bestselling cosy crime writer

After long months of pounding away at the keyboard, I'm always glad to make the most of the festive season. As the song goes, it's the most wonderful time of the year. Some people think that because I'm always writing about murder, I must be a hard-bitten soul. Nothing could be further from the truth. I'm a real softie, with a very sweet tooth. Yes, my guilty secret is that I'm a chocoholic. Always have been, always will be.

25

Midwinter

Daisy served afternoon tea at four o'clock. Ethan watched the guests trooping into the village hall, each clutching a sealed envelope which they handed to Bernadette one by one. So even Carys Neville had devoted her afternoon to the game. Ethan wasn't a puzzle aficionado himself, but he supposed solving riddles was more stimulating than simply watching the snow come down.

Bernadette headed up to her office to check the solutions. Five minutes later, she was back in the main hall, having a word with Daisy as she served tea and scones. Jeremy, who had been talking to Chandra and Frankie on the other side of the hall, went over to join the cook.

Ethan had a table to himself and presently Bernadette sat down opposite him, cup in one hand, folder clutched tightly in the other.

'How did they do?' he asked.

'Full marks. Five correct answers out of five.'

'Impressive. And what is the solution?'

'*Kristy was poisoned by cyanide.* I've tried not to make the puzzles too fiendish. But figuring out a solution takes time and a bit of trial and error.'

He nodded. 'Just like so much of what we do.'

She smiled. 'Exactly.'

'The sad loss of Baz Frederick doesn't seem to have affected their interest in the game.' He gestured towards the guests, who had tucked into Daisy's scones with enthusiasm. 'Or anyone's appetite.'

'Good to see. It's quite a relief.'

'Be thankful for small mercies, huh?'

She smiled. 'Things could have become... difficult. But people have taken the news as well as could be expected. You deserve some credit for that yourself.'

Ethan raised his eyebrows. 'Flattering, but I'm not convinced.'

'You didn't have a huge amount of information to go on before they arrived here, but the key point in your evaluations was spot on. All five of them have been badly bruised by their recent setbacks. They simply aren't in the mood to worry about anything as much as winning the game. Let's see how they get on.'

She got up to address the guests and Ethan found himself admiring the skilful way in which she talked to them as if nothing untoward had happened. Whatever else might be said about Bernadette, she was a professional.

'I can't say I'm surprised that all five of you solved the riddle,' she said after congratulating them on getting the right answer. 'As you'd imagine, one of the criteria we looked at when deciding which guests to invite was mental agility. You all scored highly in your evaluations. So well done, but you mustn't rest on your laurels. There's no time to waste. Already you know who has been murdered, and how. So you're in the same position as the police when they arrived at Midwinter to investigate the sudden and shocking demise of Kristy Winkelman. Now I'll hand out some background information for you to digest about events leading up to the murder. There's more to come, of course, at dinner time.'

Once she'd distributed the latest batch of paperwork, she rejoined Ethan.

'That should keep them out of mischief for a while.'

As he finished his tea, Frankie sprang from her seat and hurried out of the hall. Bernadette stared after her.

'Frankie looks agitated. It's not like her. Wonder what that's all about?'

'No idea,' he said. 'But I wouldn't worry too much about it. Tensions are inevitable.'

'I suppose you're right,' she said reluctantly.

The guests started to make their way out of the hall as Jeremy and Chandra went upstairs to their offices. Daisy was back in the kitchen.

'Luckily,' he said, 'your game is the perfect way to distract our detectives from fretting about… other things.'

'Let's hope so. As you predicted, Poppy, Zack, and Harry aren't natural trouble-makers. Carys and Grace are the wild cards. But so far, so good.'

'If anyone was going to upset the apple cart, it was Baz.'

'And now he's gone.'

In a voice so low that Bernadette had to lean close to hear, Ethan said, 'Finding his body knocked me sideways, you saw that.'

'Yes.'

'I'll never forget the moment I found him lying there, face down in the burn. I couldn't believe my eyes. But please don't think badly of me if I say that, in a sense, everything is actually working out for the best.'

As he bent his head towards her, the intensity of his gaze seemed to embarrass her.

'Of course I don't think badly of you. And I'm glad you think things will be all right.'

'The truth is, I bungled Baz's evaluation. I was far too quick to believe that he could let go of his investigation into Will Noone's death. I should never have encouraged you and Jeremy to take the risk of inviting him here.'

'The final decision was our responsibility, not yours.'

'Even so. I should've expressed my views more cautiously.' He sounded crestfallen. 'I hate to admit it, but I let my personal views influence my professional judgment. Chandra was right to be sceptical. She said Baz wasn't bothered about the game, all he cared about was pursuing his investigation. And she was right.'

Bernadette made a face. 'Don't let her hear you saying so. We'll never hear the last of it.'

He forced a smile. 'Don't worry. This is strictly off the record. For your ears only.'

'I'm grateful for your confidence,' she murmured.

'I trust you,' he said simply. 'Which is more than I can say for… Oh, it doesn't matter. I'm talking too much. In danger of making a fool of myself. Nerves, I guess.'

'Nerves?' She considered him. 'I wouldn't have said you're the nervous type.'

This time his smile came readily. 'For all your other talents, you'll never make a psychiatrist. Yes, I've been a bag of nerves ever since the guests started arriving. Hoping and praying that this time, nothing goes wrong.'

'Will Noone's death wasn't your fault.'

'You're kinder to me than I deserve. Ever since that day when the alarm went up and you told me Will was missing, I've been wracked with guilt.'

'You mustn't torment yourself,' she said softly.

His expression was bleak. 'Mustn't I? Sorry, Bernadette, but I don't agree. The plain fact is, I was responsible for what happened to Will Noone. I misread the man. Underestimated the fragility of his mental health. I was overconfident in my own diagnostic abilities, and he paid a terrible price. If only I'd...'

'Stop it,' she hissed. 'That way madness lies. What's done is done. You know perfectly well that, in so far as there was any blame to be attached, as the senior officers of the Midwinter Trust, Jeremy and I were ultimately accountable.'

'Yes, but—'

'You've read the Commission's conclusions,' she interrupted. 'Yes, mistakes were made. Corporate failure as well as human error, but the crucial finding was unequivocal. None of us were personally responsible for Will Noone's death. It's written down in black and white, even if the report will never surface in the public domain. Jeremy is right. Line drawn, case closed. We move on.'

He gave her hand a surreptitious squeeze. 'You're right. As usual. Thank you.'

'Nothing to thank me for. It's wonderful to see you back in Midwinter. And what matters most is that Jeremy thinks the same.'

'Jeremy couldn't function here without you.'

'He coped well enough for years before I arrived.'

'I expect he had someone else to lean on, to help him escape the consequences of his own complacency.'

She raised her eyebrows. 'I thought you admired Jeremy?'

'I did, until I got to know him.' Ethan's tone sharpened. 'I loathe the way he fawns over Daisy. And before her, Chandra.'

Bernadette hesitated. 'He is what he is.'

'That's what I detest. The way he uses people for his own ends, then casts them aside without a second thought.'

'The Midwinter Trust is all about service.'

'Not one man's vanity project?' Bernadette flinched at the sharpness of his tone. Across the room, Chandra was in conversation with Harry and Zack. Ethan slid a glance in her direction. 'What does Chandra really think about him?'

'When the Commission exonerated us all, she expected things to go back to the way they were before Will Noone's death wrecked everything.'

'In her own way, she's as selfish as Jeremy.'

'More so,' Bernadette's voice hardened. 'Whatever you may think, Jeremy's devotion to Midwinter is one hundred per cent genuine. Chandra cares only for herself. She opposed Daisy's arrival, but Jeremy gave her no choice. When he started lavishing so much time on the woman...'

'Chandra turned against him?'

'She thinks he's stabbed her in the back. In his usual, suave way, of course. She wants to enlist me as an ally.'

He eyed her with genuine curiosity. 'In what cause?'

'She'd love to see the back of him. By hook or by crook.'

'And then you'd take over as Director?'

'Who knows? That's what Chandra says would happen. I'm not so sure.'

'You're always so modest.'

'It's not just that. Maybe Chandra has her eyes on the top job herself. What if she could find a way to kill two birds with one stone?'

'It won't arise, it's academic. Presumably Jeremy isn't willing to step down?'

Bernadette laughed. 'No way.'

Ethan shrugged. She studied him with curiosity, as if discovering something in him that she'd never noticed before.

'Look how hard he's fought to preserve his reputation since Will Noone died,' she said quietly. 'Take it from me, when Jeremy Vandervell leaves Midwinter, it will be feet first.'

'Who knows what the future holds?' Ethan said.

'What do you mean?'

Ethan relaxed into a smile. 'Early retirement might prove tempting. His pension from the Trust must be eye-watering. Gold-plated, copper-bottomed, index-linked. The man isn't completely past it. He could have the time of his life, with none of the pressures.'

'What would he do? The Trust is his life. Since Sir Maurice died, he's become keeper of the flame.' She paused. 'Strictly off the record, Jeremy was offered an exit deal during the inquiry into Will Noone's death. The terms were exceptionally generous, but he turned them down flat, and not only because it might be seen as an admission of guilt. Chandra begged him to take the package, but he wouldn't entertain it. He wasn't to blame for the tragedy, he said, and nor were any of us. He was adamant that the Trust wasn't broken or unfit for purpose. According to Jeremy, what we do is more relevant and valuable than ever before. These are deeply uncertain times.'

Ethan made a dismissive gesture. 'Times are always uncertain.'

'Maybe, but Jeremy has a passionate conviction that all the good work done here over the years shouldn't be binned because of one unfortunate mishap.'

'A man died,' Ethan said softly.

'Yes, but Jeremy's fervour helped to convince people that he wasn't culpable, that the Midwinter Trust wasn't to blame. Whatever the actual rights and wrongs, that's his own unshakeable belief. And will be to his dying day.'

'So no question of a voluntary exit, then?'

'Over his dead body.'

For a few moments the phrase lingered in the air.

'Now his name has been cleared,' Ethan said, 'the man could go with dignity. Quit while he's ahead.'

Bernadette was derisive. 'That was Chandra's phrase. The truth is, however much she kids herself, she's never really understood him.'

'And you do?' he asked.

She coloured. 'He and I have worked together a long time. I'm not starry-eyed about Jeremy any longer. But I understand him.'

He gave a hollow laugh. 'Yes, you do. Might Baz's death change things?'

'No chance. Jeremy has already persuaded himself it was an accident. Definitely not another blot on his copybook. Just a personal inconvenience.'

'Jeremy sees everything from his perspective,' Ethan said. 'He's utterly self-absorbed.'

'He cares deeply about Midwinter.'

'More than he does about the people who work for him.'

'Chandra and I aren't doe-eyed teenagers. We both know what kind of man he is. The difference is, if we want to stay in Midwinter, we need to come to terms with the reality. Not fool ourselves with some romantic notion that Jeremy can't survive without us. When I told her as much, she said that, if he didn't jump of his own accord, one day he might need to be pushed.'

Ethan raised his eyebrows. 'Naughty.'

'Disloyal.'

'Would you like to replace him, if the chance arose?'

'It's a pipe dream.'

He sighed. 'You'd make a better fist of the job.'

'Sweet of you to say, but...'

'You have all the necessary experience and expertise. As well as leadership qualities. Jeremy should have bitten their hands off when he was offered a severance package. He's passed his sell-by date.'

'Don't underestimate him. Jeremy's never more formidable than when he's pushed into a corner. There's a reason why he's survived so long.'

'Agreed. But Chandra has a point.'

She shook her head. 'Remember what we tell our guests? *Trust no one*. Above all, not Chandra Masood.'

SPLIT
DECISION

specialist family lawyers

21 July

Ms Kristy Winkelman
Whodunit House
Cheyne Walk
Chelsea
(by post and email)

Dear Kristy

Great to meet you at Soho House! I hope you don't think I was touting for business after you told me about you and Mike. I was only glad I had the chance to offer a little off-the-cuff advice. Think of me as a friend in need.

As one door shuts, another door opens. That's my motto, and believe me, it's as legally sound as *res ipsa loquitur* and all that other Latin crap they used to teach in law school. You've certainly fallen on your feet with Tim Faber! I've ogled him for hours when he's been on the telly. I don't mind admitting, I'd love to consult him about the stress I'm under. Maybe over a G and T at the Ivy one evening?

Anyway, I've whizzed off the divorce petition as instructed. The conditional order (= decree nisi in old lingo) should be with us by December. And then, six weeks or so later, the final order will be issued and hey presto! You'll be free.

Mike's lawyers haven't responded to my letter. I'll send a chaser. They say it's a busy time of year in the garden, but I recognise a time-wasting tactic when I see one! Don't worry, I'll buzz around them like a really annoying wasp in the flower bed.

More from me soon. Meanwhile, here's my interim account. The hours don't half clock up early on in proceedings! But it's money well spent, I promise.

Let's do lunch?

Cindy

26

Harry Crystal's Journal

'Do They Know It's Christmas?' Band Aid enquired as I arrived at the village hall for afternoon tea. To be honest, events since my arrival at Midwinter had made me forget this was supposed to be the most wonderful time of the year.

I was on edge, but my strategy was simplicity itself: keep my ears pricked and my eyes peeled. If old-fashioned snooping was good enough for the Midwinter Trust, as Grace maintained, then it was certainly good enough for me.

Daisy Wu offered a choice of teas. I opted for camomile and sat on my own in a corner of the village hall, doodling idly in my spiral-bound notebook. My brain wasn't exactly in overdrive. At least I'd solved the latest riddle. But so, it turned out when Bernadette announced the answer and gave us the next batch of information, had my four rivals. There's nothing so transient as a feeling of superiority.

Jeremy and Daisy were deep in conversation, not for the first time. The American cook was basking in the warm glow of the Director's undivided attention. An attractive woman, with cheekbones you could cut glass on. Surely she could do better than a man old enough to be her father?

Chandra Masood was chatting with Frankie, but every

now and then she looked over towards the Director and the chef. Each time, she glared.

Meanwhile Ethan and Bernadette seemed to be getting up close and personal on the other side of the room. There was a sizeable age gap between them too, but Ethan hung on her every word. Bernadette was wearing a shapeless cardigan and a staid expression, as if impersonating a 1950s schoolteacher, yet more than once, something Ethan said made her eyes light up. In those fleeting moments, her professional mask slipped and she looked less like a frumpy representative of the establishment and more like a love-struck adolescent.

My opponents made quite a contrast. Poppy was chattering away nineteen to the dozen while Carys sipped her Darjeeling and gave occasional sarcastic rejoinders whenever Poppy said 'awesome'. Not that the young woman was fazed by her companion's grouchiness. Poppy undoubtedly had a thick skin, but what lay beneath it? Every now and then she glanced over towards me with a thoughtful expression, as if trying to figure out why I hadn't sought company. Perhaps she felt sorry for me. Harry No-Mates.

Grace and Zack were deep in conversation. About *Miss Winter in the Library with a Knife*? Somehow I doubted it. Zack's expression was flirtatious, while Grace seemed deadly serious. Every now and then, she jabbed her finger to reinforce a point, prompting a hasty nod of agreement from Zack. Even with my rudimentary skills at lip-reading, I detected his repeated response.

'Cool, yeah. Cool.'

To my surprise, something that Chandra said appeared to upset Frankie Rowland. The driver got to her feet. Her cheeks were flushed, though whether with embarrassment, temper, or distress, I couldn't tell.

'I'd best be getting on with my work.'

Her voice was louder than usual. Chandra murmured something, trying to calm things down. Inviting her to sit down again and finish her tea?

'No, no, it's all right. Really. I've got plenty to do.'

And with that, she strode past me and out of the village hall.

Telly Geek

What's On Tonight?

*Madge Miller Mysteries, series 9, episode 1 Orange TV
Allotment with Death*

Telly's favourite sleuth (if you believe Orange TV) is back
with yet another farrago about a death in a locked room,
except this time the corpse is found in an allotment shed
with barred windows. When the deceased, disgraced
former plot holder Bill Foulkes, is found, local cop Sergeant
Sharma (Rishi Mehta, whose talents are, as always, wasted
in this bumbling role) is prepared to take things at face
value and put the death (a pitchfork is involved, messy)
down to natural causes, accident, or even suicide. Anything
but murder, in fact. As usual, neighbourhood nosey parker
Madge Miller (Bethan Kirtley, probably even crosser with
Sharma than usual after recent reports revealing Rishi as
a love rat) has other ideas. Bill was as unpopular as all
victims in this series, and his enemies include Jim Battle,
who has a perfect alibi (though he's played by Oscar
nominee Jude Lavelle, this week's guest star, hint, hint).
Based on the novel by bestselling 'independent author'
Kristy Winkelman.

Our verdict: Bill lost the plot. So did the scriptwriter.
Expect it to soar to the top of the ratings as usual. And
let's hope the whispers that this is the last series aren't
simply wishful thinking.

27

Midwinter

Ethan wondered if he was the only person who found the atmosphere over dinner unbearably strained. Daisy's choice of music didn't help. Bing Crosby's nostalgic maunderings about a white Christmas seemed, given recent events in Midwinter, verging on offensive.

Ethan thought several people had noticed Frankie's abrupt exit at teatime. Although the chauffeur returned in good time to help with preparations for the evening meal, she had very little to say for herself. Ethan overheard Bernadette asking her if she was all right. Frankie responded with a curt nod and carried on laying the tables.

During the meal, Ethan sat opposite Frankie, but made no effort to engage her in conversation. There was no point. Instead, he spent most of the meal chatting to Poppy, on his right, while having an occasional exchange with Harry Crystal, seated next to Frankie. Once or twice, he looked up and caught Bernadette looking in his direction. Each time he returned her gaze before glancing hurriedly away. *It was so much fun*, he thought, *playing a secretive game.*

As Daisy served coffee, Bernadette handed out more

information – evidence sheets, as she liked to call them – about her mystery.

'Are you giving us any other clues?' Poppy asked archly.

'All the facts you need will be in the evidence I distribute to you all.' Bernadette considered. 'I suppose I can add one point. A question you might like to ask yourselves is this. Whoever murdered Kristy Winkelman must have been able to get hold of cyanide somehow. That isn't easy in this day and age, but it isn't impossible, either. Are there any characters you can safely eliminate on the basis that they couldn't *conceivably* have got hold of the poison by some means or another? Or are they all viable suspects?'

Grace said, 'So if the clues suggest that a person might have been able to access cyanide, however unlikely that might be in practice, we can't rule them out?'

Bernadette smiled. 'You've got it.'

Poppy turned to Ethan. 'Something tells me we won't be able to cross any of the suspects off our list.'

'You don't want the mystery to be too easy to solve, do you?' he murmured.

'I suppose not.' She drank some coffee. 'So awful about Baz. Makes you think, doesn't it? This time last night, he was tucking into his first meal at Midwinter.'

Not to mention getting stuck into the mulled wine, Ethan thought. This evening, people were going easy on the alcohol. He guessed that even those who felt in need of a drink were anxious to keep their wits about them. Nobody was close enough to Baz Frederick to mourn him but his death had made everyone think. Including Ethan himself.

Luckily, it hadn't taken too long for him to get over the shock of discovering Baz's remains. After talking things over in private, he was coming round to the view that the man had brought his death on himself.

Aloud, he said, 'You're a resilient bunch. We've all had a horrible shock, but I'm confident none of you will let a tragic accident distract you from the reason you came here in the first place.'

'Sad coincidence, isn't it?' Harry asked out of the blue.

Frankie looked up sharply, while Ethan stared at him.

'What is?'

'From what I hear on the grapevine, this isn't the first tragic accident to happen at Midwinter.'

There was a short pause. Poppy's gaze switched between Harry and Ethan, like a spectator watching a rally at Wimbledon.

'What you have to realise,' Ethan said smoothly, 'is that a bad winter here can be quite extreme. Dangerous.'

'Is that right?'

'Yes, most of us simply aren't accustomed to weather of this severity in England.'

'You can say that again,' Poppy interjected. 'I've never seen so much snow in my life.'

'Now you see why the Trust attaches such importance to health and safety,' Ethan said. 'And why Chandra asked each of you to fill in a medical questionnaire, provide a confirmatory letter from your GP, and complete an online psychological profile. All that wasn't needless bureaucracy, as some people may have thought. The Trust was merely undertaking due diligence before choosing which people to invite here. Thankfully, all five of you are in good shape to play the game.'

Harry nodded, as if admiring the skill with which Ethan

had nudged the conversation away from the delicate topic of Will Noone's death.

'Just as well, I guess,' he murmured.

'I can promise you,' Poppy said brightly, 'that I certainly won't be tramping around outside in the dark tonight. You're right, Ethan. In these circumstances, it simply isn't sensible.'

Was there a faintly menacing ambiguity, Ethan wondered, in that seemingly bland phrase *in these circumstances*? Best to ignore it, he decided. He was probably hypersensitive, knowing what lay ahead.

'Glad to hear it,' he said affably. 'Better safe than sorry.'

There was an awkward pause. Harry's brow was furrowed. Trying to dream up an elegant means of switching the conversation back to the subject of Will Noone? Ethan pre-empted him by getting to his feet.

'Lovely to chat, but I ought to help clear up. Daisy will want a hand getting things ready for breakfast tomorrow.'

'Christmas in Midwinter!' Poppy exclaimed. 'So exciting!'

Ethan ground his teeth. He'd almost said too much.

EXCLUSIVE: TV's hunky Doc hits back after **love cheat romp** with top writer

After bombshell *Shout* interview where TIM FABER answered cheating claims, he now reveals full truth about love affair

In his first exclusive interview since news broke of his romp in a six-star hotel in Dubai with top crime writer Kristy Winkelman, handsome telly doctor Tim Faber told Shout *reporter Trixie Oosterhuis that the pair are soulmates and now 'everything makes sense' for the first time in his life.*

'It was love at first sight,' Tim told me in the husky tones that won him thousands of adoring fans. 'Kristy and I met on the set of *Early Bird News* when I was doing my usual weekly slot on the show and she was promoting the latest series of *The Madge Miller Mysteries*, alongside stars of the show Rishi Mehta and Bethan Kirtley.'

Tim said that he was blown away by multi-millionaire Kristy's warmth and vibrant personality. 'I've never met anyone like her before,' he added adoringly.

Is it true that Kristy was secretly seeing Rishi at the time?

'All I know is, they had a great friendship. This gossip that she hit on me to pay Rishi back after an argument is total b*******.'

Tim smiles magnetically in the way that makes us all go weak at the knees. So does he think the rumours about the fling with Kristy affected Rishi's relationship with Bethan?'

'No way!' he insists confidently. 'Rishi and Bethan are great together. They do wonderful work for charity, volunteering in hospitals. Making good use of their medical backgrounds. His dad was a doctor and she used to be a nurse; they have so much in common.' Tim beams. 'If you ask me, they're the perfect couple. Same as Kristy and me.'

And the generation gap? Kristy is coy about her precise age, but she is rumoured to be old enough to be her lover's mum.

'It's never crossed my mind,' he insisted defiantly. 'Kristy's so young at heart.'

What about his then-partner, glamorous flame-haired jeweller Harriet Linaker, last seen by viewers in early summer on *Antiques Road Trip*, the show where she made her name?

'Hattie and I had something very special together,' Tim confided, adding with his trademark boyish grin, 'I've often said she's a real gem! She and I will always be best friends.'

Reminded about Hattie's furious social media rants about Kristy when she found out about the pair's romance, Tim was in forgiving mood.

'She was in shock, you have to understand that,' the famously charismatic doctor told me.

What about feisty Hattie's scathing remarks online about Tim's new-found interest in shop-soiled and over-sized antiques?

'Kristy and I actually had a real giggle about all that,' he claimed fervently. 'She's got a great sense of humour, as anyone who has read her bestselling books will tell you.'

And the shocking rumours about Harriet suffering a serious illness? Did she really take an overdose?

'I can't comment on medically confidential stuff, obviously,' Tim said earnestly. 'The bottom line is that Hattie is absolutely fine now. Glowing with health. How wonderful that she's found a new love of her own.'

So what do Tim and Kristy make of stories that Harriet is now seeing Kristy's ex, hunky landscape gardener Mike Sherwin?

'Mike and I have spent time chatting on the sofa since the news broke,' Tim said cheerfully. 'Mean-minded critics say he's not the brightest, but who needs a PhD if they've got green fingers? I say Mike has a wonderful inner calm. He and Hattie are great together. Mike's companionship is just what the doctor ordered for her! Kristy and I wish them nothing but the best.'

Isn't it a tad awkward when he and his ex's new boyfriend bump into each other in the TV studio?

'Definitely not, we're the best of mates,' Tim said adamantly. 'Mike advises me on my window boxes and I give him tips on how to ease his backache. Everything has worked out so wonderfully well for all four of us. We're truly blessed.'

28

Harry Crystal's Journal

Turning the key in the lock of my front door, I settled down to spend the last hours of Christmas Eve in Pool View Cottage alone with my thoughts about sudden death.

Was I wasting my time by speculating about Will Noone and Baz Frederick? I'd come here for one reason only, to win the game, but Bernadette hadn't yet given us enough information to come to any firm conclusions. Meanwhile I felt an irresistible urge to delve into the events of five years ago. There must be a connection, however oblique, between whatever had happened to Will Noone and the game we'd been invited here to play. No way did I believe that it was a coincidence that nearly everyone else in the village seemed to have some kind of association with the story of Will Noone's death.

To my disappointment, I didn't learn much over dinner, as I found myself close to the end of the table, with Frankie and Ethan as well as Poppy. Frankie was reticent in the extreme. I found her monosyllabic answers to my conversational overtures puzzling. Did she feel inhibited by Ethan's presence? And why had she apparently had a minor altercation with Chandra at teatime? On the way to Midwinter, despite all the talk of the confidentiality agreements we'd signed, she'd struck me as a potential help-mate. Since then, she'd retreated into her shell.

Baz Frederick's death must have shaken her severely. I couldn't think of any other reason why a woman who struck me as naturally forthright would want to brush me off. She was definitely worried. The uncomfortable thought flashed through my mind that twenty-four hours earlier, Baz had seemed equally distracted.

Ethan was friendlier but equally determined to give nothing away, so I drifted to the bar, where Zack was ordering a gin and tonic.

'I hadn't realised condolences were in order,' I murmured. 'I gather you were Baz Frederick's agent?'

He glared at me. 'Who told you that?'

'Heard it on the grapevine.' I tried to look enigmatic. Mysterious.

Zack was obviously unimpressed. 'Bloody Grace Kinsella!'

I rested my hand on the snow globe. 'Is it true?'

'Yes and no.' For a moment he sounded more like a solicitor than a literary agent.

'Meaning what, exactly?'

Zack lowered his voice. 'Baz approached me about a project he was excited about. We had a conversation, but nothing came of it.'

'This project,' I said, easing into cross-examination mode. 'Presumably it concerned the sad story of Will Noone's death in Midwinter?'

'No comment.'

I was exasperated. 'Come on, Zack. You're not being interviewed under caution. I do think...'

'Think what you like,' he retorted. 'I've said all I'm going to say.'

Browbeating dodgy witnesses at the Old Bailey is one thing. Cross-examining someone at a bar is quite another, especially if a third person comes along. Before I could put in another question, Poppy joined us in quest of fizzy water to take back to her cottage, and I'd lost my chance. Despite what Grace had told me, I felt as if I knew less about Midwinter than everyone else. The only way I could hope to tease out more information was to speak to people one-to-one and hope they'd let something slip.

Grace Kinsella wasted no time in making herself scarce after the meal. So did Carys Neville, not that I relished the prospect of questioning her. Sooner or later, I'd need to grasp that nettle. But my preferred option was later.

What about Poppy? She was a book publicist. Perhaps she knew about Baz's project. I reminded myself that she might be much less innocent than she looked. *Trust no one*. But she disappeared off to bed before I could work out a suitable line of questioning.

As I was leaving the village hall, Wham were crooning in the background. Yet it wasn't last Christmas that interested me, but Christmas five years ago. As I made my way out, I was jerked back to the present when I overheard a whispered question from Bernadette to Chandra.

'Where's Frankie?'

CELEB CONFIDENTIAL

– November issue

24/7 – My Day
This week – jeweller Harriet Linaker

Morning

I'm not really a morning person, so I'm lucky that my gorgeous boyfriend Mike brings me breakfast in bed. He looks after me soooo well. Of course he's a fantastic gardener and so much of what we eat he grows himself. Very green.

My workshop is at home and on a good day I'll have one or two orders to progress. I love working with gold – makes me feel like a wealthy lady, which I'm definitely not (sad face)! I'm quite practical, so technical processes like bombing don't faze me, but of course when it comes to manual skills, I'm not in the same league as Mike. He really is hands-on in every sense of the word (happy face)!

Afternoon

I've not had much telly work lately, as a result of being ill this summer, and since I'm on a tight budget, I often spend time mooching round antique shops or fairs, looking to pick up bargains. I'm a bit of an obsessive. I always love doing the quick crosswords in *Celeb Confidential*, of course. And I can't rest content until I do my 10,000 steps each day – that's the influence of my ex, Tim Faber – so I'll go for a long walk, rain or shine. It gives me time to think and decompress. Just what the telly doctor ordered! Tim and I are fine now. He's chosen his own path, for better or worse. I'm the lucky one. Mike is my dream man. He's even persuaded me it can be fun to potter around in the garden!

Evening

Mike usually cooks dinner. He is amazing. Then we'll watch a gardening programme on telly, maybe two or three. There's nothing Mike doesn't know about horticulture. We never watch crime shows. I get bored with them, because I always guess whodunit. When my eyelids start to droop, it's time to head upstairs. Let's just say that Mike really is an expert in bedding (happy face)!

What I Wish I Knew When I Was Young

What goes around, comes around.

29

Midwinter

'Have you seen Frankie?' Bernadette asked Ethan as the door closed behind Zack, last of the five guests to depart the village hall.

Ethan rubbed his chin. 'I sat across from her at dinner. Since then... Why do you ask?'

'Usually, she's the first to start clearing the tables and shifting them back into place. But there's no sign of her, and Jeremy wants us all together for a short briefing at ten. Chandra's gone to see if she can find her.'

He glanced at his watch. 'Plenty of time for her to come back. I shouldn't worry if I were you. She's perfectly capable of looking after herself. I expect she's taking a well-earned break. Don't forget, she's in a peculiar position here – neither one of us, nor one of the guests.'

Bernadette sighed. 'You're right, as usual. Baz's death is a hammer-blow. I can't believe the four of us are back here again for Christmas, and within a matter of hours, one of our guests has died.'

'We've already discussed this,' he said with a hint of exaggerated patience. 'Everyone was unanimous, his death was nothing more than a dreadful accident. Terrible luck, especially for the man himself, but he'd had too much to drink and staggered out into the snow to have a crafty smoke. Big mistake.'

Chandra walked in and shrugged off her coat. Her face showed signs of strain. She hurried over to join them.

'I nipped round to Frankie's cottage, rang the bell, and rapped on the door. No answer.'

'Odd,' Ethan said. 'Is it still snowing?'

'Not really.' Chandra shivered. 'Still freezing out there, though.'

'Did you check the garage?'

Chandra shook her head. 'I never thought of that.'

'She might be doing some maintenance work on the car.'

'At this time of night?' Bernadette was aghast. 'When she's had all day to muck about to her heart's content?'

Ethan shrugged. 'I dunno, maybe she's just popped out to make sure the car is all right for the night.'

'It's a limousine, not a child who can't get to sleep.'

'Okay, maybe she got bored and went outside to stretch her legs.'

'In the dark? After what happened to Baz?'

'Frankie doesn't give me the impression of scaring easily.'

'She doesn't give the impression of being stupid, either,' Chandra said tersely. 'I don't know what she's playing at.'

They looked at each other in silence before Bernadette spoke again.

'We ought to do something.'

'I agree,' Chandra said.

Another pause. Daisy emerged from the kitchen, and at the same moment, Jeremy appeared on the mezzanine floor. Ethan saw him tapping his watch.

'Are you coming?' the Director asked. 'It's almost ten.'

'We were wondering about Frankie,' Bernadette said. 'None of us have seen her for a while.'

Daisy nodded. 'I saw her leaving the hall after dinner. She didn't speak to anyone, just slipped out when she thought nobody was looking. I was surprised. I didn't expect her to be so... furtive.'

'Secretive?' Ethan asked.

'Well, yes.' Daisy rubbed her chin. 'I might be wrong.'

'She was very quiet at dinner. It seemed out of character, but I didn't attach much importance to it. Something like Baz's death affects different people in different ways.'

'She drove the man here from the station,' Chandra said. 'Other than that, she didn't know him. Unlike several other people here.'

'You spoke to her, didn't you?' Jeremy asked. 'The conversation seemed to end rather abruptly.'

Chandra flushed. 'I... I asked how she was finding life in the village, and she was quite abrupt with me. She seemed unhappy. It was very strange. I couldn't understand what had upset her.'

'Is that all?'

She folded her arms and gave him a defiant look. 'Yes.'

'Baz's death may have shaken her more than any of us knew.' Ethan made an anguished noise. 'I should have realised. Made it a priority to offer her counselling.'

'Don't go blaming yourself again,' Bernadette said. 'Frankie is the robust type. I bet she'd say counselling is for wimps.'

'Mentally robust, yes,' Chandra said. 'Don't forget she has a heart condition.'

'True,' Jeremy said judicially.

'What exactly is the problem with her heart?' Bernadette asked.

Ethan closed his eyes for a moment. 'She told me that, a year or two ago, she was diagnosed with a heart murmur. Her GP advised her it might disappear on its own. These things can be an after-effect of fever and fade away of their own accord.'

'But hers didn't?'

'When I conducted her medical examination as part of the induction process, I found the murmur was still present but she displayed no worrying symptoms. None.'

'So you weren't concerned?' Chandra asked.

Ethan shifted in his chair. 'No, not really.'

There was a short silence, broken when the clock struck ten. Eager as a footballer responding to a referee's whistle at kick-off, Ethan sprang to his feet.

'She can't be far away. I'm going to look for her.'

'Wait!' Jeremy said. 'I'll come with you.'

'No need,' Ethan said over his shoulder.

'There's every need,' Jeremy said. 'I can't let you go out on your own.'

Ethan turned to face him. 'Honestly, it's something and nothing. Frankie will be fine.'

Bernadette joined them. 'Let's hope so. But you should both go out together.'

'Come on,' Jeremy said. 'The sooner we find her, the better.'

The two men threw on their Barbours, pulling torches out of the pockets.

'Won't be long,' Ethan said. 'She can't have gone far.'

Outside the hall, a bitter wind was blowing. Ethan thought it would start to snow again at any moment. He looked at Jeremy.

'What do you think? Shall we start by looking round the back? I suppose she might be in the garage.'

Jeremy's hooded head dipped in agreement. Ethan's long strides took him past the Director, and he led the way, following the same route he and Bernadette had taken the previous night. The garage stood behind the reading room, past the shed, ice house, and diesel tank. The door wasn't locked, but there was no sign of Frankie inside or out.

Ethan shone his torch this way and that. The beam lit the wall of the ice house, now a makeshift mortuary with Baz Frederick's body lying on a shelf in an alcove. Beyond was the burn. A short set of steps led down to the garage.

Jeremy was a few strides behind. 'See anything?'

The Director was hanging back, Ethan realised. Predictable. The man talked a good game, but couldn't face the prospect of stumbling upon another disaster.

'Wait a moment.'

'Make sure you don't fall in the burn! We don't want another...'

'Corpse on our hands?' Ethan muttered to himself as he moved forward briskly before coming to a sudden halt.

'My God!' he called.

'What is it?' Jeremy's voice cracked with apprehension.

'There are two trekking poles lying in the snow.'

Ethan ran down the steps and crouched over a figure sprawled out at the bottom.

'Frankie! *Frankie!*'

Behind him, Jeremy swore wildly. Ethan had never heard him sound so frantic. Not even five years ago, when he came back to Midwinter bringing the news of Will Noone's death.

'What's happened to her?' He couldn't see through Ethan and was keeping a safe distance. 'Has she fallen down the steps?'

Ethan sank to his knees. 'I'm checking her pulse.'

'Is she injured? For God's sake…'

There was a short silence before Ethan turned his head and looked up at the Director.

'I'm afraid it's worse than that.'

'What do you mean?'

'She's dead.'

SPLIT
DECISION

specialist family lawyers

20 December

Ms Kristy Winkelman
Whodunit House
Cheyne Walk
Chelsea
(by post and email)

Dear Kristy

Here as promised is a copy of the conditional order. Like I told you, 'Breaking up isn't Hard to Do'! Not long to wait now!

Glad to say that Mike's lawyers have finally stopped dragging their feet. Seems that after hooking up with Loonyker (you are soooo naughty!), he's reconciled himself to the divorce at long last. We've still a lot of hard yards ahead, haggling over cash, and you'll need to make a new will asap. The fact you didn't have a prenup is a problem, but at least the marriage wasn't so lengthy that his financial claims on divorce are ginormous.

Speaking of prenups, you really must sort something with Tim. Yes, I know he's a keeper and the sun shines out of his you-know-what, but I've picked up some goss on the grapevine, and though I'm sure it's all down to envy and Tall Poppy Syndrome, you need to protect your interests in case the worst happens, which I'm sure it won't. So please talk to him about it. I know he's sensitive and apt to fly off the handle, but he's met his match in you, sweetie. Anyway, it's best to sort these things out before you trot down the aisle.

I'd love to take up your invitation to come along to this divorce party over Christmas. Sounds like a blast! But Julio and I will be in Mustique, and anyway, I'd rather not be stuck in a snowbound village with Rishi Mehta. He still blames me for persuading Samira to sign him up to a prenup. He didn't come out of that marriage with anything like the cash he expected. So glad you saw through the guy. A woman with your wealth can't be too careful of gold-diggers.

By the way, I'm enclosing our interim account. A bit more than I forecast, sorry about that. Let's do lunch in January. My treat. Lots of chocs!

Cindy

30

Midwinter

'How did she die?' Bernadette sounded hoarse and weary.

'There was a contusion on Frankie's right temple,' Ethan said. 'Looks like she lost her balance and let go of the trekking poles. She didn't fall far. There are only four or five steps, but it looks as though she hit her head. Whether that killed her, or the cold, is hard to say.'

Jeremy rapped on the table. The four senior representatives of the Midwinter Trust had gathered again in Chandra's office. A weird kind of déjà vu.

'What's your best guess?'

The Director's face was stripped of all colour. Tonight he looked his age. If not ten years older. No trace of the accustomed polish and poise. The man had metamorphosed into a haggard has-been.

Ethan puffed out his cheeks. 'A question for the coroner, of course, but I'd say the fall knocked her unconscious. The combination of shock and freezing temperature did the rest. The padded jacket would have given her some protection, but prolonged exposure to severe cold is too much for even the strong to survive. Let alone a woman with any kind of heart condition.'

'You said the heart murmur was nothing to worry about,' Chandra retorted.

Ethan compressed his lips. 'Her own doctor thought it was benign, and in every other respect, she was as fit as a fiddle. She made a joke of the condition. Said she lived life to the full, knowing she might drop dead at any moment.'

'You're sure it was a joke?'

'Yes! If you ask me, she expected to live to one hundred.'

'If only,' Chandra said.

In a whisper, Bernadette said, 'I can't believe this is happening.'

'None of us can,' Ethan said.

'How can we be so bloody unlucky?' Jeremy muttered. 'You're right, it's utterly incredible. And so unfair. After all we've been through.'

Ethan shot him a sharp glance. 'Especially unlucky for Frankie Rowland, don't you think?'

Jeremy gave him a hard stare before making a visible effort to soften his manner.

'You're right, Ethan, that goes without saying. Forgive me if my words sounded insensitive. My intention was quite the opposite. I simply wanted to make the point that this is a dreadful tragedy for everyone touched by it.'

Ethan gave a brisk nod. You had to hand it to Jeremy, his survival instincts were even more finely honed than his diplomatic skills. The man wasn't done yet.

'Above all, Ethan, I'm concerned for you,' Jeremy continued. 'I'm acutely conscious of the stress you must be labouring under. In a very short space of time, you've come across the bodies of two people in the cold and dark. Utterly nightmarish. Even worse, you've had the unspeakable task of laying the pair of them to rest, however temporarily.'

Ethan bowed his head.

When he'd announced that Frankie was dead, Jeremy had made a perfunctory offer to help him to move her remains to the shelter of the ice house. Predictably, it hadn't taken much to persuade him that the priority was to let Bernadette and Chandra know what had happened without delay. Jeremy had tweaked a shoulder muscle trying to manhandle Baz's body the previous evening, and in any event, Frankie weighed much less than Baz. Ethan could manage to shift her body on his own. The sleeping bag that the previous night had been too small to accommodate Baz's corpse was the right size for Frankie. She joined the podcaster, laid to rest on one of the wide shelves in the underground alcove.

'At least the job is done,' he said.

'Jeremy's right,' Bernadette said. 'Your concern for everyone else is admirable, Ethan. But you mustn't neglect your own well-being. Now more than ever, we're depending on you. When the guests find out about Frankie...'

'What are we going to tell them?' Chandra asked.

'Sadly, Frankie has suffered a fatal accident,' Jeremy said quickly. 'What else?'

'Can we be sure it's an accident?'

His eyes narrowed. 'What on earth are you suggesting, Chandra?'

'Two deaths in two days? You don't have to be a conspiracy theorist to think it's a hell of a coincidence.'

'These are extreme climatic conditions. Nowhere in England is as remote as Midwinter. What has happened is an appalling double tragedy, but clearly a dreadful consequence of horrendous weather.'

Chandra made no attempt to conceal her impatience. Turning to Ethan, she said, 'How do you think Frankie died?'

'My working theory,' he said slowly, 'is that there was some kind of freak incident, maybe a chance in a hundred. Frankie went out to the garage. Possibly she was worried about the effect of the extreme cold on the engine of her car, I've no idea.'

'If that was the case,' Chandra said, 'why not walk round the far side of the reading room and approach the garage from that direction? That route is better lit.'

Ethan shrugged. 'Human nature? She took a short cut instead, but that meant going down the steps. In normal circumstances, it's not much of a drop, but a different matter in pitch darkness, even though she did have a torch. In the icy conditions, easy to lose your footing and tumble down head first.'

'Like Baz did?'

'Probably. Not disastrous if she hadn't taken a knock on the side of the temple. The shock, the cold, the heart trouble, who knows which was the decisive factor?'

'In other words,' Jeremy said, 'she had an accident.'

Quite an achievement given the situation, Ethan thought, *to manage to convey smugness and irony in seven words*. But the Director of the Midwinter Trust was quite something. His hide made the average rhino look thin-skinned. Perhaps that was what made him a natural leader. To have the confidence to tell other people what to do over a long period of time, you couldn't waste precious time on anything as indulgent as self-awareness.

'So that's what you're going to tell the guests?' Chandra asked.

'It's the truth.'

'What about the game?'

Jeremy thrust out his chin. 'Despite everything that has

happened, the fundamentals aren't affected. Nothing has changed. If anything, people are more in need of distraction than ever. Tomorrow is Christmas Day, don't forget. The game goes on.'

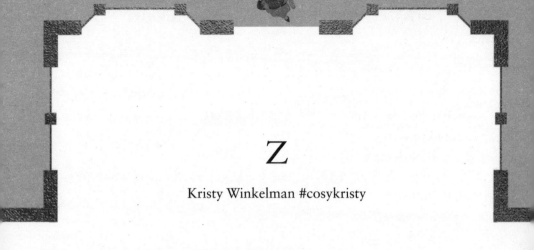

Z

Kristy Winkelman #cosykristy

Detective writer. Cosy as a cobra when crossed. Chocaholic.
Lives: Chelsea, Guernsey, California. Site:
kristywinkelmanbooks.com
Following 2 Followers 2.3 million

Z: 23 December
Heading north tomorrow for a Christmas party with a
difference ☺

Z: 21 December
#cosykristy quoted:

#timthetvdoc:
Together, forever, that's how it will be

Z: 20 December
#cosykristy quoted:

#cindysplitdecision:
Breaking up ain't so hard to do

Z: 20 December
Hi, everyone, I'm back! And I just got given some great
news ☺

Z: 6 November
Taking a break from Z to start working on something new.
##freshstart

Z: 5 November
Remember, remember the fourth Madge Miller mystery.
Guy Fawkes set ablaze before everyone realised it was the
village greengrocer 😊

Z: 1 November
Just discovered the love of my life is allergic to chocs 😊 All
the more for me, eh? ##perfectman

31

Harry Crystal's Journal

Opening the bedroom curtains on Christmas Day, I allowed myself the luxury of feeling child-like excitement. The superbly decorated tree and snow-covered landscape gave the village a perfect festive feel.

A white Christmas in Midwinter.

Make the most of your time here, I told myself. Marcus Midwinter and his son Sir Maurice were far-sighted men, believers in education and progress and determined to make society better. Yes, there had been setbacks. The death of Will Noone and now Baz Frederick's accident. Today of all days, though, I didn't want to dwell on negatives. It was time to look ahead, not back. Bernadette had even promised there'd be presents for everyone under the Christmas tree.

I put on my Christmas jumper, adorned with cheery reindeers, but my upbeat mood didn't survive breakfast. It fizzled out before I'd so much as buttered a slice of toast. Having spent so long musing in the cottage, I was last to turn up at the village hall. When I did arrive, it was obvious at once that something was wrong.

In the background, the choir from King's College,

Cambridge trilled 'Once in Royal David's City'. Delightful, but nobody was humming along. Instead, my fellow guests muttered under their breath while the downcast faces of the people from the Midwinter Trust made me wonder if Santa had been kidnapped.

I wandered over to take a closer look at the Christmas tree, and felt disproportionately relieved to see presents scattered around it, wrapped in brightly coloured paper. However, Chandra and Ethan were laying the tables in complete silence, no trace of seasonal jollity in their body language. Both of them were, I realised to my surprise, stiff with tension. Their greetings were scarcely effusive.

'Happy Christmas, Harry,' Chandra said, but plainly her heart wasn't in it.

I was about to ask a question, but she turned away. Brusque to the point of rudeness and completely out of character. Had she and Ethan quarrelled? Both of them had faint dark rings under their eyes. Neither of them could have had much sleep last night.

Strange. The previous evening they'd seemed fine, as if they'd put the shock of Baz's death behind them. Bernadette came downstairs from the mezzanine floor, but she was equally subdued.

Zack, Poppy, and Grace were sitting together, engaged in desultory conversation. Carys was skulking in a corner on her own. I decided to join her.

'What's up? You look like kids who have just found out that Santa is a figment of the grown-ups' imagination.'

She treated me to a vintage specimen from her stockpile of withering glances. 'Why do you think?'

'I've no idea.'

My candour seemed to startle her. Beneath the misanthropic carapace, the woman was floundering.

'The people from the Trust are obviously rattled. My guess is, it's something to do with the driver. Can't see her anywhere.'

I looked around. She was right. No sign of Frankie.

'If the woman has done a flit,' Carys muttered, 'who knows how or when we'll get out of here?'

'She can't be far away. It's not as if she could jump in her limo and drive off into the sunset.'

'What if she's fallen sick? A virulent bug.' Behind the large spectacles, Carys's eyes widened. 'We're confined here like caged animals. A contagious disease could spread like wildfire. Our lives might be in danger.'

I tried to suppress a groan, with limited success. Never mind a bug, an outbreak of raving hypochondria seasoned with paranoia was the last thing we needed in Midwinter.

'Aren't you letting your imagination run away with you?'

I thought this a commendably mild response, but she shook her head furiously.

'There's something very wrong here. A worm in the bud.'

A misquotation, I was tempted to point out. Shakespeare wrote about 'a worm i' the bud'. Rather than provoke her with literary pedantry, I switched to direct interrogation.

'What do you know about Will Noone?'

'Only what I heard from Baz Frederick.'

Having startled her into an admission, I tried to press home my advantage.

'What did he tell you?'

She shrugged. 'He called me a while ago. According to him,

Will Noone's death was no accident. He'd researched the case in depth for a podcast that never got broadcast. But he hoped to write a book about it and wanted some guidance on promotion, before he signed up with a publisher.'

'So what guidance did you give him?'

'I said I needed to know more about his book. What was its unique selling point?'

Ah, that eternal pesky question that has distressed so many authors for so long. I could imagine Baz's huge frame shuddering as he was asked to explain how his masterpiece stood out from a thousand others. Then again, he'd never published before, so his confidence had yet to be shattered.

'And?'

'He refused to give me details, and I told him to get back to me if and when he was willing to open up. I'm not in the market for giving free advice.'

I could imagine. 'He told you nothing?'

'Only that he was convinced Will's death was a case of foul play.'

Now it was my turn to be taken aback. I glanced over my shoulder, but no one was paying attention to us. Everybody seemed preoccupied with their own concerns.

'Foul play?'

Carys's sardonic demeanour reasserted itself and I realised that I'd lost the initiative.

'Foul play, yeah, surely you're familiar with the term? In his opinion, Will Noone was a victim of deliberate murder.'

'But he was frozen to death in the snow.'

'When the balance of his mind was disturbed, sure. For Baz Frederick, the crucial question was this: What made Will leave Midwinter at the height of a snowstorm, when he didn't know where he was going and his chances of survival were effectively zero?'

'And the answer?'

'He was driven out of the village. Deliberately. The man was killed by the Midwinter Trust.'

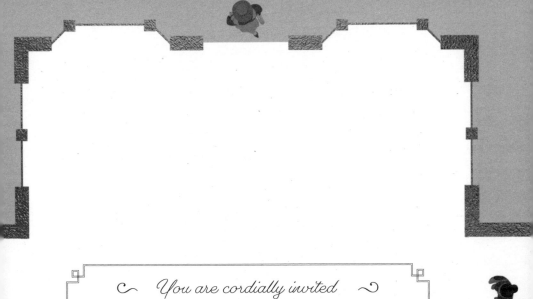

You are cordially invited ~
to

Kristy Winkelman's
Christmas Divorce Party

A new chapter for everyone!

Venue: Midwinter, North Pennines
Details overleaf

There will be a Secret Santa!

32

Harry Crystal's Journal

Christmas in Midwinter was truly unforgettable. But not in a good way.

Before I could attempt to wheedle Carys into offering any evidence for her conspiracy theory, the clock struck nine. On cue, the carollers fell silent, and Jeremy Vandervell bustled down from his office on the mezzanine floor to call us to order. To my eyes, he looked less like the head of a ruthless organisation prepared to treat people as disposable than a prosperous businessman. The chief executive of a publishing company, for instance. Perhaps this perception reflected my lack of experience of murderous cabals. Or possibly my jaundiced view of publishing companies.

Jeremy treated us to a few introductory platitudes about the most wonderful time of the year before allowing the paternal smile to slide off his face and saying that he had an important announcement to make.

'Today of all days, I am deeply sorry to be the bearer of sad tidings. There's no easy way to break this to you, I'm afraid, but it's my regrettable duty. I have to tell you that Frankie Rowland died last night.'

This bombshell was greeted by gasps followed by a shocked silence as we absorbed the news.

Two people dead in Midwinter in less than forty-eight hours. One sixth of the total population of the village. Deadwood City didn't have such a dramatic attrition rate. No wonder Jeremy sounded grim.

'Let me assure you straight away,' he said, 'there is not a scintilla of evidence that her death was anything other than an accident, or indeed natural causes.'

Despite myself, I was impressed. Not many men, faced with such a calamity, would use words like *scintilla*.

'Last night, Frankie went out to the garage to check on the state of her car. We think she was concerned about the effect of the extreme cold on the vehicle. Unlike Baz, she took her trekking poles. Unfortunately, instead of walking around the reading room, she took a short cut and hurried down the steps behind this hall. She tripped and fell and banged her head. Sadly, we think the heart condition she suffered from made all the difference. I think she may have mentioned the problem to some of you.'

Heads nodded around me. Frankie had referred quite openly to her heart problem while driving Carys and me from the station. So openly that it almost sounded like a proud boast: look at me, I've got a dicky heart, but I'm still the fittest person in Midwinter.

'When we realised we hadn't seen Frankie for some time, Ethan and I went out to look for her. Of course, her heart problem was at the back of our minds, even though Ethan had confirmed during the recruitment process that she was perfectly fit for work.'

A neat disclaimer, I thought sourly. Probably so they were covered on the insurance. But also probably true.

'Our search didn't take long. Finding her lying there was an appalling blow. Ethan thinks her heart gave out as a result of the impact when she hit the ground. A small mercy. At present, a post-mortem is out of the question, of course. All our thoughts are with Frankie's nearest and dearest at this difficult time.'

I noticed Ethan exchange a glance with Bernadette, and remembered Frankie implying she didn't actually have many nearest and dearest. Just like the rest of us.

'I realise this is extraordinarily upsetting for you, as it is for us, her colleagues at the Midwinter Trust. I've only known Frankie for a short time, but she was hard-working and enthusiastic. I'm sure you found her good company and she will be much missed.' He bowed his head. 'There's never a good time for a tragedy like this to happen, especially when it comes so soon after losing Baz Frederick. In a little while, I'll ask you to join me in a moment's silence, as we remember Frankie Rowland, but before I do so, please may I emphasise the vital importance that we place on health and safety?'

He gazed at us sorrowfully. 'Yes, the storm has abated, but the snow is deep in places, and there are patches of ice all around the village. Conditions on the ground remain extremely treacherous. I do urge you not to wander around outside unless absolutely necessary. We've already lost two people due to dreadful accidents and there's no doubt in my mind that the appalling weather is responsible.'

His expression hardened and I wondered if he was about to heap the blame on climate change. Not quite, it seemed. Just a veiled hint that Baz and Frankie might have contributed to their own deaths.

'We all need to take the greatest care to ensure there's no chance of any repeat of the tragedies that have made this

Christmas so challenging. Now, may I ask you to join me in a one-minute silence as we remember our associate, Frankie Rowland?'

Obediently, we inclined our heads. Whatever faults he might have, Jeremy Vandervell had done as good a job in breaking bad news as anyone could have managed in such dire circumstances. My inner cynic whispered that was because he'd had plenty of practice.

I sneaked a glance at my fellow guests, but their faces gave nothing away. Like Jeremy's colleagues, they seemed stunned by Frankie's death. I imagined that most of them were thinking much the same as me.

What next?

When the minute was up, Jeremy spoke again. 'Thank you very much. Now, if you have any questions, I'm happy to deal with them. Otherwise, let's have breakfast, and after that, Bernadette will give you some more information about the game.'

If he hoped that everyone would be so shocked they'd have nothing to say, he was quickly disappointed. Hands shot up, and Zack Jardine asked the first question.

'So the game is still going ahead?'

Was it on the tip of Jeremy's tongue to say that was what Frankie would have wanted? Not even he seemed willing to go quite that far.

'As you'd expect, I've discussed this with my colleagues. If we thought anything would be gained by pausing or even scrapping the game, we wouldn't hesitate. But we feel – and from the perspective of everyone's mental well-being, Ethan most definitely shares this view – that it's in all our interests to carry on as planned. So that is what we'll do.'

Zack managed somehow not to say, 'Cool.'

'What if some of us don't feel able to continue with the game?' Carys Neville asked.

Jeremy's expression was sombre. 'Is that how you feel, Carys?'

'What has happened isn't just upsetting. It's deeply disturbing. Two deaths...'

'Believe me, Carys, we're extremely conscious of that. Which is why we stayed up late into the night, debating the best way forward. The position hasn't changed. We're struggling to make contact with the outside world, and in the meantime, the reality is that we are all stuck here for at least the next forty-eight hours. So we are as confident as we can be that playing the game will be the best way to fill the time. Ethan is satisfied that, from the mental health perspective, this is the right course. Of course, if you wish to drop out, that is your right and prerogative. In which case, the agreed contractual terms will apply.'

Meaning no bonus payment at the end of the game, I thought. As well as no chance of winning the ultimate prize. No mixed feelings on my part – I hoped fervently that Carys would give up. Anything that shortened the odds in my favour was welcome.

The blunt truth was, nothing I could do would bring Baz or Frankie back. I'd come here to play the game, and Carys's wild talk about what the Midwinter Trust were capable of changed nothing as far as I was concerned. I still craved the chance to start a new life. Inevitably, the disastrous events of the past thirty-six hours or so had given me a few qualms, but not enough to make me change my mind. Not yet, anyway.

Besides, what alternative did I have?

Carys screwed up her features, as if in an agony of indecision.

'Do you need to take a little time to consider your position?' Jeremy became the voice of reason. 'Absolutely fine, needless to say. Until the end of breakfast, perhaps?'

I held my breath.

'No,' Carys said. 'You really give me no choice. I'll carry on.'

'Thank you,' Jeremy said. 'Let me make one thing clear. This is your decision and yours alone, but let me say, I'm absolutely convinced you've made the right call. This situation isn't easy for any of us, but I can't imagine a better way of taking your mind off recent sad events than by continuing to take part in the game.'

Poppy raised her hand. 'I hate to ask, but what has happened to poor Frankie's remains?'

Jeremy pursed his lips. 'Ethan is satisfied that both bodies are in the best temporary resting place available until we are able to move them out of Midwinter.'

'In other words, the ice house?' Grace made a face as she spoke. She hadn't even bothered to raise her hand.

'Indeed.' Jeremy assumed a look of injured dignity. 'There is a quiet alcove of substantial size close to the entrance, although I can assure you it's some way from the area where foodstuffs and other supplies are stored. Since you are interested in details, Ethan has made sure that both bodies are kept securely – and, let me add, respectfully – in what I might describe as fleecy body bags, originally acquired for use as sleeping bags. Earlier this morning, Ethan laid the wreath from the door of Frankie's cottage over her remains.'

I couldn't help feeling reluctant admiration for the skill with which Jeremy was playing an exceptionally difficult hand. He was giving us a masterclass in defensive management, combining a lawyer's flair for the caveat with a civil servant's knack for shuffling responsibility onto others. What's more, the even tenor of his well-modulated tones had an almost soporific quality. He wasn't *quite* lulling us all to sleep, but his reasonable, low-key manner was ideally suited to disarming hostile questioners.

He allowed himself the luxury of a glimmer of a smile. 'Is that everything? Good, thank you all very much for your co-operation and understanding. When you've finished breakfast, Bernadette will give you more information concerning the mystery game. My team and I are dreadfully sorry about what has happened, but I can promise you each one of us is as committed as ever to making sure that you have a Christmas to remember.'

Grace Kinsella turned to me and said in a stage whisper:

'He can say that again.'

News of Frankie Rowland's death hit me like a blow to the solar plexus. Unable to face Daisy's full English, I made do with cereal and coffee. It was almost impossible to believe Frankie was dead. She'd seemed so vital, so focused on doing a good job.

Might Jeremy be lying? Was it really true that both Baz and Frankie were both lying in the makeshift mortuary behind the hall? Or was this some kind of sick hoax, part of an elaborate test in the worst possible taste?

No, Midwinter was the sort of place where almost anything was possible, but if Jeremy was fibbing, the performance he'd given deserved an Oscar. Nor did I think that Bernadette and Chandra were merely pretending to be subdued, or that

Ethan was faking the nervous tension that made him nibble at his fingernails all through Jeremy's announcement.

Two dead within twenty-four hours. Astonishing. And yet that warm Geordie voice echoed in my head.

'*I need to keep my temper. Don't want to drop dead of a heart attack.*'

Had something made her lose her temper? Or had she suffered some kind of shock, severe enough to have fatal consequences? I couldn't imagine why she'd ventured out late at night. Did she really need to check her car? If so, why not deal with the matter earlier?

Bernadette broke into my reverie by rapping on a table. Her folder of paperwork lay close to hand.

'Thanks for your attention, everyone. In the unhappy circumstances, I don't want to say too much about the mystery game right now. But I do want to hand out more evidence. This is the last-but-one instalment of information that you'll receive. I'll give out the rest at lunchtime. And then, with any luck, you'll be able to solve the mystery of who killed Kristy Winkelman and why she had to die.'

As she moved between us, passing out more sheets of paper, a subversive thought sprang to mind.

Was this game a huge diversion?

Was the Midwinter Trust engaged in some highly elaborate deception, dragging our attention away from the real question we needed to answer:

Why did Baz Frederick and Frankie Rowland have to die?

~ Kristy & Tim's ~
New Chapter Divorce Party

— Christmas Lunch —

Starter
Mini Smoked Salmon and Dill Cakes

Main
Free Range Roast Turkey with all the Trimmings

Dessert
Christmas Pudding with Brandy Sauce

Coffee and mince pies
And lots of champagne!

~

33

Midwinter

'Was that all right?'

Jeremy's demeanour was modest, almost tentative. *For a hollow man*, Ethan thought, *the Director is remarkably plausible*. No wonder he'd managed to remain in post for so long. He was a cat with nine lives. But sooner or later everyone's luck runs out.

'You couldn't have handled it better.' Daisy sounded positively starstruck.

Not for the first time, Ethan found himself wondering about Daisy. The woman's credentials were first-rate, and she'd conducted herself impeccably during the recruitment process. Her demure unflappability had impressed him, and she didn't strike him as a maverick, the sort who might rock the boat if the waters got choppy. Then again, he was acutely aware that, for all his professional qualifications and years of training, his judgment of people sometimes went awry. Badly awry. Too often he was guilty of believing what he wanted to believe. And although Daisy wasn't his type, he could understand why Jeremy fancied her.

The stark reality was that, if someone seemed too good to be true, chances were she *was* too good to be true. But if

Daisy Wu wasn't what she seemed, what exactly was she? And what was she hoping to achieve?

Having allowed himself a moment to bask in her admiration, Jeremy turned to Bernadette.

'Well done to you too. The murder mystery should keep them occupied and out of mischief till the snow melts and we can start getting back to something like normality. You've piqued their interest. Not just Harry Crystal, all five of them.'

'Let's hope so.'

Bernadette sounded frazzled. Was she weary of Jeremy patronising her while he preened in front of Daisy? It had taken her far too long, but finally she was beginning to see through the surface charm. A pity that a touch of realism had come too late.

Chandra was fidgeting. No doubt equally unimpressed by Daisy's fawning. She was in more combative mood than Bernadette.

'I'm amazed the guests swallowed what you said with barely a murmur. I mean, two people killed in accidents within such a short space of time?'

Jeremy smiled pacifically. 'Remember the old comedian's catchphrase? *It's the way I tell 'em*. Besides, it's not as if I lied. I may have been a little economical with the *actualité*, but where's the harm in presenting matters in a positive light? Far be it from me to ruin people's Christmas. The last thing our guests need right now is to hear some miserable Scrooge preaching that we're all doomed. Besides, with any luck, everything from now on will go like clockwork. And it may need to, if the main power lines aren't restored soon.'

He'd gained enough confidence to risk a little joke, but for once, Chandra didn't reward him with a smile.

'Wait till they start talking among themselves. As they will, regardless of whatever they signed up to in their contracts. They only arrived the day before yesterday and already two people have died in the darkness. At the moment, they're still in shock. No way will they continue to be so meek and mild. Ethan, you're the professional. Don't you agree?'

He felt a stab of irritation at being put on the spot. Whatever private demons he might wrestle with, he had no desire to antagonise Jeremy openly at this point. It was still only Christmas morning, and there was work to be done.

'Predicting how human beings will react in strange surroundings when they are facing intense pressure is fraught with risk.'

He hated sounding even more like a cautious solicitor than Jeremy at his most guarded, but he was scarred by past experience and desperate to avoid another bad misjudgement

'But?' Chandra wasn't giving up.

'But I suggest we play it by ear. Jeremy's right, the mystery game is the perfect distraction.'

Text from first anonymous message.
Pulled from police evidence:

TIM fabEr
IS a
cOCaIne AddIcT

34

Harry Crystal's Journal

I left the village hall at the same time as Zack Jardine. Snow was still falling, but I couldn't pass up the chance to ask Zack what he made of Frankie's death. He responded with a worried flap of the hand.

'Two people dead,' he said. 'Makes you wonder who will be next, doesn't it?'

I peered at him. 'You think someone else is going to die?'

'No, no,' he said, a denial as convincing as a burglar's plea of innocence when found at the scene of a break-in with a bag full of swag. 'But you have to admit, it's scary. We only got here the day before yesterday. Since then, two people have died. Midwinter is a dangerous place, Harry. We need to watch out.'

'Do you accept what Jeremy told us? Two cases of accidental death in quick succession?'

He shrugged. 'Baz had a few drinks and he liked a smoke. All the same…'

'You were his agent, you must have known him well. His death must have come as a terrible blow to you.'

'I couldn't believe it,' he said. 'I don't think I ever met someone who seemed so alive. But I didn't know him well.

We'd only met once before the two of us happened to turn up here.'

'Only once? Seriously? An important client like that...'

His vague eyes seemed to gain focus. 'You're way off beam. I never took Baz on as a client. The guy was just a podcaster who had an idea for a book. End of.'

'What do you mean? Didn't he ever write it?'

Zack shook his head. 'Don't get me wrong. He'd done a lot of research when he was working on the podcast script. Or so he told me. But the project was nipped in the bud.'

'How?'

He frowned. 'Hey, it's all pretty raw right now. I don't want to stand here gossiping about a guy who has only been in his grave twenty-four hours.'

'He's not actually in a grave,' I pointed out. 'His body is in a sleeping bag on a shelf in an ice house.'

'Yeah, right. So let's show a bit of respect, eh?'

With that he stomped off towards his cottage, leaving me to berate myself for my failure to suppress my inner pedant. Turning, I almost bumped into Grace Kinsella.

'Something you said?' she said, jerking a thumb towards Zack. 'Don't tell me you asked him to represent your next novel? Never mind. I'm sure it will be a *succès fou*.'

'Meaning I'd be mad to dream it will have any success?' I said gloomily. 'As it happens, I'm taking a break from writing. That's why I'm here.'

'Treating Christmas in Midwinter as research?' She shook her head. 'What's happening here, you couldn't make it up.'

'Do you believe Baz and Frankie both died accidentally?'

'What do you think?'

I could have stood my ground and reminded her that I'd

asked first. But Grace didn't strike me as someone easily pushed around. I didn't want to risk a second rebuff in as many minutes.

'Everything Jeremy said was plausible,' I replied. 'Baz went out for a smoke in the dark, having drunk too much, and lost his footing in the snow and ice. So did Frankie, and her heart condition finished her off. Yes, it could have happened like that.'

'But?'

'But it's a hell of a coincidence, isn't it? Two dead in such a short space of time?'

'Coincidences happen. It's your stock-in-trade as a crime writer, isn't it?'

Taken aback, I said, 'You've read my novels?'

'No, but I've remembered what Carys said when she disembowelled them on her socials.' She grinned. 'If Carys had been found dead, you'd be my prime suspect.'

I winced. 'On the evening he died, Baz was preoccupied. So was Frankie yesterday. At one point she seemed to have a difference of opinion with Chandra. Over dinner, she wasn't as chatty as usual.'

Grace wiped a flake of snow from her cheeks. 'So what do you read into that?'

'What if there was something untoward about the way Baz died? Negligence, perhaps, or something even more sinister? What if someone was out there with him, and maybe pushed him into the burn? And what if Frankie witnessed something she wasn't meant to see?'

She nodded. 'Plausible.'

Her manner resembled a matron, noting signs of progress in a patient whose condition has hitherto stubbornly failed to improve.

Emboldened, I said, 'So to cover up the truth about Baz's death, maybe someone needed to eliminate Frankie.'

'Could be.' She shrugged. 'Who knows?'

'Suppose there's a connection between what happened to Baz and Frankie and Will Noone's death five years ago?'

'What about Will Noone's death?'

'I was hoping you were going to tell me.'

She smiled. A thoughtful, weighing-up-pros-and-cons kind of smile. 'I must admit, I'm puzzled. Are you still saying you don't know anything about Will Noone?'

'The name didn't mean anything to me until I came here.'

'Despite myself,' she said, 'I'm inclined to believe you.'

'You should, because it's the truth.'

'Well, Harry, you would say that, wouldn't you?'

I ground my teeth in frustration. 'This feels like a conspiracy of silence. Everybody seems to know about Will Noone except me. What's the big secret?'

'You're not quite alone,' she said. 'Poppy de Lisle claims not to know anything about what happened. Again, I'm not sure I believe her.'

'Why on earth would Poppy lie?'

'Why does anyone lie, Harry? Because it's in their own interests, that's why.'

'Poppy seems as honest as the day is long.'

Grace fiddled with her gloves. 'Ah, Harry, you do keep me guessing. Are you really quite so guileless? Or are you pretending, playing the part of a failed crime writer with so much gusto that at times you go completely over the top and test our suspension of disbelief beyond breaking point?'

I bit my tongue. 'Okay, let's not beat about the bush. A man called Will Noone died here five years ago. The circumstances were shrouded in mystery. Baz specialised in true crime podcasts and an unknown person encouraged him to investigate Will's death. Whatever he discovered gave him the idea that he could turn his script into a book. He approached Zack and you and even Carys for help.'

'Carys too?' She rubbed her chin. 'Yeah, makes sense.'

'Each of you possessed skills or expertise or contacts Baz thought would be useful. Before long, however, something ensured that the project was stillborn. The next thing that happens is that all four of you turn up at Midwinter. Can't possibly be a coincidence, can it? Yet, as far as I can gather, each of you was invited here separately to come along and play Bernadette's game.'

'Mmmm.' Grace was back in matron mode. 'You might just be getting somewhere.'

'All six of us have something in common. Each of us has recently suffered a serious setback in our careers. Something quite devastating. Which is why we were all prepared to spend Christmas at Midwinter rather than with our families.'

'Not that any of us seem to have close families,' Grace murmured.

'That's right! Another common factor. Like our interest in crime fiction and mysteries.'

Grace looked me in the eye. 'So what do you make of it all?'

'Not a lot at the moment,' I admitted. 'I'm even starting to wonder if Carys might be right.'

A shrug. 'Even paranoid narcissists aren't always wrong. Right about what, exactly?'

'She believes the Midwinter Trust murdered Will Noone.'

'So did Baz Frederick,' said Grace with a shrug.

I stared at her. 'On what evidence?'

'That's the snag. There is none. Will Noone's death was

investigated in depth and over a long period of time by the authorities.'

'The police?'

Grace brushed my words away with a flip of her small hand. 'The Trust came out of it all with just a slap on the wrist for not stopping the man from wandering out into the snow and freezing to death.'

Leaning closer to her, I said, 'Then why did Baz want to keep on investigating?'

'Good question. Pity he's not here to give you an answer.'

There was a short pause. 'What are you keeping up your sleeve? Don't you think you ought to tell me the whole story?'

Grace wasn't to be tempted. 'For a pound-shop Poirot, you're not doing such a rotten job. Why not carry on detecting? Good practice for solving Bernadette's murder mystery if nothing else. Now, we've spent more than enough time out here in the snow. See you at lunch. Can't wait to find out what Santa has brought us, can you?'

When I got back to my cottage, my head was spinning. I had an uneasy sense that I was missing something. Maybe quite a lot of things. Two apparently accidental deaths in quick succession were enough to put a damper on any Christmas celebrations, but what if one or both of those deaths was not an accident? Since my train had pulled into Midwinter Halt, I'd picked up quite a lot of information, much of it from sources that were not to be trusted. Yet any good detective writer knows there is an explanation for everything.

My inner sceptic whispered: *but you're not such a good detective writer*.

No, but I like a good puzzle. I could solve this one, if my reasoning was clear enough. When reading mysteries, my instinct is to empathise with the sidekick rather than the super-sleuth. Give me Watson rather than Sherlock, any day. But there wasn't a great detective in sight in Midwinter. It was down to me to unravel the tangled webs that somebody was weaving.

I don't believe in writer's block. When I'm in the middle of writing a book and my mind goes blank – a more or less daily occurrence, to be honest – I go out for a walk in the fresh air, and by the time I get back I'm always ready to pound the keyboard again.

Maybe, I thought, *there's no such thing as detective's block, either*.

Given the conditions now outside, a lengthy walk was out of the question. I didn't want to end up a second Will Noone. The obvious way to take my mind off the deaths of Baz and Frankie was to focus on *Miss Winter in the Library with a Knife*.

First, I needed to go back to the question Bernadette had posed previously. Was there anyone who could be eliminated on the strength of the information available? Someone who would be completely unable to lay their hands on any cyanide?

I studied the information and distilled the key points into a few notes which I jotted down.

Mike is a gardener.
Tim is a doctor.
Rishi and Bethan have medical backgrounds and also volunteer in hospitals.
Harriet is a jeweller and goldsmith who is familiar with 'bombing'.

Gardeners have been known to use cyanide to kill pests. So too jewellers: 'bombing' is the chemical process of brightening silver and gold. There's an outside possibility – certainly in the world of cosy crime – that cyanide may be found in a hospital: occasionally, it's used in an emergency to effect a rapid decrease in blood pressure.

So for the purposes of the game, it was reasonable to assume that any of the five suspects might have been able to lay their hands on cyanide. The real question was this: how was the cyanide administered, so that Kristy Winkelman was killed, but nobody else?

Christmas lunch was a sombre affair. Bernadette tried to lift the mood by appearing dressed as Santa Claus – complete with flowing white beard and cheeks as red as her clothes – and taking beautifully wrapped presents from her sack to put with the others beneath the tree. She even managed one or two ho-ho-hos. But her heart plainly wasn't in it.

As we were about to sit down, Jeremy asked us to join him again in a few moments of reflection, in memory of Frankie Rowland.

'These silences are becoming a regular feature,' Grace whispered to me. 'At this rate, it won't be long till we're all sitting around with our mouths zipped like Trappist monks.'

I took a gulp of mulled wine. If Daisy had made any attempt to reduce the alcohol content, it wasn't apparent. I'd sworn off drinking in the middle of the day ever since an unfortunate incident at the Mystery Writers' Association's conference gala awards lunch. But I told myself I was entitled to make an exception on Christmas Day, and anyway, I needed to keep my spirits up.

Daisy had excelled herself with the food. Roast turkey, stuffing, cranberry sauce, sprouts, roast potatoes, and lashings of gravy for most of us. Parsnip, sage, and apple Wellington for Chandra and Carys, the two vegetarians. Conversation was muted, with the subject of Frankie's death avoided by tacit consent. Even the songs on Daisy's festive playlist weren't in the conventionally jolly vein of 'Rockin' Around the Christmas Tree'. Instead, we were treated to 'Fairytale of New York', '2000 Miles', and 'Stop the Cavalry'.

Luxurious crackers had been supplied for everyone to pull. I was sitting next to Poppy, and when we pulled the crackers, the small explosions made her jump.

'It's like a bomb going off!' she exclaimed.

Ethan, sitting opposite us, raised his eyebrows. 'That's all Midwinter needs.'

I considered the joke I'd found inside the debris from my cracker. It was in keeping with the usual standard of festive witticisms.

'*Why couldn't the skeleton go to the Christmas party?*' I enquired.

'No idea,' Poppy said.

'*Because he had no body to go with.*'

She groaned and looked at the scrap of paper from her own cracker.

'*What do you sing at a snowman's party?*'

'Surprise me.'

'*Freeze a jolly good fellow!*'

After that I was more than ready for a gulp of mulled wine. I was about to get stuck into the mince pies when Bernadette –

who had changed from her Santa outfit into a plaid, long-sleeved dress – called for attention.

'I can see you enjoyed every mouthful, ladies and gentlemen. Daisy is a marvel, isn't she?' For a moment I thought Bernadette was about to invite us to give the cook a round of applause, but there was a sardonic glint in her eyes. 'As it happens, the lunch you've enjoyed replicates the Christmas lunch feasted on by Kristy Winkelman and the rest of her party in our mystery game, other than the veggie options. The crucial point for you is that all the suspects ate exactly the same meal as the luckless victim.'

'What about drinks?' Grace asked.

'All Kristy's guests quaffed champagne. No expense was spared.' Bernadette smiled. 'No teetotallers in the group, either. So I leave you to draw your own conclusions about the poisoning. But you need to get your skates on, because I'm asking you to hand in your answers just before dinner.'

'Answers to what?'

'I was coming to that,' Bernadette said calmly. 'I want you to tell me three things. First, how was the cyanide administered? Second, who was criminally responsible for killing her? And third, what was the motive? You need to write your answers in not more than two hundred words and seal them in an envelope in the usual way. In a moment, I'll hand out the remaining evidence. Two witness statements given to the police, plus two anonymous messages received by the senior investigating officer. You will then be in possession of all the relevant facts. Let's see what you make of them.'

Chandra coughed.

'Oh yes,' Bernadette said quickly. 'I almost forgot. Afternoon tea is at four o'clock sharp. And this evening, we invite you to come to dinner in seasonally themed fancy dress.'

'We realise you may not feel absolutely in the mood for a party after what has happened,' Chandra said, with smooth understatement. 'But we believe it's more important than ever to keep everyone's spirits up. We can't change what's happened, but what better way of taking our minds off upsetting news than by dressing up for a bit of festive fun?'

I glanced around at my fellow guests. Right now, nobody looked in the mood for fun, festive or otherwise.

Poppy said hesitantly, 'I suppose you're right. It doesn't do any good to sit around moping.'

'Getting back to the game,' Zack said impatiently. 'When will we know who has won?'

'I'll announce the results at lunchtime tomorrow,' Bernadette said.

'And if more than one person gets the right answer?'

'Jeremy, Chandra, and I will judge the entries. If the result is a tie, well... let's see what happens.'

She gave us a teasing smile. If I'd had any doubts about the wisdom of continuing the game after the deaths of Baz and Frankie, they were evaporating. *Miss Winter in the Library with a Knife* offered a much-needed distraction. As well as the prospect of success for at least one of us. Never mind Kristy Winkelman. Each of the guests wanted to start a new chapter in their lives.

'Now.' She pointed to the presents under the Christmas tree. 'The time has come for you to see what Santa has brought for you.'

It didn't take long for me to unwrap my gift. A handsome ceramic tankard bearing one of those quotes that writers are supposed to find inspirational.

Go where the story leads you.

Carys paused in the act of tearing open the Christmas paper to take a look at the legend. Her loud sniff spoke volumes.

'Looks like they've got you figured.'

I gave her a baffled grin.

'Sorry?'

'A big mug.'

Returning to Pool View Cottage, I wrote up my journal while the latest misadventures at Midwinter were fresh in my mind, before throwing myself onto the duvet. At first, I succumbed to the temptation to mull over the news about Frankie, along with the crumbs of information I'd gleaned from my fellow guests. Plenty of hints and allegations, I decided, but precious little in the way of hard facts. The harsh reality was that Carys, Zack, and Grace were all competing against me in the game. So was Poppy, and even though I felt I had more in common with her than with the others, I kept reminding myself not to trust anyone.

So far, I'd kept my distance from Jeremy Vandervell and his four colleagues. Now there was no chance of Frankie becoming my ally, was it time to reconsider my strategy? Tempting, but risky. There was no guarantee that any of them would respond to any overtures I made. It was hard to imagine any of them taking me into their confidence. Did I have any chance of faring better with either Daisy Wu or Ethan Swift?

I turned my attention to the latest batch of information about the mystery game. So at last I had everything I needed to solve the puzzle. Did I really still care?

Silly question. Of course I did.

I desperately needed a reversal of misfortune. What I didn't know was whether it was achievable, let alone *how* to achieve it. All I could do was try my damnedest to win the game.

If each of Kristy Winkelman's guests had eaten and drunk exactly the same things as the lady herself, the crime couldn't have been committed by poisoning the Christmas lunch. Otherwise, there would have been a bunch of fatalities.

In search of clues, I took another look at Kristy's divorce party invitation. It was lacking in detail. Even the date and the precise venue were not printed on its face.

What every recipient did know for sure, however, was that there was going to be a Secret Santa.

And as every mystery writer and reader knows, where there's a secret, there's a motive for murder.

Text from second anonymous message.
Pulled from police evidence:

KRiSTy dIDnT
wANt To
maRRy hiM

35

Harry Crystal's Journal

Ask any cruciverbalist, and they'll tell you that solving a crossword puzzle becomes so much easier once you understand the mindset of a particular puzzler. The same holds good for figuring out a murder mystery. Every plotsmith, from Dame Agatha down to yours truly, has their own way of working. As I studied the information that Bernadette had supplied, I began to see the way her mind worked.

She'd followed tradition in constructing her mystery. Each suspect had a motive to do away with Kristy, sometimes more than one. Each might have been able to get hold of some cyanide. In terms of opportunity, each had been on the scene at the vital time.

How, precisely, had she been killed? I was confident that the Secret Santa held the key. I pored over the evidence, jotting down notes, and eventually the truth began to emerge, like a hoped-for landmark coming into view as one drives through a snowstorm.

I felt a rush of excitement as I found myself solving the mystery of *Miss Winter in the Library with a Knife*.

The prize was within touching distance.

Christmas was weaving its magic. Despite everything that

had happened since my train had pulled in to Midwinter Halt, my confidence was rising. I'd lain so low for so long that I could hardly believe how energised I felt. It wasn't simply a matter of festive spirit or even the effects of a couple of glasses of Daisy Wu's mulled wine. Maybe I was kidding myself, but I'd begun to believe I was on the brink of something special. A new chapter, as the fictional crime writer Kristy Winkelman might say. I just needed to avoid suffering the same fate as her.

Yet, if there was a chance that I might break the habit of a lifetime and become a winner, one huge question remained. What did the prize really amount to, this chance to join the Midwinter Trust? And was it, after everything I'd experienced in this strange, snowbound village, as appealing as it had seemed before I set foot in the place?

I'd been so keen to take advantage of an all-expenses-paid Christmas break, and to escape from the drabness of my everyday life that I hadn't given much thought to what would happen if I did succeed in the mystery game. Winning seemed such an unlikely prospect that there was no point in building up my hopes.

From my conversations with the other guests, I suspected their attitude was similar to mine. Everyone had gone through a harrowing ordeal of one kind or another. When you're down on your luck, it's tempting to believe that any change in your circumstances will be positive, that anything must be better than the status quo. But it isn't necessarily true.

My thinking about the future had been blurred with misery, thanks to a succession of failures in life, both personal and professional. At long last, I was seeing things afresh, and with greater clarity. Time to ask myself the crucial question.

What exactly was the Midwinter Trust up to? We all like the idea of making the world a better place, but what was the substance behind the upbeat sentiments of the Trust's website? And what, if anything, could I glean from the local historian who hid behind the pseudonym of J. Doe and who had written about the Trust in such sceptical terms, until their thinly veiled criticisms of Jeremy Vandervell, in particular, had been expunged from the internet?

Since coming here, I'd learned about Will Noone and the theory that the Trust was responsible for his death. Yes, Jeremy and co had been exonerated, but questions remained unanswered. Baz Frederick had been on some kind of mission to expose the truth, and now he was dead.

There was so much I didn't know or understand. But in my mind, the hazy outlines of an explanation for what was going on in this remote little village were taking shape. For too long, I realised, I'd resembled Dr Watson at his most obtuse. Time to start channelling Sherlock Holmes instead.

What was it the great consulting detective had said? More than once, if I remembered rightly.

When you have eliminated the impossible, whatever remains, however improbable, must be the truth.

Out of the corner of my eye, I suddenly noticed something. A figure moving past the window. Hauling myself off the bed, I looked out.

Someone hurried past the back of my cottage. The person's height suggested it was probably a man. Bernadette, Chandra, and Daisy, in particular, were all noticeably shorter. So was Zack Jardine, for that matter. Carys was a possibility, but the hooded Barbour jacket looked familiar.

Ethan Swift, Jeremy Vandervell, and Zack Jardine all favoured Barbours. It might be any of them.

On impulse, I put on my own jacket, searched for my gloves, and grabbed my trekking poles, then I unlocked the back door and peered out. There was no one in sight, and snow was falling relentlessly. At least there were telltale footprints for me to follow, leading along the back of the cottages and away from the village.

Surely the man I'd seen wasn't intent on leaving Midwinter? Not after Will Noone had suffered such a terrible fate five years ago?

A muffled cry broke the silence.

The sound paralysed me. Even in my warm winter clothing, I felt cold with dread. Since my arrival in Midwinter, two people had died. I couldn't be confident they were both the victims of accidents, despite Jeremy's assurances. Was it possible that a killer was on the loose?

I dithered for a minute, struggling to decide whether I should go back to the village and call for help. But what should I say? And what if the person who had uttered the cry was injured – perhaps after a fall, like Baz Frederick – and needed my urgent help?

On the other hand, what if I were being lured into a trap?

I took a tentative step forward. Through the falling snow I could see the ghostly remains of the old village school.

Had the man I was following tried to go in there? Given that it had been derelict for decades, it might be dangerous to go in. Chances were, there had been yet another accident.

Unlucky village, Midwinter. Desperately unlucky.

I decided to risk it. If I didn't, I felt sure I'd regret my cowardice. Regrets, I've had a lot. It was time to do it my way.

Moving as stealthily as possible in the snow, I approached the building. There was no chink of light and no sign of life.

The entrance was on the far side. I edged forward, staying close to the outside wall of the school, following the footprints.

Finally, I rounded the corner and almost fell over the body.

In my time, I've lost count of the number of people I've killed. It must be over one hundred. I've employed every weapon imaginable – arsenic, automatic, candlestick, poison pinprick, to name but a few. In fiction, anything is possible. But I'd never had a close encounter with an actual dead body, never felt the gut-wrenching horror of seeing a human being who has just breathed his last.

Lying on his back in the snow was a motionless corpse, face soaked in blood.

Ethan Swift had played his last mind game.

North Pennines Police – witness statement

Case Number 54321/003

Statement of   Bethan Kirtley

Age: over 18   **Occupation:**   actor

This statement is true to the best of my knowledge and belief and I make it knowing that, if it is tendered in evidence, I shall be liable to prosecution if I have wilfully stated in it anything which I know to be false, or do not believe to be true:

Signature   *Bethan Kirtley*   Date: 26 December

My partner Rishi Mehta and I were invited to spend Christmas at Midwinter by Kristy Winkelman. Kristy is a writer whose books are the basis for a long-running television series, *The Madge Miller Mysteries*. Rishi and I are the co-stars. He plays a hapless village policeman and I am the amateur detective, Madge. Madge is the main character, but because of Rishi's success in Bollywood, he gets top billing.

I am actually a niece by marriage of Kristy's first husband, Kenneth Trewin. Kenneth was a wealthy banker who died suddenly, fifteen years ago. He was a keen do-it-yourselfer who believed in fixing the roof while the sun was shining. Unfortunately, he fell off a ladder and died of a fractured skull. The marriage had been tempestuous and there was some suggestion that the ladder might have been nudged deliberately. Kristy was quizzed by the police, but came up with a watertight alibi for the time of the accident. However, the experience inspired her to turn to writing detective stories.

Kenneth had always mocked her writing ambitions, but when her manuscript was turned down by every publisher in town, she decided to self-publish and use the fortune she'd inherited from Kenneth for an aggressive and prolonged marketing campaign. Underground walls, billboards in city centres, you name it. The rest is history.

I was the only member of Kenneth's family who didn't loathe Kristy. She is good fun when she's in the mood. Of course she knew that I was a struggling actor. I had no luck and to make ends meet I took up part-time nursing. I still volunteer at hospitals. So does Rishi, whose dad was a family GP. We're both keen to do our bit for those less fortunate.

When Kristy signed a TV deal, she put me forward for a screen test. She thought I'd make a good corpse in the first episode, but the director liked my audition so much, he cast me as Madge Miller. For a while, he and I lived together, but after some horrible allegations about his behaviour towards young women were made public, the two of us split up and he was sacked.

Luckily, the show's popularity wasn't dented. Even more luckily for me, my co-star was Rishi Mehta, the Bollywood star. He'd just gone through an acrimonious divorce from Samira Patel, who was the daughter of a billionaire. Rishi and I got involved and we've been partners ever since.

It is true that there have been bumps in the road. Kristy was always nice to my face, but I think she was jealous of my looks and my youth. She began to say that I owed everything to her, and earlier this year she wound up having an affair with Rishi despite being married to Mike Sherwin. Mike is nice enough, but he's also the most boring man I've ever met, so maybe it was understandable. But Rishi is volatile and he and

Kristy had a violent argument. They both accused each other of striking the first blow, but it was Rishi who ended up in A&E.

I was reluctant to forgive Rishi, but he persuaded me that Kristy had gone to great lengths to flatter and seduce him. He has always been very keen on money, and women with money. I don't have any of my own, apart from my earnings. Unfortunately Rishi loves gambling and wastes all his money that way.

Neither of us wanted to accept Kristy's invitation to this divorce party for obvious reasons. However, we've heard stories that she has been threatening to cancel the show. She's made cryptic comments about working on something new. In the meantime, there's talk about her trying to force the TV company to cast new actors in our parts. She has so much power, they're afraid to say no to her. So when she insisted on us joining her for Christmas, we felt we had no choice.

It was all very awkward. Tim Faber, Kristy's fiancé, is handsome and famous, but he split up from Harriet Linaker, who was one of the other guests. Hattie is now with Mike. So it's complicated. Like something out of one of Madge's stories.

Because of this, Rishi and I decided to arrive at the last possible moment and leave as soon as we could. We got to Midwinter late on Christmas Eve. We were the last to arrive. We told everyone we were exhausted after the long journey from London in bad weather and went off to bed.

We got up for a late breakfast, but the atmosphere was miserable. We got the impression that Kristy and Tim had quarrelled. They certainly weren't speaking to each other. Mike and Hattie were fine. We wanted to get Kristy on her own so that we could talk to her about *The Madge Miller*

Mysteries. If necessary, we were prepared to beg her to keep the show going, with us as the leads. But we decided to wait until later on in the day.

Kristy had said when she sent the invitations that she wanted us to have a Secret Santa, so everyone had to turn up with presents, even though we didn't know the recipients. So we had to bring one suitable for a man and one that would be okay for a woman. Or alternatively something that would be fine for anyone. Kristy just loves a mystery, and she'd asked Mike to organise the whole thing for her. Just like old times, she said.

Mike got everyone together before lunch and gave us tags so that we knew who we were supposed to be giving presents to. Then we went away to our cottages to put the name tags on the right presents, before bringing them back to be put under the Christmas tree.

After that, we had lunch, cooked by Kristy herself. It was very good, and we all tucked into each course.

Then it was time for the Secret Santa. Everyone professed to be pleased with their presents, except for Tim Faber. Kristy insisted on swapping presents with him and he agreed. As everyone enjoyed their treats, Rishi and I felt hopeful. It looked as if the atmosphere was thawing and Kristy might be in such a good mood that she'd be receptive to our pleas about the show.

The next thing of any importance was that Kristy started gasping. At first I thought it was some kind of joke. Kristy has a strange sense of humour. But it became clear she was in agony. Tim had gone back to the cottage for something, and Mike ran to fetch him to see if he could do anything for her. But within a few minutes she was dead.

36

Harry Crystal's Journal

In my horror and confusion, only one thought made any sense. I must raise the alarm and try to get help.

Waving my arms frantically, I flashed my torch and cried out for help. At once, I caught sight of a hooded figure in the distance, striding past the snow-covered village green.

The person heard me and turned to approach. For a moment, I was seized by panic.

Had I been spotted by a deranged killer?

Paralysed by dread, gripping my trekking poles as if I were about to sink into the snow and disappear forever, I could only watch and wait. Each moment dragged by like an hour. I felt I was being stalked by the Grim Reaper.

But the man in the hood didn't carry a scythe, and after a few moments that felt more like an hour, I finally I recognised him. He was wearing a Barbour – so reassuringly familiar.

Jeremy Vandervell.

The tension flooded out of my limbs. Never mind *trust no one*. I had nothing to fear from the Director. Surely?

'Harry?' he called. 'What are you doing out here?'

'It's Ethan,' I gasped.

He drew nearer, but I was blocking his view of the body.

'What about him?'

'He's dead.'

Jeremy stopped in his tracks.

'What… what do you mean? Don't tell me there's been yet another accident?'

'This was no accident.' I swallowed hard. 'Someone bashed his head in.'

A long pause, then he took a stride forward.

'You saw what happened?'

'No. I caught sight of someone from my cottage window. I was curious, so I decided to see what was going on. I followed in the direction they'd been heading. And then I saw…'

I stood aside and gestured towards Ethan's crumpled remains.

When Jeremy saw the corpse, he let out a low groan.

'I can't believe this is happening.'

An ice axe was stuck in the snow as if to mark the scene of the crime. No question, it was the murder weapon. The toothed, curved pick was dripping. Not with melting ice, but blood.

'Someone took him by surprise and battered him to death,' I muttered.

'Who would do such a thing?' Jeremy said hoarsely.

Behind us, a voice shouted out, 'What's going on?'

I turned and saw someone making their way towards us. A man, not a woman. By process of elimination, Zack Jardine.

'Ethan has been killed,' I called.

'*Killed?*'

Zack sounded terrified, and who could blame him?

'Someone beat him with an ice axe. The poor devil's face is barely recognisable.'

Zack swore. 'You're sure it is…?'

'Sure it's Ethan? Yes, no doubt whatsoever.'

'Come on.' It hadn't taken Jeremy long to recover from his shock and take command of the situation. 'We need to shift the body before it gets covered in snow.'

The next few minutes passed in a blur. Hardly anyone uttered a sound as we did what was necessary. Our immediate priority was to move Ethan under cover. This was a crime scene, but Jeremy insisted that no question arose of waiting for the police to arrive or experts to conduct a forensic examination before we took the corpse to a place of shelter. Of course he was right. We had no choice.

The task was nightmarish, but between the three of us, we managed to carry him to the ice house that had become a makeshift mortuary.

Jeremy led the way. Zack and I followed with our dreadful burden, one tentative step after another. Unlocking the door, Jeremy found the wall switch inside. Light flooded the ice house and I took my first look inside. A downward-sloping entrance opened up into a cavernous ice chamber, twenty-foot high. Ahead of us, I could see brick walls lined with crates of foodstuffs and dry goods and dark passageways beyond. You could store enough supplies here to feed an army, let alone the rapidly diminishing band who had come to Midwinter for Christmas.

'First left,' Jeremy said.

Zack and I heaved the body into the large alcove with three broad shelves fashioned from stone. So this was the final resting place for Baz and Frankie. The bulky sleeping bags containing their remains occupied the two upper shelves. A wreath had been laid upon each of the bags in a vain attempt to dignify the surroundings. I noticed that the bag on the top shelf was slightly ripped in several places. Baz Frederick's hefty frame had evidently proved a very tight squeeze. A third, empty bag was folded up on the bottom shelf. I had the ridiculous fancy that it had been put there in readiness, like a horrifically self-fulfilling prophecy.

Zack and I removed Ethan's Barbour and somehow managed the wretched task of shifting his frozen remains into the empty bag. As we manoeuvred the body onto the shelf, my elbow caught the wreath on the middle shelf, knocking it to the ground.

This felt like a bad omen, but with three people dead, what else could go wrong? Gingerly, I put the wreath back in its place. When my fingers brushed the bag, I felt Frankie's body yielding to my touch. The ghastly sensation made me want to retch.

I couldn't get out of the ice house fast enough. As I caught my breath, my mind whirled with questions.

Who killed Ethan, and why?

Should the deaths of Baz and Frankie now be treated as suspicious?

And why had both Jeremy and Zack been out in the snow that afternoon? Was one of them the murderer, trying to make a getaway from the scene of the crime?

'All right?'

Zack's voice made me jump. I hadn't realised he'd followed me out of the ice house.

'Yeah, I suppose.' I made a feeble attempt at gallows humour. 'I only hope we don't lose anyone else. We're fresh out of body bags.'

He nodded sourly. 'At least there's no shortage of holly wreaths.'

Statement of   Michael Sherwin

Age: over 18   **Occupation:**   gardener

This statement is true to the best of my knowledge and belief and I make it knowing that, if it is tendered in evidence, I shall be liable to prosecution if I have wilfully stated in it anything which I know to be false, or do not believe to be true:

Signature   *Mike Sherwin*   Date: 26 December

When Kristy decided to hold a divorce party, I wasn't sure it was such a brilliant idea. She and I weren't even legally divorced until the decree absolute came through in the new year. But Kristy was never one to bother about little details. That's why she'd never have made a gardener. She liked to say that she's a big picture person. Careless, some might say. Reckless, even. Not that I'd say that. It would be more than my life's worth.

She's also a force of nature. Not someone it's easy to say no to. I never learned how, that's for sure.

I wasn't convinced about the guest list, either. Kristy said she believed in letting bygones be bygones. But not everyone feels like that. According to her, all six of us would live happily ever after. Of course, that didn't turn out to be true, did it?

She'd had a fling with the actor from her TV series. I found out about it when a journalist from one of the nationals asked me for a comment. Whenever I'm stressed, I can't think of anything but gardening. That's why I simply said, 'People always reap what they sow.'

Despite what you may have read in the gutter press, this wasn't a threat. I'm not the type. As it happens, that's a favourite saying of mine, along with 'a weed is just a flower in the wrong place' and 'garden is a verb not a noun'.

The truth is, it was my idea to end the marriage, not Kristy's. This was back in the summer. The way she flirted with Tim Faber on screen was the last straw. Only twenty-four hours earlier we'd done an interview with *HIYA!* (months in advance) about what Christmas presents we wanted. I admit losing my temper, but I didn't lay a finger on her. She didn't exactly beg me to stay. Twenty-four hours later, Tim moved into the house she and I shared in Chelsea and I had to rent a bedsit in Clapham. It was quite a shock when I saw the piece in *HIYA!*, so long after we'd spoken to the journalist. A lot of water had gone under the bridge since then.

Harriet and I got together after we happened to bump into each other in the estate agents' office. Both of us wanted a new beginning. I'd met her once before, when I bought a bracelet from her for Kristy. Harriet was very upset about Tim's infidelity, that's public knowledge, but she's even more forgiving than me. She was the one who persuaded me that it was okay to spend Christmas with our exes. I didn't want Kristy to lord it over us, but Hattie thought it would serve the woman right to see how happy the two of us are together.

I want to marry Hattie as soon as the divorce is finalised, but at first, I wasn't in a hurry about the legalities. Kristy's lawyer, Cindy Split, is famously hard-nosed and I wanted to make sure I got a fair deal. Kristy is obviously much richer than me. Despite my earnings from being on television, gardening isn't a passport to a fortune. Hattie is in the same boat. She makes lovely jewellery, but when times are hard, people stop buying.

Finally I faced up to reality. Kristy and Tim had got engaged and I'd proposed to Hattie and been accepted. It was time to bury the hatchet. And not in anyone's back, I hasten to add.

Kristy was excited about the divorce party. I had an idea that she thought she could turn it into a new story. She might even have started work on it already. Her debut novel was based on the death of her first husband, though in the book it turned out to be murder, of course. That was a runaway bestseller and ever since then she's enjoyed turning fact into fiction. For instance, the handsome landscaper in *Up the Garden Path* is me. In that book, he gets the girl. I wasn't confident I'd fare so well the next time she based one of her characters on me.

Even so, I had no reason to kill her. I was glad to be out of the marriage. Or as good as.

When we got to Midwinter on Christmas Eve, there was quite an atmosphere. Kristy and Tim had obviously had a blazing row. Very embarrassing. Not that I was totally surprised. Tim's an odd one. Moody. And Kristy, of course, is a law unto herself.

We all had dinner together but Harriet and Rishi didn't turn up until ten o'clock. They said they'd had a rotten journey and were heading off to bed straight away.

On Christmas morning, Kristy tried to pretend that everything was sweetness and light between her and Tim, but I wasn't fooled. And if I wasn't fooled, you can bet nobody else was, because Kristy liked to point out that I'm not the sharpest knife in the gardener's tool-box. She could be quite unkind sometimes, God rest her soul.

Anyway, I was volunteered to organise the Secret Santa. At least Hattie gave me a hand. It's so easy to mess these things up. You have to arrange it so nobody would give a present to themselves. There's an easy way to do this, I found it on the internet. You create a set of cards, divide them in two, then at the top of the card you write, say, "you are number 3" and on the bottom you write "you are buying for number 3". You do this for everyone, then put the cards on the table, shuffle them around and then cut them each in two with a pair of scissors. Then all you have to do is shift the top half of the cards along by one. This guarantees that the top and bottom numbers won't match. Simple, huh?

The lunch was very tasty. Whatever her faults, Kristy was a brilliant cook. I didn't leave a morsel. Nobody did.

When it was time for the Secret Santa, there was an unfortunate fuss about the presents, but it was all sorted out.

I was waiting to pick my moment to have a private word with her. I won't deny that I wanted to catch her in a generous mood, so that we could sort out the money side of the divorce. Much better than haggling with hard-nosed Cindy Split. But Kristy died before I got the chance.

37

Midwinter

'Incredible.' Jeremy shook his head in disbelief. 'Baz and Frankie dead, and now Ethan murdered. Anyone would think this village is cursed.'

'I hear the locals used to call this place Pagans' Fell,' Daisy said quietly. Jeremy had asked her to join the surviving members of the senior management team at an emergency meeting in Chandra's office. 'Once it was a site where the ancients worshipped. When the crops failed, they sacrificed members of their community in the hope of appeasing their gods.'

'Don't be ridiculous,' Bernadette said bitterly. Her face was ashen. When Jeremy had broken the news, she'd had to fight back tears. 'What could anyone gain from sacrificing a man who devoted himself to helping others?'

'Please.' Jeremy held up a hand. 'We need to keep calm and—'

'Carry on getting killed?' Chandra asked.

Jeremy frowned. 'Think on our feet, I was about to say. We must face facts. Ethan wasn't the victim of an accident.'

'Are you sure?' Daisy asked.

'Beyond a doubt. Someone battered him to death. His features were almost unrecognisable.'

'In that case, is it possible that...?'

'That the dead body might belong to someone else?' Jeremy said wearily.

'Well, yeah.'

'Not a chance. Nobody else in the village has the same height or build or hair colour. The only person remotely comparable is Zack Jardine. And he helped to lay Ethan's body to rest.'

'What was he doing out in the snow?'

'Taking a breather on Christmas afternoon, or so he said.'

'Come to that,' Chandra said. 'What were you doing out there, Jeremy?'

He folded his arms. 'Doing what I do every day. Taking a look around the grounds. Making sure there are no trespassers—'

'Trespassers? In the middle of a snowstorm, on Christmas Day?'

'We've always agreed on one guiding principle,' he said mildly. 'In Midwinter, we can't be too careful.'

'Not that it's stopped three people dying in as many days,' Bernadette said furiously.

Making a visible effort to bite back a rebuke, Jeremy said, 'I asked Harry Crystal what he was up to before he stumbled across the body. He claimed he spotted Ethan roaming around and decided to follow him.'

'Why?' Daisy asked.

'That's a question we need to answer.'

'You think the murderer must be male?'

'Not necessarily. In my opinion, a woman could have killed

327

Ethan if she caught him off guard. Which wouldn't have been difficult. He was quite a trusting soul.' He paused. 'Too trusting, sometimes.'

Chandra glanced at Bernadette. The older woman took no notice.

Daisy wasn't giving up. 'Wouldn't it require a lot of strength to batter a man so brutally?'

'From the point of view of physique,' Jeremy said, 'anyone in Midwinter could be responsible. One well-timed swing of an ice axe would disable any victim. After that, Ethan would be at the killer's mercy. Not that they showed any mercy.'

Bernadette closed her eyes. Jeremy laid a reassuring hand on her arm, but she shrugged it off.

'Why go to such lengths?' Daisy asked.

'To make sure he was really dead,' Jeremy said. 'Possibly there was some pent-up anger, too.'

'Anger?' Bernadette hissed. 'Why would anyone be angry with *Ethan*?'

'Sorry,' he said. 'I'm simply trying to make sense of this vile crime. It's... devastating.'

'You did say that no one is indispensable.' Daisy's expression was cool, enigmatic. 'I guess the question now is whether we should look at the deaths of Baz and Frankie in a different light.'

'Are you saying they were murdered too?' Chandra asked.

'Can we rule that out?'

'Not definitively,' Jeremy said. 'However, I stick to what I said before. Their deaths were tragic accidents.'

'Seriously?' Daisy persisted.

'We've discussed this,' he said with exaggerated patience.

'Besides, why on earth would anyone want to murder Baz Frederick or Frankie Rowland?'

'And why would anyone wish to kill Ethan?' Bernadette blurted out. 'Nobody's answered that!'

Jeremy bit his lip. 'I know you're upset by this. Heartbroken even. Perfectly natural. But...'

She gave a snort of dissent, but after a momentary pause, Jeremy kept on talking.

'You may not be convinced, Bernadette, but nobody could be more distressed than me. After Will Noone died, we worked night and day, year after year, fighting to clear our names and protect the Trust's reputation, to safeguard this village so that we could keep up our good work and preserve the precious legacy of the Midwinter family. Now these terrible tragedies threaten to undo everything I've devoted my whole working life to creating.'

'This isn't all about you, Jeremy,' Bernadette said through gritted teeth. 'This is about a trusted friend and colleague who is lying dead in a bag on the shelf of an old ice house.'

'You misunderstand me,' he said hastily. 'Losing our tempers will get us nowhere. Nor will panic and recriminations. Right now, the Midwinter Trust is facing an existential crisis. We need cool heads and clear thinking if—'

'If you can keep your head when all about you are losing theirs,' Chandra said softly, 'perhaps you simply don't appreciate how bad things really are.'

Daisy said abruptly. 'The Director is right. It's stupid to backbite and quarrel. We need to figure out what is going on. And how to deal with it.'

'Thank you, Daisy.' Jeremy was always quick to regain his

composure. 'The key question is motive. You summed it up perfectly, Bernadette. *Why* would anyone kill Ethan? Answer that, and we'll know who is guilty of this terrible crime.'

Bernadette let out a long sigh. 'On second thoughts, I was mistaken.'

Jeremy nodded. His expression was solemn, if faintly tinged with satisfaction. 'No problem. After what has happened, we're all bound to be a little... overwrought. You were right, incidentally, that we should focus on Ethan. Did he say or do something to provoke a killer? Does the explanation lie in anything he saw or heard?'

'What I mean,' Bernadette said doggedly, 'is that I was wrong to say that this isn't all about you, Jeremy. The simple truth is that it must be.'

He stared at her. 'I've no idea what you're talking about.'

'No?' She didn't attempt to hide her anger. 'As you love to say, Jeremy, we need to face facts. The time for hiding from the truth is over. Actually, it was over a long time ago, but we were all too selfishly concerned for the Trust and our careers to admit it. The murder of Ethan means we can't kid ourselves any longer. None of us can, least of all you, Jeremy. Everything we hoped to achieve this Christmas has collapsed around us. Which leaves one important thing needing to be said. This *is* about you, Jeremy. About you... and about Will Noone.'

Jeremy stared at her. 'The Commission of Inquiry—'

She waved his words away. 'Was a never-ending establishment charade. They spent years looking into Will Noone's death and they never knew the most important thing about the man.'

'What do you mean?' Daisy asked.

Bernadette turned to face the American woman. 'You don't know?'

Daisy shook her head.

'Will Noone,' Bernadette said heavily, 'was Jeremy's son.'

Secret Santa Naming Code

1 = □ ⊙ ▽ ◇ ⊙ L

2 = ▽ ⊙ ◖

3 = ◖ ⊙ ⬡ ⊙

4 = ⬡ ☾ ⊙ ✸ ▽ ☆

5 = ◇ ⊙ ▽ ▽ ⊙ ⊙

6 = ☾ ⊙ ✸ ◇ ⊙

38

Poppy de Lisle's Journal

Grace burst in through the door of the reading room when I was there on my own, doodling notes about the mystery of who killed Kristy Winkelman. It wasn't too hard to solve the shape cipher and I felt sure that once I'd figured out who had given which present to whom, I'd have an idea about the killer's identity. Though there might be a twist. What was the significance of Tim swapping his present with Kristy?

'Heard the latest?' Grace demanded.

She was out of breath, and for once, she looked flustered. Her hair was in disarray and her cheeks pink with exertion, as if she'd rushed through the snow in the hope of breaking bad news. Grace, I thought, took a strange delight in disaster.

I couldn't resist teasing her. 'Please don't tell me Father Christmas hasn't shown up?'

She groaned. 'This isn't funny. Believe me... Poppy.'

On her lips, my name sounded like a euphemism for a bodily function. Time to reprise my favourite role as village ingénue, even if I suspected the pretence was wearing thin.

'What in heaven's name is the matter? Dear me, you look quite upset.'

'Upset?' She shook her head with vigour. 'Afraid for my life would be nearer the mark. There's been another one.'

'Another one?'

When in doubt, repeat what the other person just said.

'Another death,' she snapped. 'And this time there's no question of an accident.'

I stared at her. 'You don't mean…'

'There's been a murder,' she said, echoing the words of my favourite television detectives. 'Ethan Swift has been killed.'

I tossed my scribbled notes aside.

'Good grief!'

My amazement wasn't feigned. I'm not the sentimental kind, and I never mix business with pleasure, but I'd liked the look of Ethan. Well, well… so I'd never get the chance to play Cathy to his Heathcliff. Pity.

'I bumped into Zack,' Grace said. 'He helped Harry Crystal to put the body in a bag and leave it with the others. Overseen by Jeremy Vandervell in his second job as village undertaker.'

'Good grief!' I said again, unable to conjure up anything more original. 'And they are saying it's foul play? No question of an accident this time?'

'His head was beaten to a pulp with an ice axe. So no, I don't think so.'

The withering put-down was a sign she was getting her mojo back. If she'd ever lost it. I took a few moments to absorb the implications of this latest fatality. It wasn't necessary to feign bewilderment.

'Poor Ethan. He was such a charmer. Why would anyone want to murder him?'

She spread her arms. 'Your guess is as good as mine. He

was sharp-witted and he was a professional mind-reader. Maybe he stumbled across what's really going on here.'

I played for time. 'What's really going on?'

She clicked her tongue. Loudly, and more than once.

'Listen, Poppy, you're a sweet girl, but I don't believe for one second that you're as innocent as you make out. If you were, I doubt you'd be here. So let's cut the crap, shall we?'

Before I could decide how to reply, the door was flung open and Zack Jardine swept in. By his usual natty standards, he looked almost dishevelled. Forgivable, I suppose, in anyone who has manhandled a corpse through the snow before squeezing it into a body bag and shoving it onto a shelf in an old ice house.

'Grace tells me that Ethan is dead,' I said. 'How awful!'

He gave a nod. There were fresh lines on his forehead and I guessed it would be a while before he said 'cool' again. Let alone 'no worries'.

'Whoever killed him wanted to make sure he was dead. His face was quite a mess. If you ask me, there's a maniac on the loose in Midwinter.'

'A maniac?'

As if on cue, the door swung open again. On the threshold stood Harry Crystal.

Harry looked haggard and wild-eyed. Understandable in the circumstances, and certainly not *in itself* proof that he was the lunatic at large.

'Zack's told you that someone murdered Ethan?' he asked.

Grace and I nodded in unison, and he let out a sigh.

'I was hoping I'd find you all here.'

'Why?' Grace asked.

'Um... strength in numbers, I suppose.' He nudged the iron doorstop with his foot so that nobody else could simply march into the reading room. 'Better safe than sorry, eh?'

'A bit late for that, isn't it?' Grace muttered.

'Yes, three dead in as many days! Life expectancy in Midwinter is about the same as for a sapper at the Somme.'

'Don't tell me you're afraid you'll be next,' she said.

'You never know,' he said darkly.

'You're among friends here,' I said encouragingly.

Grace snorted. 'Really? What if we're all guilty?'

Harry was taken aback. 'Funnily enough, that was the plot of one of my novels. *Strangers on a Plane*. This low-budget aircraft runs out of fuel and gets stuck on an island...'

'Yes, yes.' Grace silenced him with a glare. 'Who needs artificial intelligence when your fertile imagination is coming up with carbon copies of—'

'Please!' I couldn't help myself. 'Let's not fall out. A man has died.'

'Two men and a woman, actually,' Zack said.

'You think the deaths are connected?' I asked.

Zack shrugged. 'A quarter of the village's population has been wiped out in less than seventy-two hours. Can that really be a coincidence?'

'Coincidences are commoner than you might think,' Harry said. 'After *Six Red Herrings* was published, someone wrote to say they'd enjoyed the story, but I might like to know that—'

'Harry!' Grace was simmering with impatience. 'Save your literary reminiscences for your memoirs, huh? We need to make sense of what's going on here. We know about the *means* of murder, and at present the *motive* is obscure. Let's look at *opportunity*. I suggest that we start by describing what each of us was up to at the time of the murder.'

'Which was when?' I asked.

Harry consulted his watch. 'An hour ago. I was in my cottage when I saw Ethan prowling around outside. I was intrigued, so I went out to follow him.'

'What do you mean, *prowling*?' Grace asked.

'I got the impression that he didn't want anyone to notice what he was up to. Otherwise, why take the path behind the cottages?'

'That path joins the lane after a short distance,' Zack said. 'Did you lose sight of him?'

'Of course,' Harry said. 'I had to put on my outdoor gear. That took longer than it should've done, because I'd mislaid my gloves, and I didn't want to lose my fingers to frostbite. By the time I'd found them and got out of the cottage, Ethan was nowhere to be seen.'

'You found his body at the old school?'

'That's right.'

'We only have your word for it,' Zack pointed out. 'You could have killed him with your ice axe, then taken his and pretended it was yours.'

'Why would I do that?'

'We're only looking at opportunity, remember?'

'In that case, you were almost as close at hand. The school isn't far away. Even in thick snow, it only takes a few minutes to get there. You could easily have killed him.'

'True,' Zack admitted. 'The same is true of Jeremy Vandervell.'

'What were you doing out there?' Harry asked.

'Walking off my Christmas lunch, simple as that. As it

happens, I didn't see Ethan. Or Jeremy. Or you, until after you found the body.'

'So neither of you have alibis,' Grace said. 'I might as well fess up. Nor do I. Having tucked into the mulled wine at lunchtime, I went back to my cottage for a nap.'

Everyone looked at me.

'I'm in the same boat,' I admitted. 'After lunch, I went back to my cottage for a short rest. Then I came here to have another stab, if you'll pardon the expression, at *Miss Winter in the Library with a Knife.*'

'Any of us could be the murderer,' Grace said. 'So could Jeremy Vandervell, given that he was in the vicinity.'

'He makes a daily patrol of the village,' Harry said. 'Likes to keep an eye on things. Make sure there are no problems.'

'Oh dear,' I said. 'He's not having much success, is he?'

'I wonder if he arranged to meet Ethan at the school,' Grace said.

'Why bother, when they could talk in the village hall?' Harry asked.

'Suppose they didn't want anyone to know they were having a conversation. Not even the other people who work for the Trust.'

'You think Jeremy is suspicious of his colleagues?'

Grace nodded. 'When he's with Daisy, Chandra, and Bernadette, you could cut the atmosphere with a knife. To coin a phrase. Until now, I put it down to jealousy, but perhaps there's more to it than meets the eye.'

'What if,' Zack muttered, 'Jeremy lured Ethan to a quiet spot so he could bludgeon him to death?'

'On the other hand,' Harry said, 'perhaps Ethan had vital information that he wanted to share with the Director of the

Trust in complete privacy. Something that incriminated one of the three women, for instance.'

'The possibilities are endless,' I said mournfully. 'Any of us could have killed poor Ethan, and so could Jeremy, but what about Daisy, Bernadette, and Chandra? Do we know where they were at the time of the murder?'

'Aren't you forgetting someone?' Harry said. 'What about Carys Neville?'

Secret Santa

Who Gave Which Present?

PERFUME
Person 3

SOCKS
Person 4

TIE
Person 2

CHOCOLATE LIQUEURS
Person 5

PROSECCO
Person 1

GINGERBREAD MEN
Person 6

39

Midwinter

Daisy Wu stared at Jeremy.

'You were Will Noone's father?'

The Director shifted in his chair, but his expression remained as imperturbable as ever.

'Correct.'

'How come this has never been mentioned until now?'

'Because it's irrelevant,' he said coolly. 'Will's death was a deeply personal tragedy for me. But the question everyone was concerned with was simply, did the Midwinter Trust fail in its duty of care towards him?'

Daisy shook her head. 'Unreal. Of course your relationship is relevant.'

'Why? If it had been widely known, it would only have muddied the waters. I didn't want to play the grieving parent card; I wasn't looking for sympathy on account of my loss. All that mattered after Will died was to clear the name of the Trust. We were accountable for what happened, but we weren't guilty of any crime.'

'How many people knew he was your son?'

'Only the four of us. Myself, Bernadette, Chandra, and Ethan.'

Daisy looked at the other two women. 'And you kept your mouths zipped? Never uttered a peep when the Commission of Inquiry was investigating Will's death?'

'Jeremy persuaded us that it would confuse the issue,' Chandra said.

'So it was all his fault?' Daisy didn't hide her scorn.

'He can be extremely plausible,' Chandra said. 'As I'm sure you've discovered, Daisy.'

Jeremy bristled. 'Hindsight is all very well, but I stand by what I've always said. Will's death had nothing to do with the fact he was my son.'

'How can you be so sure?' Daisy demanded.

'Because if you set aside emotional incontinence – and shouldn't we always do that? – what I say is entirely logical. Are you suggesting he was treated in a more cavalier fashion *because* he was my son? That's absurd as well as offensive.'

'All right.' Daisy chewed her lip. 'Let me try to get my head around this. Did you already know Will was your son when he came here?'

'Absolutely not. As far as I was concerned, he was a young man who had washed up here following a breakdown. He was intelligent, but... troubled. A familiar pattern. We're accustomed to people fitting that profile in Midwinter. We pride ourselves on encouraging them to take a break before returning to work refreshed and reinvigorated. We—'

'Yeah, yeah, let's skip the propaganda, huh? When did you find out the truth?'

Jeremy heaved a sigh. 'He asked for a one-to-one with me shortly after his arrival. I readily agreed. It's not uncommon for our guests to pour their hearts out to me. They hope for guidance, mentorship, advice. I do what I can to help.'

'What did he say?'

'After a few preliminaries, he came right out with it. Told me I was his father and he'd been desperate to make contact with me. I need hardly say that I was startled. The news took some processing, believe me.'

'I bet,' Daisy said. 'Tell me about his backstory.'

'There's not much to say. When I first came to Midwinter, I was a young man, footloose and fancy free. There was a young local woman who worked in the kitchen. Attractive but highly strung. Her name was Valerie. We had a fling, but it was never more than that.'

'Not for you,' Chandra said.

'I never offered her any form of commitment. There was no pretence on my part, no false promises. She always knew I was utterly committed to my work at Midwinter. Sir Maurice was still alive, but he'd seen something in me that he liked and he'd already given me reason to hope that I could carry the torch.' He breathed out. 'When Valerie told me she was pregnant, I made it clear that if she wanted to keep the child, that was her choice. I was willing to honour my financial obligations, but there was no question of marriage.'

'At least you were honest,' Daisy murmured.

'Yes!' His expression was uncompromising. 'The difficulty was that she'd fantasised about our having a happy-ever-after existence in some two-up, two-down in Gateshead or South Shields or somewhere. With no encouragement from me, I can assure you. I'd grown up in the north-east, but I was ambitious and I didn't want family ties to ruin my career prospects as Sir Maurice's heir apparent. Was that so wicked?'

Chandra shrugged. 'Matter of opinion.'

'Unfortunately, Valerie became hysterical and said she'd rather die than take a penny from me. Volatile, you see, irrational. Soon it dawned on me that I'd had a narrow escape.'

'Valerie wasn't so lucky?' Daisy asked.

'She left Midwinter and went back to live with her parents on Tyneside. I did send her a rather large cheque, but my understanding was that she didn't intend to keep the child.'

'And?'

'And that was the last I heard of her. The experience shook me to the core, I don't mind admitting. I was desperate to put it behind me. Remember, I was a young fellow, on the threshold of an exciting career. Work was my true passion. That's why I've never married.'

He looked Bernadette in the eye. Her features were frozen.

'So Valerie gave birth to Will Noone?' Daisy said. 'What did he tell you about his background?'

'As I said, Valerie was attractive. Within a few months, she married a lorry driver after a whirlwind romance. He flatly refused to raise another man's child, so Will was put out for adoption. Soon the couple had a child of their own. But Valerie never achieved that happy-ever-after fantasy she craved. The new man was an alcoholic. Drink made him violent and jealous. He beat her black and blue and eventually she snapped.' He paused. 'She suffocated him with a pillow one night while he was out for the count. Then she took a fatal overdose.'

There was a short silence, broken by Daisy.

'What happened to Will?'

'He was raised by an older couple with no kids of their own. Their surname was Noone. Highly appropriate, he told me, because he felt alone in the world and thought of himself as 'no one'. And he never used his full first name, because he was proud of his determination. His 'will'.'

'A chip off the old block?' Daisy said wryly.

He allowed himself a brief smile. 'Will's new parents gave him a decent education, but they died while he was at university in London. With no ties to this part of the world, he settled in the city and found work that suited him. By all accounts, he was extremely good at his job, but his progress faltered. He hated the rat race and all the bureaucratic red tape. Not to mention the after-hours boozing culture, and colleagues boasting about their fast cars and convoluted sex lives. I gather he'd never had a partner, male or female.'

There was a short pause. Chandra's lips were firmly compressed. Bernadette stared into nothingness.

'So sad,' Daisy murmured.

'Very. He told me that, in the end, he lost the plot. Matters came to head during the pandemic. Lockdown was the last straw. While he was on sick leave, he went AWOL for a while, causing his bosses extreme concern. When he suddenly turned up again, out of the blue, he was still in a state of serious nervous tension and unfit for work. That's when he was invited here. He was our only guest.'

He paused for a moment, as if to give them time to make sense of the picture he was painting.

'Covid was rampant. People were fleeing to the countryside, and nowhere in England is closer to the natural world than Midwinter. Nobody fell sick here. This was an oasis, a peaceful Shangri-La where you could luxuriate in the illusion of living forever.'

'Not like now,' Daisy said softly.

'Christmas was coming. Supposedly a family time, but if you have no family, this is the perfect place to stay.'

'Until the killing starts?'

Jeremy frowned. 'Unworthy of you, my dear. We have a

proud history of taking people who are seen by others as damaged goods and providing a peaceful environment where they can regain their motivation and become whole again. But we can't work miracles. Some of our guests are beyond redemption.'

'Will, for instance?'

He shrugged. 'He was in a bad way before he ever set foot in this village.'

'How did Will know you were his father?'

'His new parents had done their due diligence before taking him in. While he was growing up, he had no idea about his origins. But they left a letter with their solicitors, for Will to open – if he wished – when they were dead. For a long time, he chose not to read it. In the midst of his breakdown, he changed his mind. Very unwise. He found coping with the truth at a time of emotional turmoil far from straightforward.'

'I can imagine,' Daisy said.

Jeremy shot a glance at Chandra. 'Wearing your heart on your sleeve is fashionable these days, but it's not a good look.'

'Did reading the letter cause him to try to track you down?'

'Not initially. He'd never known he had a sibling. Or half-sibling, to be precise. So he set about tracing Valerie's other child. They met and apparently that went well. Encouraged and emboldened, he felt he must see me.'

'So he contrived an invitation to Midwinter?'

'To meet his long-lost father, yes.' Jeremy sat back in his chair. 'Not that I understood his hidden agenda until it was too late. Perhaps it would've been different if he'd come here at the height of summer, but he turned up in the midst of a snowstorm.'

'What did you say when he told you all this?'

'Frankly, I was stunned. I had no idea Valerie had actually

given birth, so the last thing I expected was for a guest at Midwinter to tell me I was his father. I suppose my manner was less than rapturous. But he'd given me a shock. I needed time to process the news.'

'Was he distressed by your reaction?'

Jeremy steepled his fingers together. 'I'm afraid so. Frankly, I found his behaviour alarming. Ethan had assured me that Will was recovering his spirits, but he'd completely misread the signs. The hysterics reminded me vividly of his mother's ranting, the day I explained we had no future together. Not that I said anything so... final to Will. I simply made clear that I had my position to think of. He couldn't simply breeze in and expect me to wave a magic wand and put everything right that had gone wrong in his life. It was incumbent on us both to behave in a professional manner. Eminently reasonable, in my judgment. I stand by every word I said, I did nothing to be ashamed of. But he over-reacted wildly.'

'How?'

'He screamed that I was about to betray him just as I'd betrayed Valerie. He hadn't wanted to believe it, even though he'd been warned that a man who abandoned his mother so cruelly wouldn't want anything to do with a by-blow of a casual fling. He had the temerity to ask me how I could live with myself.'

'And you replied?'

'That I couldn't imagine living with anyone else.'

'How did he take that?'

'Badly.' There was a tremor in his voice. 'Will flounced out of the room and I never saw him alive again.'

'Was that when he left Midwinter?'

'He didn't go immediately. He'd smuggled a burner phone into the village, and he did make one call before he vanished.'

347

'How do you know?'

'The handyman went into his cottage to replace a broken lightbulb and saw Will on the phone. He apologised for intruding and said he'd come back later. That's all he was able to tell us. Afterwards, we searched high and low for the phone, but never found it. Will must have thrown it away. So we had no clue about who Will called, or what they spoke about. My guess was that he was trying to plan his escape.'

'You make Midwinter sound like Alcatraz,' Daisy said.

Jeremy made a derisive noise. 'Quite the opposite. To me, this village is a rural paradise. Anyone lucky enough to come here should thank their lucky stars.'

'And check their life insurance?'

'A cheap gibe, unworthy of you. After Will walked out on me, I spent some time coming to terms with what he'd said. It was obvious we had things in common and I felt we could come to some sort of amicable agreement about how to move forward.'

'Like negotiating an exit deal with a troublesome underling?'

Jeremy's expression was pained. 'I decided to speak to him before dinner, only for Chandra to tell me that he couldn't be found. We searched the village, but there was no trace of him. The conditions outside were appalling, snowdrifts even deeper than they are now. Will was deeply disturbed, of that I had no doubt. He was a danger to himself and possibly others. I felt there was no alternative but to set off to look for him, and Bernadette volunteered to accompany me.'

'The boy had two hours' start.' Bernadette had been silent for so long that the sound of her voice made their heads turn. 'We knew that his life was in danger, but we never had a chance of making up for lost time. Even in the snow, he'd got a fair distance before the conditions overwhelmed him. He must have been exhausted. It seems he simply lay down and waited to die and let the snow cover him over.'

Daisy shivered. 'A horrible end to a young life.'

'Such a waste,' Chandra said.

'Of course,' Jeremy said, 'all hell broke loose as soon as his body was retrieved. I was treated as if I'd let him down. As if Midwinter had failed.'

'Are you saying you hadn't?' Daisy asked.

'Absolutely not! We spent years explaining ourselves to faceless bureaucrats. The whole business was a long-drawn-out nightmare. In the end, thank God, we were vindicated. It was accepted that what happened was deeply regrettable, but no one individual was to blame for Will's death.'

'When did you tell the others that he was your son?'

'Bernadette was the only person I confided in.'

'I told Chandra and Ethan, and swore them to secrecy,' Bernadette said wearily. 'I didn't consult Jeremy, but I felt they had to know, and I was confident we could rely on their total discretion.'

'Why did they need to know?' Daisy asked.

'They were both closely involved with Will's induction. I wondered if either of them had picked up anything about his relationship with Jeremy that would compromise us during the inquiry. There was nothing of the kind, but that didn't mean we were beyond criticism. To paraphrase, Chandra thought Will was a nice young man, and Ethan reckoned there was nothing wrong with his mental health that a fortnight in the right surroundings wouldn't put right.'

Daisy made a face. 'Unfortunate.'

'Very.'

Chandra said quickly, 'Will Noone misled me. He didn't

tell the whole truth about his background. My mistake was to trust him.'

'*Trust Noone*?' Daisy gave a wry smile. 'In Midwinter, you should've known better. As for Ethan Swift…'

'Ethan was lovely,' Bernadette interrupted, 'but he was trusting and liked to think the best of people. He admitted that he completely misread Will Noone. His much-vaunted expertise in psychological profiling let him down and he never stopped being tormented by guilt. If he'd realised that Will was so vulnerable, he'd have advised us accordingly and we'd have tightened up security so that Will couldn't simply walk away from Midwinter and freeze to death. A terrible mistake, yes, but Ethan never stopped paying for it. His conscience meant he never had a night's unbroken sleep from the day Will died until… well, his own death.'

'Enough.' Jeremy leaned back in his chair. 'We must stop this pointless self-flagellation. Ethan has been murdered. Right now, there's a killer in Midwinter and they have to be found. The questions we need to ask are like something from Bernadette's game. Whodunit and whydunit? Nothing else matters.'

'Surely the answers lie in the story you just told me?' Daisy said.

'Really?' Jeremy said.

'Yeah. Really. There's only one person I can think of who has enough of a stake in that whole mess to be a candidate for our murderer.'

'And who might that be?'

Her smile was tantalising. 'Surely it's obvious?'

Secret Santa

Who Received Which Present?

PERFUME

SOCKS

TIE

CHOCOLATE LIQUEURS

PROSECCO

GINGERBREAD MEN

40

Harry Crystal's Journal

'Carys Neville?' Zack said thoughtfully. 'Not seen her since lunch.'

Grace nodded. 'Same here.'

'Perhaps she went for a lie-down,' Poppy suggested.

'Yep,' I said. 'And perhaps she didn't.'

Poppy was agog. 'Do you suspect her?'

'Why not?'

'The reality of killing a fellow human being is deeply unpleasant.'

I pointed to the pristine copy of my debut novel on the shelf by my side. 'I should have called it *Murder Isn't Cosy*.'

Let alone *dozy*. How could I have been so naïve as to come to Midwinter without having the faintest idea of what I was letting myself in for? Time for me to get my act together. Before it was too late.

'So...'

'So if we had to pick the most unpleasant person in the village, she'd be the nailed-on favourite.' I folded my arms. 'Tell me if I'm wrong.'

Zack pursed his lips, in the manner of a *tricoteuse* waiting for the guillotine to fall. Whether he was minded to condemn me or Carys, I didn't know and hardly cared.

'Don't sit on the fence, Harry.' Grace was at her most cutting. 'Tell us how you really feel about the woman.'

'I've never heard you speak so… with such *passion* before,' Poppy murmured.

I gave a wry smile. 'Perhaps if I wrote with the same fire, my books wouldn't end up in so many charity shops. I suppose I could write a novel in which a character based on Carys is murdered. That fate I usually reserve for people who give me one-star reviews.'

'Might you be a teeny bit prejudiced against Carys?' Grace asked.

'Absolutely,' I replied. 'She ruined my career with a few well-chosen barbs on social media and I'm in good company. Carys Neville is one of those creepy individuals who haunt the internet and don't have a kind word for anyone else but whine in self-pity the moment anyone pushes back at them. I'm glad she was found out for what she was. It couldn't have happened to a nicer narcissist.'

'I'm guessing that, if Carys is found dead,' Zack murmured, 'you'll be the prime suspect. Better get your alibi dusted down.'

Poppy's eyes widened. 'You think Carys has been murdered?'

Zack shrugged his shoulders. 'The way things are going, it'll be a wonder if any of us get out of here alive.'

'Poppy is right,' Grace said unexpectedly. 'Chances are, Carys did go for a lie-down. As for Harry's opinion of her, I agree. It must get boring being so snarky all the time. Zack, you've got a point as well. We need to spend less time agonising over Bernadette's little puzzles and more time concentrating on survival. Let's put our heads together and work out what is going on. Co-operation rather than competition is the name of the game.'

'What about clause thirty?' Poppy asked.

'Fuck clause thirty. And all the other terms and conditions, come to that.'

Poppy blinked. 'But...'

'Listen.' Grace leaned towards the publicist. 'This is no time for legal quibbles, but if ever there was a case for *force majeure* releasing us from our contractual obligations, I reckon three deaths in as many days qualifies. Especially since at least one person has been brutally murdered.'

'When you say *force majeure*, do you mean, like, act of God?' Zack asked.

'God may move in mysterious ways,' Grace said sourly, 'but I doubt he clubbed Ethan Swift to death. No, the killer is someone we've dined with and talked to. A resident of Midwinter.'

He raised his eyebrows. 'Someone from the Midwinter Trust?'

'Not necessarily. Quite apart from Carys, on the basis of the available evidence, none of us can be ruled out. So, are you all going to keep mum, or shall we take a deep breath and try to make sense of what's happening here?'

'Let's talk,' Zack said. Presumably a phrase he'd uttered to a thousand authors and editors. Usually as a euphemism for *let's have lunch and claim it against tax*.

'Fine by me,' I said.

Poppy was looking pensive but she gave a nod of assent.

'Excellent,' Grace said. 'So, let's not beat about the bush. Let's go round the room. Why did you all come to this wretched place to play a game? Zack?'

'I was broke and my career was in ruins. Out of the blue someone offers to give me a free Christmas in the countryside with the prospect of a cash bonus and a special prize if I solved a mystery game. No-brainer or what? I bit their hands off.'

Grace looked at Poppy. 'Same story with you?'

Another nod.

'None of you have close families, right? Like me. So not only were we at a loose end over the festive season... if we didn't come back, we wouldn't be greatly missed.'

'Steady on.' Zack frowned. 'What are you suggesting?'

'If Carys and Baz were here,' Grace said calmly, 'I bet they'd tell the same tale as the four of us. My question is this. Why did the Midwinter Trust want us here so badly that they bribed us to come with the promise of a cash bonus and a chance to win a prize?'

'Must be linked to the podcast Baz worked on,' Zack said. 'He was dissatisfied with the official version of events relating to Will Noone's death.'

Grace leaned forward. 'Who told Baz about Will Noone in the first place?'

We all looked blank.

Zack said, 'I did ask, but he made a song and dance about needing to keep his sources confidential.'

'His very words to me,' Grace said. 'What I'm wondering is whether someone in the Midwinter Trust was a whistle-blower, leaking information to him.'

'Why would anyone do that?' I asked.

'Conscience, perhaps?'

'Do Bernadette and Chandra strike you as the types to be tormented by their consciences?'

'Not really.' Grace shrugged. 'There are other potential

explanations. What if one of them wanted to take revenge on Jeremy Vandervell? A discarded lover, perhaps?'

'You mean Bernadette?' I asked.

'Or even Chandra.'

'How about Ethan?' Poppy asked, with a glint of mischievous amusement in her eye.

'I don't understand,' I said.

Grace glared at me. 'When you die, Harry, those three words should be engraved on your tombstone. And if you don't buck your ideas up, that will happen sooner than you think.'

'That's a bit harsh,' I retorted. She underestimated how much hard thinking I'd done since our Christmas lunch. 'I mean, they are all intimately connected to the Trust. Surely, they'd only be harming themselves?'

'Ethan is an outside contractor, or so he told me,' Grace said. 'He'd been working in Newcastle since Will Noone's death and only returned to the village recently.'

'What made him come back?'

'Who could resist the prospect of a merry Christmas in Midwinter?' She shook her head. 'Not us, obviously. Maybe he had an ulterior motive. According to Baz, Ethan misread Will completely. He didn't realise how vulnerable the man was. Perhaps after the inquiry fudged its conclusions, he suffered pangs of remorse.'

'So you think he blew the whistle? Have you found any evidence to suggest that?'

Her features creased in exasperation. 'None whatsoever.'

Poppy had been listening intently during the discussion without contributing much, but now she said, 'The pattern isn't the same for everyone. I didn't have anything to do with Baz Frederick. Nor did Harry, as far as I know.'

'That's right, Poppy,' I said. 'I'd never heard of him or his podcast until I arrived in the village.'

'The Trust didn't necessarily invite all six of us here for identical reasons,' Grace said. 'What the two of you have in common with the rest of us is that you're involved in one way or another with books or crime or both. And you were down on your luck and on your own in the world.'

'So the Trust celebrates failure?'

She returned my gaze. 'Maybe they like to recruit people with nothing to lose. What do you know about them?'

'I'd never heard of either Midwinter or the Trust until a few weeks ago, when I was invited to apply to come here for a luxury Christmas break. The email came out of the blue, as Zack said. Presumably we all had the same message. At first, I thought it might be a scam, but when I looked at the Trust's website, I was reassured. It has a long history. Everything seemed above board.'

'No mention of strange deaths and murder,' she said.

'Not unless I missed it in the reams of small print I had to sign.'

'So the reason you came here had nothing to do with Baz Frederick?'

'Cross my heart and hope to die.'

'Be careful what you wish for,' she said bleakly. 'Someone may take you at your word.'

'Let's not get paranoid,' I said, although my visit to Midwinter was helping me understand paranoia's seductive allure.

'You're your own worst enemy.'

'I'd like to think that's true,' I said humbly. 'At least I know I'm not going to bash my own head in.'

She exhaled. 'I'm willing to bet the Trust played a big part in Baz's downfall. And Zack's. And Carys's. And mine.'

'But why?' Zack demanded.

'Baz's research threatened to discredit the Trust and everyone who works here. They thought they were out of the woods, but he wanted to reopen the whole can of worms. He confided in you, me, and apparently Carys. Can it really be a coincidence that we all fell to earth in rapid succession?'

Zack's face was white with anger. He certainly wasn't cool now.

'You're suggesting the Trust sabotaged our careers simply because we'd spoken to Baz?'

Her expression was uncompromising. 'Call it a direct accusation, if you like.'

'How could they do that, even if they wanted to?'

'Easy. Baz's advertisers were persuaded to pull out, leaving him with no income. Carys's computer was hacked, and her unvarnished bile made public. Zack's best client was made a better offer. And my cunning plan to make my fortune through authors who used AI was picked up by relentless in-depth monitoring of books on my list.'

I turned to Poppy. 'What about you?'

'Looks like you and I are in the same boat, Harry.'

For once I felt she was choosing her words with care. There was a hint of calculation in her eyes that I'd never noticed before.

'Really?'

'Yes. I'd never had any contact with Baz Frederick until I bumped into him at Midwinter Halt.'

I thrust my hands into my pockets. 'So how does a small outfit based in the middle of nowhere create so much mayhem?'

'Jeremy Vandervell obviously has friends in high places?' Poppy said.

'It would take some remarkable friends to do all that,' I said.

She nodded. 'True.'

Grace stared at me. 'Have you got a theory, Harry?'

I took a breath. 'Yes.'

'Care to share it?'

'You'll only shoot me down in flames. Tell me I'm letting my imagination run riot.'

Poppy said, 'I think you ought to tell us.'

'Yeah,' Zack said.

I looked at Grace. She'd closed her eyes, but her words carried a scorpion's sting.

'All right. Break it to me gently.'

For a moment I was assailed by doubt. I'd spent too long as a human punchbag to feel comfortable exposing myself to ridicule.

'I don't have much hard evidence to back my theory up.'

'Okay, disclaimer noted,' Grace muttered. 'Get on with it.'

I took a breath.

'The Midwinter Trust likes to call itself an independent not-for-profit organisation, but that's a façade. A fig leaf.'

'Covering what?' Zack demanded.

'My guess is that for Jeremy and his team, wrecking the lives of people they regard as disruptive is second nature. They play dirty tricks like the rest of us play... well, mystery games.'

Zack stared at me. 'You mean...?'

I took a breath.

'Jeremy Vandervell is a spymaster. The Midwinter Trust is tied up with the Intelligence Service.'

The Origins of the Midwinter Trust – a personal aide-mémoire by Jeremy Vandervell: I

CLASSIFIED

Maurice Midwinter was a patriot, equally devoted to his country and the tiny, remote settlement in the north Pennines where he grew up. The village which bore his family name was his favourite place in the world and he never liked to be away for long. He devoted his life to Midwinter and to England, and did everything within his power to make sure they would not only survive but thrive.

He was recruited to Intelligence shortly after Britain declared war on Germany. While studying History at Cambridge, he'd been talent-spotted by the Secret Intelligence Service. His college, Trinity, was the alma mater of traitors such as Philby, Burgess, Maclean, Cairncross, and Blunt, all of whom were recruited by the Russians, but there was never any question of Maurice betraying his country. He loathed Communism and everything that Stalin stood for.

During the war, Maurice was seconded to Bletchley Park in Buckinghamshire, where he acted as a liaison officer, linking Dilly Knox's code breakers with their masters in Whitehall. Later, he was deployed by the Special Operations Executive to Scotland, where he spent the rest of the war as senior debriefing officer at Inverlair Lodge in a remote area of the Highlands. The Lodge was home to a small number of agents who had been compromised or were unfit for continuing service, so that they could not be allowed to move freely, for fear that vital secrets would find their way into enemy hands.

Maurice's war-time activities were clandestine and he never discussed their precise nature, even half a century and more later, when he and I relaxed over a wee dram at Midwinter. Suffice to say that his knighthood was richly merited.

After the war, he felt in need of a fresh sense of purpose. On returning home to Midwinter, he discovered a new mission that would define the rest of his life.

41

Midwinter

'William Noone was a loner,' Daisy said, 'like so many people who work in Intelligence. But he wasn't quite as alone as you thought.'

Jeremy pursed his lips. 'What are you getting at?'

'After his breakdown, Will longed to find new meaning in life. He was sick of all the double-dealing that his work required and he yearned to discover his roots. Something to anchor his existence. That's why he was so desperate to talk to you. Not that you were his only blood relative. Valerie had another child, remember? Their meeting went well, you said. What if Will and his sibling rapidly became devoted to each other? That kind of bond often develops, when you trace a long-lost close family member.'

'He hardly mentioned his half-brother. Or half-sister, whatever.'

'So they didn't want to put their head above the parapet. What if they already resented you, and tried to turn Will against you?'

'Why resent someone you've never met, who is supremely unaware that you even exist?'

Daisy sighed. 'Happens all the time, Jeremy. Suppose

this person grew up blaming you for dumping their mom. When they learned you'd had no contact with Will, maybe resentment turned to hatred.'

'Completely irrational. I did what I could.'

'Who said life is rational? This person's mom was a flaky woman who suffocated her husband, then took her own life. Dad was a violent drunk. Is someone with that background likely to be cool, calm, and collected?'

'You think they turned Will against me?'

'He came to Midwinter and gave you a chance. Sounds like you blew it.'

Jeremy breathed out. 'Remember the local historian who made snide remarks about Midwinter and me? The stuff published online by a society that didn't exist? Written by someone who called themselves J. Doe? In other words, nobody. We had the site closed down, but I was curious. They chose their words with care, but they obviously knew more about me and the Trust than has ever been put out in the public domain. You think Valerie's child was responsible?'

'Obviously. Didn't you figure out their hidden message?' Daisy sighed. 'If you correct the typos, it reads: *The Midwinter Trust sacrificed Will and must be held to account.*'

Bernadette, like Chandra, had been stunned into silence by Daisy's new-found assertiveness. Now she spoke up.

'No use raking over dead coals. Ethan's murder is what matters now.'

'Sure,' Daisy said. 'Kind of reinforces what I'm saying. Ethan misread Will's mental state. Will was extremely fragile and his conversation with Jeremy tipped him over the edge. Jeremy wasn't the only one to blame. If Ethan had done his job properly, Jeremy would've known Will was extremely vulnerable. Maybe, things would have turned out differently.'

Bernadette stared. 'You're saying that Ethan was killed for revenge?'

'Why not? He was good to look at, but he was crap at his job. That's why he ended up here in the first place, rather than making a fortune in Harley Street.'

Jeremy stood up and began to pace around the room. 'So you think Valerie's other child is here at Midwinter?'

'Uh-huh.'

'But we vetted everyone before they arrived.'

'Like Ethan vetted Will Noone,' Daisy said. 'IDs can be faked. False trails laid. Isn't that what our work is all about?'

'*Our* work?' Chandra asked.

Daisy laughed. 'Don't tell me you think I'm an MI5-approved chef? I liaise between Langley and the Pentagon when I'm not roaming the world, keeping an eye on trouble-spots.'

Bernadette stared at her. 'This is Midwinter, not the Middle East.'

'Yeah, life expectancy here is even worse.'

Chandra said slowly. 'So you work for the CIA?'

'Got it in one. My bosses got twitchy about Midwinter after the Will Noone fiasco. We hoped the inquiry would close the Trust down. It would've made life simpler, but no such luck. So I was sent over here to snoop at close quarters. Like a Michelin inspector, except I had to do all the cooking.' She exhaled. 'I gotta tell you guys, this has been a Christmas like no other.'

Bernadette turned to Jeremy. 'You knew?'

He inclined his head. 'Of course. I was desperate to persuade Daisy about the good work we do.'

'You told us she was seconded from Whitehall!'

'Washington informed me Daisy's placement was on a "need to know" basis.'

'So your trysts with her were…'

'Purely professional,' he said tightly. 'Hands across the water, you know?'

'And I made it clear, it was hands off, believe me,' Daisy said. 'Ethan was more my type. Pity he was so flaky.'

Bernadette uttered a low groan.

'So where does this leave us?' Chandra asked Daisy. 'Is Will's half-sibling here in Midwinter, masquerading as someone else?'

'Uh-huh. No other explanation makes sense.'

'Who is it?' Bernadette demanded. 'We need to make sure they are…'

'Neutralised?' Daisy shrugged. 'Well, yeah. The snag is, I'm not sure who they are. We don't even know the gender of this individual, do we, Jeremy?'

Still pacing the floor, he shook his head unhappily. 'Will didn't say, and I didn't enquire. So, yes, it could be either a man or a woman.'

'Right,' Daisy said. 'We can rule out Harry Crystal. Too old. Unfortunately, the others are all in the right age range.'

Bernadette cast her eyes to the heavens. 'Grace or Poppy? Zack or Carys?'

CLASSIFIED

Towards the end of his life, Sir Maurice confided in me that – unjustified as it undoubtedly was – he'd always felt a certain responsibility for the collapse of his father's idealistic vision for the model village of Midwinter. The challenges arising from the loss of so many villagers in the war and even the economic failure of the mines they worked in might have proved surmountable. But the death of Claudia Midwinter in childbirth was too much for Marcus to bear.

Requisitioned but scarcely used during the Second World War, Midwinter was left in a derelict state. Maurice resolved to preserve his father's legacy by rebuilding the village, but not the mine. His experience in Scotland led him to believe that Midwinter, equally far off the beaten track, would form an ideal setting for a peacetime version of Inverlair Lodge. Hitler had been vanquished, but the world remained a dangerous place, and at any one time, a small number of agents were experiencing serious personal traumas. Maurice hoped to provide a tranquil environment that would enable them to recover their morale so they could serve their country once again.

Although he was still a young man, his stock was high and his influence formidable (it is said that his acquaintance Ian Fleming borrowed his initial for the spymaster in the Bond novels). Maurice persuaded the authorities to support his plan, promising to shoulder the burden of running the village as well as the cost, funded by the family fortune. In return, he secured the passage of the Midwinter Trust Act, ensuring that he and the Trust he created had more or less a free hand in conducting their activities, unimpeded by red tape and external oversight. The Trust's relationship with the security services was close, yet in critical respects, at arm's-length, so that any official connection with Midwinter was at all times deniable. This suited everyone.

During the Cold War – when the security services were severely affected by the treachery of the double agents from Trinity College – Maurice gradually rebuilt the residential part of the village while making safe the disused and dangerous mine workings and the subterranean passages which honeycombed the landscape. Eventually, the Trust became fully operational. A new chapter in the village's story was about to begin.

42

Harry Crystal's Journal

Zack stared at me.

'Seriously? Jeremy Vandervell and co are spooks?'

'Did you think they were a bunch of do-gooders with more money than sense?' I shook my head. 'You couldn't find anywhere spookier than Midwinter.'

There was a long pause. I felt the eyes of the others boring into me as they absorbed the implications of what I'd said. Or perhaps they simply hated my pun.

'Is this pure guesswork?' Grace asked. 'Or storyteller's imagination going into overdrive?'

I shook my head. 'Not entirely. Don't tell me you haven't wondered about this place?'

'All of us have, of course. Baz didn't tell us much. Not even the name of the village. He made it sound like some kind of elitist rehabilitation centre out in the wilds. I suppose we came here believing what we wanted to believe. That our luck was about to change. It's become obvious that there's much more to Midwinter than meets the eye, but everything has happened so quickly, I've been struggling to make sense of it. My question is, have you found any hard evidence for this theory of yours?'

Nothing to lose by being frank. 'Not a lot. But there was some stuff online – which quickly disappeared – that stuck in my mind. About the origins of the Midwinter Trust and Sir Maurice Midwinter's war-time work. He moved from Whitehall to Buckinghamshire and then to the Scottish Highlands. Even though he was still a young man when the war ended, he received a knighthood.'

'So?'

'So it dawned on me that Bletchley Park, the base for the war-time code breakers, is in Buckinghamshire.'

Grace looked seriously unimpressed. 'Is that it?'

'No, his next stop was the Highlands, and I bet he didn't go for the skiing.'

'What, then?'

'A place called Inverlair Lodge was a safe haven for secret agents during the war. Spies who were compromised or who had outlived their usefulness. My guess is, Maurice took charge of the Lodge.'

'That's a hell of a stretch.'

I folded my arms. 'Why else would a smart young graduate, from a Cambridge college famous for producing spies, be sent from Whitehall to Buckinghamshire to the far north of Scotland and be made a knight of the realm as soon as the war was over?'

The others looked at me. I was conscious of an unfamiliar sensation. A spurt of confidence.

'The only reasonable interpretation of Maurice's movements during the war is that he was a high-ranking spook. Once you accept that logic, it's not much of a leap to the obvious conclusion. He created Midwinter as a peacetime development of Inverlair Lodge. But he owned the place and insisted on a great deal of autonomy. The village was run at arm's-length from MI5 and MI6, and at the time, that suited everyone. The Trust's activities were deniable so far as the authorities were concerned. And Maurice had his own private fiefdom.'

There was a long pause.

'So that was what Baz kept up his sleeve,' Zack said slowly. 'He told me about this place where a young civil servant had come to recover from a breakdown. The guy was treated so badly he felt he had to flee and finished up buried in a snowdrift.'

'Civil servant was a euphemism,' Poppy murmured.

'Yes,' I said. 'Everything makes sense once you realise that Will Noone was a secret agent who had lost the plot.'

Grace glanced through the snow-smeared window.

'The spy who went out into the cold, huh?' She shivered. 'Baz said no more to me than he did to Zack. And presumably Carys. I didn't press him. He was obviously determined to protect his source.'

'Not that any of us got anywhere with the project,' Zack said bitterly. 'If Harry's right, once the Midwinter Trust was officially cleared of wrongdoing, they were determined to suppress any attempt to breathe fresh life into the Will Noone story.'

Grace closed her eyes. 'So they killed off our ability to earn a living. And set about trying to buy us off. When I got here and found who else had been invited, I couldn't figure out what the Trust's real game was. I'm still not sure, unless...'

'Unless?' Zack said nervously.

'Unless they want to... silence us forever.'

Her last three words hung in the air.

'You really think they brought you here to murder you?' I asked.

Grace laughed. 'Nothing so melodramatic. The Trust is subtler than that.'

'Or so we thought,' Zack muttered.

Grace ignored him. 'Bernadette's mystery game finally makes sense to me. The aim was to test our skills.'

I nodded. 'A time-honoured way for the security services to vet recruits.'

'I don't think so,' Zack said.

'Believe me. It's true.'

'Explain,' Grace said.

'The advantage of being a crime writer,' I said, 'is that you pick up all kinds of weird trivia during your research. When I was writing *Rogue Males*, I studied what went on at Bletchley Park during the war. They scouted people like Stanley Sedgwick to join the code breakers.'

'Never heard of him,' Zack said.

'Stanley was a humble accounts clerk, chosen on the strength of solving a cryptic crossword in the *Daily Telegraph*.'

'You're kidding.'

'Stranger than fiction, huh?'

'Incredible.'

'No, it was perfectly logical. Relying on genius mathematicians was never going to be enough to win the war. The security services needed a diverse team of original thinkers to play the great game. Maurice Midwinter studied History, so did Jeremy. The Midwinter Trust applies the same logic that was so successful in defeating the Nazis.'

'Book people fitted the bill,' Zack said, thinking it through. 'Creatives with no money but lots of imagination.'

'And twisted minds,' I said softly.

'Speak for yourself,' he retorted. 'I'm a literary agent.'

I smiled and said nothing.

Poppy spoke up for the first time in a while. 'The world of publishing is very different from clandestine operations. It's about promotion, spreading the news…'

Grace tutted. 'Ask any author and they'll tell you their book publicist resembles an under-cover agent. Someone who has taken an oath of secrecy when they should be banging the drum for your latest.'

'It's not easy to get attention in a crowded marketplace,' Poppy said in a small voice.

'The Midwinter Trust tried a daring experiment,' I said. 'Turning a problem into an opportunity. Keep your friends close and your enemies closer. We'd be poachers turned gamekeepers. I bet Jeremy Vandervell was desperate to sign us up to the Official Secrets Act.'

Grace groaned. 'And he got his way. If we plough through the endless small print we signed in minute detail, I bet we'll find we're now legally tied up. We've sold our souls for – what? An all-expenses-paid festive break?'

I said, 'Baz proved the trickiest customer. He would never sell out. Having seen through their scheme, he was determined to turn it to his advantage and put right a terrible injustice. The inquiry into Will Noone's death dragged on endlessly and got nowhere. Baz meant to expose the Midwinter Trust to proper scrutiny. Even if he'd signed a book full of terms and conditions, there was no stopping him.'

Zack looked thoughtful. 'Did the whistle-blower regret trusting Baz? Was that why he was eliminated?'

'You're assuming Baz's death was no accident,' Grace said. 'I agree. Ethan's murder suggests that neither Baz nor Frankie suffered freakish mishaps in the snow. They were killed deliberately.'

'So the whistle-blower murdered all three of them?' Zack asked.

Grace shook her head. 'There may be more than one killer, working quite separately from each other.'

Zack winced. 'This is a small village in the countryside. Not Prohibition-era Chicago.'

'No, it's more dangerous.'

I turned to Grace. 'Why do you think Baz was murdered?'

'He was the Man Who Knew Too Much.'

'And Frankie?'

'The Woman Who Knew Too Much?'

'Too Much for what? Or whom?'

'I wish I…'

She was interrupted by the sound of someone trying to open the door, only to find it blocked by the iron doorstop.

We all held our breath.

The person outside banged a furious tattoo on the door.

'Open up!'

*The Origins of the Midwinter Trust – a personal
aide-mémoire by Jeremy Vandervell: III*

CLASSIFIED

As the village was brought back to life, and the Midwinter
Trust's operations slowly gathered momentum, the
Intelligence community was on a rollercoaster ride with
serious implications for national security. A never-ending
flood of revelations about the Cambridge spies – Third
Man, Fourth Man, Fifth Man, et cetera – destroyed
confidence internally. Externally, the exploits of James
Bond and his many fictional clones created a different
kind of pressure.

Demand for the Trust's unique facilities began to rise.
What had long been regarded (when its existence was
remembered at all) as an eccentric relic of war-time
espionage came to be seen as a vital resource, all the more
useful because of that crucial advantage of deniability.
Thanks to Maurice's leadership and the efforts of a small
but dedicated staff, the Trust metamorphosed from a
curious little backwater into a safe harbour for agents
exhausted by stress and overwork. Over the years, a
significant number of gifted individuals were able to
resume their duties after a therapeutic break at Midwinter.

The value of the Trust's contribution to society's well-being is incalculable.

When I joined the Trust more than three decades ago, Maurice took me under his wing. His commitment to creative thinking inspired me, and I like to think that he saw in me just a little of himself as a young man. With his blessing, I succeeded him as Director of the Trust and continued to benefit from his wisdom until his death at the grand age of ninety-three. By that time I had recruited a capable assistant in Ms Bernadette Corrigan, who became Deputy Director in 2015. Together we have striven to ensure that Midwinter remains a beacon of best practice, a bright light in a world full of darkness.

43

Harry Crystal's Journal

'Who is it?' Grace bellowed.

'It's me.' A pause. 'Carys! Who else?'

We looked at each other. I tried to keep a poker face, but personally I was happy to leave the woman out in the snow. It wasn't simply that I was still smarting from that insult about *dozy crime*. Suppose she was a murderer on the rampage?

'Should we let her in?' Poppy whispered.

'What if she's dangerous?' Zack mumbled.

The banging resumed.

Grace went up to the solitary window and peered out into the gathering gloom.

'She's got her trekking poles, otherwise there's no sign of any other weapon. If we don't count that poisonous tongue of hers.'

'Let me in!' Carys screamed. 'I've got something important to tell you and it's freezing out here. I can barely feel my fingers! Are you trying to kill me too?'

With an ostentatious show of reluctance, I shifted the doorstop aside and heard Carys fiddling with the handle.

The door opened and Carys peered at us through her big glasses.

'What's the big idea? Barricading yourselves in?'

'Ethan has been murdered,' I said. 'Can't be too careful.'

'I know about Ethan.'

'Who told you?' Grace asked.

There was a pause. Carys was incapable of shame or embarrassment, but there was a touch of defensiveness in her reply.

'I overhead the Midwinter Trust people discussing it.'

'Where?'

'In the village hall.' She coughed. 'I was in the upstairs toilet when they were talking in Chandra's office. It's next door and they kept raising their voices. The wall is quite thin. I could hear pretty much every word.'

'That's the staff loo, isn't it?' Zack asked. 'Not the one for guests.'

'Mmmmm.' Carys seemed to debate with herself how much to say, but then the words poured out in a torrent. 'Actually, it's very nicely equipped. Gold taps, would you believe? I've kept a close eye on the people from the Trust and they pop into Chandra's room to talk when they don't want us to listen. I wondered what they made of Frankie's death. The first thing I heard was that Ethan was dead. Murdered. It's a miracle I didn't gasp out loud.'

'But you kept quiet and carried on earwigging?' Grace asked.

Carys snapped, 'If you—'

'No, no, I mean, good on you. Shows terrific initiative.' Grace gave her a conspiratorial wink. 'What did you find out?'

A sly look crossed Carys's vulpine features. 'I don't know how much I should say.'

'Tell us everything you heard,' Grace said. 'Leave anything out and you won't need to wait for the murderer of Midwinter to slit your throat. I'll do it myself and plead self-defence.'

Carys glared. 'You think you're so smart, but you don't have the faintest idea what's going on here.'

Grace clenched her fists. 'Which is why we need you to spill the beans. Now.'

Carys took one more look at her before deciding that discretion was the better part of valour.

'All right. Here's what I heard.' She took a breath. 'Will Noone was Jeremy Vandervell's son.'

Her revelation had the effect she'd hoped for. After a moment's shocked silence, people began to fire questions.

She took a step back.

'Please. I sat in that toilet listening for a very long time. I mean, there's a great deal to tell you. Why not let me do it in my own way?'

'So the bottom line is this,' Grace said after Carys had recounted what she'd heard. 'According to the Trust, Will's half-sibling could be any of us, other than Harry?'

Carys nodded. 'Right.'

Nervously, I looked around the reading room. Which of my companions was the culprit? At the moment, I hadn't a clue. No change there, then, as Jocasta would say.

Grace said, 'Anyone willing to put their hand up?'

No one moved a muscle.

'Okay.' Grace pondered. 'There's no evidence to prove that

Ethan was killed by Will's half-sibling. Harry might be as guilty as sin.'

'Hang on a minute,' I protested. 'There's no evidence to suggest I'm connected to any of the deaths in any way.'

'You found Ethan's body.' Grace cupped her chin in her hand. She was in full prosecuting counsel mode.

'Yes, but—'

'You're an expert in murder. How many people have you done to death on the page?'

'Yes, but—'

'Were any of your fictional killings disguised as an accident?'

I felt a pounding in my temples. This interrogation was causing my blood pressure to spike.

'Yes, but—'

'I rest my case.' She gave a wolfish smile. 'For the moment. We can't exclude anyone from suspicion. Let alone a detective novelist determined to win the game at any cost.'

'I wouldn't say—'

'Of course you wouldn't.' Grace swivelled round. 'Still nobody fessing up to being Will Noone's half-brother or sister?'

Carys said, 'What about you, Grace? How can we be sure you're not the killer?'

For the very first time, I found myself warming to the woman. Not that Grace was shaken.

'Not easy to prove a negative, Carys.'

'Despite everything that has happened here, you're quite unruffled.' Carys took off her spectacles and gave them a polish. Without them, she looked strangely defenceless. 'Anyone would think you're relaxing at a spa in the Bahamas rather than enduring an ordeal that makes *One Flew Out of the Cuckoo's Nest* look like *Bad Girls* or *Porridge*.'

Grace shrugged. 'I'm good at compartmentalising.'

'Yeah? Like serial killers?'

'Hey,' Zack said mildly. 'Let's not get too personal, huh?'

Carys turned on him. 'Typical agent. It's all about business, isn't it? Not people?'

'Like the agent who went ice fishing with his client?' I interrupted, desperate to lighten the mood before we all tore each other to shreds. 'A polar bear appeared in front of them and right away the agent put on his racing shoes. "Don't be crazy," the writer said, "you can't outrun a polar bear." "You don't understand," the agent said. "I only have to outrun you."'

An old joke, admittedly, and it fell into stony silence, like a pebble dropped down a very deep well.

'I was wrong about you, Harry,' Carys said. 'It's a very good job you concentrated on crime.'

'It is?'

'Could have been worse. You might have turned to comedy.'

Zack said, 'What if this stuff about a half-sibling is a blind? Can we rule out Jeremy and the rest of them?'

'Definitely not,' Carys said. 'If you ask me, Bernadette's a sly one. Not to mention Chandra.'

Grace said lazily, 'While the accusations are flying all around, aren't we overlooking someone?' She turned to Poppy. 'You've had very little to say for yourself.'

'It's hard to get a word in sometimes,' Poppy replied.

'Ah, you fly below the radar, don't you, with your sweet and ingenuous manner?'

Poppy contemplated her pink fingernails, but Grace wouldn't let go.

'You had no previous connection with Baz, is that right?'

Poppy shook her head. I'd seen her as a potential ally, but it occurred to me how little I knew about the woman.

'None,' she said. 'As I've said, I never met the man until we both got out of the train at Midwinter Halt.'

'So what brings you here?' Grace demanded. 'What's your USP that tempted the Midwinter Trust into giving you a Christmas to remember?'

'You could ask Harry the same question.'

Folding her arms, Poppy leaned back in her chair. I sensed that for all her apparent calm, her brain was working furiously.

'In his case, the answer is obvious.' Grace threw me a glance that wasn't entirely hostile. 'For all his flaws as a literary stylist, he knows a thing or two about puzzles and detective work. Whereas you work in publicity.'

She made it sound as unpleasant and useless as surgical trepanning.

Poppy said quietly, 'I wanted to make a fresh start.'

'In Midwinter?' Carys scoffed. 'You'll be lucky.'

'Got to buy a ticket to win the lottery,' Zack murmured.

'You're so right, Zack.' Poppy glanced at her watch. 'It's coming up to four. We'd better head for the village hall. It's time for tea.'

She sprang to her feet and the rest of us followed.

But I was wondering about Poppy.

Was it possible she was Will Noone's half-sister?

And if so, was it conceivable that this apparently ingenuous young woman was actually a murderer?

The Origins of the Midwinter Trust – a personal aide-mémoire by Jeremy Vandervell: IV

CLASSIFIED

The Midwinter Trust continues to evolve and grow, readying itself to respond to the new challenges posed by twenty-first-century espionage. We turn the testing physical environment to our advantage. With the effective use of technology complicated by the rugged, unforgiving landscape, we are forced to rely on our own wits rather than relying on computer wizardry to solve every problem. And this is as well. Excessive dependence on expensive kit is self-defeating. We live in an age of cognitive warfare. Phones can be hacked, pagers detonated. We need to exploit our personal resources to the maximum.

This reality lies behind our move into proactive operations. Rather than solely acting as a refuge for those suffering problems with their mental health or whose faces no longer fit, we have broadened our remit, seeking to promote the recruitment of those who may add something excitingly different to the tired and predictable mix of graduates with stellar degrees in maths and computer science.

By definition, we work in the shadows, yet whatever the weather in Midwinter, we prioritise blue-sky thinking. We pride ourselves on our flair for innovation and can-do mentality. As we aren't hidebound by the public sector bureaucracy and inertia that hobbles large agencies in the western world, we are not merely quick on our feet but accomplished exponents of thought leadership.

The specialist expertise of our Head of People, Chandra Masood, enables us to ensure that cognitive diversity is at the heart of everything we do. We seek to break free of the echo chambers and groupthink of Whitehall, with its unconscious biases and micro-aggressions, and foster the spirit of the outsider's perspective and a commitment to punching above our weight.

At Midwinter our latest goal is to find and develop those gifted individuals who will demonstrate that today, more than ever, spying is not merely a science, not even just an art, but a means of solving the greatest puzzles of the modern age.

44

Harry Crystal's Journal

If the atmosphere during our Christmas lunch had been subdued, the mood at teatime was beyond funereal. Given that we were holed up in the village with a killer in our midst, the Midwinter Trust people – those who were left – obviously reckoned they had no choice but to carry on as planned. Chandra had even pinned up a host of brightly coloured balloons.

Daisy had rustled up a few canapés but even at this most gluttonous time of the year, nobody had much of an appetite. Even I didn't have the heart to drown my terrors in mulled wine. If ever there was a time to keep a clear head, it was now.

Jeremy spoke about Ethan's death, but kept his remarks brief. Although he made no mention of murder, he wasn't foolish enough to pretend that there had been yet another accident. Or to try to discuss the implications of Ethan's murder, without being able to pinpoint a culprit.

'The snow is easing off,' he said. 'Tomorrow should see a significant improvement in the temperature. We're optimistic that a thaw will set in. With any luck, it will be rapid.'

A great deal was left unsaid. Not least, what would the police make of all this? Was there a danger that, before they arrived, the killer would strike again? When Bernadette addressed us, she didn't touch on any of the questions uppermost in our minds.

'Despite everything that has happened to disrupt our time together, we do all still need to eat.' She gave a tinkly laugh, but her heart wasn't in it. 'Dinner will be at seven this evening. After that sumptuous lunch, Daisy is only preparing a light meal. Don't forget to hand in your solutions to *Miss Winter in the Library with a Knife* before you sit down.'

She paused. 'In the circumstances, we realise that you may not be in the right frame of mind for a fancy dress party. So, we're happy to leave it to you to decide whether or not to go ahead.'

She scanned our faces. Tentatively, Poppy raised her hand, as if she were back at school.

'I think it's a good idea to take our minds off... things.'

'Thank you, Poppy. Anyone else feel the same? Perhaps we can have a show of hands for those who agree with her?'

Nobody else raised their hand.

'Very well.' Bernadette sounded disappointed. Perhaps she enjoyed pretending to be Santa Claus. 'I quite understand.'

Abandoning the party suited me fine. I'd bought a turkey costume as a last-minute panic buy before setting out for Midwinter, a purchase I'd regretted from the moment I swiped my card. Why make myself look even more ridiculous than usual?

Desperation to make sense of things for myself gnawed at me. I found it increasingly difficult to accept that Baz and Frankie had both suffered fatal accidents. Too much of a coincidence.

Say Poppy was Will Noone's half-sibling. If she was responsible for their deaths, what was her motive? After all,

Baz had wanted to expose the misadventures of Midwinter. Perhaps he had simply slipped into the burn, as Jeremy claimed. But if Frankie hadn't been murdered because she'd seen something suspicious about Baz's death, why would anyone want to kill her? In any event, why murder Ethan, if the blame for Will Noone's death should be laid at Jeremy Vandervell's door?

Conversation continued to be desultory, and Poppy was the first to leave the village hall. I hurried after her. Time for us to have a heart-to-heart.

'Poppy!'

She turned to face me.

'Yes, Harry?'

Jeremy was right. The snow had stopped falling. It felt no warmer, but in the darkness of early evening, that was no surprise. I had to hope that help might come within the next twenty-four hours.

'Can we have a word?'

'You choose your moments, don't you?' She sounded at the end of her tether, not at all like the Poppy I knew. 'Why wait until we're out in the freezing cold?'

'I wondered if we could talk in private.'

'How do I know you're not the maniac who murdered Ethan Swift?' she demanded.

'How do I know you're not?' I countered. 'You fit the age profile, remember? Which I don't.'

'You're assuming Will Noone's half-brother or sister is the villain of the piece. That's not a given.'

'Who else could it be?'

'No idea, but it may be Jeremy or Bernadette or Chandra. Daisy does fit the age profile. If Valerie was Chinese, then...'

'All right.' I waved her wild hypothesis away. 'I'd still like to talk.'

'Shouldn't you be concentrating on Bernadette's mystery game?'

'I've solved that,' I said, trying not to preen.

'Reckon you've come up with the right answer?'

'I think so.'

'Congratulations.' She peered at me through the gloom. Her tone was sombre. Out of character? Perhaps, but perhaps not. I was beginning to realise that I'd misread Poppy's character. For her part, she seemed to be seeing me in a new light too. 'We've all underestimated you, Harry. I wonder if that's a mistake we'll come to regret.'

'Shall we go to the reading room?'

'Okay.'

A voice behind us called. 'What are you two up to?'

Zack Jardine had come out of the village hall and spotted us. I swore under my breath.

'We're off to the reading room,' Poppy announced.

'I'll join you.'

'Three's a crowd, isn't it?' I said.

He made a scoffing noise. 'Strength in numbers?'

Before I could say another word, Grace and Carys emerged from the door of the hall and came clumping towards us through the snow.

'What's this?' Grace wanted to know. 'Impromptu conference?'

'Harry invited me to a chat in the reading room,' Poppy said. 'Somewhere Jeremy and company can't hear us.'

Zack threw me a suspicious look and walked straight into

the room. 'Wanted to get you on your own, did he? I wonder why.'

The moment we were settled in our chairs in the reading room, Poppy turned to me.

'So what did you want to talk about?'

Might as well be hung for a sheep as a lamb, I thought. No point in messing around.

'Can you assure us that you're not related in any way to Will Noone?'

She raised her eyebrows. 'Would you believe me if I said I wasn't?'

'Depends on how convincing I found your denial.' I sat back in my chair and crossed my legs with what I hoped was commendable nonchalance.

Poppy glanced at the others, as if seeking moral support. 'Harry's in danger of getting above himself. He's solved the riddle, you see – *Miss Winter in the Library with a Knife*. So now he believes he can figure out who murdered Ethan.'

Carys gave a sceptical grunt. Zack contented himself with raised eyebrows. Grace's face was stripped of expression.

'Only two of us claim to have had no connection with Baz Frederick's investigation into Will Noone,' I said. 'Myself and Poppy.'

Carys glowered at her. 'Didn't he speak to you about publicising his book?'

'No,' Poppy said. 'Presumably he was content to rely on your flair for social media.'

'Now, now,' Zack intervened. 'We need to tackle this business in a civilised way.'

'Really?' Poppy shook her head. 'Life here is like something out of *Lord of the Flies*.'

'*Lord of the Spies*,' I said, unable to restrain myself.

'Why not forget crime fiction, Harry?' Carys said through gritted teeth. 'A great career beckons, writing jokes for Christmas crackers.'

'Please,' Zack said. 'Squabbling won't get us anywhere.'

'Agreed,' Grace said. 'Poppy, can you explain why the Midwinter Trust invited you here? And why you accepted, come to that.'

'Isn't it enough to say I'd love to win the prize?'

Grace shook her head. 'Sorry, no.'

There was a pause.

Poppy gave a long sigh, as if reaching a fateful decision.

'I must admit, Ethan's death does change the way I see things. Until this afternoon I wasn't certain, but now there's no doubt. A killer is on the loose in Midwinter.'

Zack nodded sagely. The rest of us watched and waited. I realised I was holding my breath.

'Oh dear.' Poppy managed a little smile. 'I may as well come clean.'

'You'd better,' Grace said.

Poppy indulged herself with an extravagant wave of the hand that seemed out of character. At least for the young woman I'd come to know.

'I work for the intelligence services.' She smiled. 'Jeremy and co think I'm a wannabe, but actually I'm the real thing.'

Miss Winter in the Library with a Knife: Harry Crystal's Solution

All five suspects may have had access to cyanide, including Harriet (also known as Hattie) who used it in her work for 'bombing'. All five had good reason to wish Kristy dead. In Hattie's case, Kristy had taken Tim from her. Hattie had mental health problems – Kristy, in her brutal way, mocked her as 'Loonyker' – and she had suffered a great deal. She'd taken an overdose and hadn't appeared on TV for some time. However, embarking on a relationship with Mike after Kristy split from him gave her something to cling to.

Kristy wasn't yet legally divorced from Mike. Until the final order, or decree absolute, was issued, the marriage was still alive. So if Kristy died before the divorce was concluded, her legal husband would have a strong claim on her estate. She hadn't entered into a prenup or made a will disinheriting him, so the divorce party was not only premature, it offered a unique opportunity. If Mike inherited Kristy's millions, Hattie would reap the benefit by marrying him.

Because everyone ate the same Christmas meal as Kristy and had the same drinks, the poison must have been administered in the chocolate liqueurs. Hattie volunteered Mike, who didn't have the sharpest intellect, to organise the Secret Santa. She helped him, so that she could fix which person received which present. She arranged that she would give the chocolate liqueurs to Tim.

Hattie knew that Tim couldn't eat the liqueurs because he was allergic to chocolate. She also knew that Kristy was greedy, and a chocaholic. So she could be confident that Kristy would make sure she had the liqueurs.

Result: death by chocolate.

To muddy the waters, Hattie sent two anonymous messages to the police. One accused Tim of being addicted to cocaine (which she knew to be true). Another suggested that Kristy meant to dump Tim, which was not true. So Hattie was taking revenge on Tim for his betrayal by pointing the finger at him. It was he, after all, who had given the liqueurs to Kristy.

45

Harry Crystal's Journal

In a flash, the jolly, naïve young woman I'd met on the evening of my arrival vanished. Poppy – or whatever her real name was – leaned forward in her chair, looking as confident and assertive as Grace Kinsella.

'You work for… MI5?' Zack looked as shocked as if a client had asked him to cut his commission.

'Following in Daddy's footsteps, as it happens. My bosses knew the CIA had sent Daisy to report on what was going on here, so they decided to follow suit. They didn't want to be embarrassed by our American colleagues knowing more about Midwinter than we do. The so-called special relationship is already too one-sided.'

She nibbled her upper lip, as if wondering how far to abandon discretion.

'Jeremy Vandervell has been getting above himself. He wants to expand the Midwinter Trust's remit, which ruffled some feathers. Ever since the days of old Sir Maurice, the Trust has been a quirky anomaly. Out of date and non-compliant with modern standards. Between you and me, my managers hoped the inquiry into Will Noone's death would sound the Trust's death knell. But Jeremy is a formidable networker. He still has powerful friends to pull strings on his behalf. I could have written the inquiry's conclusions without knowing the first thing about the case. Endless guff about putting new procedures in place and learning lessons for the future. More weasel words than Prime Minister's Question Time.'

Poppy exhaled. 'So I was sent here undercover. My brief was to report on whether the Trust is still fit for purpose. Or should it go the way of Bletchley Park and be turned into a tourist attraction? Though after everything that's happened, Midwinter feels less like a rural idyll, more like a chamber of horrors.'

A messianic glint came into her eyes, giving her a faintly sinister resemblance to a political campaigner on the stump.

'If you ask me, it's time to stop the chaos and turn the page. This whole village deserves to be razed to the ground. Personally, I can't wait till the whole of Pagans' Fell is rewilded.'

I smiled nervously, as a thought sprang to mind that chilled me to the bone.

Wouldn't Will Noone's half-sibling say the exact same?

Our meeting broke up without my learning anything new. Everybody else claimed they needed time to finish working out the solution to *Miss Winter in the Library with a Knife*. The news that I'd already worked out the answer seemed to have them rattled.

Back in my cottage, I made sure to lock the front door. I doubted the murderer would try to break in and kill me, but better safe than sorry. I wrote out my entry and sealed it in an envelope, but my mind was elsewhere. Something that someone – was it Carys Neville? – had said in the reading room had triggered a memory. But I couldn't place it.

Frustrating. From long experience, I knew the best course was to stop forcing myself to remember and await enlightenment. Yet time was short.

My mind turned to Carys. Was she Will Noone's half-sibling? The woman seemed more credible as a cold-blooded murderer than Poppy. Then again, Poppy had lied to us in a way that none of the other guests had.

As far as I knew.

Christmas dinner was a bleak occasion, with nobody in the mood for seasonal gluttony. Everyone handed their envelopes to Bernadette, but I doubt if any of us cared who won the game. Jeremy left it until the end of the meal to stand up and add a few words about Ethan Swift. He was mercifully brief, urging everyone to remain vigilant and assured us that the Trust was redoubling its efforts to make contact with the outside world.

'Do you think that's true?' I asked Grace, as the now customary minute's silence came to an end. We were loitering in a corner of the village hall, keeping a wary eye on our companions.

Her smile was enigmatic. 'Trust no one, remember. Especially not Jeremy Vandervell. Let's see what Mata Hari makes of it all.'

Poppy had squeezed her leggy frame into a short Christmas jumper dress that had Zack salivating. When she joined us, she made clear she was unconvinced by Jeremy's protestations.

'I mean, how hard can it be to get help? We may be out

in the sticks, but the Trust aren't lacking in resources. It's ridiculous to be completely cut off from civilisation like this. My guess is, Jeremy is hoping against hope he can sort things out before the balloon goes up.'

On cue, a couple of Chandra's balloons popped. I jumped, as if dodging a bullet. Across the room, the Director of the Trust was deep in conversation with his deputy. The tiny explosions didn't cause his expression to flicker.

'How could Jeremy do that?' I asked. 'Sort things out, I mean.'

Poppy said, 'By identifying the murderer and making sure they can't commit any further crimes.'

'Easy, huh?' Grace said.

'The Trust is supposed to be an unofficial branch of Intelligence. Not that you'd guess, from the chaos of the last forty-eight hours. Rank amateurs, if you ask me. Jeremy's had his own way here for too long. Time for a change.'

'Given your own expertise,' I said hopefully, 'who do you think is the culprit?'

Grace laughed. 'Assuming it's none of us, of course.'

Poppy shook her head. 'I'm no detective. My specialism is conducting surveillance under deep cover.'

'Hence becoming a book publicist?'

She gave me a wry smile. 'You will have your little joke.'

'Have you managed to spot a vital clue?'

'Unfortunately not.'

'You must have an inkling,' I said.

A long sigh. 'Between you and me, I'm not sure about Carys.'

I nodded. 'I can picture her egging on Will Noone. Stirring up trouble between him and his real father. Giving him no support when he needed it most.'

'That phone call Will made, just before he walked out of Midwinter,' Poppy said. 'I bet he rang his half-sibling.'

I nodded. 'Who else?'

'Whatever Carys – or whoever – said on the phone did nothing to haul him back from the brink. Quite the opposite. If she ranted about Jeremy and said how rotten he was, a man in Will's state of emotional turmoil would become distraught. Walking out into the snow was tantamount to suicide, he knew that. But he was past caring.'

I turned to Grace. 'So who is your money on?'

'I wonder about Zack, but actually, my long shot was Daisy. Though if she's an undercover agent from the CIA...'

'That woman can't be trusted an inch,' Poppy interrupted. 'Believe me, the stories I could tell about our American friends.'

Grace looked me in the eye. 'What about you, Harry? You're a mystery man.'

'So everyone keeps reminding me.'

'You suspect Carys?'

I hesitated. 'I can't stand the woman. But is she a killer? The trouble with being a crime writer is that you're always looking for the least likely suspect. There's something too obviously sly about Carys Neville.'

Grace puffed out her cheeks and looked at us both. 'So who is the unlikeliest candidate as murderer?'

'I hate to say it,' Poppy said. 'But the answer is clear.'

Having started this conversation, I felt uncomfortably like a turkey who has voted for Christmas.

'Go on,' I said.

'Apologies, Harry.' Her tone was more-in-sorrow-than-anger. 'But of course it has to be you.'

As if to emphasise her point, another balloon popped, so loudly this time that even Chandra Masood jumped.

And a memory exploded in my brain.

I'd remembered what Carys had said that, for a nanosecond, seemed to hint at what was happening here. All I needed to do now was make sense of her casual gibe.

The dinner party soon broke up. Nobody was in the mood to linger. Three people had died in as many days and neither I nor anyone else was anxious to add to the tally.

By tacit consent, the guests began to drift back to their cottages, leaving the quartet from the Trust to finish clearing up. I hung back for a few moments and wandered over to the noticeboard. Trying to look casual, and no doubt failing badly, I took a quick peek at the sketch map Ethan had pinned up.

As I made my way outside, it struck me with a jarring thud that I couldn't get it right even when I did get it right. My success in solving Bernadette's puzzle was actually an own goal. I'd reinforced the view that I represented the greatest threat to the killer.

All I wanted for Christmas was to survive. Not much to ask. But I'd painted a target on my own back.

Distracted, I glanced over my shoulder, forgot to watch my step, and lost my footing.

I put my hands out to protect myself as I fell head first into the cold, hard, compacted snow. Quite a shock, but I was only winded. Within a few moments I was back on my feet and wiping the snow off my face and gloves.

An idea leaped into my mind.

Something odd had happened yesterday. I'd not even thought it was odd at the time. On reflection, however, it verged on inexplicable. And that was the connection Carys's remark had made in my subconscious.

No menacing shadow lurked outside Pool View Cottage. I quickened my pace. I might have discovered the solution to Bernadette's game, but this challenge was different.

My own life was at stake.

I can't recall how long it took me to work out a coherent theory about the murders of Midwinter. My thoughts whirled so fast that time passed in a blur. Finally, I understood what had happened. Now I saw the events of the last couple of days in a very different light. If I was wrong, it wouldn't be the first time. But what if I was right?

Cautiously, I opened the front door of my cottage. I was carrying my torch, but I was reluctant to use it. I didn't want anyone else to see what I was up to. The lamps, supplemented by countless small lights on the Christmas tree, meant I could see in the dark. The snag was that I was determined to venture behind the main buildings, to a part of the village with little illumination.

My destination was the service area between the burn and the village hall. I took with me the trekking poles, and also the ice axe.

I moved forward slowly, looking all around, in case I spotted anything untoward.

Suddenly I heard a cry, somewhere ahead of me.

I quickened my pace, moving in the direction of the ice

house, before something brought me to a sudden halt. For a moment I lost my balance and dropped the ice axe.

The ground had given way in front of me. I saw a gaping hole in the snow. My ice axe had plunged into it.

I remembered Jeremy's warning that the old miners' tunnels might collapse at any moment. Hardly daring to breathe, I shone my torch down into the chasm.

Ten feet below lay a sprawled body.

The position of the limbs was unnatural. There was no hint of movement, no faint breathing to disturb the silence of the night.

Death had returned to Midwinter. My ice axe was beside the corpse, too far down to retrieve.

Snow and earth covered the legs and part of the trunk, but in the beam of light I saw the head and hair. Enough to identify her.

Chandra Masood.

I let out a strangled cry of dismay at the sight of Chandra's remains. It was dangerous to make a sound, but I couldn't help myself.

Moments later, the wavering beam of my torch fell on someone a short distance away. They had turned at the sound of my voice.

The person was wearing a red Santa Claus costume, carrying a sack over the shoulder and holding a torch in one hand and an ice axe in the other.

I was paralysed with shock.

Bernadette?

As I stood there, holding my breath, it was as if Santa Claus made up her mind.

Moments later, Santa was hurrying away from me, heading towards the reading room.

I was baffled. *Bernadette...* So I'd got this all wrong? What was she playing at? Was she conspiring with Jeremy Vandervell for some secret purpose? Or had she contrived everything – including her mystery game – with the sole aim of discrediting Jeremy and everything he stood for?

Time to turn back?

No. I must discover the secret for myself.

I stumbled forward, driven not only by insatiable curiosity but also by anger and fear.

The Santa costume appeared and disappeared, moving in and out of patches of light cast by small lamps fixed high on the shed, diesel tank, and garage.

An image from a film sprang into my head.

Donald Sutherland in *Don't Look Now*. The frantic, grieving father pursuing a figure in a red coat through a maze of alleyways in Venice.

He believes he sees a vision of his dead daughter, but when cornered, she turns, revealing herself – spoiler alert – to be a terrifying woman. She smiles before slashing his throat with a meat cleaver.

The red figure was heading towards the reading room. Not hurrying, but calm and collected. Santa knew exactly what she was doing.

I hesitated.

Was it too late to change my mind and return to the warmth and safety of the cottage, and hope that tomorrow there might be a way to escape from Midwinter?

In my heart, I knew the answer. If I'd misunderstood

everything and found myself confronted, not only by Bernadette, but by Jeremy Vandervell as well, I had no chance. If they were in league together, there was no way they'd let me get out of the village alive.

Must keep going. I was sick and tired of being a loser. Jocasta liked to sneer that I'd made incompetence and failure a lifestyle choice. Her contempt had seeped into my bone marrow. I owed it to myself to trust my instincts and see this through. Wherever that led me.

Santa Claus had reached the reading room.

Summoning all my strength, I quickened my pace. As the red figure flung open the reading room door, I tripped and let out a small cry.

Swinging round, Santa Claus shone the beam of her torch into my eyes.

No chance now to turn on my heel and flee, even if my courage failed. I was committed.

No going back.

Grinding my teeth, I forced myself onward.

Santa Claus waited for me, not moving an inch.

The jolly red-cheeked mask laughed in my face.

Ho-ho-ho.

Three syllables, enough to convince me I wasn't mistaken.

I'd found the murderer of Midwinter.

The killer stood back from the door of the reading room, waving me inside with the ice axe smeared with blood.

Like the Grim Reaper with her scythe.

No time for second thoughts, far less regrets.

'Take off your mask!' I bellowed.

Father Christmas hesitated, wondering whether to indulge my curiosity.

But she was a murderer with a touch of showmanship.

Someone who found it impossible to resist the lure of a cheap thrill.

A hand came up and tugged off the mask, beard and all.

To reveal the face I'd expected to see.

Not Bernadette Corrigan's.

I was staring into the eyes of Frankie Rowland.

46

Harry Crystal's Journal

'**Y**ou don't look surprised,' Frankie said.

She shepherded me into the reading room with the ice axe, pulling a chair from behind the nearest desk. Gesturing me to sit down, she shifted the iron doorstop to one side and turned the key in the lock.

'I worked it out this evening,' I said.

If only I hadn't managed to lose my own ice axe. In a duel with Frankie, I'd come off second best, but I'd rather have gone down fighting.

She nodded. 'Ethan told me you were hopelessly inept. As usual, his judgment was way off beam. It was a mistake to write you off. I thought you couldn't be as useless as you seemed.'

Not much of a compliment. But I was trapped in a locked room with a multiple murderer armed with an ice axe, which didn't say much for my own judgment, so I mustered a feeble smile.

'The pair of you were in cahoots?' She nodded. 'You're Will Noone's half-sister?'

'That's right.'

A distant look came into her eyes. I'd seen that glazed

expression before, in the eyes of people who assured me everyone has a book in them. People with a story they were determined to tell. And right now, Frankie had a captive audience. Me.

'Will traced me. He was a very good spy, so it wasn't too difficult. He ran away from Thames House because he'd come to hate MI5 and what it did to people. Including himself. He hoped tracing his roots would help. We got on wonderfully well. I felt as if I'd only ever been half a person until he showed up at my door. I loved him, and I begged him not to go back. But he said he needed to give his career one last chance. Above all, he wanted to meet his father. The man who didn't even know of his existence.'

'Jeremy Vandervell.'

She nodded. 'They offered him the chance to take refuge in Midwinter, so he could recharge his batteries or whatever. It seemed perfect, but everything went horribly wrong. His nerves were in tatters, but Ethan said he'd be fine, and Chandra and Bernadette were too busy squabbling over Jeremy to give him all the attention he needed. Breaking point came when he revealed his identity to Jeremy. The man was so cold. Will felt he was being rejected all over again.'

'It must have been a shock for Jeremy,' I said. 'Given more time...'

'I said that to Will when he phoned me. But he was traumatised by the way he'd been treated, first at work, and then in Midwinter. Call him oversensitive if you like. A snowflake, even.' Frankie glanced at the window and gave a sardonic laugh. 'Such a sweet young man. He had all the intellectual credentials, but he wasn't cut out for the rough and tumble of spying. He couldn't see any future. Not even with me. So he walked out into the snow...'

There was a pause. I said, 'And you blamed the Midwinter Trust?'

'Of course! They had the privilege of caring for him. The chance to turn his life around. Instead, they destroyed him. All four of them were responsible. Not just Jeremy Vandervell. Bernadette, Chandra, and Ethan were all to blame.'

She stared at me, but her eyes were unseeing as she relived the torments of her past. All I knew was that I must keep her talking. Not that I had a master-plan for survival. I was simply afraid of the alternative.

'You didn't speak to the Commission of Inquiry?'

'They operated behind closed doors. It was impossible to find out what was going on. Not that it mattered. The investigators fudged their report. Took the easy way out. Getting justice for Will became my sole purpose in life. Midwinter, and the people in it, had to pay the price for making him suffer.'

Justice or vengeance? But this wasn't the moment for ethical debate.

'You conspired with Ethan,' I said.

'He was full of remorse about Will's death. Far too late, but he knew he'd messed up big time. I tracked him down and befriended him.' A mirthless smile. 'Seduced him, actually. Lots of people would envy me, getting together with such a good-looking guy, even one as flaky as Ethan. But I only had one thing in mind. Making sure he helped me destroy Midwinter.'

'I suppose it wasn't difficult for him to persuade the Trust to take him back?'

'Given that Bernadette was besotted with him, not at all. I bought off the handyman, and Ethan recommended my services as a short-term replacement.'

'You made a mistake by asking for an online review. I looked your firm up and there was no sign of Karma Kars of Kielder. At first I thought it was simply a very discreet operation. But when I came to think about the name…'

She tapped the doorstop with her axe. 'Yes… I realised as soon as I said it that I'd gone too far. Over-acted.'

'What did you tell Ethan?'

'That I wanted to discredit Jeremy. He encouraged Bernadette to dream up that mystery game nonsense. They wanted to recruit someone new. The game offered me the perfect opportunity, especially with snow forecast. Just like five years ago. Karma, huh?'

So that was why she'd called her make-believe limo company Karma Kars. A grim private joke. I tried to look sympathetic. Frankie had kept her secret for a long time and I could sense her desperation to share it with me. To make me understand the reasons for my fate, before she did her worst. Whatever that might be.

'So where did Baz Frederick come in?'

'I got in touch with him and gave him lots of insight into what really happened to Will, so he could expose Jeremy and the Midwinter Trust in his podcast. He promised to help me to see justice done, but he was more concerned with raising his own profile than helping the cause. He let me down badly. When the Trust and their pals in the security services clamped down on Baz and the others, all he cared about was restoring his career and reputation.'

'He might still have helped you to achieve your goal without… so much mayhem.'

She banged the ice axe on the floor. 'Baz had his chance and he blew it. So I took matters into my own hands.'

'Those sheets with Will's name on. You put them in

Bernadette's folder and then tripped her up so they fell out, and everyone could see.'

'That's right. A warning shot.'

'And then you killed Baz.'

'Over dinner, I'd told him something disastrous had happened. We'd agreed that he should come here for Christmas and confront Jeremy with the news that the podcast was going to be broadcast, come hell or high water. I was vague, and just said we might have to change our plans. That's why he became so unhappy and drank too much. I told Ethan I only intended to knock him out. He thought I simply wanted to cause mayhem for Jeremy and co. So Ethan was genuinely shocked when he discovered the body. But killing Baz was the first step. I wanted to rock this village to its foundations. So he had to go.'

'I suppose Ethan didn't actually hear Baz crying out, the night we all arrived?'

'No, that stuff about his amazingly acute hearing was pure fabrication. Bernadette heard nothing, because there was nothing to hear. Ethan went out to investigate at the time we'd agreed, and it was predictable Bernadette would insist on accompanying him.'

'You had some explaining to do afterwards.'

'Too right. Ethan was horrified. He was in favour of causing disruption, but murder was a step too far. I said Baz fell into the burn by accident, but actually I pushed him. He was standing stiff-legged, and I caught his ankle with this.'

She brandished the ice axe. *Unnecessarily close to my cheeks*, I thought. My own legs quivered. I toyed with the idea of doing an Ethan and pretending I'd heard something outside. But Frankie was sure to see through me, and the last thing I wanted to do was provoke her. Better to keep her in storyteller mode.

'You pretended to have a tiff with Chandra. To throw suspicion on her?'

'Yes, she didn't have a clue what was going on, which was fine by me. What mattered was for everyone else to assume that I'd seen something I shouldn't, or found some other way to upset the high-ups in the Trust.'

'So that evening, Ethan found your body and pretended you were dead.'

'It was a good plan,' she said complacently, 'and it worked to perfection. I'd told everyone about my supposed heart murmur, and of course Ethan backed me up.'

'You're really as fit as a fiddle?'

She grinned. 'Too right.'

Bugger, I thought. *No chance of her keeling over in all the excitement, then.*

She was obviously pleased with herself. 'It was one hundred per cent foreseeable Jeremy wouldn't want to get his hands dirty and inspect a corpse. He didn't do anything to rescue Will from the snow, you know. Just went back to the village and arranged for the emergency services to retrieve the body. So my poor brother was left out in the snow far longer than necessary.'

'As I see it,' I said slowly, 'the idea was to put you in a sleeping bag and leave you in that alcove inside the ice house. So you could stuff the bag with padding once the door was locked, and make your getaway through the old miners' passageways. Presumably you had plenty of provisions and somewhere to sleep underground.'

'Very good,' she said approvingly. 'How did you work that out?'

'It was the only possible explanation. And there was one specific clue which I picked up only a short time ago. Ethan drew a rough map of the service area and put it on the noticeboard. But he omitted the entrance to the mines close to the village hall. Bernadette's map includes that entrance, but he wanted to distract attention from it.' I tried to look insouciant, no doubt failing miserably. 'Like a spot-the-difference puzzle.'

She nodded. 'Yes, I was afraid Ethan was over-doing it, but he talked me into it, because he was worried that someone would wonder if the tunnels were relevant. He'd explored them when he was here five years ago. The passageways honeycomb the fell. One runs right underneath our feet as well as the village hall. The idea was that, even in adverse weather, miners could easily get back from the mines to the heart of the village. When I arrived here, a vital part of my preparatory work was making sure I could access the tunnels. In my role as handywoman, I put on new padlocks. And kept the keys.'

'There's an entrance close to the village school,' I said. 'I suppose you popped up out of there to kill Ethan?'

She mimed applause. 'You're doing well, Harry. It's not true what they say about you. Not entirely true, anyway.'

I took no notice. 'Did you always intend to murder Ethan?'

'Of course.' Her voice hardened. 'He turned against Jeremy, but far too late. He was as guilty as anyone. If he'd bothered to understand Will's state of mind, my brother would still be alive today.'

That seemed doubtful to me, but my heart was beating so fast, it was as much as I could do to keep talking. Let alone argue with a murderer.

'Easy for you to take your co-conspirator by surprise,' I murmured.

'Too right. You should have seen the look on his face. He couldn't believe his eyes.'

I shuddered. Grief had stripped her of all compassion.

My skin prickled with tension. I was painfully aware there was zero prospect of her letting me get away with a warning not to be so nosey in future.

'So,' I said, taking a breath. 'What's the plan?'

'You're the ace detective. Tell me what you've deduced. Starting with how you realised I was still alive.'

'When we laid Ethan's body to rest in the alcove, I happened to touch what I thought was your body. It yielded to my touch. I felt sick, and it didn't occur to me that a corpse in an ice house should be bone hard. What about rigor mortis? But I was slow on the uptake. Then Carys said I was only fit for writing jokes for crackers and I remembered one of the gems from our Christmas lunch. *Why couldn't the skeleton go to the Christmas party? Because he had no body to go with.* It dawned on me that your body wasn't in the bag. Just stuffing. So where were you? Were you actually dead at all?'

Her eyebrows lifted. 'Well, well. I couldn't have anticipated that, could I?'

'You took plenty of risks,' I said magnanimously. 'Inevitably one or two didn't quite come off.'

She took a stride towards me, ice axe hovering, and I realised I'd got carried away and said too much. Frankie was in no mood to take criticism, however trivial.

'You're wrong,' she snapped. 'Everything is going like a dream. I've enjoyed talking to you, Harry. At moments like this, it's good to have an audience. Only don't expect a final chapter like one of your novels, with the cavalry rushing in to save you at the last moment.'

I breathed out. 'I sneaked a look in the boot of your limousine when we arrived here. You didn't seem pleased about that, but I paid no attention at the time. This evening I've started to wonder about what I saw.'

She smiled. 'Go on.'

'The fairy lights peeping out from underneath a blanket,' I said. 'Very Christmassy, but the village was already beautifully decorated when we arrived. Eventually the penny dropped. As I told Zack today, crime writers come across a lot of weird stuff while doing their research. I recalled a case about a terrorist in the Midlands who plotted to use fairy lights to ignite explosives. All sorts of household items – cool boxes, pressure cookers, you name it – can theoretically become lethal weapons.'

'What a wealth of useless knowledge you writers accumulate,' she said quietly. 'You're on the right lines, mind. I'm going to blow up the village. Starting with this reading room.'

I swallowed. 'I suppose there's a bomb in the tunnel beneath our feet?'

'Yes, Harry. A big one.' She gestured at the overflowing bookshelves just behind her. 'There won't be much left of your first editions, I'm afraid.' She paused before adding, 'Or you.'

'You told me you'd worked for an engineer's,' I said unhappily. 'Presumably you have all the necessary expertise?'

'Enough to do what's necessary. Of course, an amateur bomb-maker needs to improvise. Hence the fairy lights. They struck me as a nice seasonal touch. I've picked up the heavy-duty stuff through the dark web. Amazing what you can find, if you look far enough.'

I nodded. If only puzzle-solving prowess was sufficient to save myself. Was there a sliver of hope of salvation?

As if to answer my unspoken question, Frankie said, 'I suppose you're wondering about Jeremy and co?'

'I saw Chandra's body.'

'Yes, she was easily dealt with.' Frankie smiled. 'During your Christmas dinner, I sneaked into the village hall via the fire escape. Crawled along the mezzanine floor on all fours, so none of you could see me from down below. Lucky the wall isn't see-through. I slipped envelopes under the office doors asking Jeremy, Bernadette, and Chandra to come to the reading room at different times and not to tell anyone. Given that levels of distrust in the village are off the scale, I was sure they'd each come alone. When that was done, I stuffed a message for Daisy under the front door of her cottage.'

'What was your plan?'

She shrugged. 'I'm not that sophisticated, Harry. No fiendish tricks up my sleeve. I simply wanted to catch them unawares and knock them out, one after the other. Worked like a dream. What happened to Chandra was a complete accident. She caught sight of me in this Santa outfit and obviously mistook me for Bernadette. She tripped, and the ground gave way beneath her. Saved me a job. I reckon she broke her neck on impact, did it look that way to you?'

'Yes,' I muttered. 'So when do you expect the others?'

'Oh, they're already here,' she said casually. 'I thought I'd done all the necessary until I saw you gaping at Chandra's remains.'

She flung open the internal door and stood back to let me see into the other room.

Jeremy, Bernadette, and Daisy were lying on the floor. Their heads were bleeding and there was an ugly gash on the Director's arm. All three of them were gagged and bound. Jeremy and Daisy appeared to be unconscious. Bernadette had a deep cut on her chin and a black eye that was closed. The other eye stared at me in disbelief.

'I recognise the rope,' I said hoarsely. 'From the boot of your car.'

Frankie beamed. 'Well spotted. I should never have let you see inside. Careless, but never mind. Anything else?'

'There was a first aid kit. Where you kept those?'

I pointed to the bandages taped over each of her three victims' mouths.

'Exactly,' she said. 'Now it's your turn. I didn't expect to deal with anyone else just yet, but don't worry. There's a spare rope behind the door.'

'So you expect me to sit here meekly and submit to being murdered?'

Frankie lifted the ice axe. The blade was sharp. Her Santa costume was bulky, but I remembered how lean and muscular she'd looked when I first saw her at Midwinter Halt, wiping the windscreen of her limousine. I was old enough to be her father and out of shape. No match for a strong, fit woman with murder in her heart and an axe at the ready.

'That's right, Harry. I could cut you up a bit first, if you force me to. Same as I did with Jeremy and Bernadette. Daisy had more sense than to resist, must be the training. Honestly, it's easier all round if you simply give in.'

Like I'd given in all my life. To Jocasta, to Saskia, to editors, agents, and everyone else with a stronger will than mine.

Actually, I was sick to the back teeth of giving in.

I leaned my left elbow on the desk. 'I still feel I've got a lot of books left in me.'

A shake of the head. 'Sorry, but they'll have to stay there. Don't worry. The literary world will survive without you.'

'I suppose it's no use begging for mercy?'

She gave the doorstop an impatient tap with her foot. 'No use at all, Harry. I'm disappointed you bothered to ask the question. And please don't jabber about the season of goodwill, either.'

'So what do you want me to do?'

'Put your hands out and I'll bind your wrists.'

'Daisy!' I screamed.

The old dodges are the best, as I used to tell my disbelieving editor. Frankie couldn't help glancing over her shoulder. At the same moment, I picked up the letter opener from the desk and lunged towards her.

I'd launched probably the least competent assassination attempt since the CIA plotted to kill Fidel Castro with a booby-trapped seashell. I only managed to catch Frankie a glancing blow on the cheek.

There was a pinprick of blood, nothing more.

Frankie gave an incoherent snort of rage. Face red with anger, she knocked the letter opener out of my hand with a single blow of her balled fist.

The ferocity of her reaction caused her to lose balance momentarily. Catching her foot on the doorstop, she stumbled backward, dropping the ice axe.

I threw myself forward, trying to reach it. Frankie stretched an arm out behind her in an attempt to save herself from falling. She only managed to claw at the crammed shelves of the towering bookcase.

I heard an ominous rumbling and froze.

Books started tumbling from the bookcase like missiles. One of them hit Frankie on the back of the head. She yelped and flailed wildly as she stumbled, while books continued to cascade down upon her, knocking her to the floor.

A hardback cracked me on the shoulder. As I stumbled sideways, I glimpsed the cover of *Endless Fright*.

I watched as, almost in slow motion, the whole bookcase fell down on top of Frankie's prostrate form.

She screamed as the weight smashed her skull.

I closed my eyes.

When I opened them again, I could only see her feet. The rest of her body was buried under the bookcase.

I rubbed my sore shoulder. To be assaulted by one of your own novels must be the ultimate indignity for any author, but never mind. I was alive, not tied up, waiting to die.

From the other side of the debris, the horror-filled eye of Bernadette Corrigan stared at me.

It took a long, long time to find my voice.

'Welcome to my version of your game,' I said, unsteadily. '*Miss Winter's Creator in the Reading Room with a Letter Opener.*'

CLASSIFIED – EYES OF RECIPIENT ONLY

Dear Jeremy

Thank you for your letter resigning as Director of the Midwinter Trust, but I am afraid we cannot accept it. The same applies to **REDACTED**'s letter of resignation.

At a time of great uncertainty, we have concluded that the work of the Midwinter Trust is too important, and your leadership skills and experience too valuable, to allow recent unfortunate events to result in an outcome that, candidly, could only give aid and comfort to those who wish to see our country fail.

I should emphasise that this decision has been approved at the highest level and has also been taken in consultation with our colleagues in Washington DC, following the return there of **REDACTED**. Just as they have taken into account the report of **REDACTED**, so we have paid close attention to feedback received from **REDACTED**. Nevertheless, we are unanimously of the view that the contribution that Midwinter makes remains indispensable.

It only remains to me to thank you for your steadfast support to this office over the years and to express the hope that, now you and **REDACTED** have recovered from your injuries, the Midwinter Trust will continue to flourish and that you will serve your country for many years to come with the integrity and selflessness that have always been your hallmark.

Perhaps dinner at my club when you are next in town?

Kindest regards

REDACTED

47

Harry Crystal's Journal

'So the rewilding of Pagan's Fell is on hold,' Grace Kinsella said.

'Apparently,' I murmured, waving for another piña colada. The bartender looked vaguely like Daisy Wu, except she was clad not in an apron but a bikini. So was Grace, and it suited her. 'I hear Poppy has quit in disgust and gone to live in an ecovillage. Maybe she'll bump into my daughter. That would be... awesome.'

'I still can't get my head round it. Five people dead, and not a word in the press, not so much as a twitch on social media.'

This was the first time we'd talked about Midwinter since flying out from England. Both of us wanted to look forward, not back.

'Too many powerful people would be too severely embarrassed.'

'Not that I'm complaining. The tax-free ex gratia compensation we've all been paid is...'

'Very generous,' I said.

'Too right. And wonder of wonders, Jeremy and Bernadette are still running the show at the village.'

'Both government and Whitehall were terrified by the rumour about Jeremy signing up Zack as his agent.'

I nodded. 'He knows where the bodies are buried. Quite literally.'

She laughed as she rubbed tanning oil into my shoulders before sitting back again. The bruise inflicted by my own novel was no more than a memory.

'Carys put a thinly veiled warning out on her socials,' I said lazily. 'She loves stirring up trouble, that'll never change. She hinted Jeremy was working on *The Midwinter Memoirs*. Publish and be damned to the Official Secrets Act.'

Grace adjusted her Ray-Bans. 'Ah, books. What was it Baudelaire said? "A book is a garden, an orchard, a storehouse, a party..."'

'Did he mention a murder weapon?'

'Poor Frankie.'

'I've worked through my grief,' I said. 'So far as she's concerned, I can't say I experienced much survivor's guilt. Anyway, it wasn't such a bad way to go.'

'Crushed to a pulp by the complete works of Harry Crystal?' She laughed. 'Surely the definition of a fate worse than death?'

'You're so good for my morale.'

'I don't want you getting too full of yourself after your deductive triumphs. There's nothing worse than an author who thinks he's smart and successful.'

'Mmmm. I guess that explains a lot about the editorial process.'

'Any plans to turn your experiences into fiction? They'd make an... unorthodox novel.'

'*Slow Hearses*?' I shook my head. 'I don't think so. The agreement we signed in return for the money...'

'Please don't tell me you've given up writing.'

'To retire here and live in the lap of luxury? I'm tempted, but no.'

'The official security services would love it if we stayed on the other side of the world.'

I gestured towards the vast expanse of sand, stretching away as far as the eye could see.

'We'd get bored to... well, death. One Hawaiian beach is much like another.'

'Not enough snow even in February, huh?' She sighed. 'You did win the prize for solving the mystery. Exactly what Bernadette and company wanted from the get-go. A potential recruit out of left field, a modern-day Stanley Sedgwick. Your lousy sales figures didn't worry them, because they reckoned you were good at puzzles.'

'You flatter me.'

'It's true. But... please don't tell me that you've decided to accept their invitation to join the Midwinter Trust.'

I shook my head. 'No fear.'

'How about building on your recent success and taking up amateur detection full-time?'

'Wouldn't that make me a professional? No.' I stretched my arms, soaking up the sun. 'Of course, if a puzzle happens to come my way...'

She said thoughtfully, 'If you intend to continue writing...'

I laughed. 'I'll need a good editor?'

'A *very* good editor. No offence, Harry.'

'None taken,' I said equably. It's remarkable what surviving a close encounter with a deranged killer and taking a quarter-of-a-million-pound bung can do for one's confidence.

'So...?'

'I'm toying with a tale of the unexpected.'

My mind drifted back to a conversation with Frankie Rowland as we drove to Midwinter.

'It's a question of solving a murder mystery. No need for a psychiatrist, really. I mean, how stressful can this game really be? A few nights in a peaceful hamlet at Christmas, trying to make sense of a puzzle?'

Grace yawned contentedly as I stroked her bare feet.

'Do you have a title?'

'You bet.'

I grinned at her.

'What Could Possibly Go Wrong?'

Cluefinder

This is a contemporary mystery but it is firmly within the tradition of British and American detective stories written during the Golden Age of Murder between the world wars. Those books were mostly written in the spirit of a game between writer and reader, and 'playing fair' was a key ingredient. With that in mind, some Golden Age novels contained Cluefinders, enabling readers to check whether they'd spotted all the clues picked up by the Great Detective. I've revived this wonderful tradition in the Rachel Savernake mysteries, and I felt that *Miss Winter in the Library with a Knife* simply wouldn't be complete without a Cluefinder of its own.

Ethan encouraged Bernadette to create the game

Page 10 – 'Thanks for your confidence.' She smiled. 'And for persuading me to come up with it. I'd never have managed to keep going without your constant encouragement.'

Ethan's sense of guilt about Will Noone

Page 11 – He examined his fingernails. 'You know I haven't always got things right.'

Jeremy's connection with Will Noone

Page 3 – 'I don't have a choice.' A pause. This is *personal*.'

Midwinter's connections with the world of espionage and its links with the Special Intelligence Service (SIS)

Page 12 – She hated any form of betrayal
Page 14 – 'Deception, in other words?'
 She shrugged. 'Isn't that our stock-in-trade?'
Page 16 – 'Just as well I never became a cryptographer, eh?'
Page 23 –
 • service
 • integrity
 • sanctuary
Page 144 – 'It's not as if I don't know better. I've been trained until I've got safety protocols coming out of my ears.'

Frankie's personality, experience, and motivation

Page 39 – 'Luckily, I'm very patient.'
Page 39 – 'Bernadette Corrigan strikes me as a real stickler. Keen to make sure everyone does the right thing.'
 In the mirror, Frankie's lips curved in a faint smile. 'You reckon?'

Page 42 – I can turn my hand to most things. After I left college, I worked in an engineer's for a bit. But I've always loved cars, and fiddling about with electrics and what-not. Jill of all trades, that's what they call me.'

Page 42 – I laughed. 'Sounds as if you're looking forward to the next few days?'

'Can't wait. It's the chance of a lifetime.'

Frankie's connection with Will

Page 42 – 'I lost Mam and Dad when I was young, and I've not got any close relatives left,' she said quietly.

Frankie's involvement in the incident with the word WILL NO ONE

Page 106 – Possibly Frankie tripped her on purpose

Frankie's opportunity to talk to Baz on the night of his death

Page 129 – He spent the rest of the meal chatting with Frankie.

Ethan's hidden agenda and connection with Frankie

Page 90 – Ethan didn't need an in-depth psychological profile of Jeremy Vandervell to know what the man was capable of.

Page 96 – Yet he'd been asked to interview Chandra, Daisy, and even – hilariously enough – Frankie Rowland.

Page 120 – In truth, he despised Jeremy

Page 122 – 'Except that it's impossible to forget,' Ethan said sotto voce.

Page 143 – 'I'm one of life's marionettes, not a puppeteer.

Page 156 – Baz's death had shocked him to the core. It wasn't in the script. Was it?

Page 204 – Things were tricky enough already, especially given Baz's death. He'd said as much to Frankie when they'd had a conversation earlier.

Page 250 – After talking things over in private, he was coming round to the view that the man had brought his death on himself.

Page 252 – He was probably hypersensitive, knowing what lay ahead.

Ethan's knowledge of the village and the circumstances surrounding Baz's death and the 'discovery' of Frankie's body

Page 148 – Ethan had explored the subterranean alcoves when he'd first arrived in Midwinter. He'd discovered that, in addition to a drain to take away the meltwater, a passage connected with the old mine workings further down the slope, a sort of ancient subway for village workers to use in bad weather.

Page 148 – 'Who is it?' Ethan shouted.

But he already knew the answer.

Page 159 – Jeremy steepled his fingers. 'So no evidence of… third party involvement?'

'None whatsoever,' Ethan said quickly.

Page 165 – *You can say that again,* Ethan thought. What in God's name had gone wrong? He'd never expected Baz to be killed.

Page 170 – To say that this evening hadn't gone exactly as planned, despite the fact he'd given everything so much thought in advance, was the ultimate understatement.

Page 265 – The Director was hanging back, Ethan realised. Predictable.

Page 265 – 'What's happened to her?' He couldn't see through Ethan and was keeping a safe distance. 'Has she fallen down the steps?'

Ethan sank to his knees. 'I'm checking her pulse.'

Page 271 – When he'd announced that Frankie was dead, Jeremy had made a perfunctory offer to help him to move her remains to the shelter of the ice house. Predictably, it hadn't taken much to persuade him that the priority was to let Bernadette and Chandra know what had happened without delay. Jeremy had tweaked a shoulder muscle trying to manhandle Baz's body the previous evening, and in any event, Frankie weighed much less than Baz. Ethan could manage to shift her body on his own.

Page 293 – It was still only Christmas morning, and there was work to be done.

The reason why Frankie felt Ethan had to die

Page 238 – The plain fact is, I was responsible for what happened to Will Noone. I misread the man. Underestimated the fragility of his mental health. I was overconfident in my own diagnostic abilities, and he paid a terrible price.

The secret of the ice house

Page 321 – When my fingers brushed the bag, I felt Frankie's body yielding to my touch

Daisy's work as a spy based at the Pentagon

Page 81 – Later on, I moved to Frederick, Maryland. Very different, but not far from DC. Incredible city. I worked in a big office the other side of the Potomac.'

Page 90 – 'Our small size and aversion to bureaucracy makes us quick on our feet. Adaptable, innovative, forward-thinking.'
Daisy's expression struck Ethan as hard to interpret. Was she *amused*?

Poppy's scepticism about the Midwinter Trust

Page 101 – I wouldn't put anything past the people from the Midwinter Trust. They are mavericks, loose cannons.
Page 130 – 'Spooky,' Poppy said, with a bright smile.
Jeremy winced.
Page 216 – 'Gosh,' Poppy said lightly, brushing intrusive snowflakes out of her eyes. 'It sounds very cloak and dagger.'

Poppy's family connections with Whitehall

Page 134 – Daddy was an absolute stickler, you see. He was very senior in the civil service

Maurice's war-time connections with locations associated with espionage including Bletchley Park and Inverlair Lodge

Page 126 – He joined up as soon as war was declared, only to bee seconded to an office-based role, first in Whitehall, then in Buckinghamshire, and finally in the Scottish Highlands.

Author's Note

The publication of a book like this is a collective effort. I've received help and support from lots of people, including Ann Cleeves, to whose hospitality I'm indebted. I felt it was vital to get to know the area in which I planned to locate Midwinter and staying for a few days in Ann's cottage while she showed me around the north Pennines proved as valuable as it was enjoyable.

My thinking about the nature of the Midwinter Trust benefited from reading Matthew Syed's *Rebel Ideas*, which includes the story of Stanley Sedgwick's recruitment to Bletchley Park as well as a thoughtful discussion about issues like cognitive diversity. I'd also like to thank Paula Keaveney, for helping me with the Greek cipher; Roger Bullock, for engineering advice; Jonathan Edwards for advice on inheritance law; and Helena Edwards, for her great help with the maps.

For several of the jokes about the publishing world, I'm grateful to various fellow authors and I drew inspiration from witty pieces about what blurbs really mean by writers such as Terence Blacker, John Dugdale, and Robert McCrum. Above all, I'm grateful to my editor Bethan Jones and my agent James Wills, not only for tolerating the way I've poked fun at their professions but also for their enthusiasm about this project. Without their support, and that of their colleagues at Head of Zeus and Watson, Little, I couldn't have written this novel. So – thank you, everyone.

Martin Edwards

MARTIN EDWARDS:
WINNER OF THE CWA DIAMOND DAGGER 2020

Gallows Court and **Blackstone Fell** Longlisted for the
CWA Historical Dagger

'Martin knows more about crime fiction than anyone
else working in the field today. He's always been a fan
of the genre and his passion shines through in his work:
the fiction, the non-fiction and the short stories. In his editing,
he's brought new writers and forgotten favourites
to discerning readers. I'm delighted his work is being
recognised in this way.'
Ann Cleeves

'Martin's fiction alone makes him a truly worthy
winner of the Diamond Dagger. His editorial excellence,
his erudition, his enthusiasm for and contributions to the
genre, his support of other writers, and his warm-hearted
friendship are the icing on the cake.'
Lee Child

'Martin Edwards is a thoroughly deserved winner
of this prized award. He has contributed so much to the
genre, not only through the impressive canon of his own
wonderfully written novels, but through his tireless work
for crime writing in the UK.'
Peter James

'Martin is not only one of the finest crime writers of his generation. He is the heir to Julian Symons and H.R.F. Keating as the leading authority on our genre, fostering and promoting it with unflagging enthusiasm, to the benefit of us all. I'm delighted that our community can show its gratitude by honouring him in this way.'
Peter Lovesey

'Martin Edwards is a wonderful choice to receive the Diamond Dagger. He's a very fine writer but has also devoted huge energy to both the CWA and Detection Club – all done quietly and companionably, which is a rare thing. I love a man who takes care of archives. I am delighted for him, but as we always say: it's for lifetime achievement – but please don't stop what you do so well!'
Lindsey Davis

'Martin Edwards is not only a fine writer but he is also ridiculously knowledgeable about the field of crime and suspense fiction. He wears his learning lightly and is always the most congenial company. He is also a great champion of crime writing and crime writers. His novels feature an acute sense of place as well as deep psychological insights. As a solicitor, he knows the legal world more intimately than most of his fellow novelists. He is a fitting winner of the Diamond Dagger.'
Ian Rankin

About the Author

MARTIN EDWARDS is an award-winning author and life-long fan of books and mysteries, puzzles and games. He has won the Edgar, Agatha, H.R.F. Keating, Macavity and Poirot awards and, in 2020, he was awarded the Crime Writers' Association Diamond Dagger for his outstanding contribution to crime fiction. He is the President of the Detection Club, a position previously held by crime-writing royalty Dorothy L. Sayers and Agatha Christie, and he is a consultant to the British Library's bestselling Crime Classics series. Martin is the author of the Rachel Savernake Golden Age Mysteries as well as several other works of fiction and non-fiction. *Miss Winter in the Library with a Knife* is his first Christmas mystery.

Follow Martin on Twitter and Instagram
(@medwardsbooks) and Facebook
(@MartinEdwardsBooks).

Did you love
Miss Winter in the Library with a Knife?

Then don't miss the Rachel Savernake Golden Age mysteries.

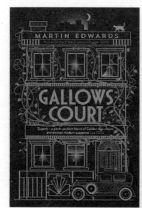

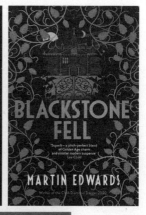

Play detective. Check the Cluefinder.
Test your wits against the modern King of Classic Crime.

Available to enjoy in paperback, eBook and audio.